KNIVES IN YOUR EYES

KNIVES
IN
YOUR
EYES

M. Loyd Gohty

FRICTION PRESS

ISBN 979-8218135058 (paperback edition)

Printed in the United States of America
First printing 2023

Cover and interior art by Danika C.
Design and typesetting by helwolves

friction-press.itch.io
patreon.com/frictionpress

*For your second family, and your first, and your third,
and the ones in between those too.*

Author's note

Some of the characters in this book switch pronouns. Sometimes it happens between scene breaks. Sometimes it happens between chapters. Sometimes it happens in the middle of a sentence. There are undoubtedly typos in this book—I'm only one person—but fluctuating pronouns are not one of them. Enjoy.

Part I
THE TWINS

Val spends a good fifteen minutes scraping mud off of his shoes in the woods outside the home of Professor Williams. He straightens his tie on the walk up a boot-trodden dirt path, and pushes his bangs off his face right before he knocks on the front door. Perked like a sunflower at noon, he puts on his best smile as footsteps sound from within the humble house. Resisting the urge to grab the edges of a strip of peeling paint and *rip*, Val tucks his hands neatly behind his back.

It's a beautiful spring day, three miles from the outskirts of Prosperity. The last meal Val had was a handful of insects and what were very likely poisonous mushrooms he found last night in the woods.

Two locks rattle loudly before the door pops open, held taut against a large black boot. Val's gaze immediately hinges on a deep scar like a ravine that pinches the flesh of a man's cheek, leading up to his left eye. Val meets irises of sharp gray, like surgical steel, and straightens his shoulders.

"Who the hell are you?" The Professor's voice is low, burned through, carrying the vestiges of an old accent from the western border that Val's never heard in person.

Val opens his mouth, quickly arranging his words as he gives a short bow. "Hello there, I'm Valerie. I'm a transfer from the Northern University. I suppose you could say I'm your new student."

The Professor leans his shoulder up against the door frame, digging into belted trousers for a pack of cigarettes and a box of matches. "I don't teach dead kids."

Val keeps a tight grip on his smile, despite the strange joke, and touches his chest as the Professor lights up. "Well we're in luck then. As I'm perfectly alive and healthy."

Professor Williams takes a drag, eyes relaxing from their dubious stare, before he blows thick smoke between them. Old tobacco burns its way inside Val's nose. "No. Pretty sure you're dead. If not now, then in a couple weeks. The stupid hangs off you like a stolen jacket." He shrugs at Val. "Too big for your shoulders."

Val swallows the first real twinge of annoyance, weaving his fingers tightly together against the small of his back. "Would you like me to provide a letter of recommendation from one of my other professors?"

Professor Williams waves his cigarette like a pointer toward the road Val just walked up. "I would *like* you to leave. I don't give a shit about any university. You'd know that if you actually went there. They cut me off years ago after one too many students died on my watch. Which means . . ." Another lazy puff of his cigarette wipes the smile off Val's face. "You're some fucking orphan who doesn't know what I do. And I'm not looking to adopt."

Val lets his breath out quietly. "I suppose that saves me from lying."

"Go back to wherever you came from, boy," the Professor says, angling away like he's going to close the door, but Val shoves his own foot in the way of it.

"Perhaps I can reason with you after all? As one outcast to another?" Val asks, a bit of desperation caught like embers in his throat.

The Professor's eyes narrow at that, his dark hair falling over his forehead. "Hm."

"I know very well what you do," Val tells him. "That's why I'm here. I want you to teach me how to wield a knife."

There is no real silence out here in the woods, but Val can hear a frog's croak from start to finish as he waits for a response. Reaching his cigarette forward to ash it outside the house, the Professor grunts. "You seemed to have missed the memo. It's no longer acceptable for proper boys like you to do that sort of thing. It'll only cut you down in the prime of your . . . rosy-cheeked life."

His gray eyes sweep up Val's body once before the Professor blows another face full of smoke at Val and kicks the door shut with enough force that Val goes stumbling off his front step. Anger bites Val's tongue as he stares at the wooden door, hearing the sound of the locks rattling back into place. It's only politeness that keeps people from destroying flimsy little doors like that in broad daylight. Politeness and the fear of getting caught.

Val straightens his perfectly neat tie and stalks back into the woods where he left his things. Luckily, the Professor is a shut in. Val knows that, because he's been watching this house from his tent for the last three days. Not once has the man stepped outside. The only thing that ever changes is a window on the second floor cracking open at the same time every night, to let out steam from a bath, which then gets slammed shut at the same time every morning.

So Val goes back to his tent and settles down to wait until dark. If he can't persuade the Professor with words, he'll just have to show him. He always did better with auditions.

These woods have a hypnotic quality to them, between the constant thrum of noise and the oppressive smell of nature. Val would never elect to stay in such a place, but it does make it a little easier to pass the time until it's fully dark. A few times, he nearly nods off, but a quick prick of his knife against the meat of his palm is enough to banish the sleepy haze.

When he hears the window struggling open, Val changes out of his nice clothes, trading his dress shoes for the rubber soled sneakers that hug his feet like gloves, slicking his bangs all the way off of his face, and tying his broken knife against his bicep. The light in the bathroom remains on for roughly half an hour, the steam slowly dissipating until the light is extinguished, and the good Professor's footsteps retreat across the house. Val crouches between the thick roots of a tree at the edge of the clearing where the house stands like some kind of massive, decaying head. Val never could shake the recognition of a face in the front of every house in cities like Prosperity—doors like teeth, and eyes in every window.

Who gains comfort from resting in an open mouth?

When it's been nearly an hour of woodsy silence, Val crosses the clearing and begins testing the ledges of the first floor windows, finding one sturdy enough to hoist himself up on. It takes him longer than he anticipated to actually get himself to that second floor window, a miscalculation on the distance between the two closest ledges leading him to an overdrawn prayer to whatever demon might be watching over him as he perches on the edge of a sill that looked a lot thicker from the ground. Finally, he gets his arm through the open window, hanging like a spider from the wall of the Professor's house as he breathes a sigh of relief.

It's easy from that point. The noise of shoving the window open a few more inches briefly gives him heart palpitations, but he gets himself inside the bathroom with hardly any trouble at all. Nothing greets him, save for the skeletal groans of an old house, and Val slips out into the hallway. An old red and gold runner full of dust and ash quiets his steps for him, and soon enough, Val is gingerly pushing open the door to the old Professor's bedroom. The latches hardly even squeak, or maybe they do, but Val's racing heart makes it difficult to hear.

He *can* hear the Professor snoring in his bed. Val doesn't even bother crouching, he simply walks across the room with a frown, nothing but pity now for an old man who talked like he knew better. If what he said was true, and he really did get tossed from the University network, maybe he's lost his edge. A sad man who was once feared and renowned for his skill with weaponry, now reduced to this papery, whistling thing. It might be a blessing if Val simply put him out of his misery.

As soon as the thought occurs to him, Val cocks his head to the side. Maybe this was the real reason he was needed here. Maybe this old man *wants* to die, and he's been waiting for someone like Val to finally do it for him. A master of killing, finally submitting himself to the end. Val could take up the mantle for him, born anew in Professor Williams's shadow.

Val is trembling as he debates how to do it. He can feel the shape of the knife strapped to his bicep, but he'd rather not. A man whose life was as bloody as this one would probably appreciate a cleaner end. Val leans over the Professor's slumbering face, breath quickening. Yes, yes, he'll keep the air in the Professor's chest—a nice personal end to things. Val will witness the Professor's last breath, and help him to savor it.

He feels giddy, like the first time he was ever near a horse three times his size, and he reaches for the Professor's neck. The weight of this new purpose settles comfortably over his body, a new uniform made just for him. He's never asked someone out on a date, yet this quivering fear bubbling in his chest must be something like that hot-blooded hope. Val snaps his hands around the Professor's throat, squeezing as hard as he can as his pulse roars in his ears.

Say yes.

Gray eyes fly open, wild and tinged with red. The Professor tries to pull Val's hands off of him, so Val simply throws himself on top of the Professor, sitting on his chest to make it all the more difficult to breathe.

They lock eyes, and once the Professor sees who it is, his expression flat-lines into something more peaceful. He knows . . . he must know. The relief of acceptance in his eyes is almost too much for Val, his heartbeat pounding in his fingertips as they squeeze into the clay of the Professor's neck.

"I'll take good care of you," Val says. "You're wel—"

Val's eyes pop open. He's in his tent outside the Professor's house, nothing but a dim glow from a match illuminating the canvas walls and the face of Professor Williams himself. He's standing above Val, hunched forward from the low ceiling of the tent, but perfectly alive. He stares directly at Val with a cigarette dangling from his lips and a look of rotten bewilderment.

"So that's a good dream for you, then?" the Professor asks wryly.

Val licks at his dried lips and tries to pull his head back into reality. "I'm sorry, did you see that?"

"Every second." The Professor blows more smoke into the air, leaning heavily on the hilt of a cane. "Don't worry, the effects have worn off. You're awake now. You better come inside."

He shoulders his way out of the tent. Val remains still for one more heartbeat before he springs up out of his sleeping bag, not bothering to collect his things, just pulls his shoes on as fast as he can and runs after the Professor. He catches up halfway to the house, light spilling out of the windows on the first floor like fire between teeth.

"Does this mean you're taking me on as a student after all?" Val asks, eyes wide.

The Professor gives him a sidelong glare. "You have a dream about killing me in my bed and you think that made me soft on you?"

Val blinks. "Well, you made me have that dream, didn't you? Some kind of test or something. How did you do that, by the way?"

"That was a test alright," the Professor mutters as he pushes open the front door to his house. "You got a lot more strange in you than I thought."

Val hurries in after him, doing another quick touch over his hair to make sure it's not too wild from sleep. The Professor ambles through a doorway where he turns on another light inside of a cramped kitchen.

"In here," he barks amidst metallic clanking. Val hovers in an archway and watches the Professor filling a tea kettle with water from his sink, the cane now propped against the counter. "Alright, out with it."

Val stays where he is, not wanting to get into this man's chaotic path. "Out with what, sir?"

"What the hell are you?" the Professor asks, dropping the kettle onto his stove and turning the knob. *Click, click, click.* "Fuckin' faulty gas lines."

"I'm sorry, I'm not sure I understand your question," Val says, tightly weaving his hands together again.

Click, click, click. Finally, blue flames burst out of the stove, and the Professor leans a hand on the counter beside it, staring Val down with impatient eyes. "I've been around long enough to know you're not human. If you don't want me to hand you over to less merciful people, you should start talking. *Now.*"

Val's back straightens, mouth falling open as he looks at this decrepit man. His frame calls to mind a great tree that found its tallest height and decided it'd seen enough of the sky, bending back down to look at the ground instead, where Val now stands in his shadow. He seems much taller now than Val remembered.

"Is it true, then?" Val asks him in a whisper. "You can tell for sure? I'm not . . . human."

The professor's eyes flash with surprise, and he leans away from Val. "Why don't we back up a little. *Who* are you? And don't feed me any more of that Northern University bullshit. They haven't worn that uniform in a couple years now."

Val gives a clipped laugh, straightening his shirt cuffs. "No, sir. My name is Valerie, that part was true. I traveled through Foundation to get here, so I spent a little time on the campus of the Northern University."

"Where're you from?" the Professor asks.

"An orphanage about ten miles west of Foundation," Val answers. "Never knew any parents. Hardly knew the other kids. There was one boy I was friends with, but—"

The Professor snaps his fingers. "Why'd you come and find me?"

"Oh, well, I wanted to learn how to fight," Val says with the slightest shrug. "I thought you might be more, uh . . ."

He stares at Professor Williams, his deep scar and smoke-addled voice and walking stick, the disheveled brown hair half-strewn about his face like he'd been caught in a wind. It doesn't match up even in the slightest to any of the clean-cut professors Val had once seen on the Northern University campus. He doesn't look like *anyone* Val's ever met. Something about him is deeper than a regular person. Maybe that's why he makes so much noise as he moves around.

"Hm?" the Professor narrows his eyes, and Val stumbles on.

"I fully admit I thought I could impress a former professor by pretending to be from a higher social standing. All they really care about up there is presentation and manners," Val says, pulling a slight, apologetic face.

"Yeah, you seem to have the performance down pretty damn well," the Professor mutters. He turns back to his cabinets, moving things around and finally retrieving a mug, which he peeks inside with a scowl before turning the sink back on to rinse it. "You don't know what you are, then?"

"No, sir," Val says. "Though I've had my fair share of monstrous accusations. You'd think people would be more impressed by someone who heals from injuries in mere seconds, but it mostly puts people off in my experience. They like blood, regular people. They want to see it spill properly."

"But you prefer to choke people to death," the Professor says, shuffling over to a set of cabinets where he starts popping open tins until he finds a pack of tea bags. He tosses one onto the counter next to his mug.

"Well I've never done it in real life," Val tells him. "It was only a dream. Can't take it too seriously, right? People do all sorts of things in dreams they would never actually do."

The Professor's gaze cuts back over to Val, storm gray, thunder in the distance. "It wasn't just a dream. It was a good dream. Yesterday afternoon, when I blew smoke in your face, I was giving you a command. I asked your brain to show me something you want more than anything else. Technically I asked it to do something else, but that effect doesn't seem to work on you, which is part of how I knew you weren't *regular people*."

Val feels his mouth attempting to smile, but something gets in the way, lips parting around the surprise. Voices rise up in his head, memories of people throughout the years calling him monster. "How else did you know?"

The kettle starts to give a plaintive whine, and the Professor immediately shoves it aside and turns the burner off with a snap. "Because I'm not a regular person either. I know one when I see one."

Val perks up, eyes wide. "Are you like me?"

"No," the Professor says flatly.

"Oh." Val's shoulder slope as he slides his thumbnails together. "I didn't know there were other kinds of strange."

"More than you can count," the Professor says, and he sounds a little less aggressive, a little more tired. He splashes water into his mug, dunking the tea bag in and out a couple times before dropping it. "Listen, kid, I'm not a teacher anymore. I'm tired of that life. Frankly,

I've held more titles than any man has a right to hold, but I don't like teaching young people how to kill. Makes 'em think they can't die."

"Oh, we don't have to worry about that," Val says, hand extended out to Professor Williams. "I can't die. Literally."

The Professor turns to him, brows knit, and his back slowly straightens up.

"I'll show you," Val says, turning his palm up. "Do you have a gun or something?"

The Professor shifts his feet, standing tall like he never needed help, and trades his mug of weak tea for the cane. The hilt pops up out of its sheath with a soft sound, revealing a thin blade.

Val nods at him, eyes bright, and opens his arms like he's waiting for a hug. "Wherever you like. I'm sure a man like you knows how to make it quick."

"What's your full name, kid?" the Professor asks, pulling the knife free of its sheath, and rolling the handle in his palm until it's pointed straight at Val.

"Just Valerie, or Val if you're short on time," Val tells him. "The orphanage gave me a last name, but I never much liked it, so I left it there."

"Sure," the Professor says, angling his body. "Turn around, Val."

Val fights off a smile made of nerves and turns his back to the Professor. His skin prickles, from the top of his spine, straight down to the meat of his calves. "You *are* a professional. I knew I was right about you."

Hands linked in front of his chest, Val is grateful that the Professor can't see his chest rising and falling in quick little rabbit breaths. He's never *asked* someone to kill him before, and there's an unfair swell of excitement that's making him dizzy. The desire to keep talking about nothing at all makes his tongue flick in his closed mouth, and right as Val realizes he's sweating, pain explodes through his neck for one searing hot second. His vision goes white, and then black.

Val wakes up on the floor of Professor Williams's living room, prying his eyes open to look up into sharp gray irises and that vein of scar tissue.

"Well, shit," the Professor says. "Welcome back."

He rises up from the crouch he was in, and holds out his hand. Val takes a deep breath from freshly reset lungs, and reaches up to take the Professor's offered palm. He hauls Val up to his feet with rough strength, and Val clears his throat before reaching back to touch his neck. The blood is still wet, but the wound has closed up tight, like nothing ever happened.

"I may need to wash my shirt," Val says.

The Professor nods. "And my floor."

Val laughs, relief and adrenaline mixing in his blood. "Happily, if you take me as your student."

The Professor's eyes dull with impatience, hand flexing over his cane. "Told you I don't do that anymore."

Val stands there, listening to his own heart rattle away. It always feels like it beats twice as hard for the minutes right after he comes back. "Surely there's something I can do for you to make you reconsider?"

Professor Williams sniffs once, and Val notices dawn beginning to push its own light into the house as they stare at each other.

"I don't need another student," the Professor says. "But I could use a bodyguard."

Val's head tilts to the side, a smile breaking over his mouth. "The master of killing needs a bodyguard?"

The Professor rolls his eyes at that and turns around to head back into the kitchen, the step of his right foot twice as loud with the cane thumping into the wood. "I hate that damn title. Listen." He picks up his tea, sniffing at it once before taking a sip. "I'm not whatever you are. But I'm not unlike you. Most things don't kill me either. But a couple still do. Not to mention the threat of all the many inventive ways that humans like to torture people like us. I gotta move on from this spot, and I could use someone like you to get where I'm going a little safer."

Val steps into the kitchen, already nodding his head. "When do I start?"

The professor glares at Val over his mug, steam still pouring off of it. "I need to be clear with you. I'm asking you to stand in the way of me and a lot of pain. Throwing yourself in the way of bullets without question, 'cause I can't know anymore which ones will kill me and which won't. I'm asking you to be a shield, not a weapon. It's gonna hurt."

Val shrugs at him, his head full of memories playing like the flickering movies they screen in the smoky theater that opened in Prosperity not too long ago. He hears the sound of crickets screeching and the clinking of tools in his chest. "It sounds like the perfect job for me, sir."

The Professor takes a gulp of his tea and nods. "You're hired. Go pack up your shit."

Val nods, turning around before he can smile like an idiot, walking out of the house with fresh blood sticking his shirt to his back. The stain is still spreading like wings unfurling across the fabric as Val hurries toward the woods, though he pauses briefly at the treeline. Glancing up at the soft pink and orange that's spilling over the sky to chase away the night, Val sees birds darting like arrows through the sky, on a hunt for food. Higher up above them, wisps of clouds drift in to signal another weather-less spring day over Prosperity. Beyond that still, where the pigments of night and day mingle together, there is a hand in the sky.

Its shape is hard to discern from so far away, but Val can see fingers half-curled toward its palm. The skin is a colorless white just like the clouds, but more solid than that—looming from a distance so great that Val can only imagine it in centuries. He waves to it once before tucking back into the woods to collect his things.

When Val returns to the Professor's living room with a fresh shirt on and all his things neatly strapped to his back, he startles as the old man tosses him another bag.

"Is this for me?" Val asks, fingers inching toward the cinched opening.

"No, it's *my* shit," the Professor says. "I told you, I gotta move on from this place. We're leaving. Heading west."

"Oh." Val stops himself from prying and sets his own pack down to strap the Professor's onto it. "Why are you moving?"

"Can't stay in one place for too long anymore," the Professor says, his gaze on the windows. "Just how it is."

"I assume this has something to do with whatever type of strange you happen to be," Val says, testing the straps once more before hoisting their things onto his back again.

"Yeah," the Professor mutters. "C'mon. Let's go. I gotta get some things from Prosperity before we split. D'you need to eat or are you a set size?"

Val blinks at him. "Sorry?"

The Professor starts ambling toward the door with a sigh. "I guess we got some catching up to do. You say you can't die. What happens if you starve?"

Val follows briskly as the Professor throws the front door open and starts through the clearing at an impressive clip, despite the cane. Looking between the Professor and the wide open door, Val calls, "Do you need me to close this? And what about the blood?"

"Forget it," the Professor barks. "Not my house anyway."

"Oh." With a smile, Val jogs back to the Professor, settling into step beside him. "The most I've gone without eating is a few days. I admit it didn't feel good, though I'm not sure I starve quite the same as regular people. I hardly hunger for things at all. It's more like a lack of fuel that sometimes makes me dizzy."

"Mm," the Professor nods, guiding them up the dirt road that leads to Prosperity. It's still cool from the night air, though the world is bright blue and green all around them. "I only need to eat when I have something to heal. When I'm healthy, I'm in stasis. You, on the other hand, seem like you're in a constant state of healing. Requires more intake, I'm guessing."

Val watches him speak with widened eyes. "So you've met others like me?"

"Oh yeah," the Professor says, his wry tone curbing some of Val's excitement. "I think, anyway. Not exactly a good way to test these things. People like me tend to want to hide. And people like you don't tend to chat."

Frowning, Val grips the straps of his pack and turns his gaze to the dirt path. There are wheel tracks framing the road they walk on, the cars that Prosperity proudly unveiled a few years back still not popular enough to warrant real roads.

"Professor, how do you know that there are things capable of killing you?" Val asks.

"Don't call me that," the Professor says. "I'm not a teacher anymore."

Val looks over at him, and the quiet displeasure in his brow. "Sir."

Professor Williams's steel eyes glance over at Val and back to the road ahead. "I should've healed from this." He points at the scar on his cheek, and then vaguely toward his right hip. "But I didn't. And I was lucky. I've seen others like me die. It didn't use to be possible, we—we thought we were immortal. So none of us were expecting it."

"What is it that kills you?" Val asks, brows creased. "Some kind of material? A certain weapon? Am I vulnerable to it as well?"

They join up with a gravel road, favoring the grass alongside it to keep the Professor's cane steadier.

"I know you're not vulnerable to it, because I stabbed you with a knife made of the same shit that cut my face open."

"Ah." Val gives a tight smile. "Sorry."

The Professor gives Val a skeptical frown. "You really have no clue what I'm talking about?"

"No, sir." Val shakes his head. "I've never met anyone who isn't human."

"Why'd you come to find me?" the Professor presses.

"Well, you *are* a skilled fighter." Val gestures to him. "And as you said, humans are very inventive when it comes to torture. I don't really know how to defend myself, and I wanted to learn from someone who did. I've had a few close calls as it is. I'm lucky I have a round face. It makes people pull their punches."

Val smiles as an example and the Professor glowers at him. "About that. How old are you?"

Turning away, Val says, "Twenty-five."

Almost immediately, there's a snap of pain over his ass, beneath where the pack sits on his back, and Val startles as he sees the Professor setting his cane back on the ground. Touching the sore spot, Val pouts at him.

"Did you just cane me?" Val asks.

"How old are you *really*?" the Professor asks.

Val's face pulls into a strained smile. "Twenty-three?"

The Professor grunts. "Fine, don't tell me. But you're shit at lying, you know that?"

With a laugh, Val nods. "So it is a material, then? Something that prevents your healing?"

The Professor shrugs. "Honestly, I haven't quite worked it out yet. All I know is that there are people out there that don't resemble my kind or regular humans, and they got means of hurting me. I can't trust my healing anymore."

"Why can't you just pick a house and stay there? Seems like the best way to avoid any trouble." Val gestures back toward the house they abandoned, now home only to his bloodstain.

The Professor abruptly stops, reaches for a flask on his hip, and takes a swig of something. "Trust me, boy, I've tried everything. If the humans don't wind up turning on me, something *else* inevitably shows up to try and do it for 'em."

"Something more like my type of strange?" Val ventures.

"Mm." The Professor nods.

"Is there some way to identify them, so I can properly watch out for you?" Val asks. "That is my job now, isn't it?"

The Professor's expression is guarded, clearly weighing the options of what to tell Val. In the daylight, it's easier to see his jaw in need of a shave, and skin that looks like it'll soak up the sun much better than Val's. He's much older than Val, but he still has an undoubtedly human air to him.

"I knew right away that you weren't human," the Professor says. "And not just 'cause of the way you stare."

Val's lips barely pinch as he listens, a voice in his head belonging to one of the orphanage staff chastising him for not keeping his eyes to himself. *Gods above, you never blink.*

"I haven't spent too much time with your type," the Professor goes on. "But I know they got a knack for finding my kind. That was my first tip-off. I made damn sure that no one had a reason to find me out here. You're not a good liar, but you wear that student shell with enough conviction, I bet I was the first to call you on your bullshit."

Val nods even though the Professor isn't looking at him, the smile falling off his face as he listens.

"Humans, dogs, cats, regular living things, they all give off a certain kind of resonance," the Professor goes on. "Like tapping a fork on glass. There's an echo. Not sure if that's a pulse or heartbeat or whatever else, but it's something I recognize. And then there's you."

He looks at Val again, eyes narrowed with the incoming accusation. "You got the same presence as an insect. Hard for me to feel it coming, but once you're in front of me, I know it. Usually something like you just tries to kill me, but you didn't. You dreamed about it, but you didn't make a move." The Professor chuckles. "Shit, you even asked me to kill you. Pretty fuckin' novel for me, all things told."

He almost sounds impressed, which has Val recovering some of his composure.

"I have no intention of killing you," Val tries to assure him. "That would defeat the purpose of me learning from you. Besides, I can't go murdering my employer before I've completed the job."

The Professor gives a shake of his head and another wry laugh. "Yeah, I'm not too worried about that, kid. Like I said, the ones I've met like you, they don't stop to chat. They don't bother lying. They got a job to do, and they don't stop until it's done. You may very well be your own thing entirely."

Frowning, Val looks back to the road. He can see the outline of Prosperity in the distance, blocky little buildings that give the impression of a child's play set from such a distance. This city is lower to the ground and a lot more spread out, unlike Foundation, the last major city he was in, with its gnarled university buildings that resembled trees more than man-made structures.

"Well that's not very comforting at all," Val admits, forcing a smile back onto his face like he's pulling the strings on a marionette. "Oh well. I'm better off now than I was before, that is certainly true. I'd rather have a job than have to hide in people's basements."

"Is that where you've been?" the Professor asks. "Squatting in people's houses?"

Val turns his smile back on in full brightness. "People are very generous with the locks on their cellar doors."

"Hm." The Professor quirks his gray brow once and leaves it be. "Throat hurts. Don't talk to me 'til we're there."

"Oh, yes, of course." Val turns away from him, setting his mind on the ever-growing sight of Prosperity.

Excitement begins to brew in his stomach at the thought that he'll be employed for the foreseeable future. This was a much better outcome than he could have ever hoped for. Even if this Professor seems a little rough around the edges, Val knows it's a price worth paying for the chance to learn something, even inadvertently. The perk of not having to lie about anything is much more freeing than he anticipated. He hardly realized how long it had been since he told anyone the truth.

He imagines this is close to what wine tastes like.

The silence is lovely, as long as he knows he's not walking alone. Even though he's already sure there will come a time when this man inevitably tells Val some version of the same speech he's gotten used to hearing, the one that accompanies getting left behind or turned in as a freak of nature or a door slammed in his face, he will do as he's told and savor whatever bit of company he can get. This job is an opportunity he can't pass up.

As the sun climbs higher and the air grows warmer, the Professor comes to another abrupt stop and half slaps, half pats Val's arm to catch him. Val has no idea how much time has passed, but they're nearly to the border of Prosperity.

"Hold on, need my matches."

Val turns away from him so the Professor can dig through his pack.

"You been to this place?" he asks Val. "Ya know, aside from breaking and entering."

"No, sir," Val says. "I've hardly spoken to anyone, aside from asking directions."

The Professor lights up and keeps on walking, cigarette leaving a trail of smoke from his left hand. "Don't mention we're traveling. Don't say anything about what we are. Just try not to talk at all. I'll handle it. We're only here for supplies and a meal."

"But, sir," Val starts, rejoining him. "If you don't need food, how do you refuel?"

The Professor jabs his cigarette at Val. "Told you. Don't say that shit out loud. We'll talk later."

The Professor hunches forward as a car comes down the gravel road. It's a boxy thing, like a tank for fish, only it's got two people inside. A woman in a voluminous dress fans herself in the passenger seat, and another woman in a fitted suit holds the wheel lazily in one hand. Neither pay any mind to Val and his companion as they go rolling by, but the Professor conveniently drifts behind Val as they pass.

"Are they looking for you?" Val asks.

"Mm." The Professor doesn't look back, but he picks up his pace. "You never know. I've been here too long."

"So I take it this will be a short stay in Prosperity," Val says, turning back to the approaching cityscape. "I was hoping to see a movie before I moved on."

The Professor gives a raspy cough. "The ones in Innovation were better."

Val turns to look at him, eyes wide. "You've been to Innovation?"

"Yeah, long time ago," the Professor says.

Val hitches their packs up higher as they finally step onto a proper walking path. "The other boys at the orphanage used to tell stories of flying cars in Innovation. Obviously I knew that wasn't true, but it must have been quite an incredible city. I think if I ever saw a cluster of buildings tall enough to block out the sun, I might really be terrified."

The Professor actually laughs at that, smoky as it is. "No city's ever come close to what they built, I'll give you that."

"Shame about the wall," Val says idly. "I'm sure someone will figure out how to deal with it."

"Mm."

The Professor falls quiet, and Val follows his lead.

The edges of Prosperity are all lined with quaint residential streets. It's different from Foundation, where one house-sized building tended to have at least four homes tucked away inside. Prosperity seems to follow a more spacious template, with every house fenced off and separated, a small kingdom unto every family. There are great glass windows in the houses here, and Val can't help but feel a strange pride emanating off of every structure—as if they're daring passersby to peek inside and marvel at their idyllic lives.

Ants in their hills.

Val watches all the same, marveling instead at how terribly easy it would be to throw a stone through those windows. He wonders if they have guns here. They didn't in the last town he passed through, but these big pretty houses with their neat little families certainly have a lot of places to hide secrets.

The Professor leads them out of the neighborhood and over to a liquor store that he makes Val wait outside as he buys something. After shoving a bottle of dark liquid into his pack, the Professor takes them to a smith where Val gets his question answered: they don't just have guns, they have *beautiful* guns, ornate from the grip to the barrel, crafted with pure artistry.

Once inside, the Professor turns to give Val a cataloging, discerning kind of stare, like he's sizing up how many portions he'll get from a cut of meat.

"Sir?" Val asks.

The Professor turns to the man behind the counter and starts fishing money out of his jacket pockets. "Need a palm pistol and a sharpening."

Along with the bills from his jacket, the Professor also puts two knives onto the dark wooden counter beside the cash register, pulled from a jacket sleeve and a pant leg.

"Very good, sir." The man behind the counter nods, and Val immediately perks up.

"Oh, are you very good with metals?" Val steps forward, suffering a withering warning glare from over the Professor's shoulder. "I know this is a silly request, but is it possible for you to turn a bit of scrap metal into a proper knife? It's an old thing, given to me by my father before he passed. I think he would be comforted to know that I could use it to defend myself."

The Professor, undoubtedly aware of how many lies Val has stuffed into one sentence, just lets his breath out and gestures. "And a custom knife, apparently."

The weapon smith leans his elbows onto the counter. "Let me see that metal, son. It'd take me a day at least, but I could try."

Nodding, Val reaches into his trousers, finding the seam of the extra pocket he sewed in ages ago, and extracts a thin piece of reflective metal. He catches sight of his own eyes for a brief moment, and remembers to blink.

"It's real small," the smith says when Val passes it over. "I suppose I could case it in a handle for you, but I'm not sure I could do much else without ruining it. What is this, anyway? Looks like a scalpel."

"My father was a doctor," Val lies. "Perhaps something just to fold it into? I don't want to risk cutting myself."

The smith nods, and turns to the Professor. "Come back tomorrow morning for your knives. I'll go get your palm pistol."

"Thanks," the Professor deadpans, shelling out some more money. "And you be real careful with that scalpel. Much sharper than it looks. Wouldn't do to . . . sully the memory of the boy's father by bleeding all over it."

The smith laughs, good-natured and no doubt completely unimpressed by the potential danger. "Sure thing, sirs."

As they step back out into the street, one pistol richer, the Professor grabs Val's arm. "You little shit. You *do* have a weapon."

"I . . . sorry?" Val looks at him as he forcefully walks Val further down the road.

"C'mon, you owe me a story," he says back. "Let's get you some food and a place for us to sleep. Maybe if you're on your best behavior, I'll teach you how to hold a knife like you *aren't* trying to get yourself killed."

Val's heart leaps into his throat, and he picks up his pace. "Yes, sir."

2

Val orbits the Professor as they cross the town to get to a humble inn, where the Professor books two rooms for them, and then to a diner up the block that smells like bacon and fried dough. The Professor asks the waitress to leave him a pot of coffee, and he lines his mug with whatever's currently filling his flask.

"You owe me a story," he says as he stirs his coffee.

Val blinks, resting his hands on the edge of a paper placemat. "I'm not very good at telling them, but I'll do my best."

"How'd you get that scalpel?" the Professor asks, lifting his mug up.

Val slides his fingernail under the edge of the paper, forcing it off the table and into his hands. "I'm not entirely sure. I don't know if I can trust my memories, but I can tell you what I saw."

The Professor takes an unceremonious gulp from his mug before setting it down with a *thunk* that sends a drop of dark liquid streaking down the side. "All I want is whatever you think the truth is."

Val's gaze flicks up to the Professor's gray eyes and back to the paper mat. The more he thinks about it, the sharper the memory is, like he's bringing it back into the light after years of fading. Pain searing through his insides, spilling over onto his outsides, the touch of things he should never know the texture of.

"I found it inside me," Val says, forcing himself to meet the Professor's eyes head on—just as steel as the scalpel. "I pulled it out of my own stomach. I was much younger. In the orphanage. That's the first time I realized I didn't quite get along with death."

The Professor's fingers tighten around the handle of his mug. "Pulled it out of your own stomach."

Val nods. "I had a bad dream that night. And I woke up feeling like there was something stuck in me. So I dug it out in the bathroom. I'm fairly certain I would have died if it weren't for what I am, but, well."

The Professor pulls his jacket off, tossing it in a heap on the bench beside himself and leans his arms onto the table between them. "Did you have surgery when you were younger?"

"Not that I recall, but I can't say what happened when I was too young to pay attention," Val says. "I've thought about it a lot. It's more than likely that I was treated for something before I could remember it. Or that whoever left me in the orphanage really did give me a souvenir. But I don't really think that's it."

"Me neither," the Professor says, staring at Val with narrowed eyes. "Did you feel anything new after you pulled it out?"

Val shrugs. "There was a lot of blood. I think I was mostly trying not to die. It was before I knew I couldn't."

"Bad dream, huh?" the Professor asks, and Val is pleasantly surprised that he's not calling Val names.

"Recurring nightmare, actually," Val clarifies, the paper placemat ripping between his fingers. "Of waking up on an operating table."

The Professor taps his finger as he speaks. "You had a nightmare about getting surgery, and then woke up and pulled a piece of a scalpel out of your guts?"

Val sets the placemat back down, smoothing over the rip. "Sounds crazy, doesn't it?"

The Professor nods, leaning away from him. "You tell me if you remember anything else about that night."

Val scoots forward on the bench, eyes wide. "Do you believe me? Maybe the dream was some kind of sign?"

"I don't know jack shit, kid," the Professor says back, grabbing his mug again. "But it's a starting point."

Nodding, Val tries to temper his excitement as they wait for the food. When the Professor ordered the largest meal on the menu, Val assumed it was to share. But after the waitress sets down three different plates, Val watches the Professor take a single bite of every item of food and then put his silverware down.

"Don't waste," he says, hunching down to nurse his mug.

Val straightens his back and takes up his own knife and fork. Saliva starts to well up as he cuts everything into neat pieces. It's been much too long since he ate food from a real kitchen. Everything has such a strong taste to it, and his eye twitches at the first bite of each new thing like it stings.

He eats everything on the table in silence.

"You ever actually use a knife or a gun on someone before?" the Professor asks as he throws money on the table.

"No, sir," Val answers, sliding their packs back on with a smile. "I'll be a good student though, I promise."

The Professor heaves a sigh, hauls himself back up to his feet, and *whaps* Val's thigh with his cane. "Don't look at me like that."

Val chokes on a gasp before jogging after the Professor as he lumbers out of the diner. "Sorry, sir," Val says, even if he doesn't quite know why.

Even after it heals, Val rubs the sore spot on his thigh as they walk back to the inn. It's afternoon, and the brightness of the sun has brought out a crowd of people to fill the streets. A couple cars go drifting by, and Val finds himself drawn to the sight of a construction crew working on laying down tracks for some kind of fixed trolley. Those were popular in Foundation for all the students to get where they needed to go across the massive campus, but Val rarely had occasion or money to use them himself.

"Professor," Val says, tugging on the man's sleeve. "Why do you think humans are always trying to build bigger?"

With a grunt and a laugh, the Professors answers, "They fuck, they make more humans, they need more space. Not complicated."

He flings open the front door to the inn, and Val takes a few more seconds to look at the construction crew, so lost in their task, before he ducks in after him.

"Logically, I know you're right, but that doesn't explain the need for shiny new toys, like cars and trains," Val presses. "Dogs don't invent new ways to play fetch. They're happy with sticks."

The Professor's cane thumps all the way up the stairs. "They have dreams, kid. They see more than dogs. Can't be helped."

Val considers this for all of five seconds before the Professor unlocks one of the rooms and shoulders it open. "Sit down."

Rushing in after him, Val places their things on the floor, his pulse uncomfortably tight under his neck. "Is it time?"

"Sit, fuck's sake." The Professor locks the door and drops onto the edge of the neatly made bed, resting his cane up against the wooden nightstand.

Val gingerly takes the space beside him, putting his hands under his thighs as the Professor unsheathes the knife from inside his cane.

"Here," he says, shoving the handle at Val.

Startling, Val takes it from him, careful to pull the blade away without risk of cutting either of them. "Is it best to start with the knife that could actually hurt you?" he asks, staring at the shockingly clean surface of it.

"You said yourself you aren't trying to kill me," the Professor says back. "So I shouldn't have anything to worry about."

Turning back to him, Val nods several times. "Yes, I promise."

The Professor rolls his eyes. "This isn't a confessional, c'mon."

He grabs Val's wrist, pulling him closer so he can cup one of his hands around Val's, pressing Val's fingers into the handle of the knife.

"Hold it like you mean it," he says.

Val tightens his grip with the Professor's calloused skin insulating his own. "Sorry, sir."

"If you're too afraid of the weapon, you'll only hurt yourself," the Professor tells him. "Go on."

He pulls his hands away and Val lifts the thin blade up, rolling the handle in his palm. He tests different ways to hold it, attempting to slot the blade between his fingers to get a stronger grip.

"Don't do that." The Professor slaps Val's fist and pries his fingers back open. "That's a perfect way to slice your own hand in half."

He takes the knife back, waving it in front of Val. "Lesson one. This knife is shit. It has no protection on it. You're just as likely to hurt yourself as you are anyone who's coming at you. Shit knives like this are for last resorts, got it?"

Val nods, pressing his tongue in the indents of his teeth where a bit of powdered sugar still lingers from their meal.

"A good weapon doesn't fight back," the Professor says, sheathing the blade back into his cane. Val can see that there's a locking mechanism as he subtly twists the handle in place. Then he lifts the entire cane up. "You'll get more mileage out of the whole stick than you would from that knife."

"But you have to keep it close, because you know it can hurt you," Val says, eyes on the length of wood where he knows that steel is buried.

"Mm." The Professor pulls the palm pistol out of his pants pocket, pops open the front plate, and shakes it around to make sure it isn't loaded. After fixing the plate back on, he takes Val's hand again and slaps it onto the gun. It's a strange thing, not like a gun at all with its circular design, but Val eases his hand around it like he did the knife.

"These are squeeze action," the Professor says, wrapping both his hands around Val's and pressing the unloaded trigger for him. It *clicks* harmlessly without a bullet inside, the noise ticking inside Val's head like a clock. "Get used to that feeling. It means you're out of options."

He does it three more times, squeezing the trigger with his hands bracketing Val's around the gun. Val swallows the sugar unearthed from the ridge of his teeth, refraining from commenting that this is the closest he's ever been to holding someone's hand. The thought hits him like a clock striking noon.

"Go on." The Professor lets go and points Val toward the wall.

Val can feel the Professor's gaze as he extends his arm and slowly applies more pressure until he hears the *click*. His shoulders twitch at the sound, so he does it again.

"Sir," he says.

Click.

"Mm?"

"If you don't want me to call you Professor, what should I call you?"

Click.

The Professor shifts his weight, sighing over Val's shoulder.

Click.

"Professor's fine. Just don't go acting like I have anything for you but this. Real teachers don't get their students hurt."

Click.

Val lowers the gun, looking at the pearly inlay in his open hand. "Will the barrel burn me when it has real bullets?"

"Probably," the Professor says.

Val squeezes it idly one more time, setting off the *click* against his thigh before he turns to face the Professor. "Is there a way to stop someone like me? What will we do if one of them comes after you?"

Setting his cane onto the hardwood floor, the Professor braces himself to get back to his feet. He tosses a room key onto the nightstand and tells Val, "All we can do is buy time to get away. Can't kill what can't die." Val watches him separate his pack from Val's and sling it over his shoulder, something about his movement making him look much further away. "If you cut off enough limbs, they'll have to spend time regenerating instead of hunting. That's usually enough time to get clear of the threat."

Nodding, Val looks back at the pistol. "I suppose that's my job now."

"Don't fuck it up," the Professor says as he opens the door. "I'm across the hall. Leave me alone 'til sunrise."

"Yes, sir," Val says immediately.

It takes a few seconds of solitude for Val to realize that the inn smells like varnish and lemons. Until the Professor left the room, he could only smell smoke. With his belly still full, Val locks his door and immediately begins undressing. Unearthing his blood-stained shirt from earlier, Val takes all his dirty clothes and goes to wash them in the bathroom.

Once everything is strung up to dry around the room, he sits in the tub, clean and a little too warm. He looks at his palms, slightly pink, still soft, though there are more lines cross-hatched in his skin than he remembers. His are nothing like the Professor's hands—worn, leathery, carved with a knife of experience that Val has yet to hone. As he sits in the water, Val curls his fingers like he's holding the palm pistol, half surprised when he squeezes and there is no audible *click*.

He's not sure he wants to kill a human, but he's pretty sure he'd feel okay protecting the Professor. Even when Val thinks about the way people have turned on him, it isn't anger that surrounds those memories. He's not even sure he would recognize the feeling if it ever wormed its way into his head. That valve has been shut off, or maybe he never had it.

Even when people call him names or try to hurt him, Val can't stop himself from coming back. He doesn't mind the pain. He just wants the opportunity to watch.

As the water cools, a small shiver of movement catches his eye, and Val turns to see a spider descending on a string of silk to the lip of the bathtub. The webbing winks in and out of view as it catches the light, the spider itself like a drop of black water slowly falling from the ceiling. The longer Val watches it, the more he feels the presence of its body in the room. Such a small thing hardly registers as living, but when he allows it to take up space in his senses, it begins to produce the softest vibration, hardly noticeable at all, but peaceful in its way. The spider effortlessly walks around droplets of water as it heads for the wall, disappearing underneath the edge of the tub, but Val can still feel it, like a single strand of hair out of place.

"Get something good to eat down there," Val says, pulling the drain plug.

The vibration vanishes from his notice as he rises out of the water. Before he gets his towel, he stands with his back to the mirror, craning his head over his shoulder to make sure there's no more blood left from when the Professor killed him earlier. As he stares at his unmarred skin—no marks, no moles, nothing but fine, pale body hair—he remembers the coarse feel of the Professor's hands on his own, and Val looks down at his palms again.

Living skin. Val knows his will never feel like the Professor's does, but he'd be grateful for a scar of his own, to prove that he's alive. As it is, hardly anyone touches him, and when they do, there are no marks to show for it.

Pulling on a long nightshirt, Val lays on top of the blue floral covers of the inn's modest bed, and closes his eyes. He can still catch the slightest edges of the Professor's smoky scent, but he can also smell a hundred hands before him, touching everything in this room. He can sense the receptionist pacing on the floor below, another guest in the room to his left unpacking their bags, and across the hall, the absolute stillness of the Professor in his room. He's not moving, but his presence seems to give off the faintest warmth. Not human warmth either—more like candlelight.

Val shivers and tells himself it's time to rest.

The dream. The same one. The sting of alcohol in his nose, the sound of electronic beeping, and the hush of voices he's not supposed to be listening to. They're making an incision along his flank. They want to know what he's made of.

Eyes loom over Val's, haloed by harsh lights from above. Their face and hair are covered from sight with muted green paper. They are only their eyes, devoid of color, perfect white and perfect black, staring at him.

He can feel gloved fingers sliding in between his stomach and his liver. There is so much more space inside of him than he ever realized.

Val wakes up with the sunlight wrapped around his bare ankle. When he sits up, spider silk catches on his hair, but he doesn't see the web spinner anywhere.

"Sorry, friend," he says, brushing the strands away. "I'm too big for you to eat."

Dressed and packed, Val stands before the Professor's door, wondering whether or not he's supposed to knock. He can tell the Professor is still inside, completely immobile but no doubt alive and well. Glancing toward the fresh sunlight filling the window at the end of the hall, Val figures it's best for both of them if they get a move on before the town wakes up. He knocks as loud as he can, and presses his ear to the wooden door.

"Professor? It's morning, should we go to the smith?"

Val is answered by a rasping cough, and the sound of a match struck against a box. He smells smoke first, and then the Professor answers him.

"Punctual, huh? Gimme a second."

Val backs up against the wall to wait for him, letting his senses unwind around the slowly moving shape on the other side of the door. A minute later, the Professor steps out into the hall and tosses Val his bag, cigarette pinched between his fingers.

"Let's go."

As Val follows him down the stairs and into the lobby, it seems like the Professor is moving faster than he was the day before.

"You good on food, or what?" he asks Val as he throws open the door to the street.

"All good, sir," Val answers. "You fed me enough for at least a day."

"Good," the Professor says. "With any luck, we'll be well on our way to the Dueling Cities by nightfall."

Val grins. "Really? Are they as dazzling as everyone says they are? The boys I grew up with always talked about making a trip when they were of age."

Another beautiful day crests over the tops of the buildings in Prosperity. With hardly anyone on the streets, Val finds himself talking quietly for no real reason.

The Professor hustles along as if there's a crowd he's trying to stay ahead of. "They're easy to get lost in, I'll tell you that much. Can't say it's my favorite place, but they got everything you could ever need, so we have to go."

Val holds the Professor's bag against his chest. "I hear they don't turn their lights off, even after dark. Must be awful to live there."

"That's why there are two cities," the Professor says, rubbing his eye with the back of his hand. "Modesty has a strict curfew so Indulgence doesn't have to. It's, like—" He snaps his fingers a few times, calling the word up out of his head. "Symbiotic. One's always waking up while the other is going to sleep."

Val smiles at that. "Hardly a duel then, is it?"

The Professor laughs into his next drag on the cigarette. As they cross the empty street to get to the smith's front door, Val begins to feel something odd against his skin. The closed sign hangs askew in the window, no lights on inside, a perfectly unimposing sight. He stops to grab the Professor's arm.

"What?" the Professor asks, glaring at Val with his hair in his eyes.

Val turns toward the shop, trying better to listen. All he can hear are birds calling to one another, and someone's car starting up several streets away, but he feels something else. Cold water splashing around his ankles—an intruder stepping into his pond, raising goosebumps all across his body.

It smells sweet, like freshly baked cookies.

"Something's wrong," Val says.

The Professor makes a low sound, not breaking eye contact with the front door as he yanks Val closer, fishing out the pistol from his bag and loading it without looking.

"This is for self-defense only, you hear me? I'll go in first."

"But—" Val lurches forward, but the Professor immediately snaps his cane across Val's stomach.

"Do as I say."

Val swallows his protest, taking the bag and the gun in each hand. "Yes, sir."

The Professor picks up his cane and walks toward the door, no limp in his step as he crosses the sidewalk. Val follows after him as quietly as he can. Whatever is inside the shop hasn't moved much, but the feeling is only getting stronger, rattling up Val's spine.

"Should we call someone?" Val whispers.

"No."

The Professor tests the door, and when it doesn't budge, he reaches into his jacket for some rudimentary lock pick. It takes him all of five seconds to release the lock and nudge the door forward with his cane. He turns to Val with his finger raised to his lips. Val nods, eyes pinned wide open as the darkness of the store looms ahead.

The shop smells so strongly, it engulfs the Professor's own smoky scent and turns it to burnt sugar in Val's nose. His mouth waters up as he takes a cautious step inside. The Professor gestures at the open door, and Val quickly shuts it behind them, fixing the crooked *closed* sign on some anxious impulse.

Val steps into the middle of the shop as the Professor ducks behind the counter, quickly hunting around until he finds the two knives he left there the day before. The presence giving Val goosebumps is further back, hidden behind a drawn curtain. When the Professor points at it, Val nods several times, his hand slowly tightening around the palm pistol. When he feels his grip faltering, he sets the Professor's bag down so he can hold the gun with both hands.

Using his cane, the Professor eases the drab brown curtain aside, revealing a work room at the end of a thin hallway. Val can see someone hunched over a desk, the smith himself, wearing the same exact clothes he had been yesterday—a brown vest cinched tightly over a white shirt, slicked-back hair now pushed slightly out of place. His shoulders keep jumping up to his ears and sinking back down before jumping up once again, like the gears of a machine set to a relentless task.

As Val comes closer, he can hear mumbling.

"Sharp, sharper, sharpest. Sharp, sharper, sharpest."

The Professor takes one more step, and another, Val inching into the cramped hall after him. Putting one knife into his jacket, unsheathing another, the Professor moves in graceful motions that Val wants to be more impressed by, but his own pounding heart is getting in the way. The workshop's walls are lined from top to bottom with weapons, every available inch armed.

Val watches the Professor take another deep breath from his cigarette, chest puffing up, so he can blow smoke in the smith's direction. In an instant, the smith's body goes stock still as pale smoke drapes over his shoulders in the silence. He turns his head to look at them, neck twisting uncomfortably tight, and his body following suit, like it's on a delay.

There's a streak of red across both the smith's hands, which he holds out in front of him, open-palmed.

"Gentlemen."

His head ticks to the left once, and resettles. Val isn't close enough to see why, but he can tell from this distance that the man's eyes are wrong. Too big, or maybe too dark.

The Professor still has his knife held between himself and the smith. "What happened to you?"

"You're here for your order," the smith says, not moving. "Two knives sharpened. One custom handle. I'm afraid—"

He stops, mouth open, blood-stained hands still splayed out in waiting. Val pushes himself forward, his eyes snagging on the smith's nails. They've turned black.

"I had some trouble with the custom order," the smith abruptly picks up his sentence again. "I had some trouble. I fit it into a handle, but I had to know. The trouble. How sharp it was."

"Why don't we take that off your hands, then?" the Professor says. "My boy'll get it. Nice and easy."

Val twitches as he realizes he's being asked to do something. Walking toward the smith is like walking into a heated oven. Something is both fighting him and inviting him to get closer with every step he takes. Passing in front of the Professor brings back that brief taste of smoke, but the second Val is in front of him, the smith turns his head to Val. His eyes are solid black, shiny and unblinking as he watches. The smell of sugar is uncomfortably sweet, like a trap set just for Val. His mouth is watering again.

"Don't mind me," Val says under his breath, inching into the work room. He hugs the wall, hoping to circle around the smith and check his desk for the scalpel.

The smith's face tracks Val's movement perfectly. "I had—some trouble."

"I know," Val says, gaze flicking between the smith's eyes and the surface of his desk. The wood is covered in blood, a massive stain spread from the center of it and dripping off the edge. Val can see his scalpel, affixed now to a small handle that looks like it once belonged to a multi-tool. The smell of sugar is definitely coming from the smith's own blood, half dried on his desk.

When Val reaches for the scalpel, he takes his time, maintaining eye contact with the smith so as not to startle him. The moment the ridges of his fingerprint touch the metal, the smith claps his own hand down on top of Val's, pinning him to the bloody wood. Val tries to pull away, but the smith holds tight, and the scalpel bites into Val's palm as his hand slides forward.

"Are you going to eat him?" the smith asks, no inflection in his voice.

His eyes aren't eyes at all, but a smooth, hard shell. His fingernails are the same shiny black, like the casing on a beetle's wings. Val's mouth twitches as the scalpel digs into his fingers.

"I don't eat people," Val says, fixed on those reflective black eyes.

"If you're not going to," the smith drawls, jaw moving with too-wide sweeps, like his teeth are moving around inside his gums. "I'm quite hungry."

Val's fingers twitch around the palm pistol, and as soon as he thinks he should do something about this threat on the Professor's life, that this is his job now and he should really *get a move on*, the smith grabs Val's gun arm. He shoves Val's hand out wide, away from himself, and lurches out of his chair to sink his teeth into Val's shoulder.

Pain. Val closes his eyes as it rips through his flesh. It hurts so bad, so fresh. These teeth aren't human. They pierce deep, ripping into muscle, and lodging in bone. These teeth are strange, hot and sharp, like they're eating away at Val's sinew.

Val forces his lids back open, every inch of him wanting to scream, hoping the shock of sunlight in his eyes will help him keep it down. All he thinks is, *we're trying to keep quiet. I have a job to do. Protect, protect, protect.*

The Professor moves in so swiftly, Val only catches sight of him the moment before he sticks a knife into the back of the smith's neck. The smith's body twitches, the pressure of his grip letting up just enough for Val to get his shoulder free of those teeth.

"Knives," the Professor orders, yanking the smith off of Val and using his own body to crush him to the floor of the workshop. "The wall! Give me as many knives as you can find."

Ignoring the pain in his left side, Val immediately turns to the rows of weapons, pulling anything with a blade off the wall to toss to the Professor. One by one, the Professor drives each knife straight through the smith's body with enough force to pin him to the wood floor beneath their feet. Every *thunk* of the knife and *creak* of the floorboards makes Val's vision blurrier, like he's being stabbed too. The smith doesn't make a single sound, or maybe Val just can't hear it. He finds himself leaning against the wall in a crouch, the room spinning violently as his shoulder screams from those teeth marks. The last thing he sees before he shuts his eyes is the smith adorned with the handles of at least eight knives, his body perfectly still.

"C'mon."

The Professor slides his hands around Val's shoulders. It feels like it's been hours. How long have they been here? And why does his shoulder hurt so bad?

"We can't stay here."

Val feels calloused fingers on his face, turning his head until he's looking at the Professor's scarred cheek once again. It's the only thing he can see.

"Did . . . I do alright?" Val asks with a dry mouth. His entire left side is numb.

Now he can see the Professor's mouth, pink lips set in their ways, and a chin in need of a shave.

"You did great."

Val smiles, hoping to memorize the way the Professor's mouth moved as he said that.

"Up, up, up." The Professor's hands go firm around Val's waist, forcing him back to his feet. "You're healing. Might feel weird, but I need you to keep moving."

"Yes, sir," Val says, tongue heavy.

"No more talking," the Professor says. "Let your body do what it needs to do. Just walk for me."

Val nods, leaning against him as they shuffle back to the front of the store. The only things he can feel are his shoulder rebuilding itself with blinding heat, and the Professor's body pressed against his own. His jacket smells like smoke, no more sugar.

Walking isn't so bad when he knows the Professor is guiding him. The pain doesn't hurt the same with a hand curled over his side. Val closes his eyes, trusting the Professor to get them somewhere safe. All he needs to do now is listen.

***

By the time Val can see again, he and the Professor have disappeared into the woods outside of Prosperity. The edge of the town is just barely visible, and despite the fact that it's the same sleepy neighborhood it was just an hour ago, Val can't help but see something else in its humble architecture—rot growing between teeth.

"Your bag," Val says, blinking at the Professor. "And my knife."

"Got it," the Professor says. "Don't worry."

Val takes a deeper breath.

"Can you walk or what?" the Professor asks.

"Oh, yes, sorry." Val straightens up, pushing the two of them apart.

The Professor immediately drops the arm he had around Val and pulls his cane out of the strap of Val's pack. He goes still, feeling at his side with a look like he's tasted sour candy.

"Oh, your wound." Val startles. "I should—should I help? Can I?"

"It'll settle," the Professor says. "Just gimme a minute."

Val nods, turning back to look at Prosperity, the backs of quaint little houses full of sleeping people.

"Did you know the smith was one of them?" Val asks. "Or did we just get lucky?"

The Professor scoffs. "I'm always lucky."

Val turns to him with a frown. "I'm sorry to hear that."

With a labored sigh, the Professor starts walking again, slow but steady. "These things don't exactly have names. They hide out in humans, wearing them like cocoons, waiting for the moment when they hatch. You saw the way the smith had some pieces on him that looked more like an insect?"

Val nods, unfortunately clear memories of those beetle-shell eyes and nails still fresh in his mind.

"He was still changing. If he'd been a full hybrid, he wouldn't have bothered with pleasantries, I can promise you that. He would have taken one look at me and gone for it. This one, he was still remembering."

Val's mouth opens but no words come out. Something like nausea swirls in his guts. "Was it—could it have been because of me?"

The Professor glances over at Val, and maybe it's the pain from his old wound, but there's a shadow in his eyes. "Did you do something to him?"

"N-no, of course not!" Val starts, but he catches himself, dropping his gaze to the grass. "At least, I don't think so. But I guess I can't know for sure. I don't really know how this works."

"Hm." The Professor squeezes his side again as he starts walking. "Maybe you slowed it down somehow. Something to think about, I guess."

Val looks back over at the way the Professor is massaging his side. "Do you need to sit for a minute?"

"Gotta get further away," he says. "Too many people saw us. When they find the smith, it'll send them into a panic. If they go searching for outsiders, we have to be sure we're far enough away."

Val reaches over and pulls on the Professor's pack. "At least let me take this."

"Fine, fine," the Professor shrugs it off his shoulders and goes back to squeezing his side. The spot is right above his hip. It must ache with every movement.

"Were you stabbed?" Val asks, pointing.

The Professor gives a dry laugh. "Most people don't come right out and ask."

Val smiles. "Well I'm not most people."

"That's for damn sure." The Professor huffs, but at least he looks amused. "Shot actually. Fucking coward didn't have the guts to finish me off himself. A friend patched me up, and I've been like this ever since."

"A friend?" Val perks up. "Another person like you?"

"Yeah." With a grunt, the Professor tightens up his jaw and says, "Hush up for a while. We gotta walk."

"Yes, sir."

They fall silent, save for the crunch of their footsteps on the forest floor. The determined look on the Professor's face begins to worry Val, like he's making himself go on out of pure spite, but Val is starting to get the feeling that asking about it won't get him anywhere, so he simply slows his own pace to match the Professor's.

When he's not worrying for the Professor's hip, he's thinking about the smith. His beetle-shell eyes and whatever poison was lining his teeth. Now that his head is clear, Val is sure that's what happened. It doesn't usually take him so long to heal, but he's never been infected by something like that. It felt like acid in his blood. His own regeneration was only a little faster. Knowing that it was only a brand new, half-hatched creature puts Val on edge. He has no idea what he'll do if they come up against something truly ruthless.

"Is there a way to save someone like that?" Val asks. "The smith?"

"No clue," the Professor says. "Too dangerous for me to try."

Val doesn't ask any more questions.

They walk and walk and walk until the sky starts to turn dark blue and then they set up camp in the woods. Val puts up his tent and the Professor sits heavily on the ground, leaning up against a tree trunk.

"We gotta work on your pain tolerance," he says when Val finishes shoving their things into the tent.

"Work on it?" Val echoes. "What do you mean?"

"C'mere," the Professor gestures in front of him, so Val kneels at his feet, hands on his thighs. The Professor pulls out one of his knives from the inside of his jacket. "Give me your hand."

Val startles, his heart skipping a beat as he sticks his palm out.

The Professor's hand dwarfs Val's as he cups Val's knuckles and wrist. He sets the tip of the knife on the side of Val's finger.

"You ever notice much about how your body handles pain?" he asks.

"No, sir," Val says, his voice turning to a whisper.

The Professor pricks the side of Val's ring finger just enough to spare a drop of blood, and pain sparkles in Val's eyes. When he pulls the knife away, one droplet of red sits pretty on the side of the blade. Val's skin immediately sews itself back together.

"Still hurt?" the Professor asks.

"No."

Val hardly recognizes the softness of his own voice. He lifts his gaze from the knife to the Professor's gray eyes, his bangs curtaining over them. The Professor pulls a cloth from his pants pocket and wipes the blade off before he takes Val's hand again.

"Different parts of you hurt differently," he says. "It's good to know where to anticipate the worst, and which parts of you heal faster. If someone's coming at you with a knife, or teeth, try to guide them away from your softer parts."

Flipping Val's hand over, he uses the tip of the knife as a pointer.

"You got tendons back here. They'll take longer to heal, and you don't want a useless hand in a fight. If you're going to try to block something, I don't recommend these."

He traces up to Val's wrist, the knife scraping along his flesh without breaking the skin. "Wrist is too narrow. You're gonna hit something big here. Don't use it."

The knife leaves goosebumps in its wake.

"The meatier parts of your arm are safer, but still a gamble."

He draws a circle with the knife tip over Val's skin, above and below the joint of his elbow, and Val shivers at the lightness of it.

"If you're blocking something with your bicep, turn to the side."

He physically turns Val's shoulder toward himself to demonstrate, and Val nods several times, in quiet awe at the Professor's willingness to continue touching him.

"You remember what I said about the knife in my cane?" he asks, leaning forward to catch Val's eye.

"That it's a bad knife, because it can hurt you too?" Val asks.

"Yes." The Professor gives him a stern look, his hand still wrapped tight around Val's arm. "That's what it means to be in a fight. Doesn't matter what kind. You can't take hubris with you when someone's coming at you to kill. Pain is inevitable. You just gotta know how to negotiate that pain so it winds up in your favor."

"Thank you," Val says, breathless for no real reason. There are goosebumps on every inch of him.

The Professor lets go and leans back against the trunk of the tree. "You should get some sleep. Conserve your energy. We'll be walking more tomorrow and I'll need you alert."

"Are you expecting it to be dangerous?" Val asks.

"Moving around is the fastest way to alert any insects to where I am," the Professor says with his eyes shut, hands on his cane.

"You must need something very important to risk moving this much," Val says.

He opens one eye to glare at Val. "You're gonna mitigate that risk. Aren't you?"

"Yes, sir." Val can't stop the smile blooming on his face. "Will you be sleeping as well?"

He waves Val away. "Gonna stay out here for a while. Sleep already."

Val tells him goodnight and gets into his tent, squishing a sweater under his head for a pillow. It's a nice night, not too cold, not too warm, and he feels himself relaxing faster. When he hears the Professor striking a match, and smells smoke in the air, he can almost forget the smith, pinned to the floor of his own shop, beetle-shell eyes unable to close.

The middle of the night feels heavier. Val wakes up in pitch blackness, feeling like he's drowning. Searching through his backpack, he finds the night light he got in Foundation: a small orb that fits in the palm of his hand. He switches it on with his thumb, and a glow no brighter than a couple of matches washes over the empty tent. Concern edges into Val's pulse, and he steps out of the tent to find the Professor.

He's sitting exactly where Val left him, back to the trunk of a tree, hands on his cane, looking for all the world like he's part of the roots. His eyes are closed, and there is a peacefulness about him that Val has never seen before. He has the wild thought that this man belongs out here in the woods. Even the colors of the Professor's clothing seem to blend into the wood of the tree.

As Val looks over his sleeping form, he is sure that the Professor must have left behind a real name at some point. Even Val, who has no care for his own full name, found a way to tailor it to fit himself better. The Professor must be more lost than he looks if there are no names that suit him anymore.

Something odd creeps in around Val's senses, tickling his nose like a feather. It makes him want to sneeze, and he turns around to try to spot the intruder.

"Professor," he whispers harshly, not wanting to give them away. He crouches down, turning his light off and shaking the Professor's leg. "Get up, something's coming."

The Professor shakes awake, lurching forward to put his hand on Val's shoulder. "Where?"

"I can't tell, but it doesn't seem to care about subtlety."

If the smith felt like cautious steps into his pond, this thing is stomping into Val's waters and intentionally making waves. It's so disruptive, it's almost disorienting.

"That's a real one," the Professor mutters. "Turn your light back on. Better to be prepared than blind."

Val clicks it back on, standing up to scan the trees for any movement. The darkness in a forest is twice as impenetrable as it is in a city, and Val's eyes refuse to adjust, but he can feel that careless invasion of his senses pointing him in a certain direction. He steps toward it while the Professor scrambles through his bag.

"It's definitely coming from over here," Val says.

"Can you tell the distance?" the Professor.

"No, sir," Val says. "Sorry."

"Alright." He steps up beside Val and holds out the palm pistol. "Let's go meet it."

Val takes the gun, heart pounding in his mouth. "Alright."

Val forces himself to walk toward the disturbance, even if it feels like going to greet an avalanche. The Professor's sure footing behind him gives him a little more confidence, and he holds the gun properly in one hand, the light held tightly in the other. Slowly, the scent of the forest begins to ebb, and something else takes its place. More sugar, even sweeter than the smith, like walking into a fully stocked candy store. He can practically taste it coating his mouth.

Just as swiftly as it made itself known, it goes completely still, and Val hesitates.

"It's not moving."

"We have the upper hand since you can sense it," the Professor urges. "If it's setting a trap, we'll deal with it."

Nodding, Val keeps walking, focusing in on the suddenly quiet vibrations emanating from the darkness. They're getting softer, like whatever it is might be falling asleep, and Val hurries forward. More and more, it feels like setting his bare foot onto a nail, but the sensation is so disquieting, he can't stop himself from drawing nearer. If it *is* a trap, it's better if he's the one to spring it.

The silence puts him on edge, but Val keeps going, bracing himself as he raises the pistol. Finally, the light crests over the sight of a human leg, pants tucked into a thick brown boot. Val stops short, raising the light up to get a better look at the body sprawled over the earth. Two human legs, perfectly normal in appearance, hips and a torso he can't find fault in. It takes far too long for Val to notice the *other* legs in a strange ruddy color that doesn't catch the light. Six of them lay prone on the ground beside the man's body, half-curled up toward the sky, covered in fine hairs and ending in claw-like points. Four out of six of them look broken, hanging at odd angles and gushing fluid all over themselves.

There's a long thin blade sheathed through its human throat, not unlike how the Professor left the smith, but this creature is already starting to move again. Val can't call this human, not with its black, compounded eyes bulging out of its face, and the long bizarre protrusion sticking out where its nose should be. As Val approaches it, he can see more destruction. There are two long black pieces of shell discarded, and the pale fiber of see-through wings lay beside them, clearly ripped off the back of this thing.

"Shit." The Professor leans on his cane beside Val, taking in the sight of the hybrid, half-dead on the ground. "Someone beat us to it."

"Is that a good thing or a bad thing?" Val asks, watching one of the insectoid legs begin to heal. New exoskeleton forms up around the severed area, slowly pushing the broken piece out of the way.

"If someone's hunting these things for us, that's a gift horse that I don't need to look at. Let's get out of here before it heals." The Professor pats Val on the back roughly enough to make him lurch forward.

"Right." Val says it, but he's still staring at the hybrid. Its jaw is starting to open and close rhythmically. It can't fully close, not with the pincers sticking up past its lips, but there are human teeth and a tongue inside that mouth.

"C'mon, don't waste time," the Professor barks, already several feet back in the direction of their camp.

Val turns toward him, feeling something hard in the pit of his stomach. An emotion that he doesn't know what to do with. When he tries to handle it, it's much too sharp. Jogging back up to the Professor, Val reaches out and grabs onto the back of his long jacket.

"What?" the Professor asks, glancing over his shoulder.

"Just don't want to get lost," Val says back. "Who do you think did that?"

"No clue," the Professor grumbles. "It's not dead though. Remember that."

"You sure there's nothing we can do to stop the healing process?" Val asks. "Or truly incapacitate it?"

"If you got any brilliant ideas, I'm all ears. As it stands, I don't like to get too close to 'em. Not at the risk of them taking off my limbs," the Professor says back.

Val has the briefest impulse to go back to it, to look over every inch of the insect hatched out of a human, but he knows that would only be putting the Professor at risk.

"No, you're right, caution is better. But, I would very much appreciate you teaching me a little more about how to protect you," Val says, tugging on the Professor's jacket. "The more I know, the more efficient we'll be."

The Professor waves his hand with a grunt. "Yeah, yeah. Let's get to the next city first. Hopefully no one tries to kill us there."

"That would be nice," Val says.

He knows where they're going, but he keeps his fingers bunched in the Professor's jacket anyway. Just as suddenly as before, something brushes against the very edges of Val's senses, a shadow seated somewhere in the dark. Val turns his head toward it, letting go of the Professor as a feather-light presence just barely draws his eye. Even though he knows he won't be able to see anything, Val stares out into the pitch blackness, a naive hope that maybe he'll catch a shape emerging out of the ink. Whatever it is has gone perfectly still, and Val feels certain they're hiding from him. He must have caught them staring, or did they catch him? It is silent and warm, not an intruder at all, but an observer.

Just as Val has the thought to wave at them, they vanish.

They walk for the remainder of the night, guided by the light in Val's palm.

"Foundation, right?" the Professor asks, smacking the back of Val's hand as he's clutching the little lamp.

"Yes, it was a gift from—"

"The Northern University, I know. They give them to all prospective students. Used to teach there, remember?"

"Ah." Val's face burns. "Right."

"They love their little trinkets up there," the Professor goes on. "Nothing too fancy, mind you. The Southern University is where they played with real technology."

"It's so close to Innovation," Val chimes in.

"Yeah, most of the students used to come from there. Before the wall went up," the Professor says.

Val looks over at him, half of his body lost in shadow. "Why did you get fired?"

"Told you," the Professor says, not looking at Val. "Too many kids died."

"How did they die?"

"I had a deal with the universities," the Professor says, body swaying in and out of the lamplight with every step. "See, they'd heard the rumors about monsters wandering the country. Insect-like creatures that almost looked like humans. They wanted weapons, and people who knew how to use 'em."

Val swallows through a dry throat. "They were teaching students to hunt monsters?"

"I was teaching children how to die," the Professor says back, eyes fixed on the darkened forest ahead of them. "Made 'em think that knowing how to fire a gun would keep 'em safe. It doesn't. Just makes you stupid enough to try."

Anger curls through the muscles of the Professor's jaw as he speaks, and Val watches intently. "Is it wrong to want protection from monsters?"

"It's a bad dream," the Professor snaps. "Humans shouldn't strive for destruction. The more you go looking for monsters, the more you'll find them. And they won't always be the ones you're expecting."

Val turns away from him, watching the dawn just beginning to fight its way through the trees.

"Just think about it," the Professor's voice gets quieter. "Telling a bunch of wannabe warriors that there could be monsters lurking inside any human being they know."

A memory begins to worm up through the earth of Val's mind, and he shakes his head a couple of times, like it tickles. "There was a boy in the orphanage, the only one who was nice to me. He wasn't a monster like I was. He was just nice."

"*Was*," the Professor echoes, gaze cutting over to Val's.

Val meets his probing look and nods. "*Was*."

"Orphans don't get nice funerals," the Professor says.

"They wouldn't let me go to his," Val reminisces. "But sometimes I would sneak out to put flowers by his name. He really was very nice. Taught me a lot about how to be a nice boy."

The Professor gives a rasping laugh at that. "No wonder you play the part so well. You got the words from way up north, but not the accent."

Val turns to him with a smile, crossing one arm over his chest and giving a slight bow as he walks. "I even know how to dance."

"Yeah, you look like a good and proper lad," the Professor says.

The wry smile is a vast improvement to the lurking anger.

"Would you like me to teach you sometime?" Val asks.

"Fuck no," the Professor says. "But you find someone who wants to. Dancing's a lot better when you're with someone who likes it."

It's light enough that Val is able to turn the lamp off. He doesn't want to sully the mood by commenting on the shockingly sentimental line from the Professor, so he tucks it away instead, right inside the empty space between his stomach and his liver.

3

The Dueling Cities have an unobtrusive silhouette. Val is almost surprised by how humble they look. The most impressive thing about them is the stream of people heading in their direction. They joined up with the procession the day before, and this morning, the Professor slipped a woman an obscene amount of money to get into her truck. Now they're jostling alongside the other people who've decided to make their way inside.

"Everyone thinks this is the new Innovation," the Professor mutters. "They're hoping to get in early and watch it build."

"Do you think it's possible?" Val asks.

"No," the Professor says. "No sense in remaking what's already there."

"Ah, don't be so hard," the woman at the wheel chimes in. "A lot of these folks are too young to really remember Innovation. And I can tell by looking that some of these walk-ups are from the coast."

The Professor turns forward, grabbing the edge of her seat. "What happened?"

"Patience, the fishing town, it went up in flames. We've been getting people all week looking for survivors."

The Professor's eyes go wide, and then he sinks back into his seat, thumping his cane onto the floor of the car.

"Did you know someone there?" Val asks him. "Extended family perhaps?"

The Professor nods once, and Val doesn't need to ask more. Another being like him, who might still be alive.

The man in the passenger seat cranes around to look at the Professor. "There's a couple taxi services out of Modesty that'll take you out there if you need to go check, but most of the survivors are here now."

"Thank you," the Professor nods at him. "I'll consider it."

Val slides over the seat, leaning his shoulder up against the Professor's to speak quietly. "That fellow we met in the woods on the way down here?"

"Mm." The Professor gives Val a stern look.

"D'you think he'll want to meet us here?" Val asks. "Or will he be content to stay where we found him?"

The Professor sniffs, looking back out the window. "Pretty sure he said he wanted to stay out there for at least another few days. Get himself back in order. And he's shy, so he won't travel during the day. I'd say we got about a solid week before he comes knocking."

"Understood." Val nods and straightens back up. "What was it you were looking to buy while we're here?"

"Information," the Professor says, and his curt tone tells Val that they're done talking about this with other people around.

They get dropped off in the middle of Modesty, the quiet part of the Dueling Cities. Val looks around the surprisingly flat landscape of the town, wondering where the *rest* of it is. Modesty looks as though it is one long building, stretched endlessly into neat zig-zags. The blocky, uniform architecture is only distinguished by different colors on the front of each unit, like the segments on a finger.

"Seems like paint color is the most exciting duel happening out here," Val says.

The Professor laughs. "The rest is downstairs. Come on."

They take to the sidewalk, but when the Professor puts a cigarette in his mouth and holds up his lighter, instead of the click of the mechanism, they hear someone loudly clearing their throat. A man in a buttoned-up uniform mimes the Professor with two fingers like he's holding his own cigarette.

"No smoking topside."

The Professor holds his gaze for a smoldering few seconds and then puts it all away. "Right."

They go walking past him, the Professor's scowl a few meters deeper than it was before. Val almost laughs, but bites his lip instead. Modesty is, in a word, *uniform*. It makes Val feel like he's seeing double. He can understand the impulse for organization, but he has the feeling that if he had to live here, it would drive him toward chaos with a much sharper edge.

There's an archway leading to an underground tunnel, similar to the trolley stations in Foundation, but with depth instead of height. Val is expecting to find some sort of underground transit system, but the Professor guides them toward what looks like a massive elevator. The architecture is markedly more industrial the moment they're out of the sunlight, and Val keeps his hands to himself as the Professor finally lights up. There are a couple more strangers standing with them, dressed in what Val can only think to describe as party clothes.

"Is everyone in Modesty so uptight?" Val asks.

The Professor smirks and blows smoke toward the open roof of the lift. "Only when they're on the clock."

The elevator sinks down for a surprisingly long time, so much so that Val starts to get a prickle of claustrophobia up his spine.

"I didn't expect Indulgence to be so hidden," he says, inching closer to the Professor.

"Far enough that the noise doesn't bother Modesty," Professor says back.

The lift is getting warmer as they descend, and when the doors finally open, several more people in slightly less crisp party attire wait for everyone to clear off. Val passes a couple of undoubtedly hungover people clinging to each other for dear life. The scent of fried food and tobacco and something mildly chemical mingles in the air, turning it heavier than it was on the surface.

The Professor takes off at a steady clip, and all Val can do is follow in his wake. Almost immediately, they're thrust into a river of people walking through car-less streets. Colorful lights blink from nearly every angle, and Val has the sudden, inexplicable urge to hold his breath. The vibrations of so many moving bodies threatens to dissolve Val under all that motion.

The two of them fight their way onto what appears to be a main road, lined with advertisements for every manner of vice and entertainment. Val forces his gaze onto the back of the Professor's jacket just to keep from getting dizzy. Excitement turned into an entire city, pulsing all around him with life.

"This place is very loud," Val says for no real reason, compelled to join the sudden constant buzzing.

"Yeah," the Professor says. "We're almost there."

With his gaze fixed on the Professor's duster, the city of Indulgence becomes a blur of brightly lit paint in the corners of Val's eyes, until the Professor pulls him inside a dim lobby. Val doesn't even see what this business is advertising, just follows the Professor, grateful for a slight damper on the noise and sights.

They find themselves in a cozy but cramped parlor, the sharp smell of incense permeating the air and ridding it of the congregation of scents from outside. Val lets go of the Professor and takes a deep breath as a beautiful young man saunters up to a desk and leans his forearms onto it.

"Welcome, boys. Are you here together or separate?" His lips are shiny and dark red, like the skin of an apple.

"Not here for business," the Professor says, fishing out some money which he puts on the counter between the man's arms. "I'm looking for your boss. If you tell Lux that 'dream came for a visit,' she'll know."

The man looks amused, but he takes the bills with a little smirk and tucks it down the front of his shirt where Val can see the edges of tightly fit straps laced over his body. "I'll do my best, but no promises."

"That's all I can ask," the Professor says.

The man steps away, dashing up a narrow flight of stairs, but as he vanishes around the corner in a pair of dizzying heels, Val sees someone else's face poking out from behind the wall. A braid dangles down from his head, five fingers curled over the corner of the wall. As soon as Val makes eye contact with him, he disappears with bare feet thumping softly on hardwood.

Despite the fact that this entire city is vibrating with life like a self-contained earthquake, that boy Val just saw was silent, still, and so utterly unnoticeable. Val stares at the empty space he left behind right up until the man from the front desk rounds the corner again.

"You're in luck, boys," he calls, inviting them up the steps with a single finger. "She'll see you."

"Great." The Professor starts up the stairs, and Val tries to shake himself out of his own daydream as he follows along.

The stairwell is *just* big enough for the Professor's body, and the hallway they step into is only a few inches wider than that. Paintings hang along the wall with lovingly portrayed bodies in strange contortions. Every painting is a different body, different shape, different color, different pose, but they all have the same air of intense focus on one bend of skin. Val can hear music playing softly above them, and footsteps scurrying around them from out of sight.

The man from the front desk holds open a door and gives Val a wink as he walks by. Val tilts his head, like someone addressed him in a language he doesn't speak. The man just laughs.

"He's not a customer, Opal, don't tease him."

Opal gives an overly dramatic, "*Oops.* Do you need anything, boss?"

"No, thank you. Keep guarding the door for me."

"Yes ma'am," Opal says, giving a slight bow before closing the door, his steps carrying him down the hall.

Val turns to see an imposingly beautiful woman, a large presence even while seated behind a desk. She has a pen in one hand, papers scattered in front of her, and a dark glass bottle by her elbow. Her thickly drawn brows arch up as she gives a glance at Val and then to the Professor.

"Lux," the Professor says, dropping himself into a chair across from her.

She's not just taller than him, but more solid as well, like a statue draped in thick velvet.

"Dream," she says, looking right at the Professor. "You look so . . . old."

The Professor gives a grunt of a laugh. "You haven't changed an inch."

"You have a boy," she says pointedly. "Why do you have a boy?"

The Professor waves Val over. "You wanna show her your trick?"

Val steps up beside the Professor's chair, looking around the room full of impeccably kept things, and Lux herself in clothes that probably cost more than anything Val has ever owned, paired with the artful arrangement of her black hair in perfect, loose curls. Even the thin band of gold through her nostril looks too nice to risk. "I don't want to get blood on anything."

The Professor holds his empty palm out, and Val dutifully puts his hand in the Professor's. He grabs a knife and a rag from within his jacket, and then stretches Val's arm across the desk for Lux to see clearly as he raises the blade up. It cuts so quickly and so cleanly up Val's arm, it hardly hurts, or maybe that's just adrenaline. The Professor quickly wipes away the bit of blood, and all three of them have a perfect view of Val's skin sticking itself back together, not even leaving any scar tissue behind.

"Well, well," Lux says, setting her pen down. "What's your name, hon?"

She looks at him with eyes lined in gold and Val stutters. "I'm. Val. My name is Val."

"He's not like us," the Professor says quickly. "Something else."

Lux's eyes flash as she looks back at the Professor. "Insect?"

"Doesn't look like it," the Professor says. "But he can pick up on 'em. And he doesn't die."

"Dream." Lux's curiosity shifts into something more urgent as she stares at the Professor, and Val realizes by her scolding tone that she is calling him by a name. *Dream.* "Does this have anything to do with Mare?"

The Professor starts putting all his things back into his jacket. "That's what I'm trying to find out."

Lux breathes an elegantly quiet sigh and folds her hands onto the desk, her bracelets clacking against the wood. "He could be dead for all we know."

The Professor—Dream?—shakes his head. "Not dead. I'd know."

Lux accepts whatever concession that is with a shrug. "Well I can't help you find him."

"Not asking you to come with us," the Professor says, hooking his cane on the edge of her desk and leaning on his forearms. "Have you had any pest problems lately?"

"No," she says. "And if you cause one while you're here, I might just shoot you myself."

The Professor raises his hand. "I don't want that either. Look, we ran into one in the woods on the way out here. Someone else got to it before us, but they didn't bother to say hello. You know anything about that?"

She tilts her head before spinning in her chair and pulling a necklace up out of her neatly buttoned black shirt. Isolating a small key amid a collection of pretty charms, Lux unlocks a safe on the other side of her desk.

"We get all sorts in here, of course. And, not to brag, but I do run the nicest houses in Indulgence." She sits back up, and places an earring in front of the Professor's withered hands. "This was left behind by someone claiming to be a monster hunter. Would you believe it?"

Her eyes shine with amusement, and the Professor plucks the shiny black earring up to inspect it. "What's it made of?"

"No clue," she says. "The guy was nice. Tipped well. *Very* high pain tolerance."

"Healing?" the Professor asks.

Lux shakes her head, her dangling earrings making a pleasant song. "Definitely human, just odd. Keep it."

The Professor passes the earring to Val. "Can you tell if this is anything like my knife?"

Val takes the little droplet of black stone, and waits as the Professor unsheathes the blade from his cane. "I don't know how to tell that."

"Just look at 'em," the Professor shoos Val toward another chair against the wall. "Don't think too hard about it."

"Yes, sir," Val says absently. He takes their packs off and sinks into the other armchair, a few feet away from Lux's desk, to stare at the two objects in his hands. The knife is shiny steel, much more like Val's scalpel than the earring in his palm. Val lifts the piece of jewelry up, inspecting the thin metal part that sticks through cartilage. It looks dull as compared to the Professor's knife, completely nonthreatening, showing signs of wear. There's no way they can be the same, but he feels like he's missing something.

"Are you going back to that cursed city, then?" Lux asks.

The Professor sighs. "It's the last place I saw him. Unless you have anything interesting to tell me, it's the only lead I have."

"Dream," she says with a layer of *soft* that catches Val's attention.

"Be careful. If he's still with them, he's been there for a long time. Do you think you'll be able to pry him loose now?"

The Professor stares at Lux's pretty face, looking like he's slowly sinking further into the chair. "If I don't get him out, we're both headed for the ground. I'll get caught eventually, by humans or insects or time. I'm tired of waiting."

She leans her chin onto her hand and gives him a smile tinged with an old familiarity. "Maybe it's silly of me, but I'm glad to see you alive. He may not be my favorite, but I hope Mare's okay too."

"Well that's a better turn than I expected," the Professor says.

Lux smiles. "Do you need anything for your hip?"

The Professor sits upright. "Since you brought it up."

"Come on, old man." Lux rises up from her desk and crosses the room. Val can't stop himself from staring at every flawless inch of her, the tailored fit of her lace jacket, blouse tucked neatly into her trousers, which are in turn tucked neatly into the softest looking boots Val's ever seen.

She opens the door to her office and calls, "Where is Sapphire?"

Opal's voice carries up from the bottom of the steps. "She's got a two o'clock, I sent her to Third Street."

Lux calls back, "Can you get Moon to let her know she has a priority for this evening? I'll buy her dinner as thanks."

A door opens somewhere and the same silent boy who stole a glance at Val earlier appears in the doorway, tugging at the edge of a pair of boots. He's built like a fawn, and his clingy clothing only accentuates that. "I heard you, ma'am. I'll head out now."

"Thanks, love." Lux waves one hand at him, and he snatches another look at Val before running off. Lux leans in the open door frame, crossing her arms to look at the Professor. "Do you have a place to stay yet?"

The Professor stands up and shakes his head. "Figured I'd get something cheap top side."

She gives a roll of her eyes. "Honestly, Dream, you still expect to visit me and not stay in my house? How long have we known each other?"

"Too long," he says without missing a beat. "The boy's not too much trouble, is he?"

Val startles at the mention of himself, but Lux shakes her head. "Of course not. We'll have a nice dinner and get to know each other later. Opal will give you the spare key. Don't be late to your appointment, you hear me? I'll have your head if you make my girl wait."

The Professor smiles, but Val is fairly certain there isn't an ounce of jest in Lux's threat. As sharp as she is beautiful, she stands there like a gilded sword. Val can only think you'd have to be mad to try and get close to her, but when the Professor starts to walk past her, she gives a tug on his jacket, and brushes his bangs out of his eyes before sighing at him.

"What'll I do with you?" she asks. "You get filthier every time you come here."

The Professor, or maybe Dream, gives her a smug type of smile, the kind that the other boys at the orphanage used to give each other at the end of a bad joke or a messy prank.

"Not my fault the ugly sticks to me like glue," he says.

Lux gives a full-chested laugh, head tipped back, mouth wide open. "Right you are. Get out of here already. You'll scare off my gems."

Val hurries to gather their stuff, returning the knife to the Professor's cane, and pocketing the strange little earring. As they're walking back toward the stairs, Lux starts to close the door but stops midway and calls, "Give Rez a kiss for me. Tell him I'll be on time."

The Professor stops in his tracks, takes a deep breath, and nods. "No such thing as a free meal, huh?"

Lux laughs as she closes the door to her office.

As the two of them walk back out of Lux's building, Val braces himself for the sensory onslaught that is the city of Indulgence. It still washes over him in continuous waves, but he manages it a little better the second time.

"Is that your name?" Val asks. "Dream?"

He gives a shrug. "I guess."

The implication seems to tire him, but he doesn't look uncomfortable. This is more like he hasn't thought about it in years, and he forgot how it makes him feel.

"Is Lux a childhood friend or something?" Val asks.

"Let's get to where we're staying," he says back. "Too many people out here."

Val nods and resumes his silent walk beside his teacher. He wants to say a lot more. Namely, he wants to think about the boy, Moon, who has absolutely no presence. Not human, not hybrid, not whatever Lux or Dream or any of their friends may be. Lux in particular has a vibration that feels *extra* human. As if she is many different people all poured into one form. There's also warmth to her, the same sun-dappled warmth that the man beside him occasionally carries.

Frowning, Val glances over at him. The teacher who insists he isn't a teacher. Val won't force a name onto him if he doesn't want it, but it thrills Val in a quiet way to think that Dream is a familiar title that only certain people get to know or say. The word doesn't exactly suit the haggard man in his beaten duster with his knives and his walking stick, but Val certainly has no opinion on how a name *should* feel.

He'll keep the name to himself for now.

Dream.

"Professor," Val says.

"What?" he drawls, probably expecting another uncouth question in public.

"Are there movies down here?" Val asks.

Dream actually laughs, a snorting, unexpected laugh. "Most of the theaters down here don't play real movies. Unless you got more blood in you than I realized."

Val tilts his head at that, and Dream barks out another laugh. "I'll ask Lux later, alright?"

"Thank you," Val says.

Dream walks faster down here, despite the soreness in his hip, and Val thinks maybe he likes this place more than he wants to admit. When they get back to the main road, they find a rail station to wait at. This place has neither taxis nor trains, just a simple trolley system that resembles a sideways moving elevator more than anything else. It has no walls, only several poles to hold onto, and moves slow enough to allow people to hop in and out as they need to, anchoring down at a couple stops for people like Dream who don't want to test a cane like that.

There is no inch of the city that isn't vivacious. Standing on the lift and watching it slide by is a lot more tolerable for Val, but he is still in awe of so many people. Over a thousand beating hearts and chattering tongues surround him. It's not just how densely packed the city is, but how alive it is. The vibrations feel like they will break him apart if he stays down here for too long.

And then there is Dream, standing beside Val with one hand on his cane and the other on one of the metal poles, his eyes closed and his face blank. He looks like he's sleeping, but Val knows that can't be true. Even the scar on his face looks less angry for a moment.

The rail operator calls, "East point!" and Dream steps off the platform without missing a beat. Val just hurries after him. They seem to be close to the city limits, given the looming rock wall at the edge of Val's vision.

"The only people who live down here are some of the business owners, and Lux of course," Dream tells Val. "This is her city."

"The whole thing?" Val asks, eyes wide. "Is she like the mayor or something?"

Again, Dream laughs, and Val finds himself more hinged on the look and the sound of it each time. "She's no mayor, but she's been here longer than anyone. It's an unspoken thing. Everyone knows who she is, and knows not to piss her off. Indulgence doesn't need a mayor, long as she's around."

They make their way up the only semi-quiet street in the whole city, with a couple utterly beautiful houses built around the edges of what looks like an underground lake. The bright lights of Indulgence make the water look like a rainbow of impossible colors. Val is glued to the sight.

"Are there fish down there?" he asks, pointing.

Dream smacks Val's calf with his cane, startling Val as he realizes he drifted too far away. Much too easy to get distracted here, Val thinks as he jogs back to Dream's side. When they start up the steps to the biggest house Val's ever seen, he starts to worry that they're in the wrong place, but Dream doesn't hesitate.

"Lux is very wealthy, isn't she?" Val asks.

"Swear to god, boy." Dream shakes his head with a smirk. "Maybe cool it with the questions when we're staying on someone else's dime."

"Yes, sir," Val chirps as they take the steps up to the front door.

Dream knocks twice with the handle of his cane and sets it back down with a thump. "Rez! It's Dream!" He looks from the door and then to Val. "Listen, Rez is a little high strung, so try not to be too weird around him. He likes things a certain way, you understand?"

Val nods, straightening his back. "Perfectly."

"Thought so," Dream says, dropping the smirk from his face.

Quiet steps sound from within the large house, and a slight man opens the door with a tight-lipped smile. In perfect contrast to Lux's curtain of loose curls, this man's black hair is styled against his head in perfect finger waves, not a strand out of place. He's an inch shorter than Val, and yet his presence is a raucous thing, idle strings on a perfectly tuned violin, just waiting to be plucked.

"Dream," he says, looking at him, and then to Val. His eyes are the most vivid hazel Val has ever seen, every fleck of emerald visible through the warm brown "And a guest, I assume?"

"This is Val," Dream says, pointing at him. "He's my, uh, apprentice."

The man gives a mildly aghast expression, blinking at Dream like the word is caught in his lashes. "Well, haven't you been a busy bee. Come inside. I assume you've seen Lux already."

Dream uses his cane to push Val into the house first, and then steps in after him. "Of course, she gave us a spare key."

The man turns to them. "Please take your shoes off." Pausing, he looks over the two of them with more scrutiny and then sighs. "Maybe you should just take everything off and bathe before we do anything else."

"I would love a bath," Val says to him, tucking his hands behind his back. "We've been traveling for a few days, and honestly, I won't feel like myself until I've washed the forest off me."

The man seems one degree more relaxed to hear that. "A sensible boy. Where are my manners. Val, was it? Lovely to meet you. You can call me Rez."

Val smiles at him, like he's back at the orphanage, meeting another prospective family that will never in a million years consider taking him home with them. "I'd offer to shake your hand, but, well, maybe after that bath we can try again."

Rez puts his hand on his waist and gives Dream a strange expression. "My my. To think you found yourself such a polite student. Maybe you can learn a little from him."

Dream turns to a rack full of shoes and props his foot up to try and get the laces undone without bending over. "Maybe I've finally gone soft."

"There are much worse things to be," Rez says.

Val sees Dream swatting at his boots, and his lips twitch in pain as he tries to bend, so Val steps over and nudges the man's hands out of the way.

"If your hip is hurting, just say," Val scolds.

He kneels at Dream's feet and unlaces both his boots, glancing up to see Dream scowling at him, white-knuckle gripping the handle of his cane. Val has a brief vision of huddling before the trunk of a massive willow tree as it considers crushing him just because it can.

Val takes his own badly worn dress shoes off and lays them amongst a startlingly huge hive of shoes by the door. Dream kicks his boots toward them, revealing the most hideous pair of socks Val has ever seen on another person, and Rez gives them both another attempt at a smile.

"You know where the guest rooms are, yes?" Rez asks.

Dream nods, and starts ambling toward a huge set of stairs. "C'mon, kid, this way."

"Meet me in the kitchen when you're all washed up," Rez calls. "I'll see about getting you some less disgusting clothes to wear."

He adds the last part with a pleasant lilt to his voice, like he's already mentally piecing together outfits. Padding up the stairs on socked feet, Val glances down at the indents that Dream's cane leaves in the carpet as they go. He takes them down a lengthy hallway of perfectly uniform doors and stops in front of one on the left side.

"I'll be in here. You can grab the one next to me," he says. "Should have its own bath. Just stay away from the right side of the house. A bunch of the gems live there."

"They do?" Val immediately looks down the hall toward the other side of the house. As soon as he does, three heads go vanishing around a corner, and Val swears he can hear laughing. "That's nice of Lux to house her employees."

"Listen," Dream turns to Val, his hand anchored to his hip. "I'm, uh, a little tired. Gonna wash up and hibernate before my appointment. Just don't cause trouble, all right?"

Val nods at him, recognizing the increasing tics of concealed pain in his expression. "Of course. We can talk later."

With a soft noise, Dream steps into his room and Val heads for the closest door, but not before checking the end of the hallway again. Someone is sneaking another glance at him, and Val gives a wave. They wave back before someone else yanks them out of view. Smiling, Val shuts himself into his new temporary room. It is the nicest place he's ever seen, and he hardly has a mind to notice any of it.

His head is buzzing from being around so many people, and he's grateful for the excuse to go take a bath in peace. Val retreats into the bathroom to sit in the tub, trying to appreciate the warm, clean water of the shower, but he can't turn off all the vibrations crowding him. This city is beautiful, and it feels like it's going to rip him apart.

Pushing his fingers through his hair, Val tries to focus on Dream in the room next door. The usual comforting warmth of his presence falls a little short when there are thousands of other bodies vying for his attention. It sounds like the rustle of cicada wings, and as he's sitting there, Val starts to smell sugar again. Breathing through his mouth, he feels an ache in his jaw and his fingers and his eyes. Mounting pressure that seems like it will crack open his bones if he doesn't do something.

Pulling himself out of the tub, Val blindly grabs a towel and throws open the door to the bedroom, trying to escape the oppressive steam. Slapping the towel to his face, he breathes through fabric instead, deeply inhaling the distant scent of soap to clear his head. Throwing it over his hair, Val opens his eyes to find someone staring at him. Moon, the boy from Lux's office. He resembles a deer even more when he's been caught where he's not supposed to be.

"Oh." Val looks at him, and the pile of clothing in his hands.

Moon starts to smile and pulls his gaze off Val's naked body. "Sorry, I should have knocked. I wasn't thinking."

He sets the clothes down on the edge of the bed, his gaze darting back to Val's and then back to the floor. The look on his face isn't embarrassed at all, more like he's trying not to laugh.

Val pulls the towel off his hair, but pauses with it held in his hands. "Does it bother you?"

"Do you mean you being naked or you being unbound?" He points at his own hips as he says it.

Val's eyes go wide. "Is there a word for it? I thought I was just a very good actor."

Moon does laugh at that, a quiet sound but he still covers his mouth. "Lux has a lot of people working for her who don't care about that stuff. Apparently one of her older gems came up with the term and it stuck. Being unbound by what people think your body should look like."

Val walks over to Moon, startling halfway as he remembers the towel, and cinching it around his waist. "Is that why you wear a skirt?"

Moon nods, hand on his hip. "Also because it looks good."

Val can't remember the last time someone saw him naked and it wasn't met with accusations of lying. It puts him at ease to speak so frankly about it.

"I actually wanted to talk to you," Val says. The closer he is to Moon, the more his quiet presence pervades the space, like a brilliant vacuum in the air, removing all desire to look at him. Moon's entire body feels as though it's repelling Val's gaze in favor of blending into the background.

"Yeah, thought you might," Moon says. He smiles at Val from half a foot above him with the palest eyes Val has ever seen. "Can you feel it on me?"

Val nods immediately.

Moon meets Val's gaze with a touch of hesitance, but there's a spark as well, like he's about to break a rule he knows he shouldn't. He sets a hand on Val's bare shoulder, and Val's breath catches at the firm touch, but Moon only uses him to keep his balance as he lifts his foot off the ground and unzips one of his knee-high boots.

Val watches the dark material parting over the pale skin of his leg, only it's not skin at all. Where there should be flesh to match his thighs and knees, Moon's calves are covered in a pale green membrane that looks like fabric, or maybe a leaf. Val immediately touches his finger to it, shivering at the unmistakable feel of a moth's wing.

"Wow," Moon laughs quietly. "No manners."

"I'm sorry!" Val quickly pulls his hand away, folding both his arms behind his back. "Are both your legs like this?"

"Yeah," he says, zipping his boot back up. "I was down here before I knew Lux. Just doing what I could to get money and survive, you know? Some guy got nasty with me when he saw my legs, and Lux found me afterwards. She didn't know I could heal, so she had her doctor fix me up. Now I'm one of her assistants."

Moon puts his foot back on the ground and takes his hand off Val's shoulder, and suddenly Moon feels twice as big as he was before. Val looks up at him, his heart pounding. "Have you ever found something inside of your body that wasn't supposed to be there?"

Moon's eyes peel open a little wider, lips parting as his gaze flicks between Val's eyes. He lowers his voice to answer. "Like thread from a surgery you have no memories of getting?"

Val's breath leaves his chest in a rush, and he nods over and over again.

Moon straightens up, folding his arms and giving another hushed laugh. "I have to get back to the office, but do you want to see me later? Maybe when your friend is at his appointment?"

"Yes, I think I would," Val says back, breathless.

"Good." Moon takes a step back. "I'll meet you there, so don't go wandering off, okay?"

"Yes, sir."

Val watches Moon walk to the door and step into the hall, but he sticks his head back in the room to add, "Sorry for seeing you naked."

Val just waves at him, not a care in the world about that. He can still feel the soft tissue of Moon's mothwing skin against his fingertip. As far as he's concerned, they're more than even.

As soon as Val dressed himself in a new crisp white shirt, new vest, and trousers, he wandered down the steps and was immediately intercepted by Rez, who stationed Val in the kitchen to chop vegetables for him while they waited for Dream.

"Are you like him, then?" Val asks, glancing over at Rez while he monitors a huge pot of soup stock like it might fight back at any moment. "Dream?"

"Yes, I suppose I am," Rez says without looking over. "And I suppose that means you know our secrets."

"Honestly, I'm not really sure," Val admits. "I was hired for a job. It's not really my place to ask questions or uncover secrets."

Rez meets his gaze at that, tilting his head and quirking a lovingly sculpted eyebrow. "Well, I appreciate that. Dream gives the impression that he couldn't care less about anything, but the truth is that he is one of our more cautious siblings. If he brought you here, then I'm not worried. Lux and Dream both have a fondness for strays, but Dream at least understands the risks of making strange friends."

"On the way over here," Val starts, returning to the onion that Rez painstakingly instructed him on how to dice. "We heard about a town on the coast. Patience."

"Mm." Rez turns away from the stock and quickly moves in to adjust Val's grip on the onion, tucking his knuckles in tighter so Val doesn't cut himself. "We haven't heard whether or not she made it out alive, but if it's taken this long, I don't have high hopes. Lux wanted to check herself, but it's too dangerous. I barely convinced her to stay. Maybe Dream will be able to see for himself if Patience is still alive."

Val stops with the knife half-buried in the onion to look at Rez. "Patience is a person? I thought it was the town."

"It's both," Rez answers simply. "It was her town, just as this one is Lux's, and Modesty is mine."

Val looks at him, delivering such wild information with the same calm he had for his brief lecture on kitchen knife safety. "Does every town have one of you to thank for it?"

"Most of them, yes," Rez answers. "Humans don't know that, of course. It would be gaudy and unnecessary to show off like that. But we are parasitic creatures at our core. We need humans more than they need us."

Val tries not to show his utter fascination on his face, simply nodding and looking back at his onion to finish pushing the knife through. "I never knew."

"It's really not as impressive as it sounds," Rez assures him. "And with these insects running around now, I'd say we're downright vulnerable these days. It's best to blend, and keep to ourselves. Why disturb what isn't broken?"

He sounds like he's talking to someone other than Val, and they both fall back into silence as Rez flits around the kitchen, prepping dinner for the gems who live in this huge house. Val doesn't expect to feel as much satisfaction as he does at the growing pile of neatly diced vegetables on his cutting board, but Rez nods his approval, and Val actually smiles back at him, feeling several years younger—finally getting approval from one of the orphanage hands.

Dream announces himself with the thump of his cane on the floor.

"I like your little protégé," Rez says to Dream as he enters the kitchen. "He follows instructions. How novel."

Dream gives a rasping laugh. "You can't have him. Let's go, I gotta get my ass back into town or Lux'll charge me late fees I can't pay."

Val sets down the kitchen knife with reverence, and washes his hands before taking his place at Dream's side. Tugging on one of Dream's sleeves, Val says as quietly as he can, "I have something to talk to you about."

"C'mon." Dream ambles toward the front door and uses his cane to pluck his boots out of the lineup. Val doesn't wait for him to even try, just kneels down and does his laces for him.

"There's someone here like me," he whispers, looking up at Dream with a knot half tied.

Dream nods. "Yeah, one of 'em felt like you. Not quite the same though. Louder."

"You think he's loud?" Val asks, finishing up and getting the door for Dream. "He felt so quiet to me."

"I could smell him," Dream says as he walks out. "Somewhere between you and a hybrid. Right?"

Val steps out after him with a contemplative nod. "Yes, I suppose I could smell him too."

"You hardly have a scent at all," Dream says, looking at Val with his usual scrutiny. "Tell me about the other kid."

Val relays what Moon said to him, describing the wings around his calves as they walk back to the station. Dream massages the wound on his side as they go.

"You both had weird shit inside you, huh?" For a moment, he seems like he has less wrinkles on his face, and Val stares at him, wondering if he's seeing things. "That can't be a coincidence."

"What are you thinking?" Val prompts.

"The weapons that can kill me and mine," Dream starts. "I used to think the hybrids made 'em themselves. Now I'm thinking it's not that simple."

Val frowns at him. "Do you think those weapons came from *inside* of the insects, like mine did?"

"Maybe," Dream says. "Would certainly explain why there's only a limited amount of them, and why I usually only see them on or near a hybrid."

He looks at Val again, and Val stares back at him, unsure what equation Dream is trying to solve, but Val just hopes it comes out in his favor.

"Insects growing inside of humans," Dream says. "With objects stuck inside of them. Maybe the object is the reason for the change. Like a tuning fork."

"So Moon got his object out before he forgot how to be human?"

"Maybe," Dream says. "Or maybe he just has a stronger will. That's probably why he didn't turn on Lux immediately."

"But what about me? I don't have any insect parts," Val adds, lowering his voice as they rejoin with a proper road full of other pedestrians.

They come to a stop at the back of the crowd waiting for the next lift into town, and Dream leans down to whisper, "Sounds like you got to it before it could get to you. Maybe this Moon got his a little after yours. Could just be a matter of how long it has to hibernate inside you that determines how bad it gets."

Val doesn't like the fit of that truth—it itches to think that he is anything like the insect they found in the woods, or the smith from Prosperity with his beetle-shell eyes. But then there is Moon. He found a place for himself well enough. As the two of them board the lift, Val hops up first and holds his hand out to Dream, who takes it without question and lets Val brace for him as he pulls himself up. Dream stands beside him, and Val lets himself think that perhaps he has a place too, right here in Dream's shade.

"What will they do at your appointment?" Val asks.

Dream shrugs. "Ah, Lux has a doctor who knows about us. She

can clean and set my old wound. Make it a little easier on me until I need to do something stupid again."

"Sorry," Val says to him. "For making you do something stupid."

Dream shakes his head with a laugh. "Better a little blood loss than someone sneaking up on me. Don't think on it."

Val doesn't, happily.

The two of them come to the entrance of what looks like a spa, but with some kind of charged energy in the air that Val can't quite put his finger on. It's probably the anticipation emanating from everyone waiting their turn.

"Will you be alright?" Val asks.

Dream snorts and heads for the doors. "Yes, thank you. Don't go causing trouble, you hear?"

"Yes, sir," Val calls back to him as he heads inside. As soon as the doors close, he starts to feel that miserable buzzing in his skull, every moving body in the city suddenly whispering into his ear, right up until a thin arm loops around his shoulder and he sees shiny pink lips in a smile.

"Got you," Moon says.

"Hi," Val blurts the word out, smiling back. "I'm all yours."

"Great. Let's go talk somewhere quieter."

Moon guides Val like an arrow weaving effortlessly through the crowds. They move so quickly, Val doesn't have time to ask where they're going or really anything at all. When Dream walks, it's as if he's creating space for himself, but Moon moves like he knows exactly where everyone *isn't* looking. Huddling under Moon's arm feels like clinging to a shadow.

When they dip inside an unassuming building that almost resembles a small tea shop, Moon takes them right up to the counter where a girl gives him a dubious expression, head tilted.

"What trouble are you causing, Moonstone?" she asks.

"None." He gives an angelic smile and squeezes Val to his side. "He's not a customer. He's a friend. Just wanted to talk to him somewhere quiet while he's stuck in the city. His boss is a friend of Lux."

The girl leans her arms on the counter, brushing her hair aside. "That sounds so fake I guess I have to believe it. Go on, I'm guessing you already know we're slow today."

"Yes, ma'am," Moon says, pulling some bills out from a pocket on the inside of his skirt to put into a glass jar on the counter. "Thank you."

She smiles at him. "I knew I raised you right."

With a laugh, Moon hustles Val through a dim hallway and down a set of steps. Val feels like he's in a play, but no one else seems to be aware. They have lines memorized, choreography down pat, and give effortless performances. Val just watches it all happen, a bystander pulled onto the stage. Moon takes them to a closed door and finds a piece of chalk hanging from a string which he uses to draw a crescent shape onto the black paint before opening it.

"After you," he says, gesturing for Val.

Val just scurries inside, feeling truly out of his depth. "Thank you."

Moon shuts the door and walks right up to Val, only a few inches away from him, and suddenly his lack of noise seems to crackle against Val's. Dream was right, Moon isn't silent. It's just that his noise sounds more like Val's.

"I've never met anyone like me," Moon says. Val only realizes right then that his hair is hanging loose around his shoulders, free from the braid he had it in earlier. "Do you mind if I take my boots off?"

Val shakes his head. "Will you let me touch your wings again?"

Moon gives a hushed laugh. "Yeah."

He takes Val's hand, pulling him toward a sliding door in the wall where he flicks the light on in an austere, but still intimidatingly nice bathroom.

"This place is actually pretty expensive, so don't tell anyone I brought you here," Moon says, sitting on the edge of a large tub and unzipping his boots.

Val drops to his knees at Moon's feet, eyes already fixed on the pale green of his calves.

"You're a little weirdo, huh?" Moon says, but he's still smiling.

Val waits until he's set the boots aside, and then reaches for one of Moon's legs. He touches as softly as he can, afraid that the material will rip like a real moth's would, but it appears to be firmly affixed to his skin. There are thin pink edges to the wing that line the muscles of his calves. Val traces one of them to the back of Moon's leg, and there he finds an eye inlaid in the fabric of his wing, a small orange and white circle, like a pattern in a piece of cloth.

"I don't have any insect parts," Val admits. "I think I pulled my knife out too soon for that."

"Knife?" Moon echoes.

Val sets Moon's foot gingerly onto the tiled floor and pulls the scalpel out of his pocket. He took it with him, just in case, and he carefully unfolds the blade from the makeshift handle that the smith made for him.

"I found this piece of metal inside me when I was very young," he says, showing it to Moon. "The silver part here."

Moon leans down to look at it, brows furrowed. "Oh my god. I only had thread in me."

Val looks at it closer, turning it over in his hands. "I had a dream that someone was performing surgery on me, and when I woke up, I was convinced they had left something behind. I couldn't get the thought out of my head, and the more I thought about it, the more it started to hurt. So I dug it out myself. I'm sure if I had been human, it would have killed me at least a couple of times."

His laughter is hollow even to his own ears.

Moon sets his big toe onto Val's knee. "I got roughed up a lot before Lux found me, but I never really thought twice about it, because I healed so fast. Once the wings started growing on me a few years ago, I think I kinda spiraled. Started looking for dangerous people just to see if any of the pain would stick. 'Course it never did, but when Lux found me in a truly sorry state, I was so done with it, I even tried to hurt her. But, instead of throwing me away, she brought me to her physician instead. The doctor found the thread while she was fixing me up. She figured I'd just gotten desperate in some other town and went to a surgeon without proper training, and it was just easier to let her believe that than to try and explain that I've never needed to be under a knife."

"Is Lux protecting you?" Val asks.

"Guess so," Moon says with a shrug, but the barest hint of embarrassment creeps into his cheeks. "I've been good since she took me on. I don't get into fights. And the wings haven't grown anymore."

"Since the thread was pulled out of you," Val says, touching Moon's ankle again. The pink seams all along the membrane suggest where they might unfold, if they ever could. Val touches one with his thumb, tempted beyond reason to try and peel it back.

"You think the thread is what caused this?" Moon asks.

Val nods, pulling Moon's foot up onto his thigh so he can look closer at the way the green of the wings blends with the sunless skin underneath it. "Your thread, my knife, yes. Something we have no memory of, trying to change us from the inside out. It makes me wonder what I might have become, if I'd left the knife inside me . . ."

Moon presses his painted toes into Val's thigh. "For what it's worth, I think you came out pretty nice."

Val looks up at him, eyes wide, lips parting as he tries to put a response together. "Humans think I'm creepy."

Moon shrugs, tucking some of his hair behind his ear. "They think bats are creepy, and snakes, and spiders. I've been hurt a lot worse by humans than I have the things they find creepy."

"Be careful," Val says, gripping Moon's leg tighter. "I've seen versions of us that aren't okay. They have some kind of drive that makes them want to hurt people like Lux, Rez, and Dream. Watch out for them, alright? You and I won't get hurt, but they could."

Moon nods at him, the playful smile gone from his lips. "I owe Lux a lot more than just my health. I'm not about to let something happen to her, or her brother."

Val lets his breath out and looks back at Moon's legs, frozen in the middle of transformation he never asked for, beautiful, like stained glass that will never crack. Leaning down, Val touches his cheek to Moon's wing-skin, smiling at the softness of it.

"You're like a cat," Moon says, laughing again. He reaches down to run his fingers through Val's hair. "Does it feel nice?"

Val nods against him. "I know you can heal, but they feel so soft. It makes me want to be careful. Have you ever touched a baby?"

Moon shakes his head as Val lets him go. "God, no. Babies terrify me. Too fragile."

Val puts his hands on his thighs, letting Moon put his boots back on. "Do you think we could be friends?"

Glancing up at his pale eyes, Val goes still while Moon adjusts Val's bangs for him. "We already are."

Val smiles at him, feels his eyes crinkling and his teeth showing. Moon laughs again. "You should get back to your Dream, and I have to get back to the office. Let me walk you to the spa."

"Oh, it's alright, I can find Dream anywhere," Val says, picking himself up off the floor. "But thank you."

Moon takes his arm as they head for the door. "Your man does feel strange, even compared to Lux and Rez. Old, you know?"

Val nods. "Like the oldest tree in the oldest forest?"

"Yeah, kinda like that," Moon says.

He erases his chalk mark on the door, and walks Val to the front of the house again. "It's not a big deal if you want me to show you back to the spa. Some people get rowdy around here, and you're pretty cute, so I'd rather not leave you alone."

Val smiles, puffing his chest up. "Nothing can hurt me."

"Alright, show off." Moon laughs. "You keep your Dream safe. I'll watch out for Lux and Rez."

"Thank you, Moon. It's Val, by the way, I don't know if I told you."

"Stay safe, Val. I want to see you again," Moon says, his eyes cooling into something more serious. "It was nice talking to you. I never get to show anyone my wings."

Val grins. "I promise I'll be back so you can take your boots off again."

Moon opens the door for him, sending Val back into the city with a kiss on his cheek. Val waves at him until the door swings shut, and he enters the crowd with a renewed vigor. Yes, this city is so full of life that it feels like it's knocking on his skull, but he's not alone anymore. The knowledge makes him feel like his lungs can breathe twice as much air.

He doesn't remember the way back, but as he walks, he tries to focus on the feeling of the bodies and their vibrations as they pass by him. Channeling Moon as best he can, Val doesn't fight the crowd, but moves alongside it. He searches for Dream's presence among all the other heartbeats, waiting to grasp onto that calm like a rock in a churning river. It's far off in the distance, sending those comforting signals back to Val like a lullaby leading him home. He knows he's too far away to catch that scent of smoke, but he still finds himself breathing deeper, hoping to find the edges of it in the air.

Val follows that lullaby all the way back to the spa, where he gets informed that Dream's appointment has only just begun, and could he come back in a couple of hours?

"Uhm," Val puts his hands on the desk where another beautiful gem is seated across from him. "Are there any fun movies playing?"

The gem gives a laugh. "Fun?"

Val nods, smiling.

They touch their chin as they think on it, but then they nod. "The big theater on Sixth Street has a couple screens, I'll bet you'll find something you like. They get all the movies that Modesty gets. Try there."

"Thank you!"

With directions from the gem, Val finds himself in a large, densely decorated theater that appears to be divided into two sections, one with an actual stage, and one for movies. With the last of his own money, Val buys a ticket to see the first movie that they'll allow him into without any identification. He buzzes pleasantly for the entire time that he sits in a plush chair, watching smartly dressed people on a huge, bright screen trying to solve a mystery that Val is hardly paying attention to. It is only in a movie theater that Val can watch people without feeling them. He savors the moments, searching for anything to steal for his own performance as Dream's bodyguard.

A bit of sweeping music is still ringing in his head when Val steps back onto the streets of Indulgence. It's a lot less frightening now that he knows exactly where to go. He walks slower, focusing on the memory of the actors and actresses up on that screen pretending to be other people. He wonders if it's a strenuous process, to constantly take on new roles like that. Do they get a thrill from pretending, or does it tire them out like it sometimes tires Val? He doesn't feel tired from Moon or by Dream though. It's a lovely feeling, bright and warm and soft. He imagines it like one of the music cues from the movie.

If only all humans came with their own instructions.

As Val turns onto the main road, he begins to search for Dream's lullaby once more, only to find something else pervading his senses. Underneath the decadent, careless air of Indulgence, another presence pings on Val's radar. It isn't at all like the plodding, mechanical steps of the hybrid from the woods, but a shark headed right for him. This sensation sets Val's teeth on edge, but as soon as he thinks to pick up his pace and run, someone's hand claps down on his shoulder, and a knife jams into the flesh of his back.

Val goes stock still as fireworks explode behind his eyes, raining molten sparks through his chest. His eyelids close without his permission and his arms go slack at his sides. It hurts in places and in others there's nothing at all, not even cold.

"Easy." Someone speaks in his ear, a whisper like rain on stone. "I expect you just lost some feeling in your body. Looks like your arms and your eyes at least. You'll get it back when I pull this out, but until then, I'm going to need you to walk with me. Your legs still work, right?"

Their voice is low, and sets every hair on Val's body upright. Val has never been able to say what *danger* sounds like, but this might be it.

"S . . . scream. I could scream." Talking is suddenly very different as the person starts to nudge Val forward. His back is on fire, his spine made of lava.

"Do you feel that?" The person asks, their mouth on Val's ear as they nudge the knife in Val's back. Immediately, Val coughs like he's trying to hack up the metal through his throat. "That's your body attempting to heal around the blade. If I break the tip off inside you, it might just prevent you from ever healing this damage. Unless, of course, you want to explain to someone what you are and let a mob do my job for me."

Val puts one foot in front of the other.

"Thank you," the person says, steering Val forward with the knife in his spine.

"You . . . know . . . who I am," Val manages.

"I know *what* you are," they say back. "And I know you're a threat to everyone down here, but most of all, you're a threat to the Pillars. I can't abide that."

Val swallows, numbness beginning to claw its way up his throat. "You're . . . human."

"Yes," they say back. "And you are an insect."

That word keeps Val silent. He can't argue against it. The two of them walk for so long, Val can't sense where they started or where they're going. It all comes to a blunt end when the human removes their knife, only to plunge it back inside Val, much lower, and Val crumples like a broken doll as the world goes silent.

There is a terrible ringing in Val's ears as he slowly fights for consciousness. His body is heavy, and his limbs feel like they're full of sand. His hands in particular feel like they're being eaten by acid.

When he opens his eyes, he is cast in the shadow of a very large person looming over him. He's kneeling over Val's torso, staring at Val's face.

"There you are," the man says.

Val looks over at his own hands, and sees the handle of a knife protruding out of each of his palms, anchoring him to the roots of the tree beneath him. His legs are bound together with rope, and as soon as he tries to move them, the guy sits on Val's stomach and the weight of his body is enough to keep Val still.

"Sorry about all this, but I can't exactly take chances with someone like you," he says, and his voice is far too calm.

"I could still scream," Val says.

"Go for it," he says back. There's thick, dark circles under his eyes, an almost sickly quality to his skin, wearing all black clothing that Val can't immediately trace to any city. The style of loose fabric doesn't look familiar to Val, but the shiny black jewelry dotting every feature on his face does.

"I think I might have your earring," Val tells him.

"Hm." He touches his left lobe and Val can see an obvious empty hole where the jewelry must have fallen out. The guy nods, picking himself up and rolling his shoulders. "Guess it was meant to be."

"What was?" Val asks, thinking in his head that he can return this man's earring and start fresh, like he did with Dream.

The guy looks down at Val with his deeply sunken eyes, blocking the dying light with his broad shoulders draped in black. From his neutral expression, to his nearly bloodless skin, and the knot of black hair on his head that doesn't even shine in the light, the man looks like a corpse brought back to life. There isn't a single vibration coming off of him now as he speaks with his lips barely moving.

"I'm here to kill you."

4

Val's eyes are open wide from the echo of the man's words. "You want to kill me?"

"That's the job," he says, reaching behind him for a jagged edged knife. "Wouldn't do well to half-ass it."

Val's heart is pounding. "You think you can really do it?"

"I can," he says, kneeling down by Val's side with the knife in his hand. He seems human, but his vibrations are nothing so simple. He hardly registers as alive, more like a wrinkle in Val's awareness. "Nothing's truly immortal. Not you, not me, not the sun or the moon."

Val can't stop from staring at this person, his pulse racing on his own tongue as he tries to figure out if this is all an attempt to frighten him. "You're just saying that."

The guy slides one hand through Val's hair, an alarming lack of aggression as he tilts Val's head back. "What happens if I cut clean through your neck?"

Val hears his own breath catch, aware of every muscle in his throat as he swallows. "The parts will grow back. Whichever part of me has more."

For the first time, there is a flicker of *something* in those deadened, sleepless eyes as the man tilts his own head. "Someone already tried?"

"More or less," Val tells him.

"What happens if I cut you into pieces and feed you to a wake of vultures?" he asks next. His eyes look completely black, almost as if there is no iris, only pupil. "They'll eat anything if they're hungry enough. If you keep healing from their bites, they'll keep coming back for more. You could become their new roost."

Val can almost picture it—his body getting assimilated into a cycle of life, providing an endless food source for creatures that do neither good nor bad. He should be afraid of this, shouldn't he? A human would, but something about the genuine threat delivered to him with such calm isn't making him scared.

"It's . . . almost a nice thought, isn't it?" Val asks.

"You're not thinking ahead," his captor tells him, pulling Val's head back toward him. "That ability of yours will hit a limit eventually, without food or water or sleep. Not even gods last forever. The Pillars know that better than you do."

Val's breath leaves him in a hush, holding the merciless gaze of a trained hunter. Realization hits him swiftly as he recognizes the almost imperceptible vibrations coming off of him.

"You're the one from the woods," Val says. "You pulled that hybrid's wings off."

"I didn't just pull its wings off. I made it so it can't ever grow its wings back. Or, at least that was the intention, before you interrupted me," he says in an inflection-less voice, hollow eyes boring into Val's. There's absolutely nothing in his gaze, and Val is overcome with the horror of recognition. This person is empty, but not like Val is. This is something else.

"I shaped it, as I'll shape you. Nothing personal. Just the job."

The job, like Val's. That's right. He can't be wasting time up here when Dream is down below, without protection. This person might be going after Dream too for all Val knows. Val can't let this person change him, even if there is something darkly alluring about that thought. Val isn't allowed to stop yet, so it doesn't matter. He'll deal with *that* feeling later.

His hands are slowly but surely forcing the knives up out of his palms as they heal.

"Did someone pay you to kill me?" Val asks. "Someone from the orphanage?"

"I don't know anything about an orphanage," the guy says, studying Val's face. "And I don't get paid."

Val tries to press against the knife that's in his hand directly behind the man's back, and the immediate kick in the teeth from the pain covers his surprise at hearing those words. "Then why are you attacking me?"

"Some work is more important than money," he says back, simple, pulling on the skin around Val's eye.

Val grits his teeth and presses again, slower, trying to force the knife free of the tree roots. "Oh, so you're broken? Is that it?"

The hunter's face doesn't register the taunt. "Do you even have any insect parts?"

Val hopes he looks like he's furious with this person, and not just trying his hardest to disguise the pain of the blade moving around in his hand. He is a little angry, if he's being honest. He thought he was doing a better job of pretending. "I'm *not an insect*."

When he manages to pry his palm up from the roots of the tree, his whole body lurches with the released tension, and the hunter simply turns and grabs Val's freed wrist.

"Increased adrenaline when you're in pain," he says, dispassionate. He bends Val's hand around, knife still embedded, and gently sets the tip of the blade over Val's own chest. "Maybe I should fuse your hands together ..."

He kneels there, holding Val's wrist, gaze unfocused while he debates his options and Val's blood drips onto his white shirt from the tip of the knife. The hunter goes silent for much too long, his brows slightly furrowed as he looks at nothing at all. It's hard to track his gaze when it's not directly on Val's, and his lips part slowly, giving the impression of some grand revelation taking place in his head.

Val stares in utter confusion as the hunter looks at Val's hand, and then at Val's eyes, and a smile begins to warp his previously expressionless features. The smile doesn't quite fit right, and if they were anywhere else, Val would think the man was inebriated for how misshapen it is on his face. The hunter is fighting it as his lips begin to curl, breath pinching his lungs, and then he claps his hands over his own mouth as laughter begins to force its way from his throat.

His eyes are deranged from a glee that does not belong.

Val bites the handle of the knife in his palm and wrenches his hand free of it, moving faster than he's ever moved before to pull the second knife free, dragging himself away from the hunter laughing into his own clasped hands. Val has no idea what is happening to this man, nor does he care, he just needs to cut the ropes from his legs to get free again. Stumbling back to his feet, Val holds one of the knives out in front of him, hands slicked with blood, fully prepared for this man to try and jump him at any moment.

The hunter is staring at his own hands now, that misshapen smile wider than ever, and his shoulders begin to twitch as some unknown emotion wracks him. Val thinks he will not get this opportunity twice, so he braces himself and starts walking toward the hunter with the knife outstretched. The vibrations coming off of him are wild, but not aggressive. It's more chaotic than that, movement in all directions, like he's forgotten how to be subtle. A noise to rival that of Indulgence. It feels as though it will peel Val apart if he doesn't do something fast.

But he's not trying to attack anymore. Val takes another step closer, gripping the knife in both his shaky hands, reminding himself that letting this dangerous man go could put Dream in harm's way. He can't allow that, but he hates approaching this laughing stranger who isn't even wielding his knife anymore. There are tears in the hunter's eyes as he tips his head back, exposing his own throat, and Val's vision sharpens around the expanse of vulnerable skin.

Val could kill him so easily. *Should* kill him, to spare Dream. Isn't that his job?

There's a ringing in Val's ears as he watches the hunter's throat pulsing with bizarre laughter. Val's jaw aches, arms frozen in place as he pictures himself jamming the knife into this man's neck. In that moment, Val has the thought that human throats were designed to be broken, or else they would not look so elegant, or so fragile.

"*Stop.*"

Val comes to an ice-cold halt at the sound of Dream's bored voice ringing out like a shotgun through the darkening woods.

"Easy, kid, he's not gonna try that twice," Dream says.

Val searches around for the familiar voice, and spots Dream's uneven steps coming up from the other side of the hunter. It's definitely Dream, from the scent of smoke to the lullaby vibrations, but there is an extra layer to his presence, textured in a way Val doesn't recognize.

"He tried to kill me," Val says to him, quiet. "I think I tried to kill him too . . ."

"Yeah I can see that," Dream says, ambling up to Val to slap the backs of his hands with the cane. "Put that down."

Val lets his hands open up, dropping the hunter's knife to the grass, but the ache in his jaw has only gotten worse. It feels like his own teeth are cutting into his gums, growing at a rapid clip, and Val lurches forward with his hands outstretched.

"There's something wrong with my teeth," he says, wanting to grab Dream's coat, but he sees his own bloodied fingers and stops short. "Professor, please, can you see?"

He opens his mouth wide, sure as he's ever been that his mouth is somehow rearranging, turning itself inside out.

Brows pinched, Dream glances at Val's mouth and back to his eyes. "Kid, you're fine."

"Are you sure?" Val asks.

"Have mercy, *yes*. Get a grip," he says back. "The fuck happened up here anyway? When you weren't waiting for me outside, I went looking for your scent. Wasn't expecting you to be all the way out here."

Forcing himself to take a breath, Val runs his tongue over his teeth, determining that nothing has actually shifted. He lowers his hands and tries to tell Dream about getting accosted in the crowd.

"He really seemed to think he could kill me," Val says.

"He probably can," Dreams says, glancing over at the hunter, now shivering on his knees with his eyes closed, arms around his own chest. "He's toothless now."

Val checks to see how his hands are healing. "Didn't seem very toothless when he stabbed me in the back."

"He didn't know you're with me," Dream says. "Promise you'll play nice when I release him."

"Tell *him* that," Val says, pouting.

Shaking his head, Dream faces the hunter, and whatever the extra presence was that had been layered into Dream's lullaby snaps like a bow string. The hunter's back straightens, eyes opening wide as he comes back to himself. Val nudges the stray knives away with his shoes as he waits for the hunter to react.

Val's captor turns his head toward Val and Dream, but before he can fully face them, his breath catches, and he claps both his hands over top of his eyes, his fingers woven together to block out the light.

"Forgive me. I'm sorry."

Dream rolls his eyes. "You're part of that group, right? The Eyes?"

"Yes." The hunter's voice sounds entirely different than it did when he was speaking to Val. What previously lacked tone or inflection before now sounds like it's getting pulled up from the very depths of his stomach. He sounds reverent, kneeling with his hands locked over his eyes, facing Dream but refusing to look at him. "I'm sorry, I shouldn't be talking to you."

"Well it's too late for that," Dream says. "What do you want with my boy?"

"Your . . . oh f—" The hunter bites back the curse that was on his tongue and takes a deep breath through his nose. "He is an insect. I'm sorry to be the one to tell you."

"I know what he is," Dream says.

The hunter's lips part and, even with his eyes covered, he looks like he's lost for words. "You know?"

"Yeah. He's not like the others. Still has his wits in him, as I'm sure you saw. Which means if you kill him, all you'll be doing is pissing off me and mine."

"I'm sorry," the hunter says again, sinking into himself. "I have . . . failed entirely . . ."

Dream narrows his eyes, not in anger, but in scrutiny. "What do your people do with failures?"

"Forgive me, I am not allowed to discuss with outsiders. Even you, Pillar."

Dream chews on his lip for a moment, glancing at Val, and then back to the miserable hunter. "You know how to fight insects."

"I do," he says.

"And you're *usually* good at stealth," he adds.

The hunter doesn't respond to that, and Dream grumbles quietly as he stares at the stranger shrinking further toward the ground.

"Professor," Val says quietly.

"Shut up, I'm thinking," Dream says, dragging a hand over his face. "These people, the Eyes, they're not known for kindness. I don't know how much that extends to their own people, but if this idiot's about to get himself maimed or killed because of this, I don't want that on my conscience. I can't exactly judge him for going after you, you're an anomaly. He *should* have the right to kill you."

Val looks back at the hunter, letting that sink in. Is Val this man's prey? Is there some kind of bond in that? And why is he now blinding himself for Dream?

With a groan, Dream takes a step closer to the hunter. "What's your name?"

"The Eyes don't have names," he says back.

"Then pick one," Dream snaps at him. "You're coming with us, and I already have a boy."

The hunter's mouth falls open. "Wh . . . what do you mean?"

"C'mon, I'm not stupid," Dream says, nudging the guy's legs with his cane. "Your people are supposed to help mine, aren't they? So, do you want to go back home a failure, or do you want to work for me directly? The choice is yours, but you have to know that I won't like it if you leave here just to lose a hand for a rule you didn't even know you were breaking."

The hunter tilts his head forward, breathing heavily through his nose. "You would offer me work . . . after I tried to kill your companion?"

"Yeah, well, we've all had shit introductions, haven't we?" Dream says, looking at Val's own puzzled expression. "*You* have no right to complain either."

Val folds his arms. "Fine."

Turning to the hunter again, Dream heaves a sigh. "You have useful skills, and besides, I can't have any more of your people showing up trying to murder my charge here. Consider yourself hired. Keep Val out of trouble, ya hear me?"

"Val . . ." The hunter angles his head toward Val, and Val has the unsettling feeling that this person can see him perfectly clearly, despite his closed eyes.

"And pick a fucking name," Dream adds, turning away. "Unless there's anything else you want to tell me about Indulgence, Val and I are due for dinner. You stay wherever you want, but I'm guessing you don't want to sit with more of my family."

"I don't . . . think I'm ready for such an honor," he says.

Dream waves his hand. "Then stay here. We'll come back in the morning, alright? I could use your help with Patience. If you leave before then, that's your business."

Val starts after Dream, but the hunter leans toward them. "There is another insect down below."

"That's Moon," Val says to Dream. "He's good."

Dream nods, and points his cane at the hunter. "Don't go near that one, he's also under my watch. He's harmless, got that?"

"Yes . . ." The hunter nods, fingers still laced over his eyes.

Dream looks profoundly uncomfortable, his expression similar to one that Val had seen on a few young men who came to tour the orphanage with their brides—men who were not ready to take on this particular role, and yet, found themselves walking among hungry children all the same.

"Just don't kill anyone while I'm gone," Dream says, starting off through the woods. "You don't have your light, do you Val?"

Val hurries after him. "No, sir, my bags are back at Lux's."

"Figured," Dream mumbles.

The sunlight is nearly gone, but Val can see the very distant lights of Modesty guiding them back to the city.

"Am I allowed to ask?" Val says, glancing behind, as if he'll still be able to see the hunter.

"Let's get out of the woods."

Val stays by Dream's side, nervousness creeping into his shoulders. "I'm sorry, I shouldn't have wandered off. I just wanted to talk to Moon one more time."

Dream gives a low grunt. "It's fine. Indulgence is pretty safe for someone like me anyway. And Eyes back there confirmed that

Moon's the only hybrid downstairs besides yourself. You learn any-thing useful?"

"Moon said his wings stopped growing ever since he had a myste-rious piece of thread removed from him," Val tells him. "Lux's doctor fixed him up and pulled it out. And he's been fine since then."

Dream gives another drawn out sigh as they walk. "Shit . . ."

"What?" Val asks. "Isn't that a good thing?"

"It's a complication, is what it is," Dream says. "How the fuck are we supposed to find out if someone has an object inside them that's not supposed to be there?"

Val frowns into the darkness as they trudge toward the dim light of Modesty. "I was able to feel Moon. And that hunter was able to feel us both. Maybe we can figure something out."

"Maybe."

Dream goes quiet until they pass out of the treeline and start making their way over the fields surrounding the humble outline of Modesty.

"If you don't want to work with him, tell me now," Dream says. "I'm not gonna force you to stay together if he scares you."

Val's eyes open in surprise. "You said he was useful."

"He is, but that doesn't mean we need to keep him close," Dream says back. "He'd probably prefer to work from a distance anyway."

Val doesn't know what surprises him more, that Dream is making allowances for Val's discomfort, or that he was considering hiring someone to protect Val in the first place.

"Can you tell me more about the Eyes?" Val asks. "I've never heard of this."

Dream shrugs. "No one knows about them except a couple of my older siblings and I. I don't know what you'd call 'em. An order, or maybe just a cult. They're a bunch of humans who, as far as I know, think it's their job to watch out for my family. They train their whole lives for it. I'd be lying if I said it didn't rub me the wrong way, but part of the problem is they're very good at not getting seen, so it's not like I can ask 'em to stop. I'm not sure they'd listen anyway."

"He called you a pillar," Val says.

"Yeah, that's the word they use for us," Dream says with a wave of his hand. "Humans use it, I guess."

Val takes another look back at the forest receding behind them. "If you think we can trust him, I don't see why we shouldn't use him. He is very efficient, I'll admit. Moved so fast, I couldn't even react."

"You're not scared of him?" Dream asks.

Val shakes his head. "No. I think I might like to talk to him more. Maybe he can teach me how to sense better."

"Look at me, I almost forgot you're a freak," Dream says in a dead-pan voice. "Alright, then. We'll see how useful he is tomorrow when I go looking for Patience. We can decide after if he stays with us."

"Of course," Val replies. He smiles to himself at the notion that he gets a say in this at all. *We* is beginning to sound like one of the nicest words.

Dinner with Lux and Rez and some of the gems is a loud, but peaceful affair. Val feels calmer than he was when he first entered Lux's house, and he thinks it was probably the brush with death that cleared his head. He doesn't speak much, choosing instead to watch the way they interact with each other. There is a familiarity to the way the gems treat each other, almost like the kids at the orphanage, except they don't look at Val with suspicion or fear, and they treat Lux and Rez with far more respect than the kids ever gave to the people who ran the orphanage.

Val is seated beside Dream, who takes a methodical three bites of his dinner before pushing his bowl over to Val.

"You need it more than me," he says. "How're your hands?"

Val shows him his perfectly healed palms, washed and free of blood. "Like nothing happened at all."

They wait until the gems have all left and the table is cleared before Rez, Lux and Dream really start talking.

"Looks like Saph treated you well," Lux says to Dream from her chair at the head of the table. "You look twenty years younger."

Dream smirks at her. "Whole hell of a lot that does for me now."

Lux chuckles. "One or two crow's feet, maybe."

Dream leans his arms on the table, pulling a flask from his pants pocket and upending the contents into his empty glass. "We're going out tomorrow to see Patience. Tell me everything."

Lux leans back in her chair, glancing once at Rez. "I wish I could tell you anything useful, but it's exactly what you think it is. Suddenly a bunch of survivors from the coast began showing up in town, claiming that a monster had ravaged their town. None of them got a good look at it, and no one has seen Patience herself."

"What name was she using out there?" Dream asks.

Rez bridges his fingers together. "She'd been signing her letters as Etienne."

"Are you sure you want to go?" Lux asks. "I don't like to watch you walk off to dangerous places. We might be able to rustle up a few others to help us. Stronger together, you know?"

Dream shakes his head. "This is why I have Val. The kid can't get hurt by the hybrids, and we can both sense them. Plus I ran into someone in the woods who can help us. The three of us stand a much better chance."

"Look at you. A sudden fount of friendships," Rez says.

Dream shrugs. "Not a friend. Hired muscle."

"Still, it's unlike you," Lux says. "Working with so many strangers. Almost like you're pining for your teaching days."

"Please." Dream takes a gulp of his drink and sets it down with a heavy *thunk*. "Desperate times is all. I'm not getting any younger, and neither is Mare."

Lux and Rez both look away as Dream says that name, and Val squirms under some invisible weight he can't quantify.

"Who is Mare?" Val finally asks.

It's like Lux and Rez are both trying to hide that they've been pinched, but Dream just swirls his glass around, staring into the contents.

"He's one of us," Dream says. "Been missing for a long time."

"Well that's not entirely accurate now, is it?" Rez chimes in.

Dream glares at him from across the table, and Rez shrinks away.

"He fucked up, alright? Not saying he didn't. But no one knows where he is, and that still counts as *missing* in my book," Dream says. "But Patience is closer, so I'll look for her first."

It takes Lux a couple of seconds to break the silence. "I wish I could give you the names of any other nearby family, but Patience was the closest one. Hardly anyone else kept in touch with us. Liz swans in and out, but you know how she is. No letters when she's on the road."

"There was a rumor about Vann staying somewhere near the southern coast," Rez adds.

Dream scoffs. "The fuck is he gonna do for me?"

"That's what I thought you'd say," Rez finishes, pulling his hands into his lap. "I suppose that's that. You know you can come back here whenever you need to. Otherwise, try not to do anything stupid."

With a smile, Lux reaches over and puts her hand on Dream's shoulder. "We'd rather not lose you too."

Dream turns to Val, and he really does look somewhat younger. Not *young*, but like a few years of hardship have been buffed out of his face. "You hear that, kid?"

"Yes, sir," Val says, nodding.

"Let's not fuck up tomorrow."

Val almost laughs, unused to this familial atmosphere, neither part of it, nor outside of it. "I'll do my best."

Without really meaning to, Val winds up helping some of the gems as they clean up after dinner, not minding at all as they ask him a couple questions about his life. He's surprised to find that they're less interested in finding out how he wound up with Dream, and more interested in his being *unbound.*

"Is the old man paying your tuition?" one of them asks.

"Oh, I don't get paid," Val says. "I found *him.*"

That gets a ripple of quiet laughter, and some kind of silent understanding passes over the gems, solidly skipping over Val, who has no idea why this makes sense to any of them.

"Long as he's good to you," another adds with a wink.

Val doesn't feel like prying, not when the gems feel so friendly. He has never been in a house as warm as this one. "Thank you. He is."

When the gems send him back to his room, Val heads toward the staircase with a wandering eye, taking in all the details of such a well loved home. He doesn't mean to spy, but when he sees the open doorway into what looks like a study, his gaze sweeps over a huge armchair where Lux is seated, and Rez is perched on the armrest like a sleek raven. Lux says something Val can't hear, pinching Rez's chin between her thumb and index finger with an affectionate smile. Rez responds with his hand placed on Lux's cheek.

Val isn't sure how he knows he is not meant to view this scene, but he hurries back to his own room, hoping no one saw him.

Dream's door pops open as Val walks by. "Kid."

Val turns to him. "Professor?"

He leans against the doorway, peering down the hall, probably to check for listening gems. "Listen, uh." His gaze fixes back on Val, gray eyes sharp and focused. "About Mare. You should know, if you're working with me, he's the one who cut my face."

"Oh." Val's eyes jump over to Dream's scar as if on command. "This is who you're looking for?"

Dream nods. "He got caught up with some unsavory people. That's all. I wasn't in any shape to help him when it happened. And I admit, I took a pretty damn long time to decide to go looking for him. But I know I won't ever rest easy until I know for sure if he's dead or alive."

"He's dangerous though." Val reaches up to touch his own cheek where Dream's scar is. "If he's working with those weapons."

Dream grunts. "It won't do me any good to lie. There's a chance that looking for him is gonna get me killed. And if that happens, all I ask is that you come back here and you tell Lux and Rez what happened. Can you do that?"

Val feels his face drawing into a frown even as he says, "Yes, I can do that. I don't want to, but I can. If you die, that means I failed."

"Well, telling my family what happened is enough to balance the scales for me," Dream says. "Get some sleep. I need you at your best tomorrow. Don't want to keep our Eye in the woods waiting."

"Yes, sir." Val says the words even though his mind is slipping down a different conversation. *Why are you more prepared to die than you are to teach me?*

Getting back into his room, Val changes and crawls into bed with a tornado swirling through his mind, scattering all his thoughts into an incoherent mess. The sound of Dream's resignation is more painful than any wound. There is still so much Val doesn't understand about Dream, or about himself.

Like why Val can't stop thinking about the hunter's dispassionate claims to be able to kill Val, or shape him irrevocably. Surely those words shouldn't fill Val with a strange, flickering adrenaline, but he spends a near sleepless night wondering how this person could change him. The hunter's voice is in Val's ear until the morning.

I shaped it, as I'll shape you.

The little sleep Val does get is swiftly ruptured by a nightmare he has, leaving him with the feeling of something crawling around inside of his mouth. In a panic, Val rushes to Dream's room, knocking on the door repeatedly until Dream answers.

"Professor, there's something in my mouth."

Val opens his jaw wide without waiting for a response, and Dream stares at him, brows cinched. With a quiet grumble, Dream grabs Val's face and tilts his head back.

"Did that Eye do something to you? Besides stab you?"

Val shrugs while Dream looks inside his mouth.

"Looks the same to me, kid." Dream lets Val go, still frowning. "What's going on with you?"

"I don't know," Val says quietly. "I'm sorry . . ."

"It's fine," Dream mutters. "We can ask when we meet back up. You *can* come with me, right?"

"Yes," Val says, nodding several times. "Of course I can. I'm sorry. I think the city is getting to me."

Dream gives Val a light shove on his shoulder. "Go get dressed, fuck's sake."

Val smiles to himself as the door shuts. He'll have to do better, but it does feel nice that Dream appears concerned for him. Nice, like rain while the sun is still out.

When Dream and Val leave Indulgence, the streets are mostly empty. The sun is barely out as they leave Modesty's town limits, and Val feels the warmth of another spring day as the two of them cross the treeline once more.

The Eye is already waiting for them just a few yards into the woods. They stand at their full height, sunless hands woven neatly over their face once more.

"Enough of that," Dream says. "If you're working with me, you're gonna have to look at me eventually."

The Eye lets his breath out slowly. "It isn't for you. Apologies."

"Whatever." Dream leans on his cane with both hands. "Did you do something to my boy? Not the knives, something else?"

"No," the Eye says, firm. "Regular poisons don't work on insects anyway. That would be a waste of supplies."

Dream's brows raise and he glances at Val. "He's got a point."

Val turns to the Eye, fully taking in how large their body is when they're standing in front of Val. They're even more imposing when the two of them are facing each other directly. Val's head only comes up to their chest.

"I guess it's something else," Val says.

"Should I tell 'em to stay out of sight or what?" Dream asks, hand on Val's shoulder.

Val looks at the Eye with their strategically wrapped clothing, bound tight at the waist and around their shoulders, but looser over their arms and thighs.

"How many weapons do you have on you right now?" Val asks them.

The Eye takes a longer breath in, and their lips move just slightly. ". . . five, six, seven? Eight."

"I think he should stay with us," Val says. "We should strategize as a group, right?"

"Guess so," Dream concedes. "Did you pick a damn name already?"

Their arms shift a little at that, and even Val can pick up on their discomfort. "I don't care what you call me."

Dream rolls his eyes, so Val chimes in. "Why don't we just call you Hunter for now? A little less confusing than 'eye' anyway."

"Fine by me," they say.

Dream gives Val a relieved look and turns back toward Modesty. "Yeah, alright. Come on, Hunter. We have a ride to catch out to the coast."

Val follows a step behind Dream, to keep his eye on Hunter as they lower their hands from their eyes. They immediately position themselves directly behind Dream, walking like a shadow in Dream's wake. Val digs into his pocket and holds out the little black earring to them.

"You left this somewhere downstairs."

Hunter turns their gaze back on Val, and just like that, their eyes enter the same utterly emotionless tint from the day before. They swipe the earring from Val, barely touching his skin, and affix it to their ear in a fluid motion, like they've done it a thousand times.

"You sure have a lot of piercings," Val says, walking half sideways as he tries to stay between Dream and Hunter.

"Mm." Hunter keeps their gaze on the back of Dream's head. "It helps."

"With what?" Val chirps.

"Killing things," Hunter says.

"Ah." Val spins back around and sticks his hands into his pockets. "Should have guessed that."

"Do you know anything about the hybrid by the coast?" Dream asks, not bothering to look behind him.

"I asked around the refugees," Hunter says back. "It burst out of a house, searching for the matriarch of the village, the Pillar of Patience."

"Right inside the center of it." Dream rubs at his jaw. "Got any descriptions?"

"Sounds like a clean half situation," Hunter says. "Human torso, insect legs. It's going to have speed on us at least."

"Fucking great," Dream says. "Val, you got your gun."

"Yes, sir," Val nods, touching the lump in his pants pocket.

"Order of operations." Dream takes a deep breath, throwing a glance at Val as they circle around the residential edge of Modesty. "Insect parts heal faster, but you want to cut down on mobility as much as possible. Aim for limbs. They can still swing at you without a head."

Val tries to memorize everything he's saying.

"That about line up with your methods, Hunter?" Dream asks.

"Roughly," Hunter says. "Unless of course it spits acid. In which case, priority goes to breaking its jaw. Better yet if you can get it to hurt itself with its own supply. Forcing it to heal slows it down."

Val looks over at Hunter. "Can you shape this one too?"

Hunter's eyes widen, and Dream comes to a full stop just so he can turn to look at them. "What is that? Shaping?"

Hunter immediately closes their eyes. "It is a . . . method for dealing with healers."

"Yesterday he said he was going to fuse my hands together," Val says, showing his palms to Dream.

Brows furrowed, Dream takes another look at Hunter. "That one in the woods between Prosperity and here, was that you?"

"Yes," Hunter answers, head tilted away from Dream.

"You didn't kill it," Dream says. "What did you do?"

Hunter's body is turned toward the road Val and Dream walked to get to the Dueling Cities. "If you can get close enough to an insect while it's healing, you can bend the body and change the shape of it. Blunt its edges."

Dream stares at Hunter, eyes narrowed. "Do you know about the objects inside the hybrids?"

"Inside?" Hunter's brows furrow as they turn back toward Dream.

"See Val and I have a theory about what drives the hybrids to kill," Dream starts, taking another step toward Hunter. "I think you might be able to help us prove it. When we get to the coast, we'll need to work together to immobilize this thing so Val can go searching."

Val grabs Dream's arm, a whirlwind of emotion inside him, too wild to properly feel. "Do you think we can stop it from hurting people?"

Dream fixes him with a razor-sharp stare. "You understand that if this doesn't work, we're all at risk?"

Val nods.

Dream's gaze softens again and he starts back toward the entrance to Modesty, his cane sinking into the grass. "C'mon. Patience isn't getting any closer."

The taxi service toward the coast is just a large, rattling truck that Dream begrudgingly forks over money to the driver for three passengers to sit in the bed of. The driver tells them no one wants to go out there ever since people started claiming there was a monster running around. Of course, the driver also claims to have no fear, and Val refrains from telling her that the three of them are, in fact, on their way to a fight.

Once they're all in the truck bed, bouncing and rattling toward the coast, Dream takes a swig from his flask and tells Hunter about how there might be objects inside of the hybrids causing their transformations. Hunter listens with their hands back over their eyes while Val studies his scalpel.

"It makes the most sense that these objects would be in the human torso," Hunter says. "But if it's something as small as a piece of thread, it could be impossible to find. Where did your knife come from?"

Dream unsheathes the blade from his cane just to look at the silver. "I don't know. I took this from someone like me, not a hybrid. Someone gave it to him."

Hunter pulls their hands off their eyes, lids opening slowly, though they keep their head angled down. "Does this have anything to do with Innovation?"

Val can see the stiffness in Dream's shoulders. "Maybe."

"The Eyes have been watching that cursed city for years, but no human can get through the wall. Insects though, they come and go as they please."

Dream nods. "That I do know."

"It's watched by a number of trained inse . . . hybrids," Hunter adjusts, glancing at Val with their tired, black eyes. "Ones more like you, but better at fighting. No offense."

Val shakes his head. "None taken. I haven't been taught yet."

Hunter gives Val a blank stare. "You're better off not knowing."

Val shrugs. "We'll see. I think I could be quite good at it. Don't you, Professor?"

He nudges Dream's arm with a small smile, but Val's expression vanishes at the first sign of plodding, mechanical footsteps at the edges of his awareness. Not two legs, but six, and they are running right for them.

Hunter slaps their hand on the roof of the truck a couple times. "Let us out! Now."

"Is it coming?" Dream asks.

"Yes." Val pulls on his arms. "We have to let the driver get away."

Dream bangs on the glass window between the bed and the cab, and the truck finally comes to a stop. The driver leans her arm out the window with a scowl as Hunter jumps onto solid ground and starts running toward the direction of the hybrid.

"Get out of here," Dream snarls at the woman. "And don't come back until you hear it's safe. There's a killer in these woods."

Val goes running after Hunter, fishing the pistol out of his trousers. He won't allow anything to happen to Dream. He won't.

With Dream's resonance behind him, Val runs as fast as he can toward the mechanical steps of the hybrid drawing ever closer. All they have to do is intercept it before it gets close enough to hurt Dream. Before he realizes it, Val has lost track of Hunter's presence, and he finds himself standing in the direct path of the hybrid, completely alone. He can hear it now, crashing through the forest with legs too big and too unwieldy to be quiet. Val aims the pistol in the direction of the sound and the wild vibrations, waiting to see its body.

The trees shake as it emerges from the shadows of the forest. Val sees its torso and arms first, red-stained hands extended out in front of it, pushing aside branches as it goes. Its spindly, black legs are harder to see, but the bright orange markings on the long torso catch Val's gaze as it goes. Val aims the gun, knowing he's not good enough to get its legs, so the best he can do is try to shock it. The hybrid doesn't even seem to notice Val in its path, its eyes wide open and fixed on a point in the distance.

Val does his best to shoot for the human torso held aloft by its many legs. Squeezing the trigger, the single bullet pops off with surprisingly little resistance or recoil. Maybe getting stabbed in the spine was more than enough to prepare Val for the kickback, but the hybrid doesn't stop. It doesn't even startle. Val can't tell if he even hit it as it comes crashing through the brush. Pocketing the useless pistol, Val braces himself to try to grab onto the creature's torso as it passes by, figuring he'll have to slow it down himself if he wants to have any real effect.

As Val raises his own hands up in a mirror of the hybrid's, something flicks out from a tree and the hybrid's human arms cinch against its torso as Hunter drops down onto its back. Val hears something *crunch* and the hybrid begins to scream.

All the will to fight drains out of Val's body as he watches Hunter loop the rope even tighter around its human torso, forcing it to a confused stop as it yells into the empty forest. Its human body twists in protest to the rope, but Hunter just turns with a knife in hand and starts to hack away at the leg closest to them. The sound it makes is worse than the cacophony of Indulgence. This is a human scream from a mouth that doesn't know it used to be human.

Either it's easier than it looks to break those legs, or Hunter has done this enough times to make it look effortless. With its two front legs severed from its body, the weight of Hunter on its back begins to unbalance the whole thing, and Hunter braces themself, crouching down as the hybrid struggles to keep itself up. With another hack of their knife, Hunter breaks a third leg, and the hybrid tips over with Hunter steering it onto the grass beneath. Hunter yanks on the rope, using their own arm to brace the excess so they can keep the hybrid from lashing out.

"You." Hunter looks at Val, face still utterly blank. "Come here."

Val snaps out of his stunned awe and walks closer.

Hunter produces a length of what might be leather, which they toss around the hybrid's face, catching the hybrid's open mouth with it. Val watches human teeth immediately bite down on it as Hunter pulls that taut too.

"Can you sense the object?" Hunter asks, both arms occupied with the ropes. "Not much time before the legs heal."

Val runs forward as he sees the edges of its severed body parts already beginning to rebuild themselves. The hybrid's eyes are human in shape but filmy and harder to see details. It watches Val approaching, breathing hard around the leather in its mouth. For some reason, Val hates looking at it all bound up and restrained more than he did when it was bearing down on him with single-minded aggression.

"Sorry," Val mutters, struggling to look away from those filmy eyes.

Hunter pulls tighter on the ropes as Val gets close enough to study its human torso. It's still wearing whatever shirt it had on before this transformation took place, a now muddied dress shirt with several buttons missing and the sleeves torn off at different lengths. Val doesn't know where, or how, to begin looking for whatever object is inside this thing, so he just puts his hand on the hybrid's chest.

The veins in its neck bulge under its skin as it jerks its head back, and Val startles at the motion.

"Faster," Hunter says, both his arms straining to hold it in place.

"Sorry," Val says again, louder.

He rips the shirt free from the remaining buttons to put both his hands on the hybrid's skin. Its heart thrashes under Val's palms, but Val tries to ignore that, searching instead for some *other* resonance. The only thing that makes any sense to him is that, if the objects are responsible for the insect bodies, then they must be in the human flesh, like Hunter said. Perhaps there is something meaningful in the distribution of flesh and chitin. Dragging his hands further down, Val tries to feel the human anatomy underneath the skin, and the closer he draws to the place where its belly juts out from the shell below, the harder the hybrid fights against the ropes that hold it.

Val puts one hand on the hybrid's stomach, and one on its back, closing his eyes. The hybrid seems to hate that he's searching, which can only mean he is close.

"*Before* sundown would be preferred," Hunter says, and Val can hear the effort in their voice as they hold the hybrid back.

He can't explain it, but Val swears he feels a strange lack of heat from the hand on the hybrid's stomach. Holding his breath, Val pulls out his scalpel, flipping it open and setting in on the hybrid's skin.

"Did you find it?" Dream's voice drifts in from somewhere behind Val.

The hybrid jerks around, its remaining legs kicking at the ground and a nearby tree trunk, but Hunter holds it still while Val cuts into soft skin.

"Stay out of sight," Hunter bellows back to the forest. "It knows you're here."

Blood pours out of the slice on the hybrid's stomach, and Val is fixed on the sight, his eyes wanting to blink, but he can't seem to get them to work. There is that sweet smell again, assaulting his senses, like he's stuck his head into an oven with a pie baking. Mouth watering, gums aching, Val has the overwhelming urge to put his mouth on the open wound of this creature. His hand which holds the scalpel trembles so slightly.

He doesn't see Hunter moving, just feels their hand crack across Val's cheek with dizzying force. Val feels like he's snapping back to reality as Hunter pulls on the leather bit again, staring daggers at Val from behind the hybrid.

"Don't make me kill you after all this," they say through gritted teeth. Their eyes show another spark, the light of anger directed at Val, completely ready to follow through on their threat if Val disappoints.

Val springs back to life, Hunter's anger leaving sparks lingering in its wake. Val puts the scalpel away, thinks about rolling his sleeves up, panics, then pulls his whole shirt off just to keep it from getting dirty. Kneeling in front of the hybrid, Val whispers one more apology in his own head before he slides his hand inside the hybrid's stomach.

He knows this feeling. He's done this before, on himself, in the bathroom of the orphanage by the light of a candle he stole. He knows the wet warmth and pulsing life and hard bone found underneath a person's skin. As soon as his fingers are once again pushing past organs and blood, it's as if he is a child again, searching in fear for the thing he knows does not belong—a poison that needs to be removed before it tears him apart from the inside. Closing his eyes, Val probes past familiar sensations, ignoring the hybrid thrashing and Hunter uttering demands, until finally, his fingers brush against something he doesn't recognize. Something thin and hard, a loop of metal that Val slips his middle finger into, working it down his knuckle like a ring before the hybrid bucks hard enough that Val is shoved back.

Val's hand pulls free from the hybrid's guts, and he looks down at his dripping wet fingers to see one half of a very small pair of steel scissors hanging from his finger. As soon as Val separates from it, the hybrid stops its fighting, its whole body going slack. Hunter's rope falls to its waist with the lack of tension as it folds forward, and Val scrambles away from it.

Hunter hops onto the ground, still holding onto the rope, but studying its sudden passivity. "What did you find?"

Val holds his hand up to show them the single scissor blade. "This."

Their brows barely twitch in recognition before they turn back to the hybrid. "It's still healing."

"Professor!" Val shouts into the woods. "I found the object!"

"Shit, kid, I'm right here," Dream says, nudging Val's back with his boot.

"Oh." Panting, Val shows the scissor to him as well. "Do you think . . . ?"

Dream doesn't take his eyes off of the hybrid. "I don't think anything yet. Don't let your guard down so soon."

Hunter affixes their rope tighter around the hybrid's middle, keeping its arms held in place while they all watch it heal in silence. Val picks himself up off the ground, moving to stand in front of Dream while they wait. Slowly but surely, like the ticking hands of a clock, the hybrid begins to move again. It doesn't strain against the rope, but dips its head further toward the ground.

"Ah, gods above or below . . ." Its voice is pained and quiet, and even as its missing legs begin to reform, it does not try to get up. Raising its head, the eyes that had been covered in some kind of film now find Val's with recognition. "Have you come to kill me?"

Val startles, dropping both the scissor blade and his own scalpel. "No!"

Its eyes flash wide, confusion in its brow, grief in its open mouth. "I've done something terrible."

Val takes a step toward it, surprised to find that what he feels more than anything in that moment is anger, raw and jagged in his hands. "Is that what you *want* to do?"

The hybrid's eyes widen, shoulders sloping. "Of course not. One moment, I was a visitor in my family's home, and the next, I was something *else*. I didn't . . . I didn't ask for this. But if I couldn't stop it once, how am I supposed to stop it from happening twice? I think I would rather die than risk it."

Val doesn't recognize his own voice, hardly feels his own body as he stomps forward and grabs this person's face and asks much louder than he means to, "What is your name?"

They slowly blink, fear and confusion filling their eyes with water. "My name is Matthew."

"Who are you?" Val asks, knowing full well that he's practically yelling, but he can't temper himself. "What were you doing here?"

"I—I am a student. I was vi—visiting my parents. I'm from Patience. I grew up in those waters."

The tears spill over Val's hands where he holds Matthew's face.

"I didn't mean to." Matthew touches Val's wrists with bloodied hands. "Please, I don't want to think about it. I don't want this body. I don't want these memories."

Val squeezes Matthew's face harder. "It wasn't you. You had no choice."

"How do you know?"

Val feels his own eyes stinging, his teeth clenched in his mouth. "I couldn't kill you even if I wanted to. You can't die anymore. Not the way you want to anyway. So . . . so you should get up, and help us deal with whatever mess there is in Patience."

Matthew's hands fall from Val's arms, and Val can see the breath rattling in Matthew's chest.

"You don't have to be Matthew from Patience anymore," Val says. "But you have to be *someone*. I'd hope you'd be a nice person, so my friend here can untie you in good conscience."

Matthew's eyes open wide, head nodding repeatedly. "I don't want to hurt anyone."

Val turns back to look at Hunter and Dream. They both look as shocked as either of them could possibly be; Dream's head tilted, slack-jawed; and Hunter's eyes gone bright with the embers of deep thought.

Val holds his arm out, shaking from the adrenaline. "This is Matthew. Do you think we could try untying him?"

5

Hunter was reluctant to let the rope go, not entirely sure how to handle the blood-thirsty beast turned humble, so they settled for keeping the rope loose around Matthew's waist instead. When Val told him they were headed to look for survivors, Matthew asked to come along.

"I'm not sure I trust myself to be alone," he'd said quietly.

Val had smiled. "I trust you."

After they regrouped, Matthew first brought them to a stream in the woods where Val washed his hands and his tools, before he packed the scissors and scalpel away in his bag and put his shirt back on. As he turned to face Hunter and Dream, ready to assure them that he was prepared to keep going, his legs simply buckled and he fell to his knees without warning.

Which was when Matthew scooped Val up and set him on his own hard-shell back.

And that is how Val winds up hitching a ride into Patience, red-faced as he clings to Matthew's back to stay steady on the slippery shell.

"How did this object get inside of me?" Matthew asks as they walk toward the coast.

"I have no idea, but I believe that you had nothing to do with this," Val tells him. "It was out of your control."

Sighing, Matthew looks at Hunter and Dream, and then over his shoulder at Val. "Who are you?"

"I'm like you," Val says with a smile. "I had something inside of me. The scalpel I used to cut you open. Sorry about that, by the way."

Matthew shakes his head. Now that the chaos has begun to wear off, Val can better see Matthew's long, shaggy hair, and his suntanned skin, and his slender shoulders. He doesn't have the build of someone used to hunting and killing. He looks like the university students Val had once seen in the streets of Foundation. He also no longer carries the scent of sugar, which Val is grateful for.

"It sounds like you freed me from hurting more people," Matthew mumbles, his brown gaze flicking across Val's face. "Does this mean . . . could I look like normal again one day? Like you?"

Val shrugs. "I don't know. You're the first person we've rescued. Maybe!"

Matthew gives the ghost of a smile as the trees begin to thin out around them. There is a sudden drop from the grass beneath their feet to a sandy beach that extends out toward the pawing waves. Matthew hesitates, shoulders raised.

"These legs . . . they're not as good on sand."

"Mind putting me down?" Val asks.

Matthew obliges, sinking to the grass to let Val back onto solid ground. Val tugs on the rope still in Hunter's hands.

"Is this still necessary?"

"Mm." Hunter looks at Matthew, who shies away from the gaze of the person who single-handedly restrained him. "Pull it off, then. Would be a waste to cut it."

"Thank you," Matthew mumbles while Val loosens the rope from his torso.

"Val, you keep an eye on your new friend," Dream says, already hopping down to the sand. "Tell us if he runs."

"Yes, sir." Val jumps down after him, and Hunter follows Val with one more withering glance in Matthew's direction.

"We can both feel you," Hunter assures Matthew.

Matthew twists his hands together, nodding several times.

The three of them walk along the beach, finding a wooden archway sticking out of the sand with the word *Patience* painted along what is now a cracked in half welcome sign. Dream walks fast, undeterred by the feel of the sand under his cane.

"Do you feel your friend?" Val asks him, catching up to tug on his sleeve.

Dream has a scowl smeared over his face. "No. Which means I expect her body is somewhere out here."

"I'm sorry," Val says quietly. "Thank you for not killing Matthew."

With a gruff sigh, Dream shakes his head. "You're right. It's not his fault. Long as he never does it again."

"I can feel him watching from the trees," Val says, turning toward them. "I think he's scared to see what he's done."

"Yeah, I don't blame him for that," Dream grumbles. "Stop talking. My side hurts."

"Yes, sir."

Val falls a few steps behind Dream as they enter the charred remnants of the fishing village. There are buildings on stilts over the water, long piers that criss-cross the ocean, as well as several more structures tucked into the woods. The breeze rolling in from the water sends goosebumps skittering down Val's arms, though it cuts through the smell of burning wood.

"There's no one here alive," Hunter says, quiet enough that Val thinks it wasn't for Dream.

Val nods. "Well at least the Professor's safe."

"Why do you call him that?" Hunter asks.

Dream steps up onto the pier, but Val stays on the sand.

"Because he's my teacher."

Hunter narrows their eyes at him. "You have no idea what he is, do you?"

Val shrugs. "What does it matter? He said it was fine to call him that, so I will."

Hunter takes a step away from Val. "I'm going to check the woods."

Val watches them walk away, a drop of ink over the sand, and his mind briefly replays the moment where Hunter wrangled a hybrid all on their own with ruthless efficiency. The slap to Val's face echoes in his ear as Hunter stalks toward the treeline.

Hunter really could kill Val. This feels truer than ever before.

The sound of Dream's boots draws Val's eye and he watches Dream cross the pier with a bright blue ribbon in his hand.

"She's either been consumed, or kidnapped. Bottom line, she's not here," Dream says.

Val points at the ribbon. "Something of hers?"

"Yeah," Dream says, easing down the steps back to the sand. "Something she wouldn't leave behind. Where's the big one?"

"Hunter went to check the woods," Val says. "Maybe they hit their limit on looking at you."

"Pfft," Dream snorts. "Don't hold it against 'em. Part of their whole deal. C'mon, I'm tired. We're gonna have to walk back, and I don't want to do it yet. We can build a fire and take a minute before we go."

"I'm sorry," Val says again. "About your friend."

Dream just nods, and Val feels his willingness to talk drying up like blood on his hands.

They find Hunter in one of the abandoned houses with a fire going in the hearth. When Hunter says they knew Dream would need to rest, Val tries not to feel jealous that they can so easily predict everyone's movements. Dream saunters in, and Hunter disappears, like they're on some kind of rotation. Just when Val is thinking *at least I can be here with Dream*, Hunter comes back with a fish they apparently caught themself.

"Did you use me as bait when Matthew was coming at me?" Val asks as the fish simmers over the fire.

"Of course," Hunter says, calm as ever. "You're not a fighter."

Val folds his arms. "Could have warned me."

"You don't trust me," Hunter says, refusing to look away from the fish. "What does it matter? Worked out, didn't it?"

"We didn't lose anyone," Dream says. "That's a victory in my book. You, Hunter, make sure Val eats a little. I'm taking a rest in the other room. Val, go check on your new friend."

Hunter nods, and Val goes back outside, grateful for the fresh air once again. As if on cue, Matthew comes rustling out of the trees, the bright orange markings on his shell standing out like a flare in the middle of the night.

"Are your friends okay?" Matthew asks, hands clasped.

Val nods. "Yes, thank you."

"Are you?" he asks next.

Val steps away from the house, and Matthew lowers himself closer to the ground, concern etched into his face.

"Would you like me to find you a clean shirt?" Val asks.

Matthew's mouth opens and it takes a moment, but he gives a choked sort of laugh. "I suppose that makes sense."

"Which one was your house?" Val asks. "I can go inside for you."

With hesitant directions, Val goes back to the beach to find the house that Matthew says he grew up in. The inside is chaotic, but not completely destroyed. It looks like there was a fight, the remnants of someone's dinner splattered across the wall. One of the bedroom doors has been ripped off the hinges, and Val goes in there to find a suitcase open on the floor and clothes neatly packed inside. He drags the whole thing back to Matthew, who waits just barely out of sight in the woods.

"How did the fires start?" Val asks.

Matthew sinks down until the length of his shelled body is entirely on the grass, picking through the suitcase. "I . . . changed. My memo-ries are hazy, but I remember this ringing in my ears. It was deafening, and for some reason, I became convinced that the matriarch, Etienne, that she was causing it. All I wanted was for it to stop."

Matthew's hands go still, gripping a jacket with the emblem for the Northern University on the front. "I went straight for her. I know I cut her, I felt my hands around her throat, but I can't really remem-ber specifics. One moment she was there, and the next, the ringing was getting quieter, and then I couldn't see her anymore. I wanted to just lay down right there and sleep, but the other villagers were scared. They came with weapons, and I just . . ."

His gaze snaps up to Val's, watery and so painfully human. "Do you really believe it wasn't my fault?"

"Of course," Val says immediately. "There's no doubt in my mind."

Matthew wipes his eyes with the back of his hand.

"Why don't you come with us?" Val asks. "You could help. Dream, the old man, he's looking for someone. I bet we could use a person as fast as you."

Matthew's breath shudders out of him and he closes the suitcase. "Thank you, truly. But I don't think I should. I might make things harder for you, looking this way."

Val opens his mouth to protest, but Matthew shakes his head.

"I need to . . . be still. Just for a little while anyway. But, I promise I'll think about what you said." He lays his hands on the suitcase, fingers tracing along a seam in the trunk. "Maybe a new name will help."

Val sticks his hand out. "I picked a new one a long time ago, and it definitely helped me. People still look at me strange, but at least I like my name. It's Val, by the way."

Matthew takes Val's hand in both of his, squeezing tightly. "If you find yourself back out here . . ."

"I'll come and see you," Val finishes for him. "Who knows, maybe by then you'll have figured out how to walk on sand. You could be a whole new person."

Matthew's hands tremble, and when he speaks, Val barely hears him. "I hope so."

When Val returns to the house, Hunter is sprawled over the couch with his eyes closed, and there is a bowl with a child-sized portion of fish and mushrooms. Val eats it in three angry seconds and nearly throws the bowl into the sink. This frustration he feels is entirely new and more uncomfortable than getting stabbed. Val goes into the other, smaller bedroom, and fights the urge to slam the door shut just to disturb Hunter. For Dream's sake, he doesn't.

Sitting on someone's abandoned twin bed, Val kicks off his shoes and stews in his own discomfort. Wasn't he the one brought on to protect Dream? He has a right to be upset that someone else is now doing better than he ever could. Hunter is more skilled, more experienced, and more composed than Val ever could be in a real fight. Val hardly needs to be here if Hunter is around.

Val touches his cheek where Hunter slapped him. Ruthless, efficient, driven. Hunter is as deadly as the hybrids, only worse, because he can predict both Val's stupidity *and* the single-mindedness of the hybrids. Val's anger begins to wane as he pictures Hunter lassoing Matthew from the trees. He made it look simple.

Maybe Hunter should teach Val to fight instead . . .

Val collapses into the borrowed bed and tries to give himself over to the exhaustion he felt when his legs quit on him earlier. For all he knows, Hunter will leave them now that this job is done, and Val won't have to think about this anymore. The one person who could actually kill Val, and feel nearly nothing about it.

Curling in on himself, Val remembers Hunter's hands on his face when he bound and pinned him in place. He also remembers the bizarre glee that overtook Hunter from whatever Dream did to subdue him. Val almost forgot that Dream has some kind of power over humans that doesn't work on him. That must have been it, some kind of emotional release that renders a person useless.

Dream and Hunter are both powerful in their own ways. They seem to fill each other's blind spots perfectly. When Val pictures the two of them in his mind, they are both as big as mountains. But where Dream feels somehow untouchable, fragile in his own way, Val knows Hunter to be human. He also knows that Hunter was in one of Lux's shops. Which means Hunter is decidedly *touchable*.

Val feels much too warm in this stolen bed, lying in an afternoon sunspot, remembering what Lux said when she first brought Hunter up. *Very high pain tolerance.* Val can't begin to imagine what Hunter looks like without his clothes, or what he paid one of Lux's gems to do for him, but trying to picture it is as chaotic and wild as staring down a monster in the woods.

Do they hit him? What good does that do? Val bends his knees up toward his chest and thinks that, yes, actually, he might let Hunter slap him again, but Val heals without scars. Hunter doesn't. As Val forces his eyes shut, he thinks Hunter must be covered in the marks of old wounds. A body that large could have whole histories carved into it.

Val is starting to sweat, which is new. He pushes himself out of bed and goes into the living room where Hunter has taken up the couch. Val starts crossing the room, and Hunter pulls a knife out so fast, Val hardly sees the movement.

"What?" Hunter asks, opening one eye.

Val feels a spark of fear, knowing Hunter might actually cut him, but he forces himself to keep walking until he's standing by Hunter's chest.

"Who are you?" Val asks.

Hunter's eyes open fully, and he reaches into the folds of his clothes to pull out a small stone. "It's fine if you don't trust me. I don't need you to."

He's sharpening the knife, Val realizes, dragging the blade's edge over the rock.

"You're even more sunless than me," Val says, not entirely sure why.

"Mm." Hunter's gaze is fixed on the knife. "I *usually* work at night."

"Do you have scars?" Val asks.

"Obviously."

"Can I see?"

Hunter pauses, gaze drifting back up to where Val is standing.

"I just . . ." Val swallows around an inexplicably tight throat. "I don't have any. I can't."

Hunter carefully sheathes the knife back where it was strapped to his bicep and tucks the whetstone away.

"I can give you scars," Hunter says, voice empty of anything other than fact.

Val's eyes widen, and the heat he tried to leave behind comes searing back down his body, from his neck to the apex of his thighs. Never, never has anyone done something like this to Val.

"Really?" Val's voice comes out strained and small.

Hunter sits upright, his back to the armrest, forearms propped on his knees. "You first. Who are you?"

Val's heart is pounding uncomfortably fast in Hunter's steadfast gaze. "I'm not really anyone, to be honest. Grew up in an orphanage. Got a very nice boy killed before I left, because he was nice to me. I've been chased out of two or three towns for being a monster that heals after getting his limbs severed. People think I'm creepy. I pulled a scalpel out of my belly when I was a child, no memory of anyone ever putting it there, so I suppose I can't really blame them for thinking I'm bizarre. I'm just . . . Val."

Hunter listens with no change in his face, but he nods at the door that Dream has locked himself behind. "How'd you find the Pillar?"

"I'm not really sure," Val admits, sitting on the couch by Hunter's feet, the weight of invisible tension too heavy to stand under. "I found out about a man who used to teach students how to fight and kill, and suddenly it was like I wouldn't know peace until I found him. But when I finally tracked him down, he wasn't a man at all. He was something else. More like me than human. He hired me to help keep him safe, but I think maybe he was just worried I'd get into more trouble on my own."

Hunter leans forward, drawing Val's gaze back to him. "The Pillars aren't yours to protect. The fact that he's allowed you into his company is a blessing, but don't mistake his sympathy for anything more than a giant's hand shielding you from the rain."

Val shies away from Hunter's colorless eyes. "Why do you call them pillars?"

"They are the Pillars of humanity," Hunter says, unblinking. "They're made of the rawest parts of us. Everything that makes a human *human*. There is, or was, a Pillar for all of the things that separate a human being from an insect, or a plant, or the weather. Emotion, inspiration, desire—"

"Dreams?" Val asks, pulse racing.

"Exactly," Hunter says. "Every one of those beings represents a piece of humanity. They are precious, and powerful. And something is hunting them down. The Eyes have watched the Pillars for nearly as long as the Pillars have existed. We gave up some of the things that make us human just so we could help keep them safe. I might have broken my own tenets, but I won't fail him." Hunter points to the door that Dream is behind. "I will do whatever he asks of me, because he's more important than I am."

Val almost smiles through a rush of warm adrenaline. "I think maybe you and I have that in common."

Hunter doesn't look remotely impressed by that, just lowers his hand. Val has the distinct impression that he is sharing a couch with a huge animal, like a wolf or a bear.

"So the Eyes protect the pillars," Val says. "What do the pillars do?"

"They keep the gods from crushing us," Hunter says, plain and simple.

Val feels his back straighten, like Dream snapped him with the cane again. "Have you ever seen something in the sky along your travels? Something that looks like a cloud in the shape of a human hand?"

Hunter's eyes narrow, tilting his head away like he caught a bad scent in the air. "No."

"Oh." Val tries to smile, but it feels broken on his face.

"You see human hands in the sky?" Hunter presses.

Val pulls his socked feet up onto the couch. "Maybe I shouldn't talk about it . . ."

"Tell me," Hunter says, and suddenly his knife is back in his hand, pointed at Val's throat.

"Mercy," Val says, raising his hands, and staring directly at the jagged edge. "It's just something I see from time to time. Like hands wearing white gloves in the sky. I don't know what it is."

Hunter flips the knife around in his hand, catching it by the tip as his face turns pensive. He lets the handle tap against his cheek. "Maybe you have some connection to the gods of this world."

Val's brow furrows. "That might mean they're the reason I had that scalpel inside me."

Hunter shrugs, holding the knife with both hands now, and Val wonders if this is like his version of smoking a cigarette. "Didn't say the gods were good. Maybe they hate the Pillars. Maybe you just hallucinate sometimes. I don't know. It's not my job to know."

"And you're fine with that?" Val asks. "Doing your one job and nothing else?"

"Yes."

Val touches his own ankles, holding his feet together on the couch of this abandoned house. He feels smaller than ever sitting beside Hunter, but he also feels a little like that jagged knife.

"Would it leave a scar to shape me?"

"Yes."

"How much could you change about me?"

"It's not fucking surgery," Hunter says.

Val bites his tongue.

Hunter gives a barely audible sigh. "Why do you want a scar so bad?"

Val shrugs, staring hard at his own two feet, the bottoms pressed against each other, heel to heel. "People have scars. It means they've lived through something. The more I see of this world, and walk away completely clean. I don't know, it frightens me. I wish—" Val swallows without meaning to, like his body is trying to consume the words before he can say them. "I feel broken, but I'm not. I feel dirty, but I'm not. I just want to know what the difference is."

Hunter points the knife at Val again, but there is no aggression in his grip. He merely holds it like he doesn't feel the difference between the blade and his fingers. "There's a man out there, one of the hybrids who watch the borders of Innovation. He looks and dresses and talks just like a man, save for the fact that he has knives sheathed in his eyes."

Hunter uses his own knife to point to each of Val's eyes. "He doesn't fight with them, he just lives like that. Surely he could take them out and let his eyes heal, but he doesn't. The shaping isn't instant, either. You have to hold them there long enough for the healing to stop trying to force out the foreign object and bind with it instead. Someone did that to him. Convinced him it would be better to be blind. And now he serves whoever lives behind the walls of Innovation. That's a version of shaping."

Val looks at the knife again, thinks about how bad it would hurt to stab himself like that, and shakes his head. "I don't think I want knives in my eyes."

"Didn't think so," Hunter says, rising to his feet. "If you're not using the bedroom, I will."

"Oh, sure." Val gestures to it without thinking, hand hanging between them. "All yours."

Hunter snatches up Val's outstretched hand in his, and draws a line on the side of Val's palm with his knife. Val feels the pain before his eyes catch up to the motion, and suddenly he's bleeding. Hunter sheaths the knife once more, and quickly pinches the cut between his fingers, twisting the skin as blood drips down Val's arm.

"Ouch," Val says, more to assert his presence than to actually complain. It's not the pain he feels most in that moment.

His skin trying to heal with something in the way is like walking against the tide, and the tide has shards of glass in it. There's more shock than anything else as his body tries to work around Hunter's influence, but it's not pleasant either. A slow burn of discomfort puts tears in Val's eyes, his arm going cold as more and more blood drips down his wrist. As dizziness begins to sweep over him, his body gives in to the new direction, and the pain begins to fade away. His blood stops dripping, and Hunter lets his hand go so Val can lick the blood off.

"There," Hunter says, walking away as Val looks down at his healed palm.

The door to the other bedroom snaps shut and Val sees a ridge of imperfect skin embedded in his hand. He draws his finger over it, as if it will peel away with a little encouragement, but no, it is part of his hand. There are nerves in that piece of new skin, and it hurts when Val presses his thumbnail into it. Val's heart races, staring in awe at how easy it was to mar this container of his.

A scar, just for him.

Dream stays shut up in his room for an hour more before they pack up to walk back to Indulgence. Matthew says goodbye to Val before he leaves, wearing a new shirt and looking like he washed and brushed his hair. Val waves, committing the scent of this salt water forest to memory, so he can come back and check in on Matthew when all of this is done.

Dream is still clutching the blue ribbon he found on the pier.

"You know, Matthew has no memory of killing Patience," Val says to him. "What if she threw herself into the ocean before he could get to her?"

Dream blinks, lifting the ribbon up like he forgot he was holding it. "Shit. I guess there's always a chance. If the currents were strong, she could have been carried out anywhere."

"How often do boats come in and out of this town?" Hunter asks.

Dream shrugs. "No clue. Here." He shoves the ribbon out toward Val. "You hold onto this for now."

Val accepts the ribbon from him, knowing this represents some kind of bond between Dream and one of his family members, quietly panicking at how best to make sure it stays safe without mindlessly shoving it into his pocket. He settles for tying it around his own throat, the slight press of the fabric serving as a reminder that he is here for Dream first and foremost.

"Be honest with me," Dream starts, casting a hard look in Hunter's direction. "How many of your rules have you broken by being out here with us?"

Hunter has their gaze fixed on the forest in front of them. "If I went home now, they wouldn't allow me to hunt again."

"You good with that?" Dream asks.

"Not really," Hunter answers, voice swinging low with resignation.

"I could use your help," Dream says. "You probably figured out by now that I'm heading for Innovation."

"I have. It's a terrible idea."

Dream laughs, and Val is glad to see that he's less disquieted by Hunter's presence than he was before. "Yeah, well. Didn't say I was smart."

"You could definitely use my help then," Hunter says.

Dream nods. "Consider yourself hired. Do you need to take care of anything before we leave the Dueling Cities?"

"I need to signal for another Eye to take my territory," Hunter says. "Won't be long."

Silence grows around them like moss, and Val itches as it sets in.

"Professor, what was that thing you did to Hunter? Is that something all of your family can do?"

"Oh, uh." Dream looks behind him at Val, and then over to Hunter, mild regret etched into his brow. "It's different for all of us. And it only works on humans. Sorry, Hunter."

Hunter just shakes their head.

"It depends on how we, uh, specialize, I guess."

Val starts to smile. "Professor, we both know what you are. You can be honest."

Dream rakes his hand through his hair. "Right, sorry. Not used to it."

"Take your time," Val chirps.

Dream goes quiet again, probably deciding how best to talk about it with people who aren't his family.

"We were born of humans, ya know?" Dream says, and Val can see Hunter watching him speak out of the corner of their eye.

Dream takes a breath. "The oldest of us, we all came up at the same time. We're not human, but we're made of human things. And we bring those things out in humans when we're around them long enough. Most of us came in pairs—opposites, ya know? Like Lux and Rez. There's meant to be balance. Never too much of one or the other. We're not supposed to be on our own. It's bad for us *and* for humans."

His voice gets quieter as he says that, petering out into silence.

"Is this how you made me have that dream?" Val prompts.

Dream seems to stutter back to reality. "Yeah, like that. The other thing, it doesn't work on you, Val. It's like bringing on the feeling of a dream while you're awake. Euphoria. It's usually harmless, but convenient when you're trying to distract someone."

"So that's what it was," Hunter mutters.

Euphoria. Val stares at the back of Hunter's head, wondering what that must have felt like on such a calm person.

"Anyone ever teach you about the old war?" Dream asks, taking a look at the two of them. "I can guess Hunter already knows."

"The old war? Does that have to do with the deadlands?" Val asks.

"It's the *cause* of the deadlands," Hunter adds.

Val gives a laugh. "Sorry, the orphanage didn't spend a lot of time on my history lessons."

"You seen it?" Dream asks, glancing at Hunter.

"In passing," Hunter says. "The Eyes don't bother watching over places the Pillars avoid."

"Why do you avoid it?" Val asks.

"Can't grow anything out there," Dream says. "The ground is too unstable for building. It's a shit stretch of land with nothing on it, which means my family can't survive out there either. We need humans to live."

Val perks up. "Rez said something like that."

Hunter turns their blank expression toward Dream, adding, "You're leaving out the part of the story where the Pillars saved humanity from destruction hundreds of years ago."

Dream waves his hand at Hunter. "That's old hat. Humans have been doing just fine without us since then."

Hunter's eyes narrow a degree or two, and they turn toward Val to explain, "The last time monsters were in our world, they fed on humans. The Pillars showed up to save us from them. Their fight created the deadlands, but it also bought humans centuries of peace. And now, monsters are back to hunt down the Pillars. Seems like a pretty clear cause and effect to me."

They say that last part like an accusation at Dream.

"You think the pillars are getting punished?" Val asks.

Hunter shrugs. "We watch over the Pillars as a way to thank them for what they did. It's been so long, most humans hardly remember or care about what happened. Our Tongues preserve that history, our Eyes protect the Pillars, and our Hands take care of our own."

"It's not that I don't appreciate what your people do," Dream starts, speaking carefully, his hand raised in a placating gesture. "But there's a flaw in your logic."

Hunter looks at him.

"If the insects are trying to punish us, they wouldn't want to work with us," Dream says. "One of ours defected to their group a long time ago. He might not be the only one they've turned by now. This isn't about divine retribution for the old war. This is just an argument at the fucking dinner table. Just so happens it's been going on for half a century."

Hunter's brows cinch, and they slow their pace as Dream's words sink in. "One of the Pillars defected?"

"Oh yeah," Dream says, not breaking stride in his path toward the Dueling Cities. "Got the busted hip to prove it."

Val nudges Hunter as he passes, forcing them back into motion.

"I . . . didn't know," Hunter says.

"Obviously," Dream grumbles, but he seems to catch himself getting angry and heaves a sigh instead. "Don't blame yourself. He's kind of the black sheep of the family. The people who do know don't talk about it."

"Is this Mare?" Val asks.

"Yes," Dream says. "No more talking. I'm tired."

The three of them drift back into silence and Val swallows against the ribbon tied around his throat.

When Modesty comes back into sight some hours later, Dream doesn't offer options, just tells the two of them that he's going down to get their stuff and he'll meet them in the woods later.

"But I—" Val starts toward him, but Hunter snags Val's shoulder.

"No bugs down there anyway. Let him have a minute. He's been stuck with you for days."

Flagging, Val pouts as Dream ambles off toward the entrance to Indulgence.

"Come on." Hunter just turns back to the woods, walking at twice the speed without Dream setting the pace. "If we separate now, he'll only get angrier."

Val slinks after Hunter, knowing they're right, but disliking it all the same. Every piece of information he learns about Dream feels less like closeness and more like rust.

Hunter's things are well hidden in the hollow of a tree deep in the woods. Val gets an eerie feeling as he follows their massive frame deeper and deeper into solitude, but it isn't the same fear as getting threatened. This feeling is jumpier than that, and it drives Val to run his thumb along his new scar.

Of course there's little fanfare when Hunter gets their things, strapping two pouches to their hip and securing a pack across their back. They dump out a small bottle of liquid that immediately fills the air with a sharp scent that forces Val to take several steps back. Wrapping a length of black fabric around the trunk of the tree, Hunter lets out a long breath, their shoulders sloping, and Val suddenly feels like he's intruding on something private.

"Are you okay?" Val asks.

Hunter turns away from the band of fabric, walking back toward Modesty. "I should be lucky that I'm not actually dead."

Val blinks, taking one more look at the tree. "Is that the equivalent of you telling someone you've died?"

Hunter shrugs. "Leaving the black band can mean a lot of things, but mostly it means the territory has been abandoned. And it means that no one will expect me to come home."

"I'm . . . sorry?" Val offers.

"Don't be," Hunter says back. "Serving a Pillar directly is a rare opportunity."

"Why do your people have so many rules?" Val asks. "Honestly, it's worse than the orphanage."

Val laughs awkwardly, but Hunter doesn't give him a glimmer of any reaction.

"We have to have rules," they say. "Or else there won't be order. Every organ in your body operates to a specific function. Why shouldn't we?"

"But why aren't you allowed to approach the pillars or work with them?" Val asks.

"Because we're human," Hunter says. "If I stay with him, I'll be changed by what he does. I won't be an Eye anymore. I'll be . . . Hunter."

Val doesn't quite understand the tangled expression on their face, so he looks away. "Was Dream right? That if you went back to your home, they'd punish you?"

"It's not punishment," Hunter says. "I've been given knowledge of the Pillars that none of the others have. It's not that I can't go back, but if I did, I would have to accept that I'm more valuable to them as an archivist than I am a fighter."

"Has that happened before?" Val asks.

"The Tongues are a mix of storytellers and Eyes that have seen too much," Hunter says. "When Eyes become too curious, get too close, or slip up, they give up their own sight and join the Tongues instead."

"You mean you blind yourselves?" Val asks, disbelief cracking his voice.

Hunter just shrugs. "The first Tongues gave up their sight in the old war. It's a sign of respect and commitment to make the same trade."

As they reach the edge of the treeline, Hunter comes to a stop and drops to their knees. "Give me a minute. Keep an eye out for the Pillar."

"You know his name is Dream, right?" Val asks.

Hunter weaves their fingers back over their eyes instead of responding, falling silent as the evening creeps ever closer. Val leans up against the nearest tree trunk, letting his own eyes slide shut so he can sense a little clearer. Hunter's presence is nothing but a whisper a few feet away, and Val realizes with a jolt why it's so hard for him to keep track of them. Hunter has no scent whatsoever. It's bizarre, like a void of a person knelt beside him. It must be part of what the Eyes do to keep themselves hidden. It makes Val feel like he's watching an actor from a black and white movie instead of a real person. Maybe that, too, will change the longer they travel together.

"Who do you think Mare is?" Val asks, breaking the silence. "The person that Dream is looking for?

"Are you ser . . ." Hunter doesn't finish the question, but pulls their hands off their face to look at Val. They rise back to their feet when they see that Val clearly means it. "The Pillars who live here in the Dueling Cities, Indulgence and Restraint, they're a set. Most of them are. Scales that balance each other out. The Pillar of Dreams is searching for the other half of his scale. It can only be one person."

Val's lips part with the realization. "Are you saying there's a pillar of Nightmares?"

Hunter folds their arms. "Everything that makes us human. Not just the good things. Dream and Nightmare are two of the oldest

Pillars. The fact that they've been separated for as long as they have is bad, but if Dream has decided it's time to track his brother down, this is more important than anything either of us could be doing."

Val doesn't know how to handle the weight of Hunter's gaze. "Do you think it's had an effect on humans? That they've been apart from each other?"

"Yes," Hunter says. "The Dueling Cities thrive because both their Pillars are intact and in concert. The walled city, Innovation, it's completely untouchable. When humans get too close to that place, they start acting strange. It's like the entire city is buried under a veil of misery. Knowing that Nightmare has been working for the insects for the last couple of decades gives me suspicions about what's causing that wall. Dream might be the only person who can undo it."

Hunter puts their hand on Val's shoulder, an iron tight grip on the meat of his muscle, and Val's pulse thrums in his neck at the sudden closeness.

"Dream thinks you're a valuable companion, so I'll trust his judgment for now. But if I suspect for even a moment that you're thinking of turning on him or getting in the way, I'll bury you alive."

Val's eyes widen, blood roaring in his ears, and it feels as though he has a second heartbeat between his legs as he realizes that, yes, he is afraid of Hunter. Not just afraid, though. If it were only that simple, Val could just run away rather than attempting to bridge the distance between them, like a child reaching for a candle flame that he knows will only burn his skin. It's going to hurt, but what if something else happens?

"I'd never betray the Professor." Val remembers to answer, his voice thinned down to a papery whisper.

"Good," Hunter says.

They start walking toward Modesty just as Val becomes aware of Dream's presence pawing at the edges of his own. All of the lights begin to flick on in the windows of all the houses that line the edges of the humble city, like the eyes of hundreds of nocturnal creatures just about to begin their hunt. Dream comes shuffling steadily toward them, and Val rushes over to take his backpack from Dream's arms.

"Thank you for getting my stuff," Val says.

"Yeah, yeah, let's get going," Dream says. "I'd rather put as much distance between us and the twins as possible. If any other bugs are lurking, we should let them target us first while Hunter's people figure out a replacement."

"Yes, sir." Val nods, falling into step beside him.

"I'll scout ahead, if that's alright," Hunter says.

Dream nods at them, and Hunter almost immediately vanishes. As soon as they're out of sight, Val leans closer to Dream.

"Hunter has no scent."

"Yeah, I noticed that," Dream says. "It'll work in our favor, in case someone sneaks up on us."

"Do you expect them to?" Val asks.

"No idea," Dream says. "But the closer we get to Innovation, the less I know about the land. It's been too long since I've been out there. I'll take whatever edge we can get."

"Hunter says the Eyes gave up some part of being human. Do you think this is what he meant?"

Dream shrugs. "No clue, kid, it's not *my* cult."

Val keeps himself from asking more, knowing he really just wants to ask Hunter, but he isn't sure how to do that. He would ask Dream about his brother, but that also feels out of his depth. It wouldn't do well to upset Dream any further with questions he hasn't earned.

"How hostile is it?" Val asks instead. "Between here and Innovation?"

"Well, if my memory isn't completely outdated, we can take the long way around the deadlands and make a few stops along the way in some small towns. That way none of us will go hungry."

He tells Val about a couple of the towns he remembers from his teaching days. Good Fortune will be their first stop, a village that

Dream describes as strange, but kind. Beyond that lies Design, a city of artisans and metal work, and further out lies Inspiration, the city where the Southern University is, and where Dream plans to rejoin with the old road that leads to Innovation. There are smaller settlements scattered around, but the major towns will allow them to stay better prepared.

"Rez brought up someone named Vann? Is that another of your siblings?" Val asks.

Dream gives a gruff laugh. "Yeah. Vanity. He won't want to help with this."

Val stops to get his hand-held lamp out again as the darkness grows thicker. "Why not? Aren't you trying to help a family member?"

"Vanity isn't much of a fighter, and he never got on with Mare anyway," Dream says. "It's too risky a job to bring someone on as dead weight."

Val flicks the little light on, holding it between Dream and himself. "Do you have any siblings who *could* help?"

Dream scratches at his chin. "Sig could be useful, but no one's seen them in ages. They helped build Innovation *and* Good Fortune. They probably still have the maps memorized. Ry, now she'd be an ace up my sleeve, but I have a feeling she's been avoiding everyone on purpose. Rae too. The problem is that a lot of us aren't exactly good at reigning ourselves in."

"These names," Val starts, playing with the little globe of light. "They refer to the human thing you were born from, right?"

"Yeah," Dream says. "Some of them changed their names out of convenience, or to hide among humans. Some of them don't want to be associated with the thing they feed on. Can't really blame them."

"Can you tell me who they really are?" Val asks, looking at Dream's face, half in shadow.

Dream weighs this in his head for a minute before deciding. "You're helping us. May as well. You can probably guess with me. I feed on dreams. Good dreams, specifically. When people are around me, they tend to have nice ones, and I can skim from those, but if I take too much, they'll have nightmares instead. That's why I don't stay in the same place for too long. Patience was going by Etienne, but you can figure that out for yourself. Her sister, Impulse, she's a bit of a wanderer. Rez changed his name from Restraint a long time ago, and Lux switched over from Indulgence around the same time. Didn't want him having all the fun."

Val smiles while Dream talks, picking up the subtlest difference in his tone of voice. It's gruff, but in a way that feels like it's been smoothed down by affection and familiarity.

"Vann shortened from Vanity pretty quickly, but that might have been from some of us teasing him. Hes obviously doesn't like going by Hesitance, and Ry doesn't love being called Fury. Mare was one of the first to switch his name so humans wouldn't get uncomfortable. It was us who wound up shortening Remembrance to Remi. Sig changed their name from Foresight just so people would stop bugging them about what was gonna happen in the future."

Dream gives a short laugh. "Sig started carrying around a deck of these handmade cards so they could pretend they got all their insight from some otherworldly presence, and now you can buy recreations of that deck. Humans call 'em sight seals. They place the card down onto their hands, like sealing their fate. Might be done differently now though."

Val frowns at him. "Sight seals aren't real? One of the kids at the orphanage had a deck. He used to read our futures for us. Though he did it with six cards at a time."

Dream glances over at him and back to the woods, hanging onto the edges of his smile. "Maybe they are real. Guess I don't really know."

"Who else?" Val asks. "I like hearing about your family."

Dream lets his breath out, the shadows of the woods deepening around them as nighttime settles in. "A lot of them have died since the old war. Some from humans turning on them. When we're on our own too long, we tend to overstay our welcomes. If humans start to figure out that they've been keeping a parasite under their roof that's giving them night terrors, they can get ugly."

Val opens his mouth, trying to find the least painful way to ask if that's what happened to Mare, but Dream startles back with a curse.

"Fuck, don't sneak up like that," he snarls at Hunter.

"Sorry," Hunter mumbles, emerging from the darkness. "You're edging toward the deadlands. Didn't want you to wander too close."

"Shit, really?" Dream leans on his cane and slaps Val's pack, searching for his cigarettes. "Last time I walked down here, it was clear for at least another day's walk."

"When was the last time you walked this path?" Hunter asks.

Dream lights up, taking a deep breath of smoke. "I don't know . . . twenty? Thirty years ago?"

"It's spreading," Hunter says.

"Well that's shit." Dream takes another puff and gestures to Hunter. "Lead the way then."

Hunter nods, staying just close enough to the edge of the pool of light that Val can see the back of Hunter's neck where their clothes don't quite cover their skin. The rest of the walk is mostly spent in silence, until Hunter shuffles around in their pack and pulls out a handful of something, which they start popping into their mouth.

"Oh, right, you need food regularly," Val says. "What are you eating?"

Hunter just crunches quietly in lieu of a response.

"His damn mouth's full, let him chew," Dream says, slapping his cane against Val's leg.

Val laughs. "Sorry . . ."

"Seeds," Hunter mutters into the dark.

"See, he doesn't mind answering," Val says to Dream, gesturing at Hunter.

Dream sighs. "You're a fuckin' pest."

Val smiles at him.

They walk for what feels like hours, though Val is unable to tell in the shifting darkness. He can smell the air around them changing as they move further and further from the coastline—less salt, more sap. He can also see the trees getting thicker and taller as they head southward. The space between the trunks is wider, which makes the darkness all the more impenetrable.

"Can you see in the dark?" Val asks, looking at Hunter's broad back.

"Yes."

"That's very impressive."

"Mm."

Val makes a noise as Dream snaps him with the cane again. "Hush up. You trying to make us targets?"

"Oh!"

Val shuts his mouth, face burning hot. He never used to mind silence, so he's not sure why he feels more compelled than ever to break it, but he forces himself quiet until Hunter determines a suitable place to make camp. Dream is rubbing his hip by the time they settle down, sitting among a tangle of thick roots once again, and Hunter starts stringing up some kind of thin hammock between two trees. Setting their packs down, Val sits on the grass beside Dream and pulls his sleeping bag out.

"No tent?" Dream asks.

Val shrugs. "Too much effort. You'll wake us up if something happens, right?"

Dream takes a swig from his flask. "'Course."

"Why do you . . ." *drink so much?* Val bites back the rest of that question as Dream looks at him with his brow raised.

"What?" Dream asks.

"Why do you want to avoid the deadlands?" Val corrects. "Wouldn't it be faster to cut through it?"

"Faster, yeah, but no people for me to feed off of out there. My wounds will only get worse if I'm away from humans for too long."

"Ah, that makes sense." Val nods, taking his shoes off and setting them on top of his pack before sliding into his sleeping bag. "You can take my dreams if you want."

Dream snorts. "Would if I could, kid. I can't take yours."

Val dreams, not of the time he performed surgery on himself, but of the boy he led to slaughter in the orphanage. He had a perfectly round face that Val would touch sometimes, before he told Val that, usually, that was not something nice boys did without warning. Thus began their lessons on how to be a *nice boy*. Val cut off the last two syllables of his own name in commitment, grateful to be shepherded into a role that made some sense.

His name was Chase. Val can still feel the soft press of his cheek under Val's thumb when he thinks about it hard enough. When Chase smiled, it was a similar feeling to looking at a full moon, so bright against a deep night sky. And when Val tried to play with the apples of his cheeks, he would only smile wider, even while he tried to insist that proper boys didn't do this sort of thing.

It turned out that proper boys did not do hardly anything Val wanted to do, but Chase made concessions for him when Val asked politely.

Val is already awake when the sun comes out. So is Hunter. He can feel them like the very tip of a feather against his fingertips. Dream sits in his chair of roots, eyes closed, his cane resting over his legs, and Hunter is sitting against the opposite tree trunk, like a massive crow watching over a nest. Val quietly puts his sleeping bag away before approaching Hunter while they're tossing what looks like dried mushrooms into their mouth.

"Breakfast?" Val asks.

"Mm."

"Is it getting any easier for you to look at Dream?" Val drops down to a squat in front of Hunter, peering up at them with his hands wrapped around his legs.

Hunter's colorless gaze locks in on Val. "What do you want from me?"

"Well, since you asked." Val inches closer to them. "I was wondering if you could teach me a little more about fighting?"

"Thought he was your teacher." Hunter nods at Dream.

Val smiles. "He doesn't actually teach anymore. Retired. Said so himself."

"Sorry, I'm not looking to start," Hunter says. They pick themself back up and turn toward the woods. "I have to fill my pack. Watch out for him while I'm gone."

They take off without looking back, leaving Val with the inexplicable feeling like he's been slapped again. The morning is uneventful after that. Dream hauls himself up out of his sleep right before Hunter shows back up, presumably with more seeds or plants in his bag. They take a faster walking pace in the daytime, and Val attempts to hold his tongue for longer.

Shockingly, it's Dream who next breaks the silence. "It's going to rain tonight."

Hunter's shoulders slope. "Let me scout ahead and see if there's better options to sleep."

Dream waves them off and casts Val a glance. "Your aim was shit back on the coast."

Val scrubs at his neck. "Yes, well. You haven't exactly been instructing me."

Dream smirks. "All your talk about learning how to fight and kill, and you go and save someone instead. You're the worst student I've ever had."

Val nearly trips over his own feet as he realizes that Dream is teasing him. Dropping his head so he can grin at his shoes, Val jogs up a few steps ahead so Dream can't see his face.

"We can discuss my progress at the end of the term," Val says.

"Yeah, yeah."

———

Hunter manages to find an impressive tree for the three of them to huddle underneath and wait out the rain. Val builds his tent, though Dream still opts to perch on the roots so he isn't sinking into damp grass. Hunter leaves his packs in a dry spot with Dream and slinks off into the rain, saying he wants to wash something and that he'll be back soon.

"How can you sit in such a hard chair?" Val asks Dream as he stabilizes the tent pole.

Dream tuts at Val, closing his jacket tighter around himself. "It's perfectly good for me. You're the one with a delicate tailbone."

Sitting under the cover of the tent, Val keeps the flaps open to wait for Hunter to come back. To his surprise, Hunter reemerges from the woods with most of his clothes hung over his arm. The only remaining pieces of his outfit are his tightly laced boots and a pair of clingy shorts that Val has to pry his eyes off of. Hunter pulls out a cloth from one of his packs and dries himself off in the shade of the tree before he starts strategically hanging his wet clothes from the branches with the help of what looks like fishing line.

There are more scars on his body than Val can count. He stops trying as his gaze shamelessly flicks between all the healed wounds and the cords of muscles and the way his shorts fit him.

When Hunter is finished, Val croaks from within the safety of his tent, "Do you need someplace dry?"

"Sure."

Hunter crawls in beside Val, taking up far more space than Val anticipated as he pops more seeds into his mouth. Not that Val minds the warmth of an extra body, but he's worried he can't stop himself from studying. Hunter's hair is still wet, tied up in another bun, but he has the cloth draped over his shoulder to catch any water dripping down his scalp. Val's mouth opens, trying to come up with something to say that isn't going to be met with annoyance or a stone wall. When it takes him much too long, Hunter holds his cupped hand out to Val without looking, offering a handful of striped seeds.

"Oh . . . thank you," Val says, taking a couple for himself. It's not what he intended, but he eats them all the same, to spare himself further embarrassment. "Have you ever been to Good Fortune?"

"Passed through a while back," Hunter says. "Good tea."

"Will there be another Eye out there?"

Hunter shakes his head. "No Pillars there, so no reason for Eyes. The old Pillar of that town hasn't been seen for a long time."

Val nods, giving an awkward laugh. "Good to know."

Hunter pops the rest of the seeds in his mouth and curls up on his side, facing away from Val. Face heated, Val just lays down and tries not to stare at the mountain range of Hunter's back. There are scars that Val can't even begin to guess what caused them. Then again, the hybrids are built with all sorts of weapons that could never be predicted.

The rain lets up in the middle of the night, but Val hardly notices when he wakes from another nightmare with the feeling of legs filling his mouth. Blind from the darkness and the haze of sleep still clinging to him, Val stumbles back outside, guided only by the scent of smoke to Dream's perch, where he buries his head in Dream's lap.

"Professor, are you awake?"

"Huh?" Dream takes a moment to shake himself out of it, flicking on his lighter in the darkness.

Val kneels on the roots of the tree, a fear he can't explain taking hold of him. He peers up at Dream, breathless from a nightmare about trying to eat someone. It wasn't self-defense. He did it because he was hungry. He can still taste the blood.

"Professor, do you think there's a chance that I'll change? Even without the scalpel in me?"

"What are you talking about?" Dream asks. He fishes out his cigarettes, lighting one up with a frown.

"I keep feeling like there's something in my mouth," Val says. "Like there's something trying to crawl out of me, or-or like I swallowed something wrong."

"This again." Dream shakes his head. "Go get your damn light. I'll look."

Val scrambles to his pack in the tent, fishing out his lamp and taking it back to Dream. The soft, low light washes over Dream's tired face, the cigarette hanging from his mouth, and the knife he has in his hand.

"C'mere," Dream says, waving Val closer. "If there really is something in there, I'll cut it out, alright?"

Val inches up to kneel between Dream's knees, tilting his face up with a pounding heart. He's not sure which thing he wants more—proof that his fears are valid, or proof that it's in his head. What if Dream finds evidence that Val really did eat someone? He'd get left behind for sure. Not just that. Hunter would probably kill him, vindicated at the end.

Dream wedges the light onto a shelf of bark behind him and grabs Val's face. "Open up."

Val lets his lips part, eyes on the serrated edge of the knife as Dream leans closer, squinting into Val's mouth. Gripping his own thighs to keep himself from twitching, Val tries to open his jaw as wide as he can. When Dream brings the knife tip closer, setting it on Val's tongue like a doctor with a depressor, Val tries not to gasp.

It's like a kick to the chest to realize that, even though Dream could hurt him at any second, he *won't*. Val isn't expecting that thought to bowl him over so intensely, but he's trying to not to smile while Dream sticks a knife into his mouth. He's only using it to keep Val's tongue out of the way, but Val still feels adrenaline at the shape of the metal that could so easily cut him.

Even knowing that Val will heal from anything, Dream is careful with him, and Val can hardly stand how good that truth feels. Would Dream still be gentle if Val really did change? Is there a version of Val that could turn him rough, or is it just at Dream's core to be nice? Dream probably wouldn't even be angry if Val turned out to be a real monster. He'd probably be sad, and that is something Val has never considered before.

Is it possible that Dream could grieve for something like Val?

Thinking about Dream's gentle hands is poor timing as Val swallows a mouthful of saliva, his tongue pulsing against the jagged edge of the knife. Dream may have calloused skin, but he might just be soft underneath that.

"Looks pretty normal in there," Dream says. "I don't know, maybe gargle some salt water when we get to town."

He pulls the knife free, but Val's hands move on instinct, clasping around Dream's wrist to keep him close. Dream's brow quirks up, and Val meets his gaze with a panicked gasp.

"What?" Dream asks.

Pure embarrassment surges through Val's legs as he staggers away from him, rising to his feet just to drop into a hasty bow. "Nothing, thank you, sorry!"

He bolts back into the tent with half his body on fire. Crawling into the darkness, he curls in on himself with his senses going haywire. He doesn't want to think about Dream, not with this urgent heat coursing through him, but as he shuts his eyes in the dark, the only things left are Dream and Hunter looming over him.

Turning his back to Hunter, Val tries to keep his breathing quiet as he grips his thighs again. He can still taste the metal of the knife, but now he can also feel the sting of Hunter's hand across his cheek. Despite the rain-cooled air around him, Val is flushed with heat that he wants out of him. Reaching into his pack, Val pulls his jacket free, sticks the sleeve into his mouth to bite, and slips his hands down the front of his pants.

Just a little relief, to let the poison out.

Part II

THE BRIDGE

6

They make it to Good Fortune the next day as the sunlight begins to thin down. The trees, on the other hand, are getting thicker, and *much* taller. They stand like massive knights towering over the earth, and when Dream says, "Finally," it takes Val too long to realize that the town is *above* them. Distant platforms cut through the sky, anchored to the formidable tree trunks all around them. It's high enough that Val can't tell if he's hearing people talking in a crowd, or just the shifting of branches in the wind.

They pay for access to a rickety wooden lift that has Dream visibly uncomfortable to stand on.

"Not a fan of heights?" Val asks.

Dream frowns with his eyes closed, muttering under his breath, "Just because the fall won't kill me doesn't mean I want to tempt fate."

Hunter, too, drops to a crouch in the dead center of the platform, as if that will make it shake less. A metallic rattling follows them all the way up, and Val notices several pipes snaking down the length of the trees, their noise blending into the orchestral sound of forest.

"Does this place have rooms to spare?" Dream asks the lift operator.

"Ah, sure, we got an inn a couple bridges down." The guy jabs his thumb behind him. "Just walk south, you'll see the sign."

As they reach the edge of the walkway connecting to the rest of the town, Val feels a brief tightness in his throat before he takes a deep breath of wood-scented air. Despite how high up they are, the density of the trees' crowns cast shadows over most of the walkways, necessitating several large glow lamps strung up through the branches like constellations. It's cooler as well, and Val takes a second to fish out his jacket before they all start walking.

"This place is beautiful," Val says, peering over the edge of the walkway as they make their way out of the lift station. Neither Dream nor Hunter respond, and Val turns to them with a grin. "Just me then? Wonderful, I'll take the lead."

Dream grumbles and Hunter narrows his eyes.

It takes crossing two breathtakingly long bridges before they find the sign for the inn of Good Fortune. More than one person offers Dream a hand when they see his cane, but he only waves them off. As they approach the open doors to the Hollow Inn, a thick scent of sweet smoke comes wafting out of the lobby. Val has the thought that building into the center of a tree trunk would surely kill it, but he notices that the inside of the tree is no different from the outside, thick bark on both sides.

"Welcome," a young woman calls from behind a squat desk. "Looking for a place to stay?"

"Yes, ma'am," Val chirps, marching up to her. "This place is amazing. How do you preserve the trees to live inside of?"

She rises up from her chair with a smile, tightening the shawl around her shoulders. A bit of blue paint colors her eyelids, matching the two uneven earrings jangling happily as she moves. One of them is long enough to brush against her shoulder. "This town is the result of very careful planning over many, many years. We don't build into the trees, we just encourage them to grow around us."

Val beams at her.

"Looking for separate rooms or are you okay with sharing?" she asks, looking past Val at Dream and Hunter, who both look ready to wilt inside the safety of the lobby.

Val is about to say he doesn't care, but Hunter answers, "Separate for me."

"It'll cost you," she says with a smile.

"Fine." Hunter reaches into his pack and slaps what looks like a pure gold coin onto the counter. "I can pay."

She whistles, scooping his coin off the counter. "Rare to see universal currency these days. One more of these and I can upgrade your room."

Hunter shakes his head. "I don't care about that."

The quality of her smile changes as she smirks up at him. "Privacy?"

Hunter holds her gaze, and Val is quietly astonished at how Hunter's completely expressionless face can somehow look different when he's looking at a curious stranger who *isn't* Val.

The woman is very pretty.

"I'll show you to your rooms. If you want a reading from the best in town, Lady Violet comes in at sundown. That's the quiet hour, so be mindful. I hate having to tell people to keep it down."

She guides them to two adjoining rooms, and Dream hustles inside without a second glance, but while Val waits to follow after him, he can see the girl talking to Hunter.

"My name's Anna, by the way," she says, leaning up against the wall beside his door. "Let me know if you need anything."

Hunter has his hand on the doorknob, but he turns to her after a few seconds to say, "It's Hunter."

Val can see her smile as Dream barks at him to close the door.

"Don't bother with Lady Violet," Dream says as Val puts their things down. "It's just sight seal shit. I don't want to stay here too long anyway. This place makes me jumpy."

"Why?" Val asks, pulling things out to go wash himself.

"We're trapped up here," Dream mutters. "If a hybrid can climb the trees, they have a lot more movement than we do."

"You could just fall to the ground, couldn't you?" Val asks. "You'd heal from that."

Dream throws him a withering glare. "If you push me, you're fired."

"Why don't you let me do the errands this time?" Val asks with a smile.

Dream sheds his jacket and sits on the edge of one of the beds with a grumble, and Val retreats to the bathroom. Washing the woods from his skin is wonderful, but Val's mind keeps wandering back to the look that woman gave Hunter in the hall. She wanted something from him, but now is a bad time for distractions. It makes him itchy to think that Hunter might get pulled away by a pretty girl, especially since he knows Hunter has paid one of Lux's gems in the past. Clearly he's no stranger to this kind of detour, but they need to be focused here.

When Val steps back into the room with fresh clothes that Rez gifted to them, he asks Dream if he needs anything from the town.

"I need flower oil—real strong shit, I don't care what kind, long as it doesn't smell like me. And make sure you two eat," Dream says, thrusting some scratchy paper bills into Val's hands. "Found some old southern currency. Should still spend."

Val heads to the door, but stops to tell Dream, "Don't worry, Professor. If someone comes looking for you, Hunter and I can buy you time while you take the lift back down to the ground. I won't have to push you."

Dream pulls his flask out, but Val can see the edges of his smile. "Thanks."

Val knocks on Hunter's door next, sticking his ear to it to see if he can tell what Hunter is doing, but the door pops open, sending Val stumbling backward into a huge wood carving of a woodpecker decorating the hall.

"Sorry, uh, Dream wants to make sure we eat," Val says, waving the money. "And also needs oil."

Hunter nods, closing the door behind him. "Fine. Let's go."

"You're . . . okay to come along?" Val asks.

Hunter's brows barely twitch. "Yes. There aren't any insects up here. I'll feel them first anyway, since we're higher."

"Oh . . ." Val nods like he knows exactly what Hunter is talking about, and pockets the money. "Alright then."

They take the tight stairway back down into the lobby of the inn, where Val asks Anna with the pretty smile where they can buy flower oil, which puts a funny smile on her face as she looks between Hunter and Val. They reemerge into the steadily darkening forest, following the lamps strung up along the walkways as they coat the town in warm, orange light. Little white moths orbit nearly every one, like planets to a sun.

The shop they've been directed to is one bridge down, anchored to one of the biggest trees that holds Good Fortune off the ground. There's a spiraling walkway that circles the huge trunk, a staggeringly massive thing that's large enough to have several shops attached to it, some houses inside the hollows of it, and some attached to the outside—little protrusions like extra knots in the bark. As they circle down the walkway, Hunter has one hand firmly attached to the ropes lining the path, and for once, Val feels like he is the steadiest one of their group.

They buy a bottle of oil that smells to Val like orange trees in the height of the warmest months, overripe and threatening to rain down onto anyone who walks underneath. He sticks it into his pocket and asks the vendor where they can get cheap food next, which sends them down another bridge and into the next tree. Val watches Hunter quickly and quietly scrape a huge bowl of stew completely clean before Val finishes his own small bowl of seasoned rice and mushrooms.

Val can't think of a single damn thing to talk to Hunter about that won't get met with unimpressed silence. It's only on their way back that he manages to say anything.

"You hate heights too?" he asks, turning to look as Hunter crosses one of the bridges with both hands on the ropes to his right.

"I prefer my feet on the ground," he says.

Val smiles. "Dream too, isn't that funny? Even though he'd be fine."

"Would still hurt," Hunter grumbles.

"Even pillars hate pain," Val says, more to himself than Hunter. "You sleep in a hammock though. Why does this bother you?"

"When I climb a tree, the only thing I have to trust is my own judgment," Hunter says. "Easier when I tie my own rope ..."

"I can understand that," Val says, happier than he probably should be at getting a scrap of information on Hunter.

When they get back to the inn, more of that sweet smoke has filled the air, and Val can see a room he hadn't noticed before tucked underneath the staircase. It's a modest space with more of those soft lamps, but they've been papered with something to change the color of the light into a cool purplish tint. Another person is back there, wrapped in a floor-length shawl not too different from the one the receptionist had on, but this one is decorated with what looks like threads of silver. They turn toward Val, catching him staring blatantly, but they give him a look more curious than annoyed.

Hunter stands beside Val, arms folded. "That must be Lady Violet."

"Must be." Val nods as the person crosses the lobby, their steps soft despite the heavy look of their clothes.

"Are you here for a room or a reading?" they ask, glancing between Val and Hunter.

"We already have rooms, but I would love a reading," Val says. "Not sure if I have enough money though."

Hunter gives a barely-there frown.

"First one is free," the person says, a smile amplified by the crows' feet around their eyes. They look up at Hunter with a spark in their gaze and add, "Even for skeptics."

"Pass," Hunter says.

Val holds out the oil to Hunter. "Can you bring this upstairs?"

Hunter looks like they're full to the brim with quiet judgment, but he takes the paper bag from Val and trudges up the stairs.

"Are you Lady Violet?" Val asks, stepping over to them.

They nod, sweeping an arm out to the cave-like room they emerged from. "Ah, so you already know. Perfect. Right this way, young man. Tell me your name."

"Val," he says, stepping into the room with a smile. The sweet smoke is even stronger, and he can see the dish that it's wafting from, to the left of a small table with two chairs on either side. Lady Violet closes the door to the room on their way in and fixes a heavy curtain in front of it as well, blocking out any external light.

"You're a traveler?" they ask, sweeping around to the other side of the table and pulling out a ring of keys from a chain around their neck.

"Yes," Val answers. "Could you tell from our clothes?"

They chuckle, unlocking a drawer in a cabinet pushed against the wall. "Your friend there, those clothes and the piercings, it's quite particular. Haven't seen someone like that in a long time. Last I heard, they weren't known for making friends. You must be very compelling, or very desperate."

Val laughs as Lady Violet sits down at the table and lays a deck of cards onto a soft cloth. "Maybe both."

They gesture to the empty chair. "May I ask where your destination is?"

Val thinks for a few seconds as he sits, and Dream's voice rattles in his head, warning him not to tell people who or what they are. "I don't think I'm supposed to talk about it."

"Ah, I should have guessed. Is it just you and the Eye, then?"

Val shakes his head. "Our leader isn't good with heights. He's hiding upstairs. I'm pretty sure we only stopped here to sleep in real beds for a night or two."

Lady Violet nods, beginning to shuffle their cards with deft hands.

"Understandable. We don't get a lot of visitors. Most people don't even know we're up here, and those who do tend to have second thoughts about trusting the walkways. But you walk like you were born here."

Val smiles at that. "I guess I don't fear things like falling."

"What kind of things do you fear?" they ask, separating the cards into two stacks.

Val blinks at them, his mind automatically slipping back to the forest around Patience, his hand inside of Matthew's stomach, the fear that there would not be anything to remove after all.

"I want to help people," Val says, carefully picking his words. "But I'm afraid of what will happen if I can't."

They nod, gesturing to the two stacks of cards. "Pick one."

Val gestures to the one on his left without thought. "I've never had a real reading before. How does it work?"

They set the right pile aside and pick up the left one again. "Sight seals are often written off as a way to fool people into thinking you can see the future. But no one can see the future, not literally. This entire town is a monument to someone who took the time to read signs, and to plan carefully. My ancestors didn't blindly turn trees into their component materials to build houses. They learned how to live with the trees without damaging them."

Val watches them shuffling cards so quickly and efficiently, it's like they're hardly moving. "My traveling companion said these cards are like sealing your fate."

Lady Violet gives a laugh as smoky as the room they're sitting in. "A misnomer. If you see a sign on a building that says 'keep out,' it becomes very tempting to look inside, doesn't it?"

"I suppose so," Val says, pulse racing.

The Lady stops their shuffling and begins to lay four cards face down on the table in a square. The backs of the cards all look the same, a black background with an eye drawn in white lines.

"These cards serve two purposes," Lady Violet says, placing a final card in the center of the square and setting the deck aside. "They give you permission to ask questions, but they also teach caution. The point of sight seals are not to satisfy endless curiosity, or to encourage you to pick at scabs. They're meant to bring your own sight into focus."

Lady Violet points to each of the five cards on the table, naming each one as they go. The four cards on the outside they label as *present*, *future*, *relationships*, and *work*, ignoring the card in the middle.

"You can only pick two cards on the border. The others will remain sealed," they tell him.

Frowning, Val stares at the square of cards, worming his hands underneath his thighs as he thinks about which things he wants to know more about. He didn't expect a test like this.

"I feel like I'm going to get a bad grade," he mumbles.

Lady Violet smiles. "No such thing."

Breath held, Val points at the two cards for *future*, and *work*. Lady Violet places two stones on top of the *present* and *relationships* cards, as if the eyes are now closed, and they smile at Val.

"Work, hm? You look a little young for money troubles."

Val feels like there's a vine wrapped around his heart. "The whole reason I'm traveling is for work. If I hadn't been hired for this job, I don't know where I'd be."

"You feel indebted to your employer?" they ask.

"More like grateful," Val mumbles.

Lady Violet flips over the card, revealing a stark white background with thick black lines painted into the shape of two snakes wound tightly around each other. One bares its fangs to the left, and the other tastes the air to the right.

"The Twins," Lady Violet says. "Or the Lovers, depending on who you ask. Two halves of the same whole. It could mean you're facing a big decision, or that you're torn between two things. The core of this card is that it's meant to remind you that everything has two sides. A snake with its fangs out looks frightening, but it's probably just scared. The snake that's tasting the air looks peaceful, but it's likely on the hunt."

Val stares at the snakes, wondering how long it's been since Dream last saw his brother.

With a small smile, Lady Violet puts a finger onto the back of the card for the future. "Curious where the road is taking you?"

"Might be nice to know that we'll find what we're looking for," Val says.

As Lady Violet flips it over, Val sees a bunch of scratchy lines detailing a wooden bridge suspended in the air, much like the ones strung through all of Good Fortune, though the card does not depict what is getting crossed or joined.

"The Bridge can be a good thing," Lady Violet tells him. "I can't tell you if you're the one who will be crossing one or building one, but be mindful of what's hiding on either side. Bridges are dangerous to get stuck on."

"We're in a town *made* of bridges," Val says.

Laughing, Lady Violet adjusts the thick braid of hair hanging over their shoulder. "It's usually a symbolic bridge. You know, a bridge between two arguing people, like reconciliation, or bringing together two different schools of thought. But, just because I know the bridges in this town, I still make a point not to linger when crossing them. Mercy is only mercy if you commit to it swiftly. Dragging it out risks everyone."

Val starts to chew on his lip. "All of this feels so ominous."

"That just tells me that you have a lot of thinking to do," they say back with a smirk. "Questions you ignore have a tendency to grow teeth."

Feeling a stripe of heat ignite down Val's back, he tries to push past the obvious point the Lady is making. "What's the last card?"

They touch it with two fingers, meeting Val's gaze. "This is for the question you *don't* want to ask. Whatever keeps you up at night, the thing you don't want to acknowledge, but pesters you anyway. Don't say it out loud, just ask it in your own head."

Val doesn't have to think long. It's in his mind before the Lady has even finished speaking.

What am I?

When they turn over the card, Val's eyes widen at the sight of a familiar hand. The lines are so thin, if it wasn't something Val had seen so many times already, it might have taken his eyes a minute to parse it. But this he recognizes immediately as the hand in the sky, just starting to curl inward, half blocked by clouds, colorless white, and so far away that his mind simply refuses to try and gauge it.

Lady Violet gives a small smile. "The Unknown."

Val's frown visibly deepens, and the Lady picks the card up off the table, pointing at Val with it. "Chin up. It's not a bad thing. None of these cards are good or bad, that's the whole point."

Val leans toward the card, afraid to touch it as he studies the thin lines.

"The point of the image is supposed to be that we can't know if the hand is opening or closing, reaching forward or pulling back, but whatever it is your mind jumps to first is surely an indication of whatever answer you're in search of. The Unknown works in concert with your other cards as well. On its own, it feels empty, but with the Twins? And the Bridge? It might begin to take shape."

"Who . . . drew this?" Val asks.

"These designs are older than me," they say back. "My grandparent of too-many-greats-to-remember designed all of them, along with this town. We've just been interpreting them since then. Remember what the Twins say."

They tap the card of two snakes and Val nods. *Working in concert, like the pillars.*

Lady Violet leans back in their chair a little, swiftly relaxing from a hauntingly knowledgeable reader to a conspiratorial friend in a few inches. "I like to think of the Unknown as an invitation. Maybe you've been waiting for someone else to answer your questions for you, but this may be a sign that you'll never be satisfied with someone else's words. Including mine."

Val lets out his breath, starting to smile once again. "Maybe so."

"Relax," they say. "Might be time to start trusting your own gut instead of waiting for permission from others."

Val nods, wondering how literal that is. "Thank you for this. I wish I could repay you."

"Stop here on your way back home from your trip," they say. "Spend more money at my inn."

They wink and Val laughs.

As Lady Violet rises from the table, it's as if they've put on a scarf of smoke. It uncurls around them as they move to open the door, and Val blinks at the light of the lobby in a haze.

"Take a walk," they say to him. "Clear your head. Helps to let your thoughts settle after a reading."

"Yes, s—" Val stops himself from calling them *sir*, as he would Dream, and gives a shortened bow instead. "Thank you for your time."

He steps out from a curtain of smoke and heads back outside. If Hunter is with Dream, he has nothing to fear, so Val goes for a walk along the bridges that only he can seem to cross without fear of falling. He walks far enough from the inn that he finds himself approaching a tree that looks to be purely residential, judging from the kids playing on it. The trunk itself splits in two, growing in a V, and at the center of the fork there's a series of ropes that children are hanging from, shouting in delight. The platform beneath it is huge, like the brim of a hat, and another walkway spirals beneath it, leading to small homes aglow with lamplight.

Despite how far this strange town stretches, most of it is made of bridges. There aren't that many people who live here, and Val wonders if it's a good thing or a bad thing—to be raised in a community small enough that everyone knows your name, but big enough that travelers like him still come and go.

Val doesn't finish crossing, but turns around and heads back to the inn without disturbing the children at play. The entire forest is black and orange by the time he gets back, nothing but darkness and lamplight. He can't see the night sky, but the thick canopy of branches tangled above him is black all the same. When Val gets to their room, Dream is back in that meditative stillness, and Val imagines what dreams he's skimming from this town.

Does Dream have any dreams of his own? Or are they all from the humans he passes by?

Val tries to sleep, but he finds himself staring at the ceiling and imagining that hand in the sky reaching down through the woods and crushing Val in this bed. Maybe it's been trying to do that this whole time, but it's so far away, it'll take decades to get to him.

A creak from outside startles Val, and even though he's sure it's just the massive forest shifting around them, his first thought is that Hunter is doing something. He could have brought the pretty lady back to his room. Maybe that's why he insisted on having his own. Sitting up in bed, Val tries to sense him through the walls. Dream's vibrations are quick and quiet beside him as he feeds, and a little further past that, there is the unnerving stillness of Hunter alone in his room. Val is relieved for a minute, until he thinks that maybe Hunter is restraining himself on their behalf.

He is human, after all. If touching people is part of what keeps him going, Val shouldn't judge him for that. But if he's denying himself necessary rituals just for Dream's sake, that isn't right either. Val feels certain of it. If they're going to help keep each other safe, that should extend to every part of them. Shouldn't it?

Hunter's body terrifies Val, for more reasons than one. Just as Dream once felt horribly fragile to him, Hunter is so immovable, so set in his ways and his shape, it feels like it will break Val if he gets too close. More than that, it makes Val want to stare, and that itself scares him. Val hasn't wanted to do that since he knew Chase, and it was different back then. Touching Chase felt like touching happiness, or sunlight. Hunter is a boulder, but he's also the most easily killed of all three of them. So very human.

That's what Val is thinking as he lets his eyes adjust to the dark in Hunter's room at the Hollow Inn. Even though Val knows how very capable Hunter is of hurting him, Val can't stop himself from getting closer. Even knives can grow dull without care, and Dream needs this one to be sharp.

"What are you doing here?" Hunter's voice is even huskier in the middle of the night.

Val shrugs. "I wanted to talk to you."

"Why are you sitting on me?"

"So you can't tell me to leave."

"Why, and answer this carefully, Val, *why* are you naked?"

From his perch on Hunter's stomach, Val puts his hand on Hunter's chest to feel his heartbeat. He's surprised that Hunter's pulse hasn't changed at all, but that's probably part of his training too.

"I figured if you didn't throw me out right away, you'd be okay with it," Val says.

"I thought you were being quiet so someone *else* wouldn't hear you," Hunter says. "For someone the size of my pinky, you have the footsteps of a fucking bear."

Val laughs, and Hunter's hand slaps down on the nightstand, flicking on the small bedside lamp. Squinting, Val shies away from the sting of the sudden brightness.

"How'd you think this was going to end?" Hunter asks from underneath him, eyes on the ceiling.

"I saw you looking at the pretty receptionist, so I figured I'd help," Val tells him, aware of how small he looks with no clothes on, but everyone looks small next to Hunter.

Hunter's eyes are sunken, the ever-present, sleepless bruising around them even harsher in the dim lamplight. He doesn't look pleased, but when does he ever? He's also shirtless, which is much more interesting to Val in that moment. How much time must it have taken to build up this kind of muscle? How badly did it hurt to get the metal put in his nipples? The more Val thinks about Hunter, the more questions begin to flood his mind.

"I know you hired a gem while you were staying near Indulgence," Val adds with a smile. "So, what's the problem?"

Hunter's barely opened eyes turn from bleary tiredness to anger with the subtlest change in his lids.

"You think there's no difference between you and the gems." Hunter doesn't ask, just says it, and pinpricks of regret begin to shoot down Val's spine.

"I wanted to help you," Val says quietly.

"No." Hunter barely opens his mouth to speak, firmly meeting Val's gaze. "I'm not gonna sleep with you."

Val's brows pinch together. "Why not? If you need it."

Hunter starts to shake his head just slightly. "You don't get it."

"What?"

"*Any of it.*" Hunter says the words slowly and deliberately. "Who gave you your name?"

Val's head tilts. "I picked my own name."

"Who raised you?"

"No one, not really."

"Who taught you?"

"Nobody's taught me anything," Val hears his own voice rising in defensiveness, when Hunter pushes himself up, displacing Val from his perch.

"This is why," Hunter says as Val finds himself wedged between Hunter's legs, the sheets going taut between the weight of their bodies. Val braces on his hands, legs askew around Hunter's waist, but his heart is pounding too fast to do anything but sit there as Hunter looms over him.

"You have no allegiance to anyone," Hunter says. "Nobody made you into who you are. You don't owe anyone for your title or your skills or your body or your purpose. You just *are*. Someone like you doesn't understand the weight of things. And it's not my job to teach you."

Val stares up at him, wide-eyed and searing hot with embarrassment that he can't isolate. Hunter's long black hair hangs over his shoulders, and Val realizes he's never seen it down before, but he can't even think about what that means.

"That's not true," Val whispers.

Hunter narrows his eyes.

"I owe Dream," Val says. "He gave me a purpose."

Hunter exhales through his nose, a hiss of steam.

"Someone else too." Val's mouth is open but the words feel clumsy and slippery in his throat. "A boy I grew up with."

Hunter glances away, his breath turning to a sigh. "C'mon, back off."

Val scrambles away to sit cross-legged at the end of the bed, feeling like a single flimsy match compared to Hunter. Kicking the sheets off himself, Hunter rubs at his eyes.

"You trying to get me to owe you or what?" Hunter asks.

Val's mouth pops open. "What? No! I just figured this was part of what you do. And that it would be easier for all of us if you didn't need to approach strangers. Dream's always saying we can't tell people who we are."

"Fuck, you really think you're helping, huh?" Hunter doesn't smoke, but his voice isn't all that different from the sound of Dream exhaling from a cigarette. Val half expects to smell tobacco in the air. "I pay people for a reason. I don't fuck people I work with."

"Is it . . . part of your training or something?" Val asks.

Hunter reaches over to the bedside table again, plucking a hair tie between his fingers. As he pushes both his hands into his own hair to gather it up into a ponytail, Val can't help noticing the bars in his nipples catching the light as he moves. Val's cheeks burn as he forces his gaze onto the sheets instead.

"Those of us who train to become Eyes prioritize our work above all else. That includes our bodies. I'm working right now, so I'm focused on Dream. I'm not looking to fuck anyone, let alone someone else who should *also* be prioritizing the job."

Val feels more pins and needles of regret sweeping down his neck and back. "I thought I was, but I guess I'm not."

"If I'm, uh, too much of a distraction for you—" Hunter starts, brows furrowed, but Val picks his head up and waves his hands.

"No, no, please, you need to be here. You're better at this than I am," Val says. "I'm just here to take bullets for Dream, you actually know what you're doing. You two would probably be fine without me."

Hunter doesn't react to that, resting his arms on his knees bent up in front of him. "What were you really hoping for when you came in here?"

Val shrugs. "I really thought you'd take the chance if I was willing. Most men are easier to read than you are."

Hunter gives a short scoff that might be a laugh, but Val isn't about to ask.

"Are you a man?" Val blurts out, leaning forward.

Hunter leans over the side of the bed, scooping one of his packs off the floor. "I'm an Eye. Or, I was, until you two showed up. Now I'm just."

His brows pinch and Val thinks for a panicked second that he actually upset Hunter, but the way his expression quietly vanishes as fast as it came doesn't feel like anger.

"I didn't even have a name before you," he says, digging around for a smaller pouch, which he sets onto the nightstand. "What does it mean to be a man in your world?"

Val's eyes widen, and he rubs at the back of his neck. "I'm not sure I'm the best person to ask that. People have yelled at me for lying about being a boy, but it's the only thing I know how to be. I was taught by someone at the orphanage. I don't think most men need to be taught."

"Maybe they should be." Hunter's gaze is fixed on the set of *whatever* it is he just pulled out. Carefully, he lays out a lighter, some little black pieces of stone, and a needle. There's a small bottle as well, which Val doesn't recognize.

"What does it mean to be a man in *your* world?" Val asks, watching Hunter pick through what Val now realizes are spare pieces of black jewelry.

"Nothing," Hunter says. "We're born however we're born, and as we get older, most people stop using words like 'boy' or 'girl.' All the older people back home don't talk like that. The older you are, the less you're seen as one thing or another. You just are. You do your job or you don't. You have sex or you don't. You have piercings or you don't."

Val smiles. "One of the gems told me the word for it is 'unbound.' Is that what you are too?"

Hunter shrugs. "Don't need a word for it. You came here to help, didn't you?"

Val perks up. "Yes."

"Go wash your hands."

Startling, Val bolts into the washroom to thoroughly scrub his fingers under scalding hot water, adrenaline coursing through him. When he walks back into the dim bedroom, Hunter waves him back over.

"C'mere," he says. "Since I know you're not squeamish."

Hunter rests one foot on the ground, making room for Val to kneel on the bed between his legs. Before Val can even ask if he should get dressed, Hunter passes him the lighter and the needle.

"Burn the end of that," Hunter says, using the bottle to wet a small piece of gauze, which he rubs over the very peak of his left ear. "Not gonna pass out on me, right?"

Laughing more from the excitement than anything else, Val shakes his head. It takes him a couple tries, but he gets the lighter going and sticks the sharp end of the needle into the flame.

"Steady hands," Hunter says. "Like when you cut open Matthew."

Val looks up at him, eyes wide. He's trying not to smile at the compliment buried under the instruction, and nods again. "Yes, sir. Or, sorry, should I not call you that?"

"It's fine," Hunter says, turning his head to the side. Val rises up on his knees to see the top of Hunter's ear while he takes the lighter from Val.

"See the bar at the top there?"

"Yes."

"Do it underneath that one. Here, put this on the other side."

He gives Val an old cork that already has a couple divots in it from other piercings, and Val presses it to the back of Hunter's ear.

"Space it out," Hunter says. "Not too close to the others."

Heart pounding, Val holds the needle and tries to line it up between the metal bar sticking through the very top of Hunter's ear, and the metal hoop beneath it.

"You sure you're okay with me doing this?" Val asks.

Hunter puts his hand on Val's bare waist, his skin hot to the touch. When Val glances at his face, Hunter's eyes are closed, and he almost looks relaxed. His face is wide and strong, definitely a face older than Val's, but not as old as Dream. When he's like this—not apathetic or stoic, but sort of peaceful—Hunter is a lot prettier than Val expected.

"Yes."

Val doesn't need any more permission. The last thing he wants is to shatter this moment by questioning it. Hunter's expression is serene, but his hands are closing around Val tighter and tighter. The pulse in his fingers doesn't match the empty look on his face. He tells Val when to pierce, and Val is once again shocked by how easy it is to cut skin. Even the cartilage of an ear isn't all that tough.

Hunter takes a sharp breath in the moment the needle pierces him, his eyes opening wide for an instant before settling back to their usual half-open set. He gives Val the earring and has him thread it through the cartilage with the hollow needle before putting the back on himself. Hands only mildly shaking, Val kneels on the bed again, admiring their combined efforts in the form of that little black stone.

"Fits right in," Val says, leaning over to see Hunter's other ear. "You're almost out of room."

"Plenty of space on the rest of me," Hunter says.

When Val meets his gaze again, Hunter appears twice as big as he did before. Something imperceptible has changed in his posture, or maybe just the look in his eyes. Val feels like he's been caught in a net as he stares up at a much different Hunter. That peace from before has been replaced by something sharper.

"Could I have one?" Val asks, his voice getting eaten up by his own heartbeat.

"Won't heal right on you," Hunter says. "Your body won't give it room. It'll try to pull it flush with your skin. Wouldn't be an earring, but a permanent decoration."

"Oh." Val gives a short laugh, not sure if that's bad or good.

"If you want jewelry, mine won't do," Hunter says. "Unless all you want is for me to cut you again."

Val swallows, his whole body pulsing. He can tell now what's changed about Hunter. It's not his posture, it's his *presence*. He's finally setting off Val's own awareness, slow and steady footsteps circling around him. It's not quite a threat, like the first time they met. This feels like curiosity, and it's much harder to breathe through.

Val starts nodding, manners and control slipping away as he breaks into a sweat. Hunter leans down to the floor, fishing out one of the many knives from his pile of things half shoved under the bed, and when he sits up again with a short, smooth edged blade in his hand, Val is once again acutely aware that he isn't wearing any clothes.

"Where do you want it?" Hunter asks.

Val has never felt more like a rabbit down the sights of a gun, and yet, he put himself in the cross-hairs. The rush of power and vulnerability makes him dizzy.

"Anywhere," Val says. "I don't care."

Hunter tilts his head, looking Val over with an eye that goes beneath Val's skin. Val isn't just naked, he's *exposed*. The appreciation in Hunter's face isn't at all like the way that woman looked at Hunter earlier. When Hunter puts his hand on Val's chest and guides him down to lay on his back, Val's breath catches. He doesn't know what this sensation of being threatened and unthreatened at the same time is, but it's heady and strong, like booze.

"Stay there," Hunter says.

Val just nods as Hunter picks up Val's leg, gripping his ankle tight to scan his calf. Hunter sets the flat side of the blade against Val's skin, and Val doesn't know why he's so hard but he is. It was never like this with Chase, but Val is pretty sure this is the difference between two kids fumbling around after curfew, and someone like Hunter who knows what he's doing. There's no way Hunter can't tell how excited Val is, but his calm eyes are busy tracking the knife. Goosebumps spring up across both Val's legs as Hunter painlessly drags the knife up Val's skin without cutting.

"Gonna bleed," Hunter mutters, setting Val's foot onto his shoulder so he can grab some of the gauze from his piercing supplies.

Knife in one hand, gauze in the other, Hunter pricks Val's ankle with the tip of the knife. Val's muscles tense for a split second, relaxing again as Hunter catches the droplet of blood with the gauze. He moves the knife up a couple inches, over Val's shin, and does it again. Again, Val jumps, his breath quickening as Hunter wipes the blood off again. He doesn't get all of it, two smears of red leftover on Val's perfectly healed skin, like messy brush strokes.

"Breathe," Hunter says, lifting the knife away.

Val opens his mouth to fill his lungs, feeling like he's got much more room in his chest than he ever did before. On the exhale, his vision seems to clear up. Hunter waits for him, and though his body is motionless, his presence is a rattling bell in Val's senses. He's more alive right now than he has been for the entirety of their travels together, and looking at him is dredging up memories of the moment Val learned that the moon in the sky that he could so easily cover from sight with his hand was actually bigger than anything he'd ever seen.

When Val nods at Hunter to keep going, he buries his fingers in the sheets and braces for the sting. Hunter flicks the knife so quickly, a red line seemingly opens itself up along Val's calf. Val's breath leaves him in a harsh gasp, but he gets it back watching Hunter's face. The next cut happens in the corner of his vision while Val studies Hunter's focused expression. His body still reacts with a jump every time his skin is broken, but it stops feeling like pain and starts feeling more like letting out steam that was trapped inside him.

Hunter moves his hand up to push Val's thigh back, and it's like discovering Val had a whole set of nerves he never knew about. The proximity to the center of his body is enough to send hectic, wanting thoughts crashing through his mind. Val bites his lip through another cut along the meat of his thigh, whining as he realizes Hunter is hardly even touching him skin to skin, but Val's body doesn't seem to know the difference.

What if Hunter's hands are made of gauze and metal? His fingers, sharp enough to cut, his palms soaking up Val's blood. It's almost as if the reason there are no marks left on Val's legs isn't Val's healing, but just the way Hunter handles him. Dipping in and out of a haze, Val realizes how much closer Hunter has gotten to him with Val's knee hooked over his shoulder. When did that happen? Val scans over Hunter's body again, all the wild ringing of his presence seemingly concentrating into a single, piercing note that takes up almost all of Val's awareness. It's a sound like perfectly clear glass begging to be shattered.

Val's gaze skips around, taking in the way his own body looks next to Hunter's—the thinness of his own legs, Hunter's fingers sinking into Val's skin, the way Val twitches without even meaning to. When Val finally lets himself look at Hunter's waist to find the unmistakable shape of his cock pressed against the fabric of his shorts, all of Val's thoughts immediately shift to one singular desire, and it feels like he's about to lose his balance even while he's lying on his back.

The next slice of the knife takes him by surprise, and Val tips his head back as his voice twists in his throat.

"Cover your mouth," Hunter says, voice calm but fuller than Val remembers. "You don't want to wake Dream."

Val immediately clamps both his hands down over his open mouth, waiting for another cut, only to have Hunter lean forward, bending Val's leg with him as he puts his hand on the bed. The knife is practically singing in Val's gaze, pressed against the sheets as Hunter braces himself to look at Val's face.

"Don't think I didn't hear you in the tent before we got here," Hunter says.

Val makes a muffled sound against his own hand, eyes wide as he meets Hunter's gaze.

Hunter gives the smallest shake of his head, tossing the bloodied gauze onto the floor and dropping his hand out of sight between Val's legs. The next time he touches Val, it's with his own calloused skin, dispassionately laying his fingers over top of Val's clit. Val's voice warps against his palm, the slight pressure punching the air from his lungs.

"I'm not the one who needs this," Hunter says, swiping his fingers roughly over the length of Val's cunt, and it riles Val the same as the knife—turning sparks to smoke inside him.

Val squirms in Hunter's shadow, the tips of Hunter's fingers hot enough to burn as he pulls at the folds of skin to find Val's slit. Leaning forward, Hunter puts his mouth on Val's temple to speak low.

"This is what you wanted, isn't it? It was never about helping me. You were touching yourself last night, and now you want someone else to do it."

When Hunter presses his finger tight inside Val's cunt, Val feels certain there must be actual steam pouring out of him.

"Next time, *ask*," Hunter's voice drops to a growl, and Val starts nodding his head over and over.

Sitting up again, Hunter pulls his hand free with no warning, and Val can see light caught in the fluid on his fingers.

"I don't work for you," Hunter says. "Use my bathroom if you don't want to wake Dream, but I'm not finishing you off for a lie."

Val slowly uncovers his mouth as Hunter picks himself up off the bed. He stalks into the bathroom, and Val hears the sink turn on. Trying to step back from the sheer cliff's edge he was just on, Val gets to his legs like a newborn fawn. No, he and Chase never did anything quite like that. Chase never left blood on Val's legs, or a yawning hunger that threatened to swallow Val whole.

Val picks his clothes up off the floor one piece at a time, and Hunter walks back to sit in his bed, staunchly ignoring as Val shuffles to the bathroom. The shower takes much too long to turn hot, and Val has his fingers back inside himself before it's warm enough to step into the basin. It's hardly fair how much bigger Hunter's hands are than Val's. He can't possibly make up for the difference on his own. Sinking down to his knees, Val comes apart under the shower, wishing there would be any trace of this on his body in the morning, but Hunter didn't leave him any scars this time. All Val can do now is moan into his palm while he strums his own clit, wishing these were Hunter's fingers instead.

After washing off the blood and sweat and cum from his skin, Val feels like a different person as he leaves the bathroom with his clothes back on. Hunter is propped up in his bed, long hair hanging over his shoulders again, tending to the knife he used on Val.

"Sorry for waking you up," Val says in a tired mumble.

"Thanks for the earring," Hunter says back. He doesn't look up from the knife as Val lets himself out.

7

Val doesn't go right back to his room, but decides to clear his head in the trees. There's a faint ringing left over in his hips from jerking off in Hunter's tub, but his legs are perfectly healed once again. Val's hungry too, but he can't do anything about that quite yet. He wanders off from the Hollow Inn, finding a low platform that appears to be made for sightseeing. There's a placard with what might be the name of the tree, but it's too dark to see it clearly.

Dangling his feet over the edge, Val twines his arms through the rope railings that are strung up to keep people from falling, and takes deep breaths of clear air. He wasn't expecting anything that just happened, but that *thank you* at the end took him most by surprise. Hunter uses a different type of logic from Val, and even that is exciting to learn.

If Val were to try and list the things Hunter is made of, strength would certainly be at the top. Not just physical strength, but really any kind Val can think of. They have strength that lets them leave the people who raised them, just because they believe that they're doing the right thing by helping Dream. They have the strength to pull away from something that Val knows other people would say yes to without blinking. It's a strength that harrows Val to think about. Complete loyalty, not to a person, not even to themself, but to a concept.

Are concepts stronger than people? Stronger than trees that hold up entire towns? Stronger than the pillars who supposedly keep the gods themselves from crushing humankind?

Even after what felt like a rejection in the moment, there is an undeniable spark of curiosity warming Val's chest as he thinks about what else Hunter could teach him. Humans really are the most interesting things . . .

"Late, late, late, *you're late.*"

Val's back straightens as something disturbs his awareness from underneath his dangling feet. A presence that rings with the mechanical nature of a hybrid, but without the mindless chaos that Matthew gave off when they first found him in the woods. Val quickly pulls his feet up onto the platform, right before a human face peeks out from beneath the ledge where Val is sitting.

"I have so many messages to deliver, and the hatchling deigns to waste my time. Now I must come near these awful humans. How rude."

Val stares at a thin face, barely visible in the dim lighting of the nearest glow lamp. They have no eyes, merely more skin in two smooth curves from their brow to their cheek, but the two huge, curled antennae sticking out of their head twitch about as they speak. They don't smell like sugar. They don't smell like much of anything.

Frowning, Val makes eye contact with the curves in their face and says, "I'm sorry."

"I don't care," the hybrid says. "Your job is not as important as mine."

"What *is* your job, then?" Val asks, his confusion warring with his annoyance.

"To tell the hatchling from Patience that he has a meeting with the Cardinal Major. *Not* to be near noisy humans."

Val's eyes pop open, and he clamps his mouth shut to keep himself from saying something stupid. This hybrid who can't see must think that Val is Matthew. Val must still have traces of the ocean scent clinging to him, or maybe even some of Matthew's blood caked onto his shoes.

"The Cardinal Major?" Val asks slowly.

"Yes," the hybrid says, and something inside of their mouth *clicks*. With a soft sound, they set the tip of a gray insectoid foot around the edge of the wooden platform, little hairs visible in the lamplight. They must have crawled up the tree trunk to reach him. "It is a great honor to speak with him. He will wait for you on the forest floor between here and Southern Truth tomorrow at midnight. He will not wait for more than an hour at most, so do not keep him. He, too, has important work. More important than mine or yours."

Val feels his balance tipping one more time. Playing along with this mistake feels dangerous, but he can't stop himself from asking, "How will I find him in the middle of the woods?"

Another *click* from the hybrid makes Val's shoulders jump. "You will feel him. He is special. Perfect as only a spider can be."

Val can hear their feet softly thudding over the wood as they start to pull away, but Val lurches toward them.

"Wait, what's your name?" Val asks.

The hybrid stops in their tracks, and the hairless skin over their brow wrinkles as they stick their face back into view. "I am the messenger. Do not make me come near humans again."

"Thank you, messenger," Val says. "And, I'm sorry."

Despite the fact that they have neither eyes nor eyebrows, Val has the distinct impression that this creature would be glaring if they could.

"The Cardinal Major will not forgive your lateness like I did," they say before they disappear back beneath the platform.

Val's heart is still pounding uncomfortably fast, but he sits there and waits until he feels the hybrid climb all the way back down to solid ground, focusing on the vibrations traveling up the trunk of the huge tree. Letting his breath out, Val realizes how tightly he was gripping the ropes during that entire exchange. He was ready to throw himself off the edge of the platform to catch the messenger if he felt a single flicker of aggression toward humans.

Picking himself up, Val walks back to the inn on hollow legs. He has no idea if he made the right choice, but at least no one got hurt. Not yet anyway.

As he pushes open the door to his room with Dream, Val can't bring himself to wake Dream *or* Hunter yet. They need their rest. Val may not be able to sleep any more that night, but he can at least give his companions a moment more.

Val curls up in his bed, eyes on Dream's back as he sits there in stasis, his fingers threaded over the handle of his cane, mere inches from the blade that scarred him. Val hopes the people of Good Fortune can give him some good dreams to feed on.

Neither of them have moved an inch by the time sunlight begins to fill the room. Dream doesn't wake up like a regular person would from sleep. Slowly, his head rises up from its slightly slumped position, like a flower responding to the sunlight. His shoulders pick up and his breathing deepens, and finally, he opens his eyes.

"You up, boy?" he asks.

"Yes, sir."

"You feel uneasy," Dream says, still facing the window.

"I am, sir. Something happened while you were asleep."

"Get Hunter. Don't waste your breath telling it twice."

Val slinks over to Hunter's door like a kicked dog as he knocks very lightly on the wood. He fears that the solitude will have made Hunter angrier, but when they answer the door fully dressed with the usual depth of bags under their eyes, Val doesn't notice anything different at all.

"He's awake?" Hunter asks.

"Yes, uh, I suppose we're about to have a meeting . . ."

Hunter's brow twitches, but they follow as Val retreats back into his room with Dream. The other two are silent while Val explains what happened in the night. He tells them everything the messenger said, knowing that he has the details correct because he's been dutifully repeating them in his head all night.

"There was a hybrid in town and you let it go?" Hunter asks from where they lean against the wall.

"They didn't mean any harm to the people here," Val says. "And besides, I had no weapons."

"Don't go wandering around at night unarmed," Hunter snaps, and Val twitches at the acid in their voice. *This* is what they're angry about?

"Sorry, I . . . sorry." Val folds his hands under his thighs, knowing it's pointless to argue. "I figured it was more important to get details on this Cardinal Major."

Hunter looks right at Dream, and Val keeps to himself that this is maybe the first time Hunter has been able to do that without flinching away.

"You know who that is, right?"

Dream rubs his hip, like this talk is aggravating his wound. "I have an idea, yeah. Never seen him myself, of course. I have a feeling if I had, I wouldn't be here now."

"Do I have to ask you to explain?" Val says.

Hunter's gaze flicks back over to Val's. "I mentioned the hybrids who guard Innovation. There's five of them that have titles. The Northern, Southern, Eastern, and Western sentinels are tied to the walls of the city to keep people out. Those four guards answer to the Cardinal Major. He's the one I told you about."

"The one with the knives?" Val asks.

"Yes," Hunter says. "We need to stay far away from him. Meeting up would be suicide."

"Well." Dream just twitches his fingers in Val's direction. "Mostly."

Hunter shakes their head. "A man like that knows how to shape. I wouldn't even trust Val to get away unscathed. My advice is to leave now and put as much distance between us and him before he realizes Dream is here."

Dream takes a deep breath, tips his head back, and says, "*Fuck.*"

"Sorry," Val mutters.

"No, no, you did the right thing," Dream says, scratching at the line gouged into his cheek. "As much as I want to take Hunter's advice, we don't know which direction this asshole's coming from, so it's as much of a risk to leave as it is to wait right now. We could run into him without realizing it if we take off blindly."

"The insects are worse at sensing above them," Hunter says. "But your scent . . ."

Dream reaches over to the bedside table where the bottle of oil they purchased is sitting. He shakes it at Hunter. "Cigarettes, booze, and oil do the trick just fine. That messenger didn't immediately rip me apart in my sleep last night, so we know it works. Powering down should help too. Slows the heart."

"I can do my best to scout ahead and figure out where he's coming from," Hunter says. "If I can catch a lead, we can take you in the other direction and stay ahead of him. But I think you know that it's most likely he's coming from Innovation."

Dream works his jaw, rustling around for his flask which he takes a deep swig from. "God damnit. If he's driving, there's no point in sending you out. He'll be faster than you anyway. We should stay and wait him out. You'll both be able to tell when he leaves and where he's headed."

"They think Matthew is up here in Good Fortune," Val says. "He might come looking if no one meets him. We should move you away from the people here, to keep them safe."

Dream looks like he's trying to swallow something a little too large. "Fucking, fine, I'll go up higher. Hunter, let me borrow your stupid hammock. I just need to be above him, right?"

"That's safest," Hunter says. "Someone in town might have better climbing equipment."

"I bet Lady Violet will help," Val adds. "They said they're a descendant of the person who founded Good Fortune. Isn't that one of your siblings, Professor?"

Dream's brows furrow. "The fuck are they talking about? My family can't breed."

"Oh." Val's shoulders shrug up. "Maybe they were mistaken, but I'm still sure they'd want to help you. Especially if you told them you knew Sig."

"You little rat, you went and got a reading, didn't you?" Dream asks. Val's face burns as he smiles. "Whatever, fine, ask 'em. Just get me up high enough that I can't be sensed. I don't want another Patience on our hands."

"Yes, sir," Val says. "I'll go ask the Lady."

Hunter opens the door. "I'll map out the town better."

As Hunter and Val take the curved steps back into the lobby, Val grabs the back of Hunter's shirt to stop them.

"Dream seems to be forgetting something," Val says quietly.

Hunter turns their head to look over their shoulder at Val.

"If this Major is as adept as you say he is, he'll know there's an insect here. He'll come straight for me."

Hunter's visible eye narrows.

"I can't be anywhere near Dream when he comes here," Val tells them. "You're better at fighting anyway. Will you let me distract our guest, so you can stay and protect Dream?"

Hunter exhales like a bull through their nose. "You know I won't leave Dream. Even if I *know* that you walking off is a god awful idea, I'm not going to risk his life just to keep you from doing something dumb."

Val smiles, despite the whispered vitriol in Hunter's voice. "Just wanted to make sure I understood your priorities."

Hunter jerks their shirt out of Val's grip, mumbling bitterly, "Your priorities are fucked."

Val waits for them to get a few steps ahead before seeking out the Lady. He's pretty sure this means that Hunter is somewhat concerned for him, which is miles better than anger or even apathy. Val carries that concern right underneath the blue ribbon from Patience that Dream gave him to keep safe.

As Val suspected they would be, Lady Violet is very helpful. So much so that Val has to stop and ask them why they're so dutifully providing three strangers with climbing equipment borrowed from one of their nephews who lives nearby.

The Lady smiles at Val. "I know three things, young man. You are honest to a fault. You keep the company of an Eye. And I know I've seen your older companion in my inn roughly twenty years ago, looking exactly the same as he does now. He even signed the guest book with the same fake name."

"You know about him?" Val asks.

"I know about the pillars," Lady Violet says in a whisper. "Don't worry, Val. I'm good with memories *and* secrets. I only want to ask you one question."

Val holds his hands behind his back, nodding.

"Will you be alright?"

Val blinks at them. He was expecting to be asked about the safety of the town, or even of Dream, but his mouth falls open with no answer.

Lady Violet puts their hand on Val's arm. "Take care of yourself, okay?"

"Thank you," Val sputters.

"And make sure to eat," they add, shuffling off toward the front doors of the inn. "I'll get your gear. Anna will bring some food to your room."

Lunch is a little less tense than their morning meeting in Dream's room, but that's probably because Hunter is still out scouting and instead of glaring at Val. Val sits beside Dream on his bed and offers him the first taste of tree nut pasta. Dream glances over at him, and snatches up the fork for exactly one bite before passing it back.

"You're not gonna do anything stupid while I'm roosting, right?" Dream asks.

Val shovels a huge bite into his mouth. "Mm, what do you count as stupid?"

"Talking with your mouth full, for one," Dream says, but Val only smiles wider as he chews. "Don't go trying to square off with this monster, you hear me? If he's out of Hunter's league, he's definitely out of yours. You told me you'd stay with me. Don't break your promise."

"I won't break my promise," Val says. "This job is easily my favorite job I've ever had."

Dream's brows pinch. "Thought you'd never worked."

"Yes, it makes the ranking a lot easier," Val says back.

Dream points his finger at Val. "When the hell did you get funny? That's not allowed."

Trying not to laugh, Val shrugs. "Well, since you won't teach me how to fight, I've been learning a different trade."

"Hm, I don't trust it," Dream says, anchoring his hands over his cane again. "Next thing I know, you won't even be weird. Then what am I gonna do?"

Val smiles at his pasta. "Maybe you could promote me from body-guard to, I don't know, manager?"

"And risk actually getting shit done? No thank you," Dream says back. He keeps his head turned toward Val, still scrutinizing with steel eyes. "I think I've gotten used to you."

Val puts his fork down so he can smile properly. "That's a big compliment."

"No it isn't," Dream says back. "The only people I'm used to are my family, and they're all insane."

"Does that mean . . ." Val's face feels hot. "You see me as part of your family?"

"I don't know what I see," Dream mutters, pushing himself up to his feet. "My eyes aren't so good anymore."

"Professor." Val finds the edge of his jacket, pinching the old leather between his fingers. "Can you tell me something about Mare?"

He looks up at Dream's eyes, not quite as sharp as they were a moment ago—storm gray instead of steel.

"I guess I'm curious about the person we're trying to save," Val adds. "Does he look like you?"

Dream's gaze glances around the room as he makes a soft noise. "Identical. I mean, we used to be anyway. He doesn't have the scars or the rough edges, far as I know." Dream gestures up at his own face. "Last time we saw each other was in, ah. Hm. I guess I don't know what he might look like anymore."

"Do you care about him a lot?" Val asks, pulling a little harder on Dream's coat.

Dream's breath leaves his lungs, not so much an exhale but some-one steadily pushing the air out of him. "He's . . . everything."

Dream presses his fingers together at his side, sliding his thumb along his fingertips, like there should be something there, something in between.

"I'm not *me* without him." Dream whispers, and Val holds his breath. "I haven't been *Dream* in a very long time. And my brother can only have nightmares without me."

Dream's gaze snaps back to Val's, a sheen in his eye that almost distracts from the sudden burst of anger like a flare going off in his mouth. "If I have to gag him and cut his fucking fingers off to drag him back home, I will. He's a stubborn brat but *no* isn't an option anymore." With a start, Dream shuffles toward the bathroom on his cane. "I'm gonna take a bath. Tell me when Hunter's back."

Val lets go of his coat. "Yes, sir. Oh, Dream?"

"What?" Dream asks, standing in the open doorway to the bathroom.

Val smiles. "Would you let me see your wound sometime?"

Dream's entire face spirals into an affronted frown and he shuts the door on Val while muttering, "The fuck kinda question . . ."

They wait until dark and, with Lady Violet's permission, use the window of the highest floor of the inn to get Dream onto the trunk of the tree. Hunter makes the climb first to hide the hammock among the massive branches. Dream grumbles and curses the whole way out the window, and Val waits for Hunter to come back and tell him it's secure.

"Are you going to stay up there with him all night?" Val asks.

Hunter stares back at him from their perch in the open window. "Yes. So if you're going to be an idiot, you may as well go now and keep the insect from even trying to come up here."

"Thank you," Val says.

Hunter doesn't say anything, just casts Val one more withering glare that'd probably strip the paint off the walls if Val weren't in the way. Then they climb back up to the roof of the inn with a scowl. Val only takes a few things with him: the scalpel, Matthew's scissor blade, the ribbon from Patience now tied under the collar of his white dress shirt, and the pistol Dream bought him. Val rides the lift to the forest floor with his thumb pressing into the scar Hunter gave him. He asks the lift operator to point him in the direction of Southern Truth, and then Val waits.

The forest smells like sap and the color green. Val perches on a root and closes his eyes. Lady Violet told him that Southern Truth is a three hour walk from here, so he'll only need half of that to make the trip. They also told Val that Southern Truth isn't a town, but a landmark—a defunct church that no one worships in anymore, but it stands seemingly untouched by decay.

When Val asked if the Lady was really related to the maker of sight seals, they smiled at him and said, *not all families are bound by blood*. Val felt silly for not putting it together. He should know better how true that is.

At the right time, Val starts walking on autopilot, his awareness thrown out as far ahead of him as he can manage. The more he focuses on the space around him, the less he feels his own feet marching over the forest floor. The ground tells him where not to step, and his legs make the adjustment for him. All Val cares about is finding this person and keeping them away from Dream and Hunter. Nothing else matters about this place.

Dream asked him not to break his promise, but Val never swore to stay by Dream's side. He promised to keep Dream from getting hurt. As far as Val is concerned, that's exactly what he's doing out here in the middle of the night. Even if all Val does is lie to this person and get him to go away empty handed, that will be a victory, but Val would be lying if he said that was the only reason he was marching by himself toward Southern Truth.

He's curious. Curious if this Cardinal Major has an object inside him that needs removing. Curious what a person who serves Innovation is like. Curious what the messenger meant when they said he was special, *as only a spider can be*. Who, or what, is it that even Hunter refuses to face?

When Val finally senses another presence stepping into the waters of his awareness, he goes stock still. The being takes shape in Val's head, and chills sweep down his body. *Special* is one way to describe the sensation. *Crushing* is what Val would call it. If Hunter's body feels like a mountain, this one is a gun, cocked and aimed right between Val's eyes.

It's difficult to force himself to keep walking, but a regular hybrid wouldn't hesitate. Val is still trying to play the part, even if his heart feels like it's trying to punch out of his chest. His eyes have adjusted to the dark well enough to tell tree trunks from bodies, and Val has the distinct impression that a thousand tiny insects are watching this meeting from the shadows. He breaks a spider's web as he enters a small clearing, and mutters an apology under his breath.

That is when he sees the Cardinal Major. There's a strand of silk stuck to Val's lips as his eyes focus on the shape of a man in a heavy black coat. Someone with duller eyes might have mistaken him for another tree in the darkness, but Val can see his boots, and a hat affixed to his head. Val takes each new step carefully, suddenly afraid of startling this creature. He is shaped like a man, and that is what scares Val more than anything. He looks like an ordinary human, and all Val can think is *so do I.*

They're about a bedroom's width away from each other when the man turns his head toward Val, but Val can't see his eyes in the dark.

"You failed to report to the scout in the woods east of Patience." The Cardinal Major's voice is like tires on loose gravel. There is force behind every word, enough to make Val flinch, but he's quieter than Val expected.

Val's back straightens as he remembers the hybrid that Hunter mangled, the one they ran into on the way to the Dueling Cities. His voice leaves him, as faint as crushed snow. "Someone got to the scout before I could. I found them, but they were wounded."

As the Cardinal Major moves closer to him, Val realizes why he can't make eye contact. Hunter's voice sounds in his head like a distant wind. *Two knives embedded in his skull.* Val isn't meeting his gaze, but looking at the rounded handles of two silvery knives sticking out from his eyes. He faces Val as if he can see perfectly fine, the crossbars sitting vertically against his brows, and Val wonders if his other senses are that good, or if he can somehow still see in spite of the knives.

"You are not the hatchling from Patience," the man with knives in his eyes says.

Val's breath catches. "I wasn't born in Patience, but—"

A gloved hand snaps around Val's throat, and Val grabs at the man's fingers to no effect, coughing and sputtering as his airways slowly close.

"You have no tool," the Cardinal Major says, and Val braces as though his voice will slice Val's skin for how much effort every word seems to take him.

Val's breathing shortens to little gasps with what feels like a pinprick of air getting to his lungs.

"Did you also kill the hatchling in Patience?"

Val can only shake his head, his mind getting fuzzy the longer he goes with hardly any oxygen.

"Did you take their tool?"

Val moves as quickly as he can to try and get to the palm pistol, but the second his fingers close around it in his pocket, the Cardinal Major takes Val's hand in his, points the gun away from them both, and squeezes the trigger for Val. The bullet pops off with a *crack* and lodges uselessly into a nearby tree.

"So the Pillars have turned one of ours," the Cardinal Major says. "Tell me which one has led you astray, and I will take you home unharmed."

Val gasps when the Major lessens the pressure of his hand. The lump in Val's throat bobs against the stiff material of the glove, and he tries to clear the fog from his head with deep, greedy gulps of air.

"I pulled the scalpel out myself," Val says. "When I was a child. I've been on my own since then."

The Cardinal Major's jaw is smooth and hairless, his teeth white and orderly. Val can't find anything about him that looks like an insect. Aside from the knives, he could be just any man, yet he sets off every impulse Val has to run as far and as fast as he possibly can. This is the creature that scares Dream and Hunter. A creature that looks like Val.

"Why are you here?" the Cardinal Major asks.

"I wanted to see who you were," Val tells him, and suddenly he's telling the truth. "I wanted to know if you were like me. Perfectly human on the outside, but something off on the inside. Are those knives your tools? Or did you pull yours out, like I did?"

The Major's breath turns to steam in the chill of the night air. He clamps his hand back down tight, so tight, too tight around Val's neck.

"You're not a hatchling at all."

Val can't even choke. His vision turns to blotchy darkness, slipping away as the Major crushes Val's throat, quick and decisive. Val dies while slung over the Cardinal Major's shoulders, dangling from him like a wet scarf. He revives some time later in the same position, only now his legs and wrists and eyes are bound.

"Where are you taking me?" Val asks. His stomach hurts where some piece of the Major's coat digs into him. "Are we going to your home?"

"Not yet."

The Cardinal Major walks with Hunter's steadiness, but with Dream's heaviness. He has no need for stealth when he has no reason to fear these woods.

"Do you have a name?" Val asks, pulse racing. "I have a feeling we're about to spend a lot of time together. Might be nice to be on friendlier terms."

"Names are for humans," the Cardinal Major responds. "Or those who wish to pretend. Those like us need only our work."

Val braces his elbows against the Major's back, twitching his legs to figure out if his weapons were taken from him. The pistol is gone, he can already tell that much.

"I could give you a name," Val chirps, and he knows he's talking too much out of nerves, but he can't stop. "Cardinal Major doesn't really roll off the tongue, you know?"

The Cardinal Major doesn't say anything, just jostles Val a little higher on his shoulder.

Val gives a clipped laugh, bending his tied hands up toward his throat. "How about I just call you Knives? Sorry, I'm not very creative."

No response. Val flattens his hands to his freshly healed neck, squirming against the thin rope to try and get his fingers under the collar of his shirt.

"Hey, Knives, do you know someone named Mare?" Val asks, picking at the blue ribbon tied around his throat. "I'm not sure what he looks like, but I think he has gray eyes."

With sweat between his fingers, Val finally pulls Patience's ribbon free, letting it drop to the forest floor.

"Maybe you know his title," Val says, his arms going slack. "The pillar of nightmares?"

"Stop talking or I'll have to kill you again," is the response.

Val bites his lip to keep from babbling, hoping that Patience's ribbon won't be destroyed in the woods. At best, Hunter will be able to find it and return it to Dream. At worst, no one will ever find it, but at least it won't go to the people who wanted Patience dead. If Knives is taking Val back to Innovation, then it's best to leave it behind.

They walk for some time with Val trussed up on the Major's shoulder. His senses feel muted without his feet on the ground, but he can still tell when another hybrid begins to walk toward them. This one is distinctly more insect than human, a train of small legs propelling them forward with alarming speed.

"Sir, is it defective?" they ask.

"Yes," Knives answers. "I need to examine it further."

"But, ah, sir," the many-legged hybrid stutters, their body darting around Knives and Val in manic bursts of movement. "You are due back to Innovation. Surely this can wait until we are all home again."

Knives comes to a complete stop, turning to face the hybrid, and Val feels them shying away from whatever look must be on Knives's face.

"No one is to enter the church until I'm done," Knives says, and the hybrid takes a few steps away from him.

"Yes, sir," they say to the ground.

Knives carries on, and Val hears a wooden door thrown open and then slammed shut behind them as they step inside what must be the church of Southern Truth. It smells like dust, ash, and old wood. Val pictures a wide aisle between rows of stiff benches, or at least that's what the vibrations coming off of Knives's boots make him think of.

Sometimes the orphanage took the kids to a local shrine. It was a humble box of a building without adornment, just a simple place to dwell on one's thoughts during important days or rough nights. The people who ran it welcomed anyone who asked to use it, and Val always wondered what would happen if two people sitting next to each other prayed to different gods. He thought it must be the building itself that listened, not some divine power.

This church eats all the sound inside it.

Knives flips Val over onto a hard wood surface, and Val gasps at the impact nearly knocking the wind out of him. Knives efficiently reties the ropes, binding Val to the table before he removes the blindfold. The first thing Val sees is the glow of firelight reflected in the silver pommels sticking out of Knives's face. The blades look well made, decorative even—symbols of authority more than deadly weapons, but Val doesn't want to find out how sharp they are.

"Can you see me?" Val asks, his voice a hollow whisper.

"Yes," Knives answers.

"How?"

Knives leans further down, and Val feels his skin crawl at the thought of those pommels touching him—like eyestalks made of metal, unmoving and unblinking. Val struggles to keep his breathing under control as the reflection of the fire swirls around in the silver.

He should be afraid. Hunter and Dream, they were afraid for him, so convinced that Val would get destroyed by this creature, but Val is only just beginning to understand that there are different kinds of fear.

"I see everything," Knives says. "I can even see the place where your tool once was."

He untucks Val's shirt from his trousers, only to rip open the buttons with hardly any effort. Val can see his own stomach fluttering with every wild breath he takes while Knives begins to loosen one of the gloves from his hands. Pinching one finger at a time, he snaps the black material off, stuffing it into his own jacket pocket so he can touch Val's belly with his bare skin.

"Right here," he says, the tips of two fingers pressing on Val. His nails are short and neat, skin clean and without scars. His entire hand is so unblemished, it almost looks fake. That's what Val is thinking as Knives pierces Val's stomach with his fingers, like sinking into mud. The pain rips Val's voice out of his throat in a scream that tears into the empty church. The whole table shakes, but Knives holds his fingers still inside Val's guts, turning his head toward Val's.

"How were you able to pull it out?" Knives asks.

Val can't shut his eyes, like the pain stole that function from him. He tries to calm himself down enough to speak, reminding himself that his body will heal from anything, though the filmy windows behind him swim in his vision.

"I just did," Val says. "I had a dream and I dug it out."

"A dream?" Knives prompts with a twist of his fingers, and Val grits his teeth at another swell of pain through his body. He tells himself it's fine, that he's felt this before, that nothing this man does to him will matter, but there is that fear. This fear is a slimy one. Val doesn't fear death, he can't, but more and more, he is becoming convinced that this person is just like him.

"I dr-dreamed about someone operating on me. When I woke up, I knew something was there." Fighting off the desire to pass out, Val tries to keep his eyes on those knives. "What about you? W-when did you realize?"

Val's gasping breaths are the only thing he can hear as Knives pulls his fingers out of the wound on Val's stomach. He regards the blood dripping off his skin for a moment, the pommels pointed right at his own hand, and Val can finally see what looks like a dress uniform under his heavy black coat. It's pristinely kept, shiny silver buttons lined up the front, and neatly tucked black fabric hugging his torso.

"I always knew. But I didn't remove it until after," he says, and Val's mind pulls up the memory of Hunter's hand slick with fluid after he touched Val. Knives puts his bloodied fingers into his mouth, and Val watches him in confused awe as the wound on his stomach seals itself back up.

"After what?" Val asks, his insides settling without the pressure.

Sliding his clean fingers from his lips, he answers, "The knives. I was gifted sight beyond human eyes. It made the removal much easier."

Knives pulls his hat off, politely setting it on the table beside Val's bound legs, showing neatly kept waves of brown hair, shorter on the sides than on the top. Val can see now that the hat matches the rest of the uniform, the silver lined brim and crisp black fabric. Knives takes Val's jaw in his gloved hand, forcing their faces to align, and places his bare fingers around one of Val's eyes, pulling his lids open.

"Would you like to see as I do?" Knives asks.

Val stares at him, the smooth skin of his face, the beautiful weapons buried in his skull. If Val could see like Knives, he'd know exactly where any objects were inside any other hybrid. He could save them that much faster. But he can't possibly know if there are other side effects, or what *else* Knives might do to him if he says yes. Far too many unknowns to justify, but there is an uncomfortable ache in Val's chest.

This thing, this person, he moves so smoothly.

"I have precious little time, spiderling," Knives says. "I cannot take you to Innovation, broken as you are. Either you allow me to fix your eyes, or I will put a new tool inside you, and let the healing resume."

"Is that even possible?" Val asks in a breath.

"Of course it is," Knives says. "But it will be painful."

Val's shaking his head before his mouth can catch up, realizing the answer as the words burble out of him. "I don't want to go back."

Knives pulls his hands from Val's face, pink lip curled in distaste. "You enjoy this half-formed shell? Such an ugly thing." He shakes his head, reaching to tap Val's forehead with his gloved index finger. "Always thinking. Not working. When you have purpose again, you will be at ease."

"I have purpose," Val says, his own anger surprising him as he pulls on the restraints around his hands. "I have a job and, I suspect, one or two more friends than you do."

Knives's brows furrow beneath the silver crossguards, ruining the parallel lines of his face. "What have these friends done for you?"

"They . . . they help me," Val sputters. "What do you mean?"

Knives makes a quiet sound in his throat, head turning toward Val's bare chest and stomach. He places his fingertips back on Val's skin, lightly brushing up from his navel to the hardest part of his breastbone, which Knives taps three times, like a muted drum.

"You have allowed your gears to rust," he says. "I will make you clean again."

Knives loosens his remaining glove with his teeth, tugging it free so he can put it in his pocket with the other. He takes his hat off the table and turns to hang it on the edge of the lectern behind him, the one that may have held scripture at one point. He sheds his coat too, draping it beside the hat.

"What are you going to do?" Val asks, much too quiet in this echoless church.

Knives walks back to him, his pristine uniform on full display, turning his boxy frame under that coat into a lithe whip of a man.

The silver pommels look like the final set of buttons leading up from his tailored jacket, and Val imagines the uniform stitched directly into his skin.

"I have many responsibilities as Cardinal Major," he says, laying both his hands on Val's stomach. "You should have been mine, but you took your blade out too soon."

Producing a small handkerchief, Knives wipes away the blood from Val's wound, reducing it to a light smear of pink. He puts the bloodied cloth into his breast pocket before undoing the silver buttons on his jacket, holding open one edge to reveal several small pieces of metal sewn into the fabric—a collection of small, steel scalpels in varying sizes and slightly different shapes.

Val feels like he's going to choke on his own heart. "Where did you get those?"

Knives selects one slightly longer than the scalpel that Val pulled from his own body, carefully removing the blade from the threads that held it in place.

"These are gifts," Knives says. "Gifts from a higher power. We do not know how they came to be here, but here they are nonetheless. Unfortunately, not every body is a perfect fit for tools like these. I harvest the blades from the ones that cannot be saved."

"What happened to the people you pulled those tools out of?" Val asks.

Knives doesn't answer as he skims his hand back up Val's torso, and Val doesn't know what to do with the soft feeling of this man's skin as he says such horrid things.

"Hey, *Knives*," Val snaps. "Did you kill all those people?"

He turns his head toward Val again, several heartbeats of agonizing silence passing before he asks, "Are you trying to name me, little spider?"

Val glares at him. "I just want your attention."

"You have it," Knives says, his fingers moving along Val's ribs, achingly gentle. "For the rest of your life."

The scalpel slices cleanly through Val's skin, and it is nothing like how Hunter cut him. This pain doesn't slowly bleed into pleasure, but pierces through him, through his skin and his lungs and his control. Knives slides the scalpel blade past Val's ribs, and Val tries to scream again, but there is blood in his throat, drowning the sound.

Knives lays one hand over Val's chest, and the other he uses to cover Val's mouth. Lowering his face, Knives hovers over Val, staring at him with those rounded silver eyes as Val tries and fails to scream once more.

"I'm going to kill you now," he says. "You will feel better when you wake up. Your body will heal with my knife inside of you, and then you will be *my* spider. As it should have been. No more running wild. It's time to come home."

Val dies so quickly, he doesn't even know what caused it. It's almost a relief. The last thing he feels before time stops is Knives's breath on his forehead as he hushes Val to sleep.

Val wakes up with his chest and stomach properly cleaned, and his ripped shirt now completely removed. His arms and legs are still bound, but clearly Knives took advantage of the lost time.

Val feels pressure every time he breathes.

Panic begins to set in as he thinks there is a new blade inside him. Of course, Knives could have put more than one; he could have done any number of things in Val's sleep. Pulling on the restraints, Val starts hyperventilating as he tries and fails to touch his own body to see if it's still his.

"Settle." Knives cautions, rising up from the closest pew. "It's not good to move while you're healing."

"What did you do?" Val asks.

Knives puts his gloves back on as he approaches the table. "You tell me, spiderling. Are you not in tune with your own body?"

Val grits his teeth. "Don't give me riddles. I felt you put that scalpel in me."

"Then there are no questions," Knives says, laying his hand over Val's stomach. "You're already mine."

Val swears he hears the entire church shifting around them, like someone stretching after a long nap. It's hard to read Knives's face with his eyes obscured, but the set of his mouth and the tone of his voice all say *contentment*. He's finally put something back where it belongs, and Val feels a surge of raw emotion, like a second knife buried in his heart.

Does Val belong with them? Just as the pillars are all family, perhaps Val is brother to every hybrid—or are they hatchlings? He does like that word better, but apparently Val is a *spider*, like Knives.

"When you are feeling agreeable, I will untie you," Knives says. "And we can begin the trip home."

Val hates the way his eyes sting at the word *home*. "I can't go with you. I have work to do."

Knives turns his head toward Val's, hand still anchored to Val's naked stomach. "No work is more important than ours."

"I don't want to hurt people," Val pleads. "I'm not very good at it anyway."

"We are made of violence, spiderling. You have been softened by humans, but surely you remember the days before you removed your knife?"

Knives asks it so bluntly, but Val shrinks away from the memories. "I was too young."

"Don't lie." Knives grabs Val's jaw, but Val looks away from that unblinking silver gaze. "It's not something easily forgotten."

"It wasn't me," Val says, closing his eyes. "I'm better now."

"Lies are not growth." Knives's calm voice is much worse than raw anger, and Val braces himself like he's about to get stabbed again. He isn't ready for the gloved hand sliding down his belly and over the front of his trousers. Val's eyes snap open with Knives holding him by the face and the groin, the heel of his palm pressing into Val's clit.

"I know what you are. All spiders are made of the same thing." Knives catches Val's gaze, the pommels showing Val's own shocked face reflected back at him.

"*Fascination*," Knives goes on, sounding out every syllable like the word doesn't fit in his mouth. Val's eye twitches from the pressure of Knives's hand. He doesn't want it to feel good, doesn't want to feel anything at all, but there is no one in the church but the two of them, and Val has never been very good at controlling himself.

"There must have been countless times that you thought about cutting something open just to see how it worked," Knives says, rubbing his palm over Val's body with disquieting precision. Val tries to hold his breath, so as not to make a sound, only to wind up choking on the sparks as Knives presses with his fingers.

"We are all born with the same wretched curiosity," Knives says, fingers pinching Val's jaw tighter. "Someone cannot simply tell you that blood is hot. You have to feel it for yourself."

The ropes binding him to the table bite into Val's wrists as he writhes between shame and excitement. A human wouldn't want this, but god knows he isn't human.

"Only work can calm the mind," Knives tells him. "Give us focus. Steady our hands."

His voice dies out in a hush while Val succumbs to a swell of pleasure at the steady pace of Knives's fingers penning release into Val's body. Val snaps his teeth down in vain, but he can't stop himself from giving a strangled sort of moan. Letting go of Val's jaw, Knives begins to unbutton his jacket again, his gloved hand working quickly to open the black shirt underneath it as well, until his chest is bared over the high waist of his pants. Val's gaze snaps to his skin, confused and scared and unbearably excited.

"Would you like to feel my blood?" Knives asks.

Val's legs jump with gloved fingers searching along the seam of his pants, as if Knives will rip right through the fabric just to get inside Val.

Val nods, over and over and over again. He does. He really does.

Knives withdraws his hands so he can cut the ropes from around Val's wrists with a proper knife. Sliding his arm under Val's back to help him sit up, Knives perches on the edge of the table, a soft wooden groan sounding at the extra weight. Knives uses the blade to draw a line into his own skin, right over where his heart should be. Val's mouth falls open at the sight of perfect red, and before he can even say anything, Knives cradles Val's face to his chest.

His blood tastes like steel, like Val's childhood, like cold hands slowly turning warm. When Knives touches Val again, it is with his bare skin as he wrenches open the front of Val's pants and slides his fingers deep down dark. Val's hands grip Knives's waist, but it's not him at all, it's the boy he once knew from the orphanage. The blood in his mouth belongs to Chase. Val is sucking on a shallow slice along Chase's thin finger while he watches Val with a strange look in his round eyes.

It tastes good, Val had told him, heat in his face.

I'm not sure it's supposed to, Chase had replied in a whisper. *Let's not tell anyone about this.*

Okay!

Even after the cut on Knives's chest heals, Val keeps trying to drink from him, scraping his teeth over tensed muscle as Knives forces him past the line that Hunter refused to cross. Val clings to Knives, his legs still bound to the table, shaking with wet fingers gliding over his clit until Val wants to scream again. When Knives draws that other blade over Val's bare back in a shallow cut, he does scream. It stings like the glare of all the people Val disturbed after he fled the orphanage—the gamble he took every time he asked someone for help as he traveled to Prosperity. Would they be kind? Or would his own curiosity turn their concern to fear? At least if they're afraid, he won't have to bother pretending that he isn't like them.

Knives drops the weapon to press his hand into the cut, holding Val as heat spills out of him from two different wounds.

Val feels like he's been wrung out like a wet rag as he goes limp against Knives's chest. He sees it now, the understanding that happens without being asked, like they can communicate through their skin. The beauty of it cinches his throat closed, grief settling in right beside the clipped joy of finding someone just like him. Because Knives *isn't* like Val. If they were really the same, Knives would let Val walk back to Good Fortune, and Val can already tell that isn't going to happen. So he darts his hand up to try and grab one of the handles sticking out of the Cardinal Major's eyes.

Val doesn't even brush the silver. Knives catches Val's arm, moving so fluidly, picturesque really, as he draws another, heavier knife from behind his waist, the kind of blade that Val has only seen in butcher shops. Val hears the sound of metal sinking into the wooden table with a *thunk* before his mind catches up to the sight of his hand cleanly severed from his arm.

And then the pain hits him. Pain and blood and pain, and pain—

Knives stops Val keening by forcing his jaw shut, the silver pommels back over Val's face.

"Hands are complex. It will take a while to regrow. If you try that again, I will take the other. After that, a leg."

Val can't wrist anything other than the fire in his feel. He place to leave this wants. He Dream to go back to needs, but it hurts too much. He wrong the made choice. Hunter, Hunter, Hunter was right. And it smells like smoke.

It smells like smoke.

With a short grumble, Knives turns toward the door with the dripping blade still in his hand. "Perhaps I will meet your master tonight after all."

He doesn't bother buttoning the shirt, just puts his jacket and hat back into place as the front door bursts open.

"Sir, someone is trying to set fire to the church!"

The person Val couldn't see earlier comes flying down the center aisle between the pews on what looks like a hundred legs.

"Useless," Knives mutters, stalking off toward the door. "Stay with the spiderling."

"Spider?" The human face at the end of the centipede's body quickly clamps down on their own confusion and they move their lengthy body out of Knives's way, draping themself over the church pews so as not to touch him.

Val wants to talk to them, but every time he tries, his wrist pops and sparks in new, horrible ways, stealing any words he might have had. The centipede comes closer to Val, circling the table with their body and leaning up over Val with one set of human hands worrying at their own fingers.

"Ugh, what a mess."

Val is gagging on the pain as he tries to get his voice to work. "N . . . name?"

"What?" The centipede's thick brows knit and they tilt their head. "You're delirious from the pain. Don't talk."

With fingers curled in disgust, they reach for Val's arm, as well as a pack tied around their waist, where their human flesh meets insect. Wrapping Val's severed wrist in gauze feels like a moot point, but at least he isn't ruining his own clothes with so much blood.

"Get up, get up," the centipede says, untying the ropes from Val's feet. "You're supposed to be hearty, aren't you? The Cardinal Major only wastes my time on strong ones."

They try to force Val off the table, and Val's head spins, dizzy from the blood loss and the shock. His body is working twice as hard to rebuild his hand, which doesn't leave a lot of spare energy for ambulating.

"I wanted to know your name," Val finally spits the words up, clutching his arm to his chest as he slumps against the centipede's torso. Only as he leaves a smear of his own blood across white fabric does he realize the centipede is wearing a doctor's lab coat.

"Gods above, you are annoying," the centipede says as they push Val upright. "I am a medical assistant, obviously."

"That's not a name," Val tries to say, but a bright light catches his eye. Through the filmy, stained-glass windows, a fire is creeping closer. The smoke he smelled earlier is only getting thicker, and he realizes it's not just coming from outside, but from underneath his own feet. Tendrils of thick, gray and black fumes worm their way up from the floorboards of the silent church.

"Walk, you useless larvae," the doctor hisses, forcing Val forward.

Val takes two steps before he misses the ground and tries to catch himself with a hand that isn't there, collapsing like a broken doll into one of the pews.

"Must I do everything."

The doctor hoists Val into their arms and speeds them both out of the church on spindly legs. Their curtain of perfectly straight hair turns to ribbons as they run at full speed through a cloud of smoke. As soon as they're outside, Val hears a gunshot crack through the night air, and the doctor flinches. The cool air brings a spot of clarity to his mind as he remembers that he is supposed to go back to Dream and Hunter. His job is long from finished. Shoving his hand into his pocket, Val finds the scissor blade.

"Major!" The doctor shouts into the woods as the heat of the fire begins to grow brighter.

Val pulls the scissor free while the doctor attempts to scan the forest. He doesn't have time to search for this doctor's buried tool, so he just jams the blade into their chest as hard as he can. Ribs are a lot denser than he realized. Another new piece of information to store.

With a yelp, the doctor drops Val to the ground, and Val scrambles to his feet as quickly as he can.

"Horrible thing!" the doctor shouts at him, pressing their own hands to a dark stain blooming over their white coat. When they open their mouth again, saliva visibly wells along their teeth and gums, dripping down their chin as they rise up like a massive cobra about to strike. Val has a vivid memory of the poison from the gunsmith's bite all the way back in Prosperity, and he glances around the woods for something, anything helpful at all.

Another gunshot rings out, and before Val can even try to run, something *else* crashes into the doctor through the trees in a blur of orange and black. The doctor's body writhes around as the force of the impact upturns them into the grass. Val wants to collapse out of relief as he recognizes the pattern of Matthew's shell. It's not just him, though. Val almost missed it in the chaos, and the wild brightness of the fire that is now slowly consuming Southern Truth. There is a person standing at the other end of the doctor's body, holding a hatchet over her head. It's hard to see her when her hair blends in with the color of the inferno behind her, but she looks fully human, save for the wild expression on her face.

The doctor screams when the ax hacks into their thorax. Vaulting over the split apart centipede, the woman with red hair and a blood-spattered shirt calls out, "Alright kids, time to run!"

Matthew bucks off the doctor, scurrying over to Val and scooping him up as best he can. The woman hops onto Matthew's shell, and they start sprinting through the trees.

"Nice to . . . see you again," Matthew pants as his legs propel them into the darkness.

Val latches all four of his limbs around Matthew's torso, not caring at all that he must look like a desperate child as Matthew holds Val against him. He isn't thinking about the woman, but suddenly they're face to face. She gives Val half of a smile, one of her hands gripping the back of Matthew's shirt, the ax in the other.

"Nice to meet you, Val," she says. "Hell of a friend you made back there."

"Did you see Knives?" Val asks, panic reigniting in his throat. "Is he coming after us?"

"The one with the, uh." She points at her own eyes and Val nods. "Don't worry, I sent him on a little chase with some of my blood, right after I messed with his car. The centipede will be out of commission for a while, so we'll have plenty of time to get you far away."

"Who are you?" Val asks.

"Impulse," she says, red hair streaming behind her as Matthew runs harder down a dirt path. "I'm looking for my sister. You seen her?"

Val's head lolls forward onto Matthew's shoulder. "I'm sorry, I haven't. I had her ribbon, but . . ."

"This one?" She points with the hatchet blade toward her own arm, and Val sees the blue fabric tied in a knot around her bicep.

Nodding, Val tries to hold on tight, but he feels his grip faltering. "I think I might pass out."

"We've got you," Matthew says.

"Dream and Hunter . . ." Val's tongue is getting heavier by the second.

"I remember Dream's scent, don't worry," Matthew says. "Just heal."

"No, he's hiding his scent, I don't know where they are." Tears sting Val's eyes as he realizes how big this detour really is. "I can feel him if we're close but . . ."

"Hey." Impulse leans closer, drawing Val's eye. "It's alright. If Dream feels us, he'll come out of hiding. I know a place where you can sleep. So go to bed already. We'll figure this out."

With her permission, Val slips away, like the wind itself is carrying him.

8

It's only a temporary peace. Val wakes up in an unfamiliar bed like he's just had his hand severed all over again. When someone leans over him, he expects Knives and his silver gaze boring into Val.

"Jeez, kid, am I that scary?"

His eyes focus on Impulse, her red hair now tied back with her sister's blue ribbon.

"Sorry." Val feels sweat on his brow, and his entire right arm trembles. "My hand hurts."

"Yeah, looks like you had a rough night," she says. "It's trying to build itself back, but I don't know if it's better or worse to keep it wrapped while it's all raw like that." She looks at his wrist with a smirk. "Gross."

"Miss, I hung that flag like you asked." Matthew's voice carries in through a window and Impulse rises up to her feet, planting her hands on the small of her back to stretch it out.

"I told you, just call me Liz. And thank you, you're a real gentleman."

Matthew sticks his head through a dark window across the room, arms folded on the sill. "Val should probably eat."

"Yeah, figured as much." Liz puts her hands in the back pockets of her pants. "I'm kind of a shit cook, but I'll see what I can do."

"I'm not sure I'll fit in the kitchen," Matthew mutters.

Liz shrugs with a smile. "It's alright, you stay with the kid. The other kid. Damn, you guys are both so young . . ."

She wanders into the next room muttering to herself, and Val tries to sit up, half slouching against the wall. "Where are we?"

Matthew shrugs. "I'm not really sure. She said she knew a safe place somewhere on the coast. All I know is that we're underground. I would never have found this place if she hadn't guided me. There's another one here, like Dream and her. He's, uh, less helpful than Miss Liz, but nice enough. She called him Vann?"

"Vanity," Val mutters, remembering Dream's remark that he'd be of no use to them. "Wonderful."

"Do you need anything?" Matthew asks. "Can . . . I ask what happened to you? Why aren't you with your friends?"

Val gives him a wide-eyed look that he knows must be entirely too panicked to pretend like nothing important happened. This, that, *Knives*, he can't keep that completely under the skin.

"It's, uh," Val swallows, pulling his wrapped wrist against his stomach. Liz must have changed the bandages at least twice, judging from the bin against the wall full of pink and red gauze. "We didn't realize we'd wandered close to someone dangerous, so I went to throw him off of Dream's path. Hunter agreed to get Dream somewhere safer."

"And you?" Matthew asks, his gaze dipping down to Val's hand, or lack thereof.

Val gives him a tight smile. "It was a long night. That man, the Cardinal Major, he's . . ."

Val's open mouth makes no sound. What could he possibly say to convey to Matthew all of the things that Val saw and felt in that church? There aren't any words good enough to untangle the root of emotion growing in Val's throat. Shaking as he is, Val gets to his feet and starts shuffling across the room to Matthew.

"D-don't, it's alright," Matthew tries to say, but Val goes to him anyway, putting his good hand on Matthew's face.

"I might have lied to you when I said that you and I are the same," Val tells him, voice weighed down by exhaustion. "I didn't know it when we met. I'm glad I spared you a meeting with Knives. You've been through enough on your own."

"Val?" Matthew touches his shoulders. "You should lie down, okay?"

Val pulls his hand away, nodding. "Sorry for worrying you. Just wanted to touch a familiar face."

Matthew gives a hushed laugh. "I'm glad I can be a comfort to you, but please get your rest. I think we're safe here."

Val toddles back to bed, his regrowing hand burning like he's got it over an open fire. Sinking into the covers, Val looks at the palm of his other hand, wondering if he'll ever have that kind of understanding again. He'd hoped Matthew would just sort of know, that he'd feel Val's skin and it would simply make sense.

There are things only we can do for each other.

Val grits his teeth at a piercing pain ricocheting up his arm, and he grabs his shoulder, like that'll ease the sinew and bone that are pushing out of him like fresh stems from a seed. There's probably still blood on his mouth from last night. He worries at his molars with the tip of his tongue, wondering if any of Knives's skin is there from Val scraping his teeth over Knives's chest. If Val was still hatching before last night, he's certain he has broken through that shell by now.

It isn't sleep so much as it is hibernation as Val lays there under the covers, shivering and sweating through the waves of discomfort in his right arm. There is a shape of a hand, but it is long from finished, and his gauze is completely scarlet when he hears a shout from somewhere in the house.

"Bring the boy his food, you useless layabout!"

It's Liz, reprimanding someone. Not a minute later, there is a soft knock on the door and the sound of a man clearing his throat.

"Excuse me, I have some dinner for our esteemed guest."

Val pushes himself up to lean against the wall again. "Come in."

A smartly dressed man sweeps into the room with a tray on one hand, bustling in like he wasn't just getting scolded by his sister. He approaches the nightstand by Val's bed, and his lip curls at the sight of bloodied cotton and tweezers before he simply shoves them aside to put the tray down.

"Well, there you have it. The finest crab casserole on the southern coast."

Everything about him is tailored with precision—the fit of his satiny clothes to his lean body, the almost imperceptible thin lines of makeup accentuating a statuesque face, a perfectly imperfect sweep of black curls over his head. It's as if a painting of golden beauty came to life and is now standing over Val with barely concealed disgust.

"Vanity, right?" Val asks.

He laughs through his closed mouth. "Vann is just fine."

Val turns toward the tray, setting his feet on the ground to eat with his left hand. "May I ask you, Vann, where we are?"

Vann gestures with his hand. "Oh, it's just a little family secret, tucked away under the rocks of the coast. Nothing too fancy, but you take what you can get, am I right?"

Val nods at him, not sure at all. "I'm sorry if I'm making you uncomfortable."

"Well." Vann angles his body away from Val with another laugh. "The whole point of this little getaway was to hide from the insects, so you can imagine my surprise when dear old Liz showed with not one, but two. Funny, that."

"I promise we won't hurt you," Val says. "I just want to get back to Dream. I'm working for him. I think I did a bad job of it . . ."

Vann frowns for a split second, then seems to catch it on his own mouth, turning on his heel and dropping to a crouch so he can look up at Val. "Listen, kid, there's two things I know about that old codger. The first is that his bark is much worse than his bite. The second is that no one on this miserable pile of mud is more of a sucker for stray animals than big brother Dream. You'll be fine."

He actually winks at Val as he says it, and Val startles at the sight. "O-oh. Thank you."

"If it were Mare." Vann quirks a perfectly arched brow and shrugs. "Well, he's not here, so we don't have to worry about that."

"Have you met him?" Val asks with wide eyes, leaning forward. "Can you tell me about him?"

Vann shows his empty palms. "What is there to say? He maimed Dream, got a bunch of us killed, and scurried off with his tail between his legs. And Dream *still* wants to bring him home."

Val grabs the sheets beside his leg, staring hard at Vann. "Will you please tell me what happened? Dream won't talk about it."

"Probably because they're family secrets," Liz chimes in, throwing the door open with an armful of fresh gauze.

Val shrinks away from her, dropping his gaze. "Sorry, you're right."

Vann swans out of Liz's way as she kicks a stool over to sit in front of Val. "At least, that's what I'd normally say, but not everyone goes and gets their hand chopped off for the family. So I'd say you've earned at least one story. How many of us have you met by now?"

Liz holds her hand out and Val gives her his wrapped wrist. "Not that many. We stayed with Lux and Rez in the Dueling Cities."

"Oh, it's been a dog's age since I saw them," Vann says, leaning his shoulder against the wall. "I miss Lux. We used to have a hell of a time together when she'd take me out."

"You could go see her whenever you wanted," Liz says, cutting off the matted gauze from Val's hand.

"Oh, please. Me? Trekking through the woods on foot for days on end? *Camping*?" Vann scoffs, gold eyes on the back of Liz's head. "The gin's not *that* good."

"People call you a lush, you know," Liz says with a shake of her head. "You're much too cowardly for that."

Val doesn't know whether to laugh or keep his mouth shut, but Vann just gives a wave of his hand. The air here is so much like staying in Lux's home with Dream, listening to them talk so easily, despite how different they all are.

"You tell him, Liz," Vann says. "You spent more time with Mare than I did."

Liz gets the very tips of a smile on her mouth. "We usually come in pairs, you know?"

Val nods, holding his breath while she looks over his raw, unformed hand for anything that shouldn't be there. He'd been picturing it like plant growth, but the truth is all jagged red rock, or the inside of a volcano.

"Sometimes it's a simple division, like positive and negative. Dream and Nightmare were one of the first sets. But there's not always such clear boundaries."

"I'd argue vanity is a good thing," Vann chimes in, looking at his nails.

"Same with impulse," Liz adds, glancing up at Val with sky blue eyes and a smirk. "The thing about it is that no one else values us like our other halves do. And no one else is more dishonest about us."

Val feels hot and cold at once, remembering the way Dream spoke about Nightmare. So quiet, and so raw. And then Val thinks about Knives, his own fear and curiosity, like parasites in his heart.

"I think I know what you mean," Val says quietly.

Liz smiles, gathering up the clean gauze. "Nightmare could probably do anything, and Dream would still want to bring him home. I'm honestly surprised it took him this long to try again, but I guess things are getting harder out there."

"The damn bugs are getting smarter," Vann says. "Why do you think I've been holed up here? It's not because of this charming cottage, I'll tell you that for free."

"What do you think Austen would say to that?" Liz asks.

"Oh, shoot me, you hag." Vann heaves a sigh. "If Austen were here, well . . . they *wouldn't* be here. Not for this long, anyway."

Liz looks proud of herself, wrapping Val's ring finger. "Sorry, Val, it's been a while since I've seen my adoring little brother. We tend to distract each other."

"You want to know why Mare went off the deep end, it's because he's been alive longer than any of us," Vann says, meeting Val's gaze. "Honestly, I can hardly blame him. Hundreds of years of human nightmares crammed into my head, I doubt I'd have lasted as long as he did without going ballistic."

"Dream said he can only have nightmares on his own," Val tells them. "Does he mean that literally?"

"Yeah," Liz says, fidgeting with the bandages around Val's wrist. "When they're together, it's like they filter the air in each other's heads. But it's also never that clean. Some towns have more good than bad, and you can imagine it's harder for Mare when the bad weighs more than the good, rather than the good weighing more than the bad."

Vann starts laughing. "Though, I will never forget that time in Old Mercy."

"Oh my goodness." Liz's eyes flash. "Don't think I've ever seen Dream so . . . *dreamy.*"

"He was worse than high, he was downright cosmic." Vann touches his chest as he grins at a memory Val can't see. "A good town. Shit booze, but the spirit was there."

"So, if I understand it," Val starts, gently trying to refocus the conversation. "Mare saw so many nightmares from humans over time that he just . . . lost faith in his family?"

Liz finishes with a safety pin in the edge of Val's bandages and gives a sigh. "I don't think he lost faith. I think he just got tired of trying."

"Siding with those insects—no offense, kid—wasn't about exhaustion. None of us know why he did that. Running away I understand, but going to them?" Vann scoffs. "Can't imagine they're any better than humans."

"Dream believes he had a reason." Liz rises up from the stool.

"Yeah, that reason got him shot through the hip," Vann says. "And now he'll never recover from it. Feels like a pretty succinct way to tell someone to fuck off forever."

Liz dumps all the old supplies into the trash bin and scoops the whole thing up. "Let Val eat. Hopefully someone will have seen the flag by now."

Vann pushes off the wall. "You—you put the flag up?"

"Of course I did." Liz breezes out of the room. "He's looking for Dream. No faster way to get him here than to call a family meeting."

"Oh for fuck's sake." Vann groans and follows after her with a sudden slouch to his elegant shoulders. "I hid that stupid flag for a reason . . ."

"*You hid it?*"

Their footsteps thunder down the hall, the bickering of siblings who know each other far too well, and Val tries to eat his breakfast with his head ballooning from all of the conversation. So many things he could never know, and he's right there in the middle of it. Well, maybe not the middle—he is in the shadow cast by the pillars. The one thing they didn't answer that Val feels percolating in the depths of his head is that *why*. Why did Mare go with the hatchlings and the spiders? Val can only think of one reason: he can't feed off of them.

If Innovation is truly run by the hybrids now, there'd be no nightmares for a pillar to see. There'd also be no food.

Val eats all of his breakfast and still feels a hole in his gut. Shuffling out to where he hopes the kitchen is, Val stops short of someone absently braiding and re-braiding their hair in the middle of the hall. Val's senses aren't quite as sharp from the healing, but he feels their presence in a strange way, like the ticking of a clock. They're definitely a pillar, judging by the enormity of their vibrations, Val just doesn't know which one.

"Hello," Val calls softly.

They turn their owlish gaze on Val and nod. "Are you the reason for the family meeting, or is it the centaur beetle I saw fishing for crabs in the tide pools?"

"Uh." Val shrugs. "Probably both. May I ask your name?"

With a worried sound, they shake their braid loose and fold their arms. "No offense, but you owe me a little more than that. How did not one, but two outsiders worm their way into our family hideout?"

"Liz brought us," Val says. "My name is Val, the person you saw outside is Matthew. We're, uh, I suppose we're working for Dream. We got separated and Liz thought this might help get us back together."

They tip their head back, eyes narrowed behind the length of their nose. "I don't like it."

"Which part?" Val ventures.

"All of it," they say. "Dream doesn't take students anymore. Did you lie to him?"

Val frowns, the heat in his regrowing hand traveling to his cheeks. "Dream knows me better than most people."

"Ah, so you're his pet," the pillar says.

Val feels a flare of anger like a sunburst in his chest. "Fine, maybe I am. I don't care what you or he calls me, but I agreed to do a job for him and I plan to get it done."

Their mouth opens, and then quickly shuts when another person saunters up behind them and claps a hand down onto their shoulder. "Providing a warm welcome to our guest, hm?"

Val takes a step back from the person now shadowing both he and the pillar.

With a frown, the spindly pillar juts their chin out, their whole face an arrow of impatience. "We need to be discerning of insects in our house."

"According to Liz, this one is our friend. Do you think she's a liar?"

With a childish groan, they throw their hands up and stalk in the other direction with a, "Fine!"

The other pillar, twice the size of their owlish counterpart, gives Val a much more hospitable smile. "Don't mind Sully, they're like that with everyone. I'm Gen. It's nice to meet you, student of Dream."

Val starts to extend his right hand on instinct, warmed by the title, but Gen gently takes Val's bandaged fingers, like holding broken glass. "Oh, I hope none of my siblings did that."

Shaking his head, Val smiles. "No, no. That was courtesy of . . . my family, I think."

"Hmm, no one hurts or helps quite like siblings, huh?" They smile, eyes bright, and Val can't help smiling back, even when his hand pulses with discomfort. "Sorry, I haven't seen Dream quite yet, but I'm sure he'll arrive soon. Don't worry, I'll keep Sully out of your hair."

They saunter off with a fond expression, and Val feels smaller than ever. He slinks into an oven-warmed kitchen, where Vann and Sully stand in one corner exchanging whispers, and Gen sits with an entirely new woman, just about as tall as Gen, but where Gen is all warmth and curves, this woman is jagged like a cliff's edge. Her smile is as sharp as her gaze, and though she doesn't have the distrust that Sully radiated, she nods at Val once and Val has the immediate, overwhelming sense that she knows more than anyone else in this room.

The yearning for familiarity drives Val out of the house. It's disorienting to open a door into humid darkness, and he remembers the mention of this place being underground. He can see a lamp in the distance, throwing light against a damp rocky tunnel, and goes wandering after it like a confused moth. His senses feel *erratic* in the cramped space, and he winds up sticking his hand out to hug the wall just for an anchor. When he tries to search for Matthew, he is only met with a strange mirror of his own footsteps. Whatever this place is, it's a perfect hiding spot for the pillars.

Finally, bits of real sunlight begin to light his path, and Val emerges onto a beach made more of stone than sand. The orange markings on Matthew's shell immediately catch Val's eye, and then he hears Liz. "Look at all this! You're an ace fisherman. Did my sister teach you?"

"She taught my mother, actually." Matthew gives a soft laugh, his six long legs stepping delicately over a series of interconnected tide pools. He smiles when he sees Val. "Are you feeling better?"

Val nods, ignoring the wash of pain in his hand. "Getting better by the minute. I just wanted to make sure you were alright."

"You kidding? I might have to steal this guy for myself," Liz says. "He's awesome. Patience would love him, too."

Matthew rises to his full height beside Val, though his face seems a little more red than usual. "That's very kind."

Val feels the hairs on the back of his neck stand on end, and he stumbles back, turning his face up to look at the mouth of the cave he just walked out of. Two wide eyes stare back at him, little hands gripping the rock beneath him.

"Is that one of yours?" Val asks Liz.

She looks up, hand on hip, but the person ducks out of the way, and Liz smirks. "Did I see a cat up there?"

After a short pause comes a singsong, "*Maybe.*"

Liz holds out the bucket of crabs to Val, which he takes without thinking. "Can you bring these inside? Matthew, I think it's best if you stay out here for now, to give my more skittish family members time to adjust. I'll come to get you when it's safer."

"Thank you, Miss Liz."

She holds her fingers up to her lips, taking a few silent steps toward the lip of the cave's mouth, and then leaps up to climb over the stone. "I SEE YOU!"

A squeal of laughter echoes in the distance, and Matthew sinks down beside Val. "They seem no different from humans when they're together."

Val nods in agreement.

Matthew lightly touches Val's arm, drawing his eye. "They'll come back. Don't worry. Your friends are quite capable."

"I know," Val tells him, but the whole walk back into the house inside the cave, Val can only wonder if this was the wrong choice. Who's to say Knives didn't just go back to Good Fortune and kill Dream and Hunter? What if, when they tried to run away, they ran right into Knives? What if Knives was even crueler to them because of what Val did to him? If Val winds up the only survivor of their trio, what in the world is he supposed to do?

"Are you with us, boy?"

Val snaps back to the present with the jagged woman holding her fingers in front of his eyes. "I'm sorry."

"It's alright, you just looked like you were about to run into the wall. Do you need a hand?" She holds hers out, and Val holds the bucket out to her, only realizing then that he was using his bad hand to carry it.

"Ah." Val laughs through his teeth, leaving a bloodied palm print on the wooden handle. "Sorry, I did lose this one last night."

"Did you?" She straightens up, hauling the bucket into a corner of the kitchen, sending Vann backing two steps away from a stray drop of water while eyeing his loafers. "You really are a human-shaped insect, then? I've heard rumors of them before."

Val looks at his hands, the stain of red over his bandaged one. He thinks of the knife trapped in the cage of his ribs and he thinks about how good Knives's blood tasted. "A spider."

"Is that what it is?" the woman sounds intrigued, and Val shrinks away, not fully intending to say that out loud. "Tell me more, if you can. We need all the information we can get."

She leans up against the wall, arms crossed, and Val pictures her as some kind of off-duty knight, like she can't quite fully relax without the weight of some armor. "May I ask who you are? Your pillar name?"

She gives a half-smile. "Courage. But I prefer you call me Rae."

Val nods, offering a smaller smile in return. "I'm Val. It's nice to meet you. Why do you want to know about the spiders?"

"They're the most efficient killers of my family," she says back, no anger in her voice, just blatant fact. "I would prefer to stop that from happening. If you have insight, I'll hear it."

So Val begins to tell her a mix of his own memory and Hunter's words about the sentinels of Innovation. He doesn't say anything about the connection he felt with Knives, or the things Knives did to him, but he makes sure to tell her, "If you pull out the tool inside of them, it's like turning off a radio inside our head. A radio we never asked for."

Rae considers this, black brows cinching and relaxing again. "As it stands, these *hatchlings* as you call them, they're receiving instructions. And without those instructions, they'll revert to whatever they were before?"

Val nods. "But the spiders, they're not quite the same. I don't know what will happen if you remove their tools. I don't know if anyone even could. I tried, and he cut through my wrist like it was a stick of butter. Not to mention, he's carrying a collection of instruments that can kill pillars."

Rae gives a grim kind of smirk. "Starting to feel like war again."

"You've brought rainclouds inside my house," a new voice chimes, and Rae turns to yet another pillar that Val doesn't recognize.

"It was my house before it was yours," Rae says, embracing him. "Good to see you."

Val backs away until he is pressed against the opposite wall. This house is full of familiarity and the distinct, ice-cold feeling that Val does not belong. He stands apart, watching the pillars moving through the kitchen and the adjacent dining hall and what looks like a sitting room beyond that. When he closes his eyes, he can sense them drifting around and clumping together and separating again, like an organism breathing and pulsing around him. That makes him the knife that does not belong, silent and strange amid the warmth. If he can be useful to these people, he'll be happy, but there is a small part of him that feels like he should be put back where he can do no harm.

As the vibrations of the pillars synchronize and harmonize and trill all around him, Val remembers Dream's soft lullaby sounds, his scent of sweet tobacco, and his complete lack of fear around Val. Something about him always feels so organic, like a tree compacted into the shape of a man. The more he dwells in the memory, the more it feels like it's with him here in the house, curling around him like the smoke from Dream's cigarettes. When Val hears the thump of a cane on hardwood, his eyes fly open, wondering if he's fully hallucinating, but no, Dream looks much too angry to be fake. Which means he's really here, standing in the kitchen while at least five of his siblings looking on, doing a poor job of pretending that they're not staring.

"Professor!" Val lurches forward, catching himself before he touches Dream with his blood-stained hands.

Dream looks like he's been chewing on rocks—utterly furious, steel eyes gone razor sharp, mouth twisted. He crosses the kitchen in three uneven steps and grabs Val's shirt with both his hands, threatening to rip the fabric.

"You fucking idiot, how stupid can you get? I told you not to go off and do dumb shit! Just because you can't die, doesn't mean I can't lose you!"

The whole house is silent as the grave in the wake of Dream's shouting, but Val is only embarrassed by his own red-faced smile. His eyes sting and he touches one of Dream's hands with his good one.

"I'm sorry, I'm sorry, I know."

"At least try to *look* sorry, you little shit." Dream lets go just to roughly pull Val's head against his own chest.

Val is only glad no one can see him grinning. He rests his hands on Dream's stiff coat and asks, "Is Hunter okay?"

"He's outside. Started shaking like a fucking leaf when he realized there were more of us down here."

Val gives a breathy laugh, sniffing hard so as not to dirty Dream's coat.

"The fuck happened to you?" Dream asks, pulling Val's head back and grabbing his wrapped wrist.

Val shrugs. "Had a small fight at Southern Truth. Are you two alright? Did you get away safely?"

"It was fine. Whatever you did worked. He didn't come back to Good Fortune, but one of my siblings did, to tell me there was a family meeting."

"I'm so glad," Val starts to say, but Dream snatches Val's jaw in his fingers, eyes ablaze.

"Don't ever do that again."

Val nods, breathless in the face of his angry concern. Dream shakes his head, exhaling like he hasn't breathed in two days, and his face sags into a tired relief for a few seconds, before he whirls around on his staring siblings and snaps, "It's not a fucking show! Go sit down and we'll talk, alright? Vultures, all of you."

He shuffles off toward the dining room, and Val bites his lip to stop from laughing. Dream turns back to look at Val over his shoulder and barks, "Go get Hunter. No sense starting without 'em."

Val folds his arms behind his back with a smile. "Yes, sir."

✦

Val finds Hunter by taking the tunnels deeper into the caves, away from the shoreline. He only trips a couple of times with his senses constantly echoing back onto himself, but eventually, he discovers Hunter kneeling in the perfect darkness of the caves. Well, Val doesn't so much discover him as he does stumble onto him, confusing his hulking body with a rock. Hunter places a hand on Val's stomach to stop him from toppling over, and Val yelps into the chilly air.

"What are you doing lurking out here?" Val asks.

Hunter stands up beside Val, and Val feels more than sees his body taking up space. "I'm not sure I can handle it."

"Handle what?" Val asks with a laugh. "They're just in there bickering and catching up. It's nothing grand at all."

"Do you stand in front of a burning building and say it's only wood and fire?" Hunter asks.

It's not funny, but for some reason, Val starts laughing anyway. Hunter's serious words are surprisingly comforting after spending a day worrying himself raw. Reaching out toward the shape of him, Val catches Hunter's arm and starts pulling in the direction of the house. He should probably ask if it's okay to touch him again, but now that they're back in the same space, suddenly Val needs to make sure that Hunter isn't going to vanish in these caves. Val doesn't know much for certain, but he knows he feels better when Hunter and Dream are with him.

"You have useful information, alright?" Val chirps, guiding Hunter forward. "Isn't it your life's purpose to be of use to this family? Cover your eyes if you have to, but we're expected."

Hunter makes a noise of uncertainty, but he still follows as Val drags him forward. When Val slips on a bit of wet rock and nearly cracks his head against the wall, Hunter yanks Val back against himself. His touch startles Val, mostly from the gentleness of it. *Caution* isn't what Val expects from this person, but it's nice to have Hunter steadying him.

When he thinks about the last time Hunter touched him, or how angry he looked before Val left the Hollow Inn, Val starts to shrink as he wonders if they're really okay. It's not just *nice*, it's overwhelmingly soothing to know that Hunter still wants to help Val.

Val mumbles, "Thank you."

"This place is meant to confuse things like you," Hunter says. "There's ore in the walls that can screw up a compass too."

Val nods, catches himself as he remembers that they're in the dark, and then stutters as he remembers further that Hunter can see in the dark. "I-I suppose that's why they hide down here."

"Yes," Hunter says, keeping a hand firmly anchored to Val's shoulder. He holds tight enough to make Val think that maybe he's just as spooked about Val slipping away. "I . . . can carry you if it's easier?"

Val lets his breath out with a smile. That must be it. They're both trying too hard. "If you don't mind, I'm sure Dream would rather not deal with more of my blood."

Hunter scoops Val up into his arms like a child, perching him in the crook of one arm, and they walk at twice the speed. The darkness feels strange, endless even, and Val gets a ping of fear in his gut at the thought they could walk straight off a cliff and he wouldn't see it coming.

"I'm . . . glad you survived," Hunter mutters. "Dream was angry with me for letting you go, but it worked."

Val blindly reaches for the heat of Hunter's head, accidentally disturbing his neat bun of hair. "Is that why you don't want to go into the house?"

"Partly," Hunter says.

"Are you scared of the pillars?" Val asks, quieter.

Hunter stays silent for just long enough that Val thinks he might have offended by mistake, but Hunter stops walking, and Val feels his head turning toward Val.

"I've started having nightmares." His voice is a whisper. "Don't tell him. It'll only make him feel guilty."

It takes Val a few heartbeats to figure out what he's saying. Hunter has already offered all his good dreams, which means Dream is causing him to have nightmares, because Dream can't stop feeding any more than Hunter can stop being human. And now, Hunter is about to be the only human in a house full to the brim with other pillars.

"Oh," is the only thing Val can manage to say.

"Nothing will stop me from doing my job," Hunter says, resuming their walk with a little more iron in his voice. "But I don't need this getting any more complicated for Dream. He didn't want to accept me as is. All I can do now is make this as painless as possible for him."

When the house comes back into view, it is a distant star in an endless night sky. Hunter's body slowly becomes visible again, the familiar outfit of heavy black and the constellations of piercings, and a new piece of black fabric bound tightly over his eyes.

Val touches his knot of black hair pushed askew. "I messed this up, let me fix it."

Hunter just shrugs, so Val pulls the tie from his hair. Awkward as it may be, Val knows that if Hunter didn't want him doing anything, he has more than enough tools at his disposal to stop Val whenever he wants. A shrug from Hunter is probably the closest Val will get to a *yes* for now.

"You know, it looks very pretty when you have it down," Val offers, running his good fingers through any tangles.

"Gets in the way," Hunter says back.

Val smiles. "Then chop it off."

"I like it long."

"Well, alright then," Val says, careful not to get blood in Hunter's hair as he puts it into a ponytail instead. "I'll make it prettier after I change my bandages."

"Sure."

He's holding Val unnecessarily tight as they approach the house. Val hadn't seen it from this angle before, but it is a truly strange sight to see the walls of a stone cottage grafted into an underground tunnel, as if it simply grew like stalagmites from the caves. It must have been a pain to build, but then again, the pillars have had a lot more time to figure out the best way to do it.

Before they make it to the front door, it swings open and Liz waves them in. "Come on in, we gotta talk before we can feed you."

Hunter startles at her voice, or maybe just her presence, and Val puts his hand on top of Hunter's head again. "Thank you!"

"Congrats," she says as Hunter passes through the open door. "You're the first human who's been invited into this house."

"It is . . . an honor," Hunter coughs up the words and Liz makes a guilty face.

"Sorry, we'll make it quick, okay? This must be weird for you."

When they walk back into the dining room, it is brimming with pillars. Every chair is taken up, sometimes by two bodies, additional chairs have been dragged in from other rooms, people are leaning against the walls and sitting on the floor and on the table itself. They all turn to Hunter and Val as they step into the open archway leading inside, and it's like getting stared at by twenty pairs of suns and moons. Val feels unbalanced, like he'll be knocked over by the force of their focus. He is only saved by the steadying feel of Hunter's fingers gripping him tighter and tighter.

"Alright, listen up," Dream says, ambling over to stand beside Hunter. "I'm pretty sure the only reason this meeting was called was so Liz could return Val to me. Which she did, so, meeting adjourned."

He turns his back on them, and the chorus of shouts that erupt from the room causes the hair on Val's neck to rise up.

"What?" Dream asks, wheeling around to face his siblings again. "None of you give a shit about Mare! If I tell you I'm going to bring him back home, you'll tell me it's too dangerous. Far as I can tell, there's nothing to talk about. I'm leaving here with these two." He jams his thumb toward Val and Hunter. "And I'm either going to come back with my stupid brother, or I'll die somewhere between here and Innovation. That's the end of it."

Rae steps forward from where she was leaning against the wall. "That's all? I thought you were building a team to go in and stop these insects and spiders at the source."

"I thought you wanted to break the wall around Innovation," Liz chimes in.

"No offense to all of you, but I don't give a shit about that," Dream says. "I mean, maybe we will. By accident. But this is about Mare. Which obviously none of you want to hear."

"I want to." A quiet voice drifts over the table, and Val spies the same wide eyed face that had been watching him and Matthew from the tide pools. "I miss him too."

Dream drops his head a little. "Thank you, Ozzi."

"Do you think they're using him?" The young boy, Ozzi, asks. He looks no older than ten, but Val is sure that he, too, has at least a hundred years on any human.

"Yeah, I do," Dream says. "There's a chance that pulling Mare out of that godforsaken city might bring the whole thing down. I don't know. But I have to try."

"And what's your impeccable, flawless solution to them shooting you dead within ten miles of the city border?" Vann asks, fingers steeped.

"I'm working on it," Dream says.

"No, no, no, none of that." It's Sully who stands up from their chair—no, from Gen's lap—and points at Dream. "Tell it to us in detail. At least let us help you *plan* for your miserable triple suicide."

"Quadruple, if you count Mare," Vann chimes in, and Liz punches him in the shoulder.

"My plan is to walk," Dream says, shoulders stiffening under the scrutiny of the entire room. "I'm going to walk right up to the gates of the city and tell Mare his brother is here. If he can look me in eyes and decide to finally kill me, then at least I'll know he made the choice himself. But *this*." Dream points at the scar on his cheek, and then down to his unhealing hip. "This wasn't a deathblow. It was fear. I'm not afraid of him, I'm afraid of what they're doing to him."

"I hate to say it, but what if he's already dead?" Rae asks.

Dream readjusts his fingers over the handle of his cane. "Then I don't need to be here either."

"You're really serious about . . . dying." Vann looks genuinely confused by the notion, and someone across the table from him *tuts*. They look like Vann but without any adornment, including a shaved head and better posture.

"It's not for you to judge," they say.

Vann opens his hands with a limp shrug. "Sorry."

"Most of you still have your pairs," Dream says, gesturing vaguely at the room. "It just doesn't feel right. To go this long without him."

An uncomfortable silence begins to stretch around each of them, but Val notices Ozzi's round eyes like spotlights pointed right at the three of them.

"Listen, all I'm saying is that if Nightmare doesn't want me to try for him, he should at least have the balls to kill me himself," Dream says. His words are burnt with the anger that Val has come to recognize as concern in Dream's language. Everyone seems to accept this a little easier than his sadness, and Vann's twin starts looking around the room.

"Sig isn't here, are they? They'd certainly be the most helpful one for crafting a plan."

"No one's seen them in years," Rae offers. "I worry. Ever since they lost Remi, they've been hard to find."

"Last I saw, they were spending an awful lot of time with humans," Sully says.

Gen smiles. "They looked happy about it, though. Sig took to them nicely. Taught them a lot of fancy card tricks, as I recall."

"Alright, well, if none of you have any information about Mare, then I guess we can just scatter again," Dream says.

"You haven't told us anything." Sully narrows their eyes. "Do you really expect this confrontation to go differently? And who is this human you're dragging around? Why are their eyes bound?"

"Oh, uh." Dream scrubs at his face for a moment and then gestures at Hunter. "Some of you remember that group of, uh, passionate humans that try to protect us or whatever? Hunter came from them. He's a good fighter and he's got intel about Innovation. And Val here can safely pull the objects out of hybrids that make 'em try to kill us. These two healed one out by Patience's old village."

"That's the beetle outside?" Ozzi asks, leaning forward in excitement.

"He's here?" Dream looks over at Val.

"Matthew!" Liz claps her hands together. "He's a sweetheart. Cries pretty easy though, so be nice. He's going to help me look for Patience when we're done here."

"You can *heal* insects now?" Sully looks like they're about to fly off the handle, but Gen puts their hand on Sully's back.

"That's good news," Gen says quietly. "Very good news."

"You should let the human take a break." Vann's twin rises up from the table. "They look like they're about to pass out. Vani, have you been butchering my recipe again?"

Vann follows them into the kitchen with a, "Now, now, cooking is about improvisation! Austen! Don't be mad!"

The room swiftly deflates as the pillars begin to talk amongst themselves, and Dream finally turns away from his siblings so he can heave a sigh without them looking.

Val touches Hunter's shoulder. "Are you alright?"

Hunter just gives a short nod, but Dream nudges him with the cane. "Don't lie. I need you at your best. If it's time for a break, take it. I'm gonna go outside to smoke."

"There's a bedroom you can hide in," Val says, directing Hunter through the house as Dream heads toward the front door.

They navigate the cramped halls back to the bedroom, and Hunter puts Val down to sink heavily onto the edge of the bed that Val had been sleeping in.

"How do you feel?" Val asks quietly.

Hunter looks like he's bracing against a huge weight that Val can't see. "They can't shut it off, you know? They feed automatically. All of them."

Val takes the stool that Liz had been using and sits down in front of him. "Is that why the Eyes stay away from the pillars?"

Hunter nods. "It unbalances you. I doubt I could fight like this. But . . . it's not just that. There's something." Hunter's voice goes quiet, a flame dimming. "It's satisfying, in its own way. To help them. Feed them. Makes it tempting to become part of their cycle. I never really got it before, but now."

His fingers are shaking as he sits there, palms upturned on his own thighs.

"We're supposed to keep our eyes clear, and our hands empty," Hunter says in a whisper. "Focused. Ready."

Val doesn't know what to say, but being here to listen to Hunter's strange confession puts warmth in Val's chest. They must be okay if Hunter can speak like this to him.

"Val?"

"Yes?"

"Can you touch my hair again?"

Val's breath catches at the request. Hunter has never looked quite so unsteady, and it feels not entirely dissimilar to Knives choking him in the forest. Val jumps at the chance to do something for Hunter, lurching forward until he catches sight of his own blood.

"Hold on, I'm sorry, my bandage is dirty."

"I'll change it," Hunter says, cupping his hands in front of Val.

Val offers his bandaged hand to Hunter, and puts the other one on Hunter's head, more grateful than he expected to be able to do such a simple task for Hunter. Immediately, Hunter starts sliding his fingers over the edges of the wraps, locating the pin holding them together, steadying himself with a task to focus on. As he unravels ruined gauze onto the floor in a heap of red and white, Val is shocked to see actual skin underneath. Any blood leftover is merely a stain on his freshly healed hand.

"Is it still in pain?" Hunter asks.

"All better," Val tells him, flexing his fingers in Hunter's cupped hands. "Just need to wash the blood off."

"Here!"

They both startle at the sound of Ozzi's voice as the boy comes running right up to Val with a wet cloth. "For the blood."

"Thank you," Val says, though it's Hunter who takes the cloth and rubs Val's palm clean. Val keeps his hand on Hunter's shoulder while Ozzi looks on. "May I ask what pillar you are?"

The boy gives a sparkling smile, hands behind his back. "It's a secret."

Val smiles back at him. "What if I trade you one of my secrets for it?"

His eyes are like two suns. "You go first."

"Are you agreeing?" Val asks. "I won't say anything until you agree to my terms."

Ozzi gives another cloying smile as he sways between his feet. His clothes aren't all that different from Val's outfit supplied by the orphanage, though Ozzi's are a bit higher in quality.

"Okay, fine." Ozzi walks closer to Val, bunching up the sleeve of Val's shirt. "I want to know about the man who cut off your hand."

Val's brows jump up, and the room feel much smaller now than it did only a second ago, but he nods. "What do you want to know?"

Ozzi's eyes are almost hypnotic, the way they only seem to grow larger the longer Val looks at them. "Is he your twin? Like Dream and Nightmare?"

Val stiffens, and he can tell Hunter is listening carefully, as if he's slowed his own pulse so it won't distract.

It takes Val a few seconds to pull words up out of his stomach through the emotion churning down there. "We're not the same as the pillars. But I suppose we're not entirely different either."

"You feel a connection to him?" Ozzi asks.

Val nods, not wanting to say it out loud, all the while wondering what Hunter must think of that.

"You seem nice," Ozzi says to Val. "You heal people, so that must mean he hurts them."

Val can't explain the threatening aura of Ozzi's words, but he feels pinned down like a butterfly in a display case.

"I'm not sure it's that simple," Val mutters back. "I think it's more like, we use the same tools differently."

Ozzi's gaze flicks back and forth between Val's eyes, a sparkling blue-green in each iris, and he nods. "Like two hands that work in tandem. I can feel something like that in you. A piece of someone else."

Val suddenly feels exhausted by these declarations, much heavier than he wanted them to be, but he holds Ozzi's gaze as he realizes that Ozzi must be able to feel the scalpel that Knives gave him.

"Are we even?" Val asks. "Will you tell me your secret too?"

Ozzi tugs on Val's arm, pulling him close enough that he can put his hands around his mouth and whisper right into Val's ear.

"We're twins too. Curiosity and Mischief. We used to be separate, but there came a time when we had to share. Dream likes you, so we wanted you to know. If you find Mare, but he's too weak to come with you, Dream can still bring him home."

Ozzi backs away, an angelic smile on his face. There's a dizzying quality to his presence, and Val feels like he's back in the tunnels with his no senses to guide him as Ozzi opens his mouth, and snaps his teeth down shut.

"Like that," Ozzi says. "If you're with Dream, it must mean you're good. Mare is good too. It'd be nice to see him again, so bring him home, okay?"

Val starts nodding and Ozzi beams at him before he gives a short bow to Hunter. "It was nice to meet you both."

He takes off down the hall with unabashedly loud steps, and Val turns back to Hunter, agog. "Did you hear what they said?"

"Didn't have to," Hunter says back. "They take twice as much from me as the others do. Never met someone with such a loud presence."

"Is he saying he . . . that he and his other half . . . ?"

"One of them ate the other," Hunter says bluntly. "Don't know how literal that is, but there's no doubt. That's two Pillars in one body."

"Kind of incredible, isn't it?" Val asks.

Hunter sets the washcloth onto the bedside table. "I'll find it more impressive when I'm not getting fed to them."

"Sorry." Val reaches up for Hunter's hair with a laugh. "Didn't mean to slack off. Here, I'll put this back into a bun. You don't look the same without it."

Hunter makes a barely audible sound, sort of like a laugh that he's too nauseous to follow through on.

"Dream isn't mad at you," Val tells him, his fingers buried in Hunter's hair as he looks at the black fabric where Hunter's eyes are covered. "He's worried. Worried for both of us."

"I know," Hunter whispers. "I think he expected both of us to leave by now, but since we stayed, now he has to worry about us dying in one way or another."

"Are we being unfair?" Val asks, trying to get the bun to sit in exactly the right place that Hunter always has it. "Joining along with him even though it's stressing him out?"

Hunter breathes through his nose, and the corners of his mouth twitch just a little. "To quote the man, if he doesn't want us around, he should have the balls to tell us himself."

Val almost doesn't believe Hunter is trying to be funny, but he starts laughing before he can help it. Giving up on perfection, Val settles for the closest approximation he can get to Hunter's usual hairstyle and pats Hunter's cheeks.

"Will you be alright?"

He nods. "If it's all the same to you though, I'll go wait outside for Dream to finish up."

"Would you like some company?"

". . . Sure."

As they make their way out of the house, Hunter picks Val up before he can ask, and they head toward the tide pools. When the mouth of the cave comes into view, Hunter slows down at the sound of Dream's voice. He's standing in the way of the waning sunlight, smoke drifting off the cigarette in his hand as he talks to someone leaning up against the stones.

"You seen Hes lately?" Dream asks.

It's Rae who answers, "Yeah. Found her up in the mountains, just like you said."

"And?" Dream takes a drag, and Val can see his impatience in the way he burns down the cigarette. The glow lasts much too long.

"She was half rotted," Rae answers. "Couldn't even see me. I had to carry her to the nearest settlement so she could feed. When she came out of it, she begged me to take her back."

Dream blows two lung's worth of smoke toward the ocean. "What are you going to do?"

"Whatever I have to until she comes back," Rae says. "You still drinking too much?"

"We fighting or talking?" Dream asks. "You know how hard it is to break a routine."

Hunter starts walking forward again, and Val takes the moment to call out to them.

"Professor!" Val yells. "Is that you? It's hard to sense anything down here."

Rae pushes off the wall and squeezes Dream's shoulder before melting into the shadow of the tunnel.

"Yeah, these walls are good for that." Dream flicks the cigarette aside. "Sorry, Hunter, I wasn't thinking. Shouldn't have made you come down here."

"It's fine," Hunter says immediately. "We're off course though. Should we get going?"

Dream shrugs. "You were right when we left Good Fortune. Better to let Mister Cardinal get where he's going before we do anything. Did he say where he was heading, Val?"

"Innovation," Val says as Hunter sets him back down in the sunlight. "His assistant said they were due back. I get the feeling he threw off their schedule by opting to spend time torturing me."

Dream's eyes bug out. "Fuck, I thought he just cut off your hand."

Val shrugs. "He did a bit of surgery. I'm all healed now, though there might be another knife in my chest."

"A knife? That's not going to screw you up, is it?"

"I don't feel any different," Val tells him, touching the front of his shirt. "He said it might change me, but nothing's happened yet."

Dream pokes Val in the shoulder. "You're not going near that guy ever again."

Val tilts his head to the side, a smile inching onto his face. "Aren't we trying to rescue the person who hurt you the worst?"

That seems to choke Dream, and he turns his frown toward the sea. "Well I guess you fucking got me, huh? Fine. Just don't be stupid."

"I'll do my best. Would you like to leave?"

"Yeah, yeah, we gotta take a different route if we're going to get there anytime soon," Dream says as he starts back into the tunnel. "I'll get our shit. Stay here, I won't be long."

"Dream," Val calls, waving his hand.

Dream turns to face him again, his body half-eaten by the darkness of the caves.

"Will you tell us more about Nightmare?" Val asks. "Maybe while we walk? I think we've earned at least one story."

Dream rolls his eyes and vanishes into the tunnels with a, "Yeah, yeah."

9

With all their stuff back in order, Val says goodbye to Matthew, heartened by his enthusiasm to join up with Liz.

"I was scared that she'd try to kill me," Matthew admits. "When she came to Patience, she was fierce, you know? But she saw me struggling to walk in the sand and decided to hear me out instead. We were looking for Patience when I caught your scent. I'm glad I did."

Val shakes Matthew's hand with a smile. "Me too."

"All healed?" Matthew holds Val's unwrapped hand up and squeezes it. "Be safe out there."

"You too," Val says. "I'll try to make sure the next time we meet, it's not so bloody."

"Third time's the charm." Matthew offers an awkward smile, and Val laughs, bolstered by his making any joke at all.

Val, Dream, and Hunter decide to follow the coastline in the direction of Innovation, figuring it's less likely for them to run into Knives at the edges of the continent. Val feels a lot sturdier the further they get from the caves, and some ten minutes out, Hunter pulls the black fabric off their eyes. Dream is walking faster too, which Val only notices because Hunter isn't visibly forcing themself to slow down as often as they were before they got to Good Fortune.

There is no silence with the ocean so close by, but Val stares at Dream, waiting for him to start talking.

"I can feel you staring at me," Dream snaps.

Val jogs up to walk beside him, and Hunter drifts down to keep pace at his other side.

"You do owe us a story," Val reminds him. "Unless you're still mad at us."

"I'm not . . . I'm not mad at anyone," Dream says, adjusting the tone of his voice midway through. "I know why you did what you did. You still broke your promise, but I know why."

Val tangles his fingers behind his back. "I've only ever done my job since we've met. That was the first promise I made to you. And we both know where Hunter's priorities are."

"Fucking knew you'd say that." Dream sighs. "Fine, what do you want to know?"

"Why do you think Mare went to Innovation?" Val asks.

Dream starts shaking his head, staring staunchly toward the seemingly endless stretches of rough grass. "I don't know. I've thought about it so many times. Came up with a hundred different reasons why he might have gone, but I won't believe any of them until he says it in his own voice."

"Will you be able to forgive him?" Val asks.

Dream's jaw clenches, brows furrowing, hot iron cooling into a mold, and Val thinks that if he saw Dream coming at him with *this* expression, he might be a little scared.

"Everyone thinks he's the only one responsible," Dream says. "My siblings are ready to cut him loose. It's easier to say he sided with insects over his own family because they're scared. I guess I can't really blame them. You live long enough believing you're immortal only to have that thrown back in your face by one of your own—it stings. But it's been over fifty years and not one of my fucking siblings asked me what *I* did to make him leave."

Dream's knuckles are bone white over the handle of the cane where the knife is sheathed.

"It was my responsibility to look out for him. That's been the way of things for as long as we've all been here. Those of us who have the lighter burden, we take care of our other halves no matter what. And somewhere along the way, I fucked it up so bad that Mare shot me in the hip just so I couldn't follow him."

Hunter's gaze slips over to Val's before they face forward.

"You said it was a warning," Hunter says. "So did he injure you to keep you from following, or to warn you?"

"I—I don't know!" Dream barks, waving his hand. "I've had too much time alone to think about it. You try mulling something over for half a century and tell me if it still comes to you coherently."

Val tugs on Dream's jacket. "Can you tell us about when he injured you? What you remember most clearly?"

Dream exhales, the anger beginning to burn off into resignation as his shoulders slouch. "Innovation was getting to me. It was the last place we were together, and we'd been there for a long time. It was so big, we could move from one neighborhood to another without completely drying up the dreams of the humans there. And they had some wild dreams. No place compared to Innovation for a feeding ground. People traveled from all over to live there and become part of the technological advance. Neither of you were alive when Innovation was in its prime, but the city really was beautiful. It almost drove me mad."

He gives the ghost of a smile, eyes unfocused as they follow the curve of the coastline made of beach grass.

"It was unbalanced," Dream says. "But I knew Mare was thriving there in a way he hadn't in any other place. So I stayed. See, Mare and I figured out a while ago that we rarely see our own dreams, but we see each other's when we're absorbing too much. Like spillover. Alcohol though, it makes it harder for me to dream. I don't get drunk like a human, so I started drinking more just to keep Mare from seeing the dreams I was having."

"Don't you have good dreams though?" Val asks, a strange nausea burbling in his stomach as he thinks about this not as a story, but a memory.

"I didn't know what he'd see," Dream says. "I was . . . I was scared that he'd see me wanting to leave. That he'd think I was mad at him or that I minded staying. I didn't. I would have stayed as long as he wanted me to. I would have gone anywhere with him. But eventually, he figured out that I was taking too much in, so we left. Or, I thought we were leaving."

Dream fidgets with his empty hand, touching his coat and deciding better of it. Val wonders if he's forgoing the booze, the cigarettes, or both.

"The insects were just starting to be a problem. Our family was either grouping together or scattering, for safety. There had been one in Innovation, right before we left, it tore up a whole shop, took down a bunch of humans and then killed one of us. I helped dismantle that one. That's how we learned they heal so perfectly. It took way too many of us to put a stop to it. And by 'put a stop to it,' I mean we basically did the equivalent of trapping a bug under a cup. Six of us, just for one insect. Rae still has a scar from it."

"That many Pillars were in one city?" Hunter asks, blatant curiosity on their face.

Dream lets out a reverent sigh, like he lit that cigarette after all. "Most of these cities are associated with one or two of us at most. Some are in name only, others don't even know about us. But Innovation? Innovation belonged to all of us. We all came and went, left pieces of ourselves in the people and the architecture and the plans for the future. We designed that city, and humans came to fill up all the spaces. We wanted it to be the best of both worlds. So it was all that much worse when the insects started hatching."

Val is surprised when Dream doesn't insist his hip hurts so he can stop talking, and Val has half a mind to offer him the free pass just to spare him the pain for a little longer, but Dream carries on.

"Mare was the one who told me that some of the insects are smarter than others. When he took me out of the city to give me a break from all the people, he told me that he'd met with a man who was neither human nor insect. The way he spoke about it was like he'd found religion. The silence . . . he said it was the most beautiful thing he'd heard in years. To stand with someone and not sense anything from them, to not feel the edges of their nightmares bleeding in, or the shadows that live in their soul. He was so excited, and I was too fucking jealous to care."

Dream practically spits the words.

"It was right there. He was telling me what was wrong. He was just as tired of sharing as I was. I didn't want to need humans anymore, but I think Mare didn't want to need *me*. So when he started telling me he was making friends with one of the things that killed our brother, I wouldn't hear it. I wasn't ready for it. We got into an argument and an argument spiraled into a screaming match and I realized in the middle of shouting at him that I'd *never* shouted at him before. Ever. It was like I didn't know how. When I say he's my brother, humans think they know what that means, but it's not the same. It's not *human*. That may be the word they put on us so they can understand what we are, but the truth is that it's like we're carrying each other's h—"

He stops talking, the word breaking up in his mouth as he swallows and reevaluates.

"We were on the road when I heard myself screaming at him, and it was the worst sound. The silence after wasn't much better, so I asked him if we could just go back home together. I'd figure it out, it wasn't that bad. I just wanted to stay with him. He said the city wasn't good for me, and I should stay away. When I realized he meant for us to split up, I didn't know what to do. I don't think I've ever felt so cold. It didn't feel fair. He'd found this beautiful silence for himself in the city, and I was just . . ."

Dream shrugs.

"He tried to walk away. I tried to keep him there. He cut my face. I don't think he realized it was gonna scar the way he did. It bled so much, and he actually looked scared of the mess. He looked like the old Mare. The one who reached out for me in his sleep because he was seeing other people's nightmares. But when I reached for him, he ran away."

Dream goes quiet again, and Val glances at Hunter, wondering if that's all they're going to get. Hunter quirks an eyebrow at Val as if to say, *you ask*, but right when Val thinks about clearing his throat, Dream starts up again.

"I saw him a year later. I was scared to go back, but Rae told me that there were a lot more insects there than when I left, and she was worried Mare was trapped. Humans had been fleeing the city in droves, and our family knew by then not to fuck with the hybrids, so Innovation was becoming a husk. I went there thinking I was going to rescue Mare. He met me at the border of the city with a gun. I told him to come with me, that we could try again somewhere else, and Mare just looked so fucking disappointed. I thought the gun was for the hybrids."

He gives a withered laugh.

"I saw the man Mare spoke about. The person neither insect nor human. After Mare shot me, he had that same scared look on his face, but he didn't run. This person came up behind him, and I couldn't feel them at all. I thought it was the pain, but I remembered what Mare said about the silence. He pulled Mare into it, into this complete absence of feeling. I could see Mare, but it was like looking at a picture. That day, I started feeling different. I'd looked the same for almost my entire life, but after that day, I started aging. And my hip never fully healed. Like it's still trying to kill me."

That time, when Dream stops talking, Val knows it's the end of the story, but there's so much left unanswered. Dream finally lets himself light a cigarette, pausing for a brief moment to strike a match and pull a box out of his coat pocket which he frowns into.

"Fuck," he mutters, crushing the empty box in his hand.

Val pulls the useless lit match from him and crushes the flame between his fingers, feeling his skin quickly adjust to the burn. "I'm sure we'll find more along the way."

"Yeah."

"I can scout ahead," Hunter offers, but Dream shakes his head.

"Too dangerous out here. Let's just stick together."

They keep on walking, and the silence carries them all the way until dark. Hunter guides them just far enough inland to find some woods to hide in, pointing out that a tent in the middle of the beach is only going to attract attention. Hunter puts their hammock up, Dream settles against the trunk of a pale, mottled tree, and Val sets up his camp.

"I have two questions," Hunter says, kneeling in front of Dream.

Dream only sort of frowns at the supplication.

"First, how do you plan to deal with the wall around Innovation?" Hunter asks.

Dream gives a laugh. "Val."

Hunter nods. "I figured as much."

"Wait, sorry, how do I factor into this?" Val walks over, head tilted at their unspoken understanding.

"Whatever you are," Dream tells him. "It's the same as the man I saw with Mare. If he can come and go, you probably can too."

"Oh . . ." Val folds his arms with a nod. "Spiders and insects must be able to pass through without trouble."

"Spider?" Dream's brows furrow.

"That's what Knives called it. People like me."

Dream looks at Hunter. "Who the fuck is Knives?"

"The Cardinal Major, I'm guessing," Hunter ventures, glancing at Val.

"Yes, we had a conversation prior to the torture," Val says. "There's a sort of hierarchy, I guess. Matthew and Moon are both hatchlings. You can see the parts of them that have changed. Knives, myself, and whoever that person with Mare is, we're spiders."

"Speaking of," Hunter says. "My second question. Do you remember what Mare's spider looks like?"

Dream sags against the tree trunk, setting his cane onto the grass. "Barely. I remember how clean he looked. Like he was made of marble. But that might have been the bullet in my hip."

"Hair?" Hunter asks.

Dream shrugs and gestures to his shoulders. "Bout this long, I think? He was all straight lines. Straight posture, straight nose, straight hair. But the rest is a blur by now."

Nodding, Hunter rises up and gives a quiet thank you before retreating to his hammock.

"You." Dream points at Val.

Val's shoulders jump. "Yes?"

"What happened in that church?"

Val takes a deep breath, tugging at his sleeves. "He put another knife inside me. A scalpel, like the one I pulled out of myself when I was little. He said it would fix me."

"And?" Dream prompts, gesturing at Val. "Did it do anything?"

Val shrugs. "No, sir."

It wasn't the knife Val felt the most.

"If anything changes, you let me know," Dream says. "I'll dig it out of you if I have to."

"You'll be the first," Val promises, fixing a smile onto his lips. He also knows that it will be much harder to get this one out than it was to get it in, and they don't have time for that. "Get some rest."

He nods at Val. "You too."

It's not that Val can't sleep, it's that he doesn't particularly feel like it. He lays inside his tent, listening to the sounds of this sparse, humid forest. They're so far south by then, it doesn't quite get chilly at night the way Val is used to. The air is different here, heavier from the ocean. Something catches the edges of his awareness, and Val pulls his shoes on to dart out of the tent, scalpel in hand. Despite the fact that he knows he would recognize Knives from a mile away, his pounding heart is wary nonetheless.

Of course, it's not Knives. It's Hunter.

Usually their presence barely registers to Val, but that night, they're ringing in Val's head like thunder and lightning. He puts the scalpel away as he walks over to their hammock, no sound or movement, just the disquieting feeling of *distress* rolling off of them. Just as Val gets within an arm's reach of them, Hunter bolts upright with a gasping breath, and even in the dark, Val can see their eyes wide open. Their breathing levels out into panting and they turn right toward Val.

"Nightmares?" Val whispers.

Hunter breathes at him, and Val feels a hand bunching up the front of his shirt, hauling him closer.

"Don't tell him." Hunter's voice puffs against Val's face.

"I won't," Val says, reaching out to touch Hunter's chest. Their heartbeat is wild, wild enough to call anything that can sense humans right to them. "How do I help you?"

Hunter doesn't say anything, just holds Val's shirt much too tight, breathing through the last of a nightmare-panic.

"There's room in the tent," Val offers, taking a step back and letting his shirt suffer Hunter's grip.

"Mm, wait."

They pull on Val's shirt again, unwilling to let go as they shift around in the hammock. Val waits as they find their boots in the dark and swing their legs out, step by step, like a doll controlled by unseen hands. When they've got their feet on the ground, they finally unclench their hand from Val's shirt, trudging after him as he goes back to his tent. Val finds his glow lamp and turns it on as Hunter squeezes in and sits on the other side of the tent pole, frowning into the dim light while they pull their boots off to put next to Val's shoes.

"Usually I can't feel you," Val says. "Every person has these vibrations I can pick up on, but not you. Or, not usually. Now though, you may as well be a pillar for how much noise you're making."

Hunter's eyes flash and they dip their head. "Sorry."

"Would you like me to touch your hair again?" Val asks, holding his hand out.

He can see Hunter's shoulders stiffen, but they don't move away.

"You've been having a rough time, haven't you?" Val asks. "Between regrowing a hand and endless nightmares, I think I got the lighter burden."

Val feels the hairs on the back of his neck stand on end as he reaches his hand closer to Hunter's head. There's heat pouring off their scalp as Val slides his fingers down the braid they were sleeping in.

"Are they your nightmares?" Val asks, pulling a small tie free so he can loosen the braid. "Or Dream's?"

The look on Hunter's face is anything but relaxed, and Val has the distinct sensation that he is trying to calm a wild animal that could bite him at any moment. If Val were anyone else, he'd have earned at least one broken finger for getting this close. No, Hunter would never let anyone else do this, and that's probably why they look like they're being held at knife point as Val pulls their hair over their shoulders. Hunter is more likely to pierce their own flesh than to let someone else soothe them.

"I think they're Mare's," Hunter's voice is nothing but a quiet hiss of teeth, eyes open wide.

Val's hands go still. "Really?"

"I know how to deal with my own." They talk quickly, the bags under their eyes even more prominent, or maybe Val is just worried about them. "But these. These are something else. Dream, I think he's been carrying Mare's despair with him, and it's gathering interest. Spilling over into me."

"What are you seeing?" Val asks, lowering his own voice on instinct.

Hunter's mouth opens, pink tongue rolling unspoken words around. They start to shake their head.

"I'm not sure you want to know," they say.

Val pushes his hands through Hunter's hair, turning their face toward his to offer a small smile. "Come on now, do you really think I scare that easy?"

Hunter lifts their chin. "You were scared of me."

Val shrugs. "Sorry, but I've met someone worse."

Hunter doesn't smile, but they exhale through their nose, and there might have been five percent of a laugh in it. "Fair enough."

Val runs his fingers back through Hunter's hair. "If we're going to meet Mare, I'd like to know what we're walking into. I'm not sure Dream will ever tell us. He's too busy blaming himself for everything."

With a nod, Hunter lets go of some of the tension that had their shoulders in a perfectly straight line.

"I keep seeing Dream from someone else's eyes. He's younger, before he got shot. I only knew it was him because I heard Mare calling to him. Sometimes it's simple. Mare watching Dream die over and over again while he curses Mare out. Sometimes it's a little more complicated. I can't always tell which parts of the dream are the nightmare and which parts are normal. They're . . . different from humans."

Hunter runs their teeth over their bottom lip, and Val inches closer, pretending he knows how to braid as he waits for Hunter to find the words.

"I think they were together," Hunter says.

Val's brows furrow. "Together? Like a couple?"

"Yes."

"So they're not brothers?" Val asks.

"Oh, they are," Hunter says, looking back at Val. "I don't think it's as simple as one or the other for them."

Val's face begins to heat up. "How can you be sure?"

Hunter just meets his gaze with a look of hardened exhaustion. "Do you need me to tell you everything I saw?"

"I suppose not," Val mutters, probably turning pink as his fingers fumble through Hunter's hair. "But, how do you know that's not just part of the nightmare?"

"Because it doesn't break bad until *after* Dream fucks Mare."

Val feels like he's been pinched, making what he's sure is a particularly stupid face. "I see."

"The shape of those dreams aren't about fear of his brother touching him, it's always right when things should be calm. The moments after. Sometimes Dream starts rotting in front of him, like old fruit. Sometimes Mare kills him. Sometimes it's a stranger. Those are always bad, when Mare is stuck watching someone else kill Dream. The worst ones by far though are the ones where Mare watches Dream being happy with someone else. Mare usually winds up killing them both."

Val nods, a slimy nausea in his stomach. "I doubt Mare will be very excited to meet the two of us."

Hunter looks like they might just laugh again, then tilts their head with a frown. "Wait, have you and Dream . . . ?"

Val's eyes pop open, warmth flooding back to his cheeks. "N-no, I only meant that we care about him. And he seems to care about us too."

Hunter's black gaze looks even more endless as they say, "You wish you could though. Am I wrong?"

Val pulls his hands off Hunter's hair, hot and strange and small in Hunter's shadow. "I don't know."

"It's fine," Hunter says, regaining their control once again. "I get it. He may not be a god, but he's not like us."

Val's heart is crawling up his throat, a vine of thorned memories choking him. Dream holding a knife in his mouth, Hunter cutting perfect lines into his thighs, Knives feeding him blood with fingers tucked deep inside Val's body.

"I *don't* get it," Val says back. "I just want to do a good job. I don't want to feel things like this."

"Guess you're more human than you thought," Hunter says, their face turning more and more orange in the artificial light. Val is too focused on their words to realize that his glow lamp is dying, so when it blinks out with no warning, hurling them back into pitch blackness, he startles like it's a physical thing pressing into his shoulders.

He can't feel Hunter anymore, their calm cloaking them from Val's senses once again.

"Relax," Hunter says, their voice much closer than Val was prepared for. "I'm not judging you."

"I don't like wanting things," Val says back. "It makes me stupid. I don't have time to be stupid."

"I could give you another scar," Hunter offers. Val feels warmth blooming against his side and he shivers. "Clear your head."

Val closes his eyes even though there's no difference. He can't feel Hunter, save for the spot of warmth against his hip, and someone whispers in the back of his head that it shouldn't excite him to be so vulnerable, but he doesn't so much care for those whispers anymore. Touching the side of his hand where Hunter forced his skin to heal into a firm ridge, Val takes an unsteady breath.

"I have to be honest with you, Hunter. That won't clear my head."

It's like he's speaking to a living pool of shadow.

"Maybe we could pretend we're normal for a night," Val offers. "Comfort each other like regular people?"

Val is drawn to that warmth, the only thing in the dark that makes sense to him. He brushes his fingers over the back of Hunter's hand, touching tendons and knuckles and skin that really isn't as rough as

Val expects it to be. He wraps his fingers around Hunter's wrist, their pulse wildly beating against him for only a second before Hunter snatches their hand up from the tent floor to place on the center of Val's chest. Val braces himself as he realizes he touched Hunter without permission again, but Hunter pushes Val flat onto his back against the canvas like they mean to press their own heat into Val instead.

"We're not normal," Hunter says, their voice starting to waver. "And I'm not good at pretending."

Val grins, his heart racing under Hunter's palm at the quiet, strained way they're speaking to him. "That's better, actually."

"Keep quiet."

It's not a command, but a plea. Val gladly lets his head fall to useless static while Hunter pulls his clothes off. His head is on the edge of his sleeping bag, his body only separated from the ground by the bottom of the tent. There's a chill bleeding into his back from the grass below, offset by the heat of Hunter's hands as they find Val's hips, and then their mouth as they find Val's thigh. Val was expecting another blade, but Hunter opts to use their teeth instead, biting hard enough that it seems to chase all the air out of Val's chest in a gasp.

It takes no time at all for the pain to slide right into his blood, turning to a strange hunger. Val's fingers open and close around nothing, panting at the relief that comes with the sting. Maybe this is just a favor to him, but it works all the same. Val needs this want pulled out of him, and if nothing else, Hunter is an expert at wrangling creatures like Val. With teeth sinking into his thigh, Hunter finds Val's slit in the dark, and Val's breath stutters in his throat as he tries not to make noise at the fingers sliding roughly inside him. It isn't the efficient burst of miserable pleasure that Knives excised from him, but a barreling, messy heat that turns Val to pins and needles with Hunter's thumb anchored to his clit.

Val tries so hard not to make noise that he starts to see stars on the canvas of the tent, like his own silence is exploding into light. In the cloak of the darkness, he lets his expression turn to something unrecognizable, feeling like he's about to swallow the night sky. It doesn't seem real, that there is a place to touch him that so easily erases anything but physical pleasure. He picks his leg up, the arch of his foot flexing as he forgets there's no wall here to brace against, but Hunter catches his ankle before he can kick the tent out of place.

Val sits up on his elbows, his own teeth nearly chattering with the sensation coming to an abrupt halt. "C-can you ..."

More warmth pours over him as Hunter gets closer, and Val can feel their naked skin and the brush of their hair. He wonders how many scars and piercings line Hunter's body that he can't see. He can feel the metal bars in Hunter's nipples as they crush Val against the bottom of the tent and Val has to cover his mouth as he feels much more than fingers trying to press inside him. The canvas *hisses* as Val bends his legs up to try and get them out of Hunter's way, desperate to know what Hunter wouldn't give him before. There is a distant growl of an animal and a dull flash of pain as Hunter pulls Val onto their cock.

Val's voice slices through the quiet of the night for a single second, and then Hunter seals his mouth shut with the palm of their hand.

"Shut the fuck up," they breathe against Val's temple, and it's not anger, it's that same desperate pleading, but Val's body is so full, he *needs* to let some of this pressure out through his mouth. He needs to scream loud enough to make light out of darkness. As soon as his voice catches in his throat like flint on iron, Hunter jams their fingers into Val's mouth, drowning the sound with their skin on Val's tongue.

"Quiet," Hunter hisses.

Val's lips close down around their knuckles and Hunter jerks their hips. Moaning around Hunter's fingers, Val catalogs the inside of his own body—how it pulses around Hunter's skin, how different parts of him jump and flex all their own, how his muscles seem to know to clench down around Hunter without being told. The soft groan he earns from Hunter at the extra pressure makes Val's blood rush. If his body knows how to be like this without instruction, then this must be as normal as breathing.

It doesn't take long for the tent to warm up far beyond the need for clothes, and with his legs wrapped around Hunter's waist, Val has a realization like a stray bullet. This whole time, he's been thinking about Hunter all wrong. They are not the efficient killer that Val once thought. Knives is the machine. Hunter is an animal, as all humans are, but never more so than here in the dark. Val wishes he could see Hunter's face, to match these barely restrained groans to an expression. What does a human look like when they're losing control? At least he knows what they feel like, and what they sound like, and that alone is exhilarating. There's something almost mournful in these little sounds wresting out of Hunter, but Val knows it's not sadness, not when Hunter keeps trying to move inside him faster and faster.

This is not what Knives did to him. Hunter isn't doing this to prove something to Val. They're both doing this because they have nowhere else to put this feeling; because Hunter can't pierce their flesh in a place like this; because Dream, the man they've both sworn to protect, was made for someone else, and Val wouldn't know how to touch him even if he could. But Hunter knows how to touch Val. They treat him like a wild thing, like a fire that needs containing, or a weapon to be disarmed. When Val's body takes over, planting his feet on the ground to pick his hips up, one of his hands blindly reaching out for Hunter's hair, frantically trying to figure out how to make this graceless electricity turn into lightning, he can almost believe that he's dangerous.

Like the churches patiently listening to the people praying inside them, Val listens to Hunter, their inability to pretend, their skin and their blood and their quiet cursing, the way they shiver when Val pulls their hair, until the words are running down Val's thighs.

There's drool on Val's cheek from Hunter gagging him, his jaw sore from being held open, but Val sucks on their fingers to make sure he didn't draw blood by mistake. A jolt of *something* ricochets from Val's mouth into Hunter's shoulders as they pull their hands away from him with a startle. He wonders if that's not what you're supposed to do after sex, but a moment of cricket-filled silence passes between them before Hunter puts one finger back in Val's mouth. Val can hear a deep sigh as Hunter replaces all the air in their lungs and Val licks the indent of his own teeth in Hunter's skin. Their presence is back in a low toned whisper at the edges of Val's awareness, like a radio on an unused station. Val, on the other hand, feels like a lightning rod.

"You good?" Hunter asks, taking their hands back. Val can picture the blank look on their face, not apathetic so much as neutral.

"Yes," Val says, more air than sound.

"You got a towel in that backpack of yours?" they ask, and Val gets a shiver at the realization of how messy they are.

"Uh, no actually, I usually borrow those . . ."

Another sigh and Hunter pulls their hips away from Val, letting the chill of the night air rush in to cool the fluid on his skin. "There's a river nearby. Can you follow me in the dark?"

"Yes."

Hunter shuffles around, probably for their clothes, and when they leave the tent, they take all the heat with them. Val sees a flash of his own skin in the pale moonlight as the tent flaps open and shut. His bare legs have never looked less familiar to him, all bent up as they are, frozen as if Hunter's waist is still in the way. A moment later, Hunter pushes the tent flap open and practically throws a small cloth at Val.

"Clean up and follow me. I only got a few of those so we gotta wash them."

"Y-yes, sir. Or, uh. Sorry."

"I don't care what you call me," Hunter says, starting to dig through the pile of their indiscernible black clothes. Val jolts back into motion at the rare opportunity to see more of Hunter's body. Unceremoniously cleaning up as much as he can with the little cloth, Val grabs his own underwear and shoes and slips out of the tent. Hunter rises up beside him in their shorts, jamming their feet into their boots before stalking off into the woods with their clothes hugged to their chest.

It's still nighttime, but the thin trees and the bright moonlight are enough to see the curtain of their hair, and the shape of their body as they cut a path through the darkness.

"I feel like I gave you the wrong name," Val says, gaze fixed to a pattern of healed flesh slowly emerging over Hunter's back. The longer he stares, the more clearly he can see the scars, some healed in thick lines and some in dips and swells of missing space, some splotches of permanently reddened skin from old burns spider-webbed across them.

Hunter shrugs. "It's just a sound."

Val looks up at the back of their head, touching his own bangs as he watches Hunter's hair swaying. "Your hair really is pretty. I see why you don't cut it."

Hunter glances over their shoulder at Val, confusion chiseled into their brow.

Val smiles back. "I don't think I would look as nice with hair that long. People would probably just think I was a girl."

Facing forward, Hunter tucks all their clothes under one armpit and wrangles their hair back into a lopsided knot at the base of their neck.

"Did I embarrass you?" Val asks, eyes widening. "Sorry."

Hunter huffs without looking at him, and Val's spine straightens, some of that lightning rod energy peeling back up his skin. They're silent for the rest of the short walk to the river, where Hunter kicks their boots off and immediately splashes in with no care. Val sets his shoes down neatly beside Hunter's and quietly slides in, suppressing a yelp at how cold it is.

"I thought a southern river would be less icy."

"It is," Hunter says, ringing out the wet cloth.

Val forces himself in deeper, goosebumps jumping up along every limb as his feet find the bottom of the river. "Do you pierce yourself as punishment, or do you like it?"

"Focus," Hunter says. "Clears my head."

Val stares at Hunter as they drape the cloth over their shoulder, their body going still like something snared them under the water.

"I don't . . ." Hunter seems to lose their footing in their own thoughts as their face funnels into confusion. "Eyes aren't expected to leave marks on the world. We don't take souvenirs, we don't take lovers, we try not to let anyone notice us."

"So you mark yourself instead?" Val ventures.

"Mm." Hunter turns like they're going to look at Val, but they stop short, letting their fingertips dip under the surface of the river as their arms go slack. "Never spent much time thinking about what I liked. Not sure if I know yet."

"Feel free to tell me if you come up with an answer," Val says. He doesn't know what about Hunter just standing there thinking makes his heart constrict, but it does.

"Sure," Hunter mumbles. "Maybe after we finish the job . . ."

They turn back toward the river bank, and Val smiles wide at the sight of Hunter's shoulders half shrugged to their ears. Val starts splashing after them, oddly delighted by this less rock solid version of Hunter. As he tries to come up with something else to say, wet feet slipping on the grass on the way up the bank of the river, he sees Hunter go impossibly still. Dropping to a crouch, they fish a knife up out of their discarded clothes, and Val tries to feel it too.

"Coming from the left," Hunter says, voice barely audible. "Most of my things are back at camp."

Val turns toward an ever increasingly loud presence, a thunking, chaotic vibration in the distance. The moonlight strung through these sparse woods makes everything look gray and ashen, like the life has already been sapped out of it, but he doesn't see movement yet.

"You can run faster," Val says. "I'll start toward it. Get your things and meet me."

Hunter slips their knife into Val's hand before they take off in a frighteningly quiet sprint back to camp. Val doesn't have time to feel stupid about the fact that he's only wearing his underwear and his shoes, just grips Hunter's knife and starts jogging in the direction of whatever insect has picked up on them. It feels like approaching an out of tune guitar, and Val ignores the discordant noise practically begging him to turn away.

He breaks into a run when he can feel whoever it is stalking straight for Dream. He can practically taste the determination in the air. It isn't bloodlust or anything as human as *anger*. This hatchling, this person, they're not even running as fast as they can. They walk with the surety of a machine whose only purpose lays directly ahead of them. Val though, he pushes himself to move faster, because he can, because he needs to, because if something happens to Dream or Hunter, well, he doesn't want to know what that feels like.

Maybe it feels like decades of solitude, or wounds that won't heal.

Val sees the hatchling weaving through the trees, two gauzy, crooked wings twitching in bursts of movement that don't seem to be doing anything on a body too heavy to fly. They're not much bigger than Val, which he's grateful for as he lets himself collide full force into their chest with his shoulder, knocking the hatchling to the ground. Despite his own sweating palms, Val jams Hunter's knife directly into the hatchling's neck, ignoring the sickening resistance on their flesh and muscle and bone. As he's wrestling with their arms, trying desperately to figure out how to secure their hands without rope or fabric, the hatchling lets out a sound like a water-logged scream, and spits all over Val.

Wiping his eyes with the back of his arm, Val reaches for their hands again, only to stop midway through as a burning sensation rips across his skin, sinking into his eyes. There isn't any connection between his mind and his mouth, Val just hears himself crying out in pain, like he lost his hearing and it snapped back right at that moment. His eyes are on fire, his face, neck, and chest covered in a spray of distilled stomach acid. Strangely, the hatchling doesn't take a shot at him, but simply pulls the knife from their own neck to let it heal.

"Is this . . . a test?" Their own voice is burned through, from the knife or the acid, Val doesn't know. "You are one of his spiders. Am I being punished?"

Val grits his teeth, trying to ignore the pain enough to keep his senses from completely dissolving.

"I was told to stop the Pillars." They sound so innocently confused. "Why is a spider attacking me?"

Val tries to grab the knife out of their hand, blind as he is with acid in his eyes, and cuts his palm open on the blade just to wrench it from the hatchling's shocked fingers. Val's vision comes and goes in bubbles as his own healing fights with the corrosion, glaring down at the hatchling who is looking up at him with eyes seemingly split down the middle, two per socket.

"You're making it very hard to ask your name." Val grinds the words out through clenched teeth.

"A young spider who asks for names." The hatchling's face draws in a frown, and Val groans through another match strike of pain. "He warned us about you!"

Val isn't ready for the hands around his throat or the weight of the hatchling throwing him off balance. His back slams into the ground, and Val only catches a flash of blurry movement above him as the hatchling rears back with something in their hand. Vision crackling in and out, Val barely catches sight of the hilt of another knife now buried in the hatchling's chest. The force of it landing knocks them off of Val's body, and the device they were holding goes rolling into the grass.

The smell of his own burning skin makes it harder to breathe as Val pulls himself up, giving a hoarse shout to whoever is there, "There's acid! Don't get close."

He almost steps onto the small metal cylinder as a thin rope cinches around the hatchling's chest. In short bursts of clear vision, Val watches what happens like a series of photographs developing in front of him. The hatchling's mouth is open, throat bobbing like they're working up more saliva. Hunter appears behind them in their dark clothes like they materialized out of the shadows. The hatchling gasps when the rope cuts into their breathing. Then, Hunter has their boot planted on the back of the hatchling's head so their open mouth is spewing acid into the ground where their own face is.

Hunter's expression swims and burns in Val's broken vision, but Val is pretty sure that's a new look on Hunter's face. They didn't look nearly so furious with Matthew.

Dream sneaks up on him, crouching beside Val with a pouch of water and a hand on Val's back. "Tilt your face up."

Val does, holding the metal thing out in his palms. "They were going to use this on me. What is it?"

Dream pours clean water into Val's eyes, sending tear streaks of acid rolling off his skin. Val leans forward, letting the water wash over him as Dream takes the device with a scowl. Righting his cane, Dream walks over to Hunter and the lassoed hatchling, their body twitching and writhing under the weight of Hunter's body and their own acid burning their face.

"Break the jaw," Dream says.

Hunter doesn't even look at Dream for confirmation, just nudges the hatchling's head to the side and rears their boot up higher. Val doesn't mean to close his eyes, isn't really sure why he does, considering everything else he's seen, but his eyes close on their own for the moment of impact.

"They got a limited supply," Dream says as Val lets his eyes open again. "Better if they don't have control over it."

"I could fuse their mouth shut," Hunter offers.

"How long does it take?"

"Mouths are hard. Acid won't help either."

"Hm, too dangerous. Maybe just the legs."

Val struggles back to his feet. "Wait. Don't. Let me see if there's a tool . . ."

Dream holds out the metal tube, shaking it for the both of them to see. "Chemicals in here will knock a regular human out for a good long time. On me, or Val, that's enough to get us back to Innovation without complaint. And I don't think it was for me."

The hatchling is sputtering up acid like a broken engine.

"You had this on you in case you ran into Val here, didn't you?" Dream asks the hatchling who can't respond. "Which means word is spreading a lot faster than I like."

"Dream." Val totters up behind him, pulling on his coat. "Please let me check."

"It won't matter," Dream says, his steel gaze fixed on the hatchling. "This one likes their work a little too much."

When Val looks at the hatchling again, bound and broken as they are, he can see the strange look in their eyes. Even with their smashed jaw, Val knows a smile when he sees one. The strangled noises burbling out of their throat aren't just from the acid. Even their eyes are laughing.

"This one isn't like Matthew," Dream says. "The second we let 'em go, they'll either come after us, or go crawling back home for more weapons."

Val's eyes sting all over again. His heart is beating uncomfortably fast, heat prickling down his neck like more acid. "At least let me look. It's not good to let them run around with weapons. Someone else could get hurt."

Dream heaves a sigh and nods at Hunter as he pulls his flask off his hip. Unwilling to step away, Hunter drags the hatchling to a tree so they can pin them more effectively. Val can see the hatchling is already running low on acid, but he still feels an icicle of discomfort at the thought of getting spit on again. Only after ripping their wings off, pinning their hands with knives, and weighing them down with Hunter's own boots on top of the hatchling's back, does Hunter allow Val to get close enough to look.

"They said Knives already warned people about me," Val says to Hunter as he lays his hands on the hatchling's shoulders. They're face down with their mouth to the earth. "I've gone and made things harder for you two."

"Shut up," Hunter mumbles, perched like a massive gargoyle atop the hatchling. "Don't want to hear anymore self-sacrificial bullshit from you. We're not getting into the city without you. You'll fuck us over worse if you run away again."

"Oh." Val nods, giving a muted laugh as Hunter glares at him in the dark. "Okay. Sorry."

Hunter turns their face away, and Val almost smiles as he goes back to searching. This is probably the closest he'll get to Hunter actually asking Val to stay with them. The request may be aggressive, but Val can see the warmth at the core of it. Hunter believes that things will be worse if Val leaves.

Val smooths his hands over the hatchling's back, searching for the strange ringing of one of those objects, but panic begins to set in the longer he looks with no resonance coming to meet him. Only then does Val process that this hatchling doesn't smell sweet at all. They hardly smell like anything, except stomach acid and blood.

"It can't be," Val says it more to himself. "Why would . . . why would any of them do this if they didn't have an object?"

"You don't know how long they've been in the city," Hunter says, their glare softening on Val's distress. "Raised by spiders. Can't be good for you."

The last place Val checks is their head, wrapping his hands around the hatchling's temples and turning their face to the side so they can speak again.

"Do you like doing this?" Val asks.

Their split eyes find his, just as bright as the full moon, maybe even brighter. It's a look of euphoria, of adrenaline, of a job well done.

"They'll punish you for failing," Val says. "Won't they? Isn't that frightening?"

They don't blink, they don't look away, they simply stare at Val with a gleeful, dewy eyed grin, even with the broken jaw.

"You're wasting your time," Hunter says.

Val bites his lip, bites it hard enough to bleed and force his own body to heal the split.

"I can't accept this. We can't just let them go back to that city!" He looks at Hunter as his teeth start to chatter.

"We won't." Dream ambles up, shoving his flask into his coat again. "Hunter will shape him so he can't go anywhere."

"You just want to maim them and leave them here?" Val asks. "What if a human finds them and gets burned up in their acid? What if *Knives* finds them and undoes whatever Hunter changes?"

"Then what the fuck do you want to do?" Dream snaps.

"*We're* the only ones who can manage someone like this," Val says back, rising up to his feet. "We can keep them from hurting anyone else. All we have to do is keep them restrained and drain their acid, right?"

"You're asking us to take a killer into our group?" Dream asks.

"We took Hunter!" Val gestures at them. "*You* took *me*. And you've killed more than both of us combined! I don't understand what the problem is. We just need to keep them with us until we figure out a better solution. I'll talk to them. Maybe I can help them see reason."

"It's not a fucking pet, Val—I—*fuck*." Dream pinches the bridge of his nose and turns his gaze onto Hunter. "You, tell him how stupid this is."

"It's beyond stupid," Hunter says immediately, but they give a soft sigh. "Val also has a point. We're the only ones adept enough to deal with this. And it's best not to let any humans or Pillars trip on a stray hatchling. Outside of irrevocable torture that'd take way too long, we don't really have any good solutions. Besides, if anyone in this world can annoy someone until they change their mind, it's Val."

Dream scrubs at his eyes, groaning into the first dappled bits of early morning light. "What is this, a fucking mutiny? I thought I was calling the shots."

"I'm sorry, sir, I just think this is the fastest way to keep us moving toward our goal." Val faces him with his hands balled into fists. "If you want to use them as a shield, then so be it. But I just can't stomach the thought of cutting them to pieces and leaving them here for someone else. It's not fair. I'll regret it, I know I will. I can feel it in my stomach."

Scowling with the force of a shotgun aimed at Val's face, Dream closes the distance to loom over him. "Let it be known that I hate everything about this plan, it's borderline suicidal, you're a naive idiot, and if this little shit tries anything on any of us, I'm letting Hunter fuse their feet together and throwing them into the ocean."

Val beams at him, fresh relief cracking open in that hollow place in his chest. His voice is a whisper. "Thank you, sir."

"I don't want to hear a fucking word out of you complaining about this either," Dream says, poking Val in the chest. "And why the fuck are you naked?"

Val rubs at the back of his neck. "Uh. Acid."

Dream turns on his heel and starts walking back to camp. "Fuck this night. We're not gonna get any goddamn sleep for the rest of the trip."

Carefully, Hunter pulls the hatchling up off the ground. Their wounds immediately begin to heal, but when they spit onto the ground, it mostly looks like blood and regular saliva.

"We'll have to drain the acid every couple of hours or so," Hunter says. "Maybe more, depending on how fast they heal."

Val nods, stepping over to help wrangle the hatchling as their jaw snaps back into place.

"Merciful hunters," the hatchling says with a half-healed smile. "Are you going to hand deliver me back home? Very thoughtful."

"Yes, we're kind like that," Val says to them.

"Not kind enough to let you have your hands," Hunter adds. Guiding the hatchling's wrists behind their back, Hunter skewers both their palms with a knife and drives it into their back, to sheath it all in place.

The hatchling coughs again, eyes flashing wide from the pain. "Smart little hunters, smart, smart, very smart. You *are* a spider, after all, yes sir, yes sir."

Ignoring that, Val pushes them forward, toward camp. "Just be good and we won't have any problems. Doesn't that sound nice?"

"Mm, very nice," the hatchling sings back to him.

Hunter walks behind them, rope in one hand, knife in the other, eyes practically burning holes into the hatchling's head. As soon as they get back to the camp, Hunter ties the hatchling to another tree, too far away for it to spit at any of them, but close enough that the hatchling's ear-to-ear grin is in perfect view of all three of them.

"Master of Dreams," they call. "It's you, isn't it? You have the same lullaby as your twin."

Dream goes stock still, and Val holds his breath as sugar and smoke turns to shredding metal right in front of him.

"What a pretty song," the hatchling says, practically bouncing up and down in their ropes. "Yes, we all know about you. He sings about you in his sleep. To think! Threatening such terrible things, and you were supposed to be the *soft* one."

One peel of laughter is all the hatchling gets before the crack of a gunshot rips through the air and a bullet destroys half the hatchling's face in a splatter of pink and white and red. Val startles at the sight of Dream holding a shiny, engraved revolver in his hand, the barrel pointed in a perfectly straight line at the hatchling's head.

"Should take him at least half a day to heal that," Dream says, putting the gun back into his belt, tucked out of sight under his coat. "That's a couple hours of peace by my count."

When Dream looks at Val, Val's first instinct is to drop into a half-bow, like he would when the orphanage hands caught him out of bed after hours. "I'm sorry!"

"For what?" Dream asks, chin tilted up in a mask resembling a smile. "I feel better already."

10

Hunter and Val agree to take turns watching over the hatchling, and by the time their head is back in one piece, Val is ready to take the first shift. The hatchling wakes up laughing, as if they'd only been put on pause when Dream shot them, and Val kneels in front of them to get their attention. Aside from their strange eyes and wings, they look like a pretty human, chin length hair and messy bangs that maybe need a trim but otherwise, a person Val could have seen wandering around Indulgence with friends.

"Do you have a name?" he asks.

They give him a delighted smile. "No."

"Okay, No, it's nice to meet you," Val says, patting the hatchling's shoulder. "Are you a boy or a girl or something else?"

"I'm a fly, obviously," they say, bright lights in each of their split eyes. "See the wings?"

Val notes the silvery wings twitching awkwardly between their back and the tree trunk. "Alright, then. We're walking today. I don't think I need to remind you how pointless it would be to run. Our companion is quite a good shot."

"Oh, I'm not going anywhere," they promise with a smile. "This is much too fun. The master of Dreams and his pet spider. The human is a surprise though. Who does he belong to?"

"No one," Hunter grumbles, slinging his things around his waist and securing what Val is sure are several extra knives he didn't know about. Val doesn't know what answer he expected, but he'd kind of hoped to hear something else from Hunter.

"We'll have to drain your acid now," Val says to the hatchling. "You understand, No. Nothing personal."

"Well of course," they say, rising up to their feet as Val loosens the ropes binding them to the tree trunk. He checks their hands, still firmly held in place by the knife in their back. The skin of their palms has turned an angry red as their body tries to heal around the knife, but Hunter secured it much too tight to loosen. "But how will you get rid of it when I—"

Hunter breezes up to them, taking some of the rope from Val's hands and gagging the hatchling's open mouth with it. Yanking their head back, Hunter bends the hatchling's body forward so he can gut them with one of his toothier knives. The hatchling wretches around the rope in their mouth, and Val kneels down to look at the fluid spilling onto the ground. When he sees the telltale bubbling of acid chewing up the dirt and grass, he gives a thumbs up to Hunter.

"Right on target."

Hunter shakes the hatchling for good measure, and Val watches their stomach until it's only blood dripping onto the ground.

When Hunter lets them go, tossing the ropes to Val, the hatchling gives a drunken, post-sick smile. "Efficient."

Val smiles back. "Let's talk."

Hunter and Dream walk side by side behind Val and the hatchling, the two of them poised like loaded guns as Val holds the hatchling's ropes in both hands. The hatchling doesn't resist, walking at a comfortable pace for Val, their wings twitching every so often, like a person might blink.

"Where are you from, Mister No?" Val asks.

"Innovation," they say.

"Really? You were born there?"

They smile. "I was *reborn* there. On the Cardinal Major's table."

"Have you met the pillar of nightmares?" Val asks, keeping his voice amicable, despite the hateful aura pouring off his companions behind him. "I've been curious about him myself."

The hatchling's eyes seem to sparkle. "The master of Nightmares is far too important to meet with someone like me. But we all hear him sing while he sleeps. Can't be helped."

"Have you met all the spiders?" Val asks.

"They keep us in order," the hatchling says with a nod of their head. "The Cardinal Sentinels and the Queen. They teach us and they give us work and we are very happy."

"Queen?" Val prompts. "Is that the most important one of them?"

The hatchling's face devolves into a childish sort of blush, and Val wonders just how young this person was before hatching. "The Queen was the first. The Cardinal Major is the most perfect of us, but the Queen is the most beautiful. Hers was the first face I saw. She greets everyone in Innovation."

"Let me guess," Val says. "Is she friends with the master of Nightmares?"

The hatchling nods, pink in their cheeks and a shine in their eyes. "They are the best of friends."

Val can *hear* Dream bracing, like a massive tree shifting in a harsh wind, so Val puts his hand on the hatchling's shoulder. "What is it that the Queen wants? What does she hope to gain by killing all the pillars?"

The hatchling shakes their head, brows furrowing. "You make it sound like a war. This isn't a fight. We have no conflict to settle. Do you wonder why wolves kill rabbits? Why plants drink sunlight? It's because we were built to do so."

"Wolves need food," Val says. "You don't."

"Not for me," the hatchling tells him, and Val is pretty sure they haven't blinked for this entire conversation. "For the master of

Nightmares. You see? An assembly line. We do our job, we kill our prey, and then we come home and we give the food to the one who needs it. I will do this until I die and I will die knowing I did a good job. When does your job end, spider? Who is it that you feed?"

Val flinches away from them with a frown.

"What the fuck are you feeding my brother?" Dream asks, jabbing the hatching's shoulder with his cane.

The hatchling turns their beaming smile back on Dream. "Whatever he asks for."

Dream's expression quickly collapses into impatience, the tree pulling up its own roots just to crush something, but Val snags the hatchling's sleeve. "How do you know what he wants if you've never met him?"

"The Queen tells us," they answer immediately, and Val gives a sigh.

"Rather convenient how well your Queen knows the needs of someone you can't speak to."

"Yes, isn't she great?" the hatchling asks, and Val pats them on their head.

"That's enough talking for now, No."

"Don't worry." The hatchling turns to him, imploring. "If you're nervous about meeting the Queen, I know she'll like you. She likes all her spiders. Or are you worried that the Cardinal Major will be angry—frmph."

The hatchling's voice catches on a bit of rope as Hunter gags them again.

"He said enough," Hunter growls, yanking on the rope.

Val gives him a smile. "Thank you."

Hunter just shrugs.

"Seems pretty obvious to me that this Queen of theirs has Nightmare locked up somewhere." Val looks between Dream and Hunter. "Blaming an appetite on a man under lock and key, right?"

"Yeah," Dream pats his hands down his coat and heaves a sigh.

"Swear to god, if I don't smoke a cigarette in the next twenty-four hours, I'm gonna kill this idiot again. A couple times."

"Perhaps we can find a town to get some supplies?" Val offers.

"I can scout ahead," Hunter says. "Will you be okay with them?"

Val gives a tight smile. "I think Dream can shoot faster than they can run. We'll be alright."

With a nod, Hunter takes off ahead of them, and Dream drifts up to the space beside Val. He doesn't say anything, and Val gets a prickle of nerves that makes his palms sweat. Dream looks taller than ever, heartier somehow, and Val hates that it might be from anger alone.

"Dream?"

"Yeah?"

When Val opens his mouth, he looks over at the hatchling smiling in a daze, and puts the question away, choosing instead to wrap the ropes around his left arm, and to grab the edge of Dream's coat in the other hand.

"Thank you for trusting me," Val says.

"Mm."

"I really hope . . ." Val almost lets it go, but he knows if he doesn't say it now, he might not get it out of his throat the next time. For some reason, it makes his tongue swell in his mouth to say, "I really hope we find Mare for you."

Dream doesn't say anything, and Val thinks he should let go of the man's coat and let him walk, but Dream puts a heavy hand on top of Val's head, ruining Val's bangs with a ruffle of his hair, and lets his hand fall back to his side.

"Wish I could say 'he'll like you,'" Dream starts, voice turning to an ashy hush in his mouth. "But I don't know anymore."

"You didn't much like me when we first met," Val says. "Maybe I can grow on him."

"Pfft." Dream doesn't smile or laugh, but Val can still feel the heat of his hand. "We'll see, kid."

It takes him nearly a mile of walking to realize that Dream isn't leaning on his cane nearly so heavily. Val almost says something about how much lighter his tracks are in the earth, but then Hunter comes back to guide them toward a tiny village of people, and it doesn't feel worth mentioning.

"There's an odd feeling out there," Hunter warns them. "We shouldn't stay any longer than we have to. And we definitely can't let them see the hatchling."

"The people out here are still living in the shadow of Innovation," Dream says. "Not quick to trust. Just give me an hour, I'll get what I need and come back."

"I'll watch from a distance," Hunter says, and as soon as Dream starts crowing about how he'll be fine, Hunter just repeats himself, slower. "I will watch from a distance."

"Fuck, you two are worse than family," Dream mutters, walking off with a scowl.

"Oh, Hunter." With an reassuring tug on the hatchling's restraints, Val walks up to him as Dream's mumbling gets quieter in the distance.

Hunter doesn't step back from Val, but he looks like he wants to, like he's steeling himself against an oppressive sound or smell. Val doesn't know why this makes him smile, but it does. He should probably feel guilty for unsettling Hunter like this, but Val only puffs up like a happy bird the more Hunter lets on that he doesn't know what to do with Val.

"Be careful, please," Val says. "I think Dream is very tender right now. I'm more worried about his emotions than I am about someone trying to hurt him."

Hunter nods. "I know. If he tries to fill his flask, I'll break the bottle."

Val laughs, which makes Hunter angle his body away for some reason.

"Would you like your knife back?" Val pulls Hunter's knife out by the blade from the pocket he had it in. "It's unsheathed, so I'll probably wind up slicing my own clothes off or something stupid. Best for you to have it, right?"

Hunter makes a quiet noise, reaching into one of his packs with a frown and then throwing something at Val before taking off into the woods to tail Dream. Val barely catches an empty sheath, nearly cutting himself with the knife as he flails to grab it. He supposes Hunter would rather have Val more armed with the hatchling around, even though he feels like he just proved himself completely useless once again. A small flame of an idea flickers in the back of Val's head as he thinks, *is this a gift from Hunter?* So he sheaths it with a smile.

The sound of retching draws his eye, and Val turns to see the hatchling with acid burbling out of their mouth. It sizzles against the ropes that Hunter bound them with, but hasn't quite done any real damage yet.

"Were you storing some?" Val asks, walking over with the knife. "Or do you heal faster than we thought?"

The hatchling only burbles, eyes alight with mischief. Val pushes the hatchling's head forward, feeling around the back of their neck with his fingers for a good place to cut. He tries to remember the quickest way to kill someone, like the clean and precise way that Dream did it to him the first day they met. As he's pressing into soft skin, the hatchling coughs again.

"Don't worry, spider, I'm not trying to run. I only wished to speak with you."

"Oh." Val kneels beside the hatchling, still holding their face away by their hair. "Then you won't mind spitting up any more of that acid? If you don't, I'll have to waste our precious alone time trying and failing to cut it out of you. I don't have nearly the same control as Hunter or Dream."

The hatchling's left eye zips over to Val and they give a slightly less boisterous smile. "Ah, yes, of course."

"Thank you," Val says, smiling brightly. "I look forward to our conversation."

The woods between the southern coast and the deadlands smell strongly of life. It's overwhelming in the same way that overripe fruit is, as though the trees themselves are fit to burst. As Hunter perches in the branches of a tall, pale pine, he finds himself treading more lightly than he normally might, for fear of wounding the tree. They feel as though they'll bleed at the slightest bruising.

This village feels the same. Hunter watches Dream approaching the trodden footpath, joining up with an empty road leading into a bare-bones collection of buildings, and the hair on the back of his neck stands on end. There are no visible bodies, but Hunter can sense the people hiding behind their doors. They probably scattered at the first whiff of an outsider, and now they lurk inside, waiting to see what kind of person Dream is.

Dream approaches the half-torn awning of a general store, disappearing behind the unlocked door, and Hunter moves to a different tree with the light steps of someone walking on a thin layer of ice. With a looking glass, he can just barely see two shadows moving around through a filmy window. With his breath held, Hunter can sense the pitter-patter of nervous feet, and the brash *step, thunk, step, thunk* of Dream's uncaring gait. With his eyes closed, Hunter can smell old taffy that has long since melted and reformed inside its plastic packaging, gun powder packed in glass, hair wax caked into metal tins, a human woman with sweat in her hairline, and Dream's vivid blood.

Hunter braces for the entirety of the transaction, money passing hands and cigarettes rustling into pockets, waiting for Dream to exit the building with pressure filling his lungs. Dream wants to smoke so badly, Hunter can feel a craving in his own throat. Dream lights up as he's walking back out, his cane hooked over his arm—he's been doing this more and more, his range of movement improving in degrees the further out they travel—and no one else comes out to greet him, though Hunter catches the curtains swaying in one of the windows. Dream exhales a cloud of smoke, the only person in this entire village who's actually breathing in that moment.

As soon as Dream steps off the dirt path into the woods, Hunter joins back up with him.

"Relax," Dream says. "They're just scared."

"Just because they have the right to be afraid, doesn't mean they'll be smart about it," Hunter says.

"They're just human," Dream says. "Couldn't hurt me if they wanted to."

"Who's to say Knives hasn't been through to sell them cursed bullets?" Hunter asks.

"Well isn't that a pleasant thought," Dream mutters, taking another drag.

"Are they going to come after Val?" Hunter asks next, looking at Dream's face, much as it fazes him to. There is still a constriction in his chest every time he does this, a quiet alarm that asks him to look away, but he wants Dream's honesty more in that moment.

Dream lets smoke waft out between his teeth as he thinks, like the grate over a car engine. "We're going right to Innovation. No reason for them to send someone after him if he's walking right up to the doors anyway. No, it's when we hit the city that they'll try to separate us. You know they'll kill you first, right?"

Hunter nods. Of course he knows this.

"Or, maybe they'll put a tool inside you," Dream muses, looking at his cigarette. "Damn, tobacco's still better down here."

Hunter narrows his eyes. "Are you trying to scare me?"

Dream shrugs. "I guess so, yeah. Not even good at that anymore."

Hunter looks away as the constriction returns in a painful fist at the center of his chest. "I hate to be the bearer of bad news, but you're always going to be better at inspiring others, not scaring them off. It's in your title."

Dream makes a sound, a haunted attempt at a laugh that digs into Hunter's ears. "Well, fuck me. Should've put that together a couple decades ago."

"I assumed that's why you were alone for so long," Hunter adds quietly. "To avoid people . . . wanting to be near you."

"People who follow me have a real bad habit of trying to die for me," Dream says with the bluntness of a machete. "I doubt it'll do any good for me to say that I think you'd be better off living, especially because I know you're worried about the kid too. But I'll say it anyway, useless as it may be. I think you should use this tranq on Val, sling him over your shoulder, and run as fast as you can in the other direction. Leave Innovation to me. I'm not as fragile as I look."

Pulling the metal cylinder from his coat, Dream waves the tranquilizer in front of Hunter's face, and Hunter snatches it out of his hand on instinct. It's not technically a bad plan. Hunter knows very well how sharp Dream's senses are when he chooses to use them. He's been taking care to build himself an impressive array of weaponry, hidden on the inside of that tacky coat. It must weigh twenty extra pounds on his shoulders for the bulk of it. There's a good chance that, without having to worry about others, Dream could get exactly as far as he wanted to, and therein lies the problem.

"Do you think I'm dumb enough to believe you're trying to send us away just for our safety?" Hunter asks him.

"Hm." Dream gives a husky laugh, his lips pulling into an uneven smile. "You should be mad at me for that. Maybe mad enough to take your leave."

Hunter pushes himself into Dream's path, wheeling around to stare at Dream with his cigarette half raised to his mouth. There's only a few inches of height difference between them, but Hunter takes everything he can get to force Dream to stop and look at him.

"You are a Pillar. I'm your Eye. If you give me an order, I'll follow it. If you tell me to let you die, I will. If you tell me to incapacitate Val and drag him to the eastern coast so the people in Innovation can't find him, I will. But until you order it, I'm not going to put that on him. It'd be a full time job just to stop him from coming to look for you anyway. So if the time comes and you want to send us away, you better be real specific about how you tell it to me. I'll follow your order to the letter, understood? Nothing more, nothing less."

Dream's teeth clench behind his closed mouth, and he exhales through his nose, a rusted anger in his eyes that makes Hunter glad he has the few inches he does on the man. He may not have been able to say this without it. Even now, his heart is pounding uncomfortably loudly in his own ears.

"This is why I didn't want you with me," Dream says, a sharp edge to his quiet voice, like the tip of a dagger poking out from the edge of his sleeve. "Either of you."

"I know," Hunter says. "Be mad about it when we're done, or buck up and tell me to go now. I don't take suggestions."

"Fucking unbearable," Dream says, taking a harsh breath on his cigarette, singeing away the last knuckle's length of it before he grinds it into the dirt with his heel. "I thought you'd be better at reasoning than him."

"You know I am," Hunter says, finally relaxing his shoulders as he puts the tranq away. "You also know how I work. Pretend all you want that you don't know who we are, but the Eyes all know you. You're one of the originals. I am who I am because of you."

"Ah, shut up." Dream starts moving again, leaning on the cane like he was before, and Hunter falls into step beside him.

"Don't put that on me," Dream says.

"Put what?"

"*You*. Them. Any of that. I'm not the same Dream anymore."

Hunter hears the smoke of bitterness in his voice, glancing at Dream's bunched up jaw muscles, and he shakes his head. "You're right. I'm not following that Dream. I'm following you."

"Thought I hired you to protect Val," Dream says, giving Hunter a sidelong glare, but it's starting to lose its edge.

Hunter shrugs. "You and I both know where Val wants to be. Protecting him *is* protecting you."

Dream gives a hush of a laugh, and the tension finally starts fizzling away. "You think the hatchling's driving Val crazy by now? That's gotta be what it wants, right? To get inside our heads or whatever."

"Maybe," Hunter says. "It doesn't feel as unstable as other hatchlings have, but it doesn't exactly feel human either. Matthew was worse off when we first met him, but he cleared up faster."

"If Val's smart, he'll have killed it again to save himself some breath," Dream adds. "But, well."

"It's Val," Hunter finishes.

Dream gives another, louder laugh and rubs at his eyes. "How the hell did I get stuck with all o' you?"

Hunter doesn't say anything. They've already answered that one.

The rest of the walk is a little more peaceful, if peace can exist on slowly melting ice. At least Hunter has something more pressing to focus on now. As they approach the spot where they left Val and the hatchling behind, Hunter can smell the acidity like boiling blood. It must be healing, which means Val might be in trouble, but his presence is nothing more than an unloaded gun at the moment. Every step that brings him closer solidifies Val's shape in the distance. Even the Pillars with their unmistakably vibrant auras don't compare to the pure metallic sharpness that defines Val. Dream is loud, and hopelessly bright, but Val is a weapon even when he isn't.

The silence of the two bodies puts Hunter on edge. Maybe Dream feels it too because they both start walking faster. He expected tension, or at least voices, or maybe even the death tone of the hatchling as it healed from another lethal wound, but this *quiet* is much more suspicious. Cataloging the weapons on his body, Hunter pieces together a few different routes to the tree he tied the hatchling to, so he can throw something from a distance without risk of acid getting on himself or Dream. He's making a decision about the fastest way to kill if the hatchling has overpowered Val when Dream calls out to him.

"Val?"

"Ah, welcome back!"

Hunter doesn't relax at all as the two of them come back into view. Val is sitting with his back to the very tree Hunter had tied the hatchling to, and the hatchling is lying with their head in Val's lap. Their hands are still pinned to their spine, but there are no other restraints on them. Their eyes are closed as Val pushes his fingers through their dust colored hair, and Hunter has an utterly nauseating image of a man and a dog at rest, except this man is younger than Hunter, and the dog spews acid when it wants.

"The fuck are you doing?" Dream barks, gesturing out at the two of them.

Val smiles, sunlight glinting off the tip of an arrowhead. "I've made us a new friend."

⬥

Lunch is an uncomfortable thing. They really only do it for Hunter's sake anyway, since he's the only one who needs to eat routinely. As he crouches on the grass and picks through his available stores—all of them low, he has to get more, but when will he have time—Val smiles at him.

"May I have a little?"

Hunter passes him the dregs of the berries he found on the way to the village, assuming it's for Val after he had to heal that acid. Val puts one in his own mouth and then holds a second out to the hatchling.

"When's the last time you had food?" Val asks them.

The hatchling shuffles up to him on their knees, eyes all wet and bright, their hands still pinned to their back in a picture of a helpless, supplicant creature. It turns Hunter's stomach to watch Val touch the hatchling's mouth to feed them.

"Real convenient that you waited 'til we were gone to make your little friendship pact," Dream says, pointing at the hatchling.

The hatchling *whines*, shoulders shrugging as they turn away from him, and Dream rolls his eyes.

"What did you promise, huh?" Dream asks, looking down at the hatchling. "Obedience? Treasure? Keys to the city?"

Val puts his hand on the hatchling's hair again—why must he do that—and answers for them. "I asked more about their Queen. Turns out maybe she's not so lovely after all. Poor thing hasn't been shown any kindness since they woke up a year ago. Was the berry good?"

The hatchling nods repeatedly, looking at Val with the shine of a zealot in their gaze. "I won't hurt Mister Val. I promise. I'll be good and nice."

"No offense, but Val's the only one who can't get permanently damaged by you," Dream says. "Not a very *promising* promise on your part."

The hatchling shrinks away with a pout, putting their forehead on Val's shoulder. "I'll do whatever Mister Val wants."

"I would like you to help keep all of us safe," Val says, hand on the back of the hatchling's neck. "And also to pick a name for me to call you by."

The hatchling nods again and—gods above *and* below, they're blushing. Hunter exhales through his nose.

"They haven't tried to separate their hands?" Hunter asks.

"No," Val says.

"Or spit on you?"

"Nope!" Val looks pleased as a summer's day and Hunter narrows his eyes as he rises back to his feet.

He gestures with his head for Dream to come closer, and Hunter lowers his voice to say in Dream's ear. "This one's stupid."

"No shit," Dream mutters back. "The kind of stupid that's gonna try to kill us in our sleep because it thinks we're being mean? Or the kind of stupid that does what it's asked and nothing else?"

Hunter glances back at the two of them, the hatchling with their four eyes packed into two sockets, all focused on Val with the slightest pink tinge in their cheeks as they open their mouth for another offered berry. It's embarrassing—the hatchling acting like a fucking child, and Hunter immediately realizing that he could have fed Val by his own hand and didn't.

"They're not gonna risk upsetting Val," Hunter grumbles. "Not for now anyway. If we're nice to it too, that acid could be a boon."

"Yeah, yeah," Dream huffs. "Had the same thought."

When they turn back around, Dream stamps his cane into the dirt like he's calling a meeting. "Fine. If it's good for the day, maybe we'll untie its hands tomorrow."

The hatchling perks up, their wings buzzing for a brief moment. "You *are* kindly, Dream."

Dream's face collapses like a dying star, and Val perfectly times a pat on the hatchling's head to distract. "See? My friends are good people."

The hatchling looks it's going to start weeping on Val, and Hunter feels the void between his fingers where a knife could be.

When the four of them start walking again, it's the same formation. Val and the hatchling take the lead, with Hunter and Dream behind them. The trees are getting more and more sparse as they go, and the grass beneath their feet is slowly turning yellow, as if dyed by the sunlight above. Hunter hasn't spent as much time out here in the shadows of Innovation, but he can feel the proximity like the extra acid in the hatchling's stomach.

"What would you like to be called?" Val is asking for a name.

"O-oh, I wouldn't know about names," the hatchling says. "None of us have names, only titles."

"Then you should have a fancy one," Val says. "To make up for the year without it."

The hatchling looks like a lovesick teenager and Hunter wants to gag them again just to free himself from all the stuttering, but that won't help.

"Philomena!" Val exclaims, then shakes his head. "Alexander? I'm not very good at this."

The hatchling is practically shivering. "Anything you'd want to call me is better than nothing."

Val puts his hand on the hatchling's shoulder. "You should pick your own name. It's not fair of me to give you one. And you can always change it later. It's only a sound, after all."

"You're very wise, Mister Val."

When Dream pats Hunter's chest with a gruff laugh and mumbles, "yeah, stupid is right," Hunter realizes he's hardly been paying attention to their surroundings.

"I'm going to scout ahead," Hunter says, peeling away from the group at a dead sprint.

He hears Val calling after him, "Be safe!"

The noise and the sights and the smells are unbearable. Hunter runs until he finds a tree tall enough to give him any kind of sight lines, scurrying into another layer of atmosphere so he can finally breathe again. It's been twelve hours since he fucked Val, and he's not really sure he ever walked out of that tent. He left one of his senses in there, and now it's packed neatly between Val's hands, leaving him dazed. If Val hadn't been standing right there when Hunter woke up, it wouldn't have happened. He would have laid back down in his hammock, dug out his kit, and pricked himself with a needle until his head stopped ringing. But, no, it had to be Val offering warmth and whispers of concern, fresh from a dream where Hunter was trapped behind Mare's eyes as Dream wound around him like a guilty snake.

He thought that bringing up Dream and Mare's *relationship* would have disgusted one of them enough to quell any kind of desire for intimacy, but it seemed to open the door directly to it. Even the chill of the night air wasn't enough to pull the memory of Dream's hands off of him. Closing himself off with Val was desperation. The way it lingers is something else—like sweet smoke filling his head. Hunter presses his cheek to tree bark, attempting to overwrite the sense memory crowding in. Heated darkness, soft flesh between his teeth, Val's tongue, wet between his fingers. It's a good thing Hunter couldn't see his face. He's pretty sure he'd be blind now if he also had visuals crowding in beside the scent, and the feel, and the taste, and the sound.

He can barely fucking see now anyway.

Biting his lip to focus, Hunter turns back to the landscape to look for a path. The line they've been walking is a straight shot to low, treeless fields which won't do well for cover. They need to curve back toward the archipelago of coastal towns dotting the way toward Innovation, hostile as they may be. It's a longer walk, but it'll be easier to hide in their shadows, even if they risk pissing off the locals. If the hatchling really does behave, they can avoid detection if they're careful. If it comes down to it, Hunter would rather risk humans coming after them than more hatchlings or spiders.

They are very lucky indeed that Val is on their side.

When Hunter tastes blood from biting his own lip, he climbs back down to the ground, spends five minutes scraping mushrooms off a tree stump, and returns to the others. The silence between point A and point B brings back the ghost of Mare's voice coming out of Hunter's throat. *I missed you, you oaf. Why do you always want to travel so much? I'm right here. I'm right here . . . please.*

The desperation of someone else's heart racing in Hunter's chest, Dream's smirk on a younger, sun-drenched man, and hands. Oh god, the hands. Hunter almost trips on the roots of a tree, dropping into a crouch in the middle of the woods with his own hands over his eyes. Only they're not his hands, they're Dream's, smoothing over his face, sanding down his jagged edges.

I want to stay here but I know how much it hurts you. If I could give you this silence, I would. I didn't tell it to you right the first time.

It's Mare's blood racing in his veins, deciding by the logic of a dream that if his brother can still stand to touch him, he'll be forgiven. Teeth chattering, Hunter's knees press into the grass while hands that don't feel like his drag down his chest. He braces his shoulder against the trunk of a tree, turning his face toward the bark as surely someone *else* reaches through the folds of his clothes. These hands are too big to be Val's, but as they tighten around Hunter's cock, squeezing the breath from his lungs at the same time, it's Val's voice purring in his head.

Your hair really is pretty.

And then it's his old instructor, the Eye-turned-Hand who showed Hunter how to be an animal.

Humans who set down their roots are not to be bothered. We aren't like them. The moment you stop moving is the moment you surrender. You listen well, so I know you'll be good at this.

How wrong they were. Hunter shivers with the sun on his back as he touches himself in the middle of the woods, his panting breaths unrecognizable to his own ears. It was the same with Val. He heard a sound like an angry wolf as he tried to drown himself in Val's cunt, and only after did the sound catch up to him as his own miserable growl. He will be completely useless by the end of this journey, but if he can keep Dream alive and Val free of capture, he'll at least have done something good with this body. He should have surrendered his eyes already. Maybe that's why he can't see the way he used to—his vision is past its expiration. By right, his hands will follow after, and then his tongue. The least he can do is give them to Dream and Val before they become useless.

Hunter will never understand the way Val looks at him. He doesn't even look at Dream like that. Maybe Val can sense Hunter unraveling like old yarn. Maybe that's why Hunter wants to lay at his feet.

By the time Hunter finds the others to tell them they have to adjust their path, the sun is creeping toward the horizon.

"There's some kind of campground if we start toward the mountains," Hunter explains. "Looked abandoned. We can reach it by midnight if we don't stop."

"What would we do without you?" Val asks with a shiny smile.

Hunter turns away from his diamond gaze. "Something incredibly dumb."

Val laughs. "Probably."

Hunter hears Dream twisting open the top of his empty flask.

⟡

The campgrounds are littered with the husks of big, communal tents seated on wooden platforms that are home to more wildlife than anything else. Dream immediately claims one and tells them all to leave him alone while he has a cigarette or two in *fucking peace*. Pale smokes drifts out of his tent while Val investigates the adjacent one, pointing at it with a hopeful glint before Hunter ducks his head in and assures him it is full of poison ivy.

Val laughs and scratches the back of his neck. "Oops."

Three tents later, Hunter finds one passable for Val to occupy without risking hours of precious healing energy. The hatchling promptly sits down in front of Val's tent like a guard dog, and Hunter tries not to let pettiness get the better of him as he thinks about knocking the hatchling over like a turtle onto its shell.

"Just stay with me," Val says, and Hunter is about sick to death of Val's peachy words toward the hatchling, until he feels Val's hand on his arm, and Hunter almost jumps out of his skin.

"What?" He stares down at Val as he would the barrel of Dream's revolver.

"Stay here," Val says, pointing at the tent. "I can still feel Dream so I assume you can too. If you're going to have more nightmares, I'd rather it be easier for you to get to me."

Hunter feels like he stepped on a nail, and Val covers his mouth as he laughs.

"Don't give me such a scary look," Val says. "You don't have to if you don't want. Dream won't notice if you sneak back over to him. You're good at that. Sneaking. I wish I could do that too."

"*Stop.*"

Hunter feels the fabric of Val's shirt on his fingers before he realizes he's grabbed the front of it.

"Sorry," Val breathes at him and his eyes have gone wide, but not out of fear.

"That's not . . ." *my hand.*

Hunter exhales and walks out of the tent, hoping Val doesn't follow after him. He's hungry and tired and he needs to get some of this weight off his shoulders before he can sit still again. It's not fair that Val propositions him so easily. That's obviously what he meant. Hunter will have more nightmares, he'll start to spiral, and Val will put himself in the way of it. The longer he thinks about it, the more Hunter's scalp prickles at the memory of Val pulling his hair. If he does that again—Hunter shakes the thought away.

The trees are thicker here at the base of a modest mountain, a bit like knuckles poking up out of the ground from a clenched fist, and the four of them have settled around the tallest one. Maybe in the morning, Hunter will scale it and get a better look at everything around them. That'll help. But for now, he finds a sturdy tree to climb, pulls out his lighter, and carefully inserts one of his needles into his skin. Not enough to bleed, just enough to draw his attention back to his body.

Skin, and muscle, and bone, and blood. Hunter only thinks about the places where the needle touches, dotting all down different limbs until the forest stops smelling like his companions and instead like plants and animals and atmosphere. The sharp yet soft touch of pain makes the flesh beneath it sing until everything else starts to melt away.

Hunter opens their eyes again, vision adjusting to the night, lungs full of clean air. Dream has entered his stasis once more. Val is flitting around his tent, and the hatchling is still dutifully guarding out front. Hunter comes back down to earth, wishing they could so easily pin their own hands down like they did the hatchling's, but that would be much too easy. As they head back toward Val, they make a decision: if Val is touching the hatchling again, they'll go sit at Dream's feet instead. If not, they'll make a deal with the hatchling. It's time to focus on the damn job.

Voices float through the trees before Hunter reaches the tent.

"Mister Val, would you like me to go fetch the human for you?"

"No, no, Hunter can do what he needs to do," Val says. "He wouldn't just leave us."

"Mister Val, you look anxious."

Val laughs. "Is that what it is? I suppose you would know better. You have more eyes than me."

Hunter bites their tongue, waits three more minutes to the second, and then stomps back over toward Val's tent. The hatchling leans toward them as soon as Hunter enters a pool of dim lamplight, mouth open to alert Val, but Hunter stalks over to turn them around, grab the knife in the small of the hatchling's back, and rip it out of place.

"Pick a name already," Hunter snaps.

"Oh, oh, that hurts! Oh, wait, I . . ." The hatchling brings their bleeding hands around to their front, and then shows them to Hunter, as if they don't know what they're looking at. "Did you mean to do this? It isn't morning."

"If you're going to fight with us, you'll need your hands," Hunter says, tossing them the knife. "Do you want to earn your place with Val or not?"

The hatchling clutches the handle of the knife, eyes wide, and it's not entirely dissimilar to how Val used to look at Hunter. Strange.

"Yes, yes I do," the hatchling sputters. "I'll be good and loyal. You'll see!"

Val claps his hands together from behind the hatchling, startling Hunter. "Look, see!" He drops down to crouch beside the hatchling. "A gift of trust. Why don't you go clean yourself up? Oh, I have a wonderful idea. Would you be able to watch out for us tonight? I'm afraid we're all very tired, so it might be nice for us to get a little bit of guarded rest. I'm sorry, is that too much to ask of you?"

The hatchling holds the knife to the front of their shirt, nodding at Val with feverish intent. "I'll make sure Mister Val and his friends stay safe."

"If you see anything dangerous, any other hatchlings or spiders, yell nice and loud, alright?" Val asks. "But don't hurt any humans. They can't heal like us."

"Yes, sir," the hatchling says, breaking into another delirious grin. "In the morning, will you tell me if I did a good job?"

"Of course," Val says.

Hunter feels like they're standing on shifting sand as they are thrown back to memories of first meeting Val and Dream, the strange rapport they held with each other, and how bizarre it was to witness.

As the hatchling goes running off with a childish laugh, Val pops back up to stand in front of Hunter, eye to eye for once, thanks to the wooden platforms holding the tents up. Hunter has to watch Val's face break out into a huge, horrifyingly perfect grin. Even with all his time walking outside, Val's perfectly dimpled face doesn't show a trace of it. Hunter has seen their own hands reacting to their shift in routine, color creeping into their skin that they haven't seen since they were a child, and Dream seems to drink up sunlight like a hungry plant as his skin effortlessly tans darker day by day. Val looks the most fragile of them all, but there is no marking him, not by knife or sunlight, not unless *he* wants it.

"Thank you," Val says.

Hunter's face draws into a frown and they turn their gaze. "It's better if they're helping us."

"You're trusting me," Val clarifies. "We've come so far from you threatening to bury me alive."

"Don't push your luck," Hunter mumbles, stepping past Val and into the tent.

Hunter starts setting their things down, all their extra packs, and then their boots, and some of their weapons. Val wanders back in as well, his mouth barely containing the beaming smile he obviously wants to wear. Hunter uses their hammock like a sheet over top of one of the slowly decaying cots and sprawls out, deciding to keep to themself how nice it feels to stretch their body against a hard sur-face. Reaching above their head, Hunter's back cracks like a firework popping, and Val laughs.

"Would you like me to walk on your back?" he asks.

"You don't know how to do that," Hunter says, closing their eyes to take a breath of musty air, warring with Val's own uncomfortably clean scent.

And Hunter's eyes fly open as Val sits on their stomach. "You've got me there, but I bet I could learn."

"Probably," Hunter admits, staring at Val's shamelessness.

Val slides his feet free of his shoes, peeling his socks off with his thumb. "I get covered in acid and stabbed and bitten for Dream, but it makes him feel guilty, so he doesn't ever ask for more. You don't ask me for *anything*. Ever."

Tucking his legs up, Val sits cross-legged on top of Hunter, turning to face them. "I keep trying to guess so you don't have to ask, but it's not getting me very far. Are all humans this hard to read, or is it just you?"

"You've spent more time with regular humans than I have," Hunter says. "I'm good at one thing, Val. Just . . . let me be good at that."

Val shifts forward, leaning his hands on Hunter's chest. "You *are* very good at that. But it has to take its toll on you. If I could help Dream in more ways than this, I would, but I don't think he'll let me. Will you?"

Hunter wants to turn away from Val's searchlight gaze, but they're quite literally stuck underneath of him. Moving Val means touching Val—touching Val—*touching Val.*

"I don't want pity," Hunter whispers.

Val's eyes flash and he inches up a little closer, sliding his legs to either side of Hunter's torso to straddle their waist.

"It's not pity," he whispers back.

There he goes again, bullets in the chamber, arrow nocked and ready. Hunter breathes through their nose, reminding themself what a spider smells like.

"I've always liked humans, but also I didn't. They're kind of mean. And gross," Val says with a laugh that carries the sting of cleaning solution. "I'm sure if I locked myself in a basement and never saw another person again, I'd stop feeling like this, but the more I'm around other living things, the more I want to understand them."

It's like he's taking all the air out of the room, thinning the atmosphere down until Hunter's lungs are full of him. The only oxygen on the whole damn mountain is coming from Val's slightly parted lips.

"Tell me more about you," Val says.

"You don't get it," Hunter responds, weak in the wake of Val's excitement. "There's nothing *to* me. You've already seen everything."

Val leans forward to grip Hunter's shoulders, and they flinch like Val's gaze might burn them. "No, no you're thinking about it backwards. You think you're only made up of these automatic responses, but that's the animal. That's not *you*. You're only looking through one window, b-but there's a whole house."

Listening to Val trip over his own words out of adrenaline makes Hunter wonder if this is what Val would be like under Dream's euphoric spell, if he could be affected by that. His pupils have erased the color of his irises, and Hunter sees the darkness of the tent in his gaze. There's a bit of red in Val's cheeks and Hunter can taste his skin again.

"Why are you so determined?" Hunter asks.

"Because *you fascinate me*," Val says with a breathlessness and a high-cheeked blush, like he's asked Hunter to get naked, but that's not what it is, not exactly. Val swallows, the slight swell of his larynx pushing against the thin velvet of his throat, and Hunter's body reacts without permission, warmth pooling around the muscles of their hips.

"I didn't realize it fully until I spoke with the hatchling," Val carries on, his face only inches from Hunter's as he speaks almost too quickly to understand. "Every moment since you joined up with us has been new for you. We broke your routine and you're stumbling your way around just as much as the hatchling is, you're just better at hiding it. You're learning something every single day just by being around us, and I can't stop watching. Isn't that exciting? You get to pick everything you do from now on, and I-I want to see what it looks like on you. All of it."

Val licks his lips, taking a stuttering breath like he forgot he had to do that. He probably did.

Hunter can't move.

"I'm sorry," Val adds with a clipped laugh. "You said I didn't have to pretend to be normal. The truth is that if there was a way for me to look inside your body without hurting you, I would. It's not really fair, you know? You're so strong and-and capable, but if I put my hand inside your chest, you'd probably die. I just wish I could touch even more, you know? Like if I could feel your heart beating against my own fingers, I might finally understand how it works. You could do it to me sometime if you wanted. Imagine coming back to life with your hand in my chest."

The look on Val's face is some mind-rending mix of arousal and intoxication. Hunter is worried they'll be crushed by the weight of this slender body on top of theirs.

"Val."

Their voice leaves their throat like an anvil. Val's eyes flash, and he bolts upright, slapping his hands over his mouth as the red in his cheeks flushes to a darker, more embarrassed shade.

"I shouldn't have said that," he says through his fingers.

Hunter isn't quite sure *it's fine* is the honest response, but unfortunately, nothing but dead air sits on their tongue.

With a manic sort of laugh, Val shoves his bare feet into his shoes, grabbing his socks off the floor and jamming them into his pockets. "I'm going to see if the hatchling needs help!"

"Val," Hunter calls after him, but it's not enough to bring him back.

Covering their eyes with their hands, Hunter breathes instead, trying to pick apart everything Val just said. His words pile on top of Hunter's chest, replacing the weight of Val's body until it starts to squeeze the air out of their lungs. Too many things, really, for one brain to think about without going mad. With eyes shut tight, Hunter tries to cut the mess apart until they can stand to handle the pieces. What they are left with still feels much too hot to touch, but Hunter forces themself to turn each thing over in their head until it stops burning. There are many things, kernels of strange truths that Hunter could spend days or weeks analyzing, but the thing that sticks like a sword through their gut is much simpler than that.

Val believes this is the beginning, not the end.

Hunter covers their mouth at the sudden feeling like they've cracked an egg they didn't mean to. Their skin is hot, temples buzzing, eyes wide.

How many more rooms are inside them?

⬥

Val doesn't actually go out to find the hatchling, he just tucks himself into the shadow of a tree between Hunter and Dream and tries to force his mind to stop going in circles. He really said too much. Humans would never offer to do that to one another. Just because Val feels safe with these people doesn't mean he can say whatever he wants without consequence.

Head pressed to the tops of his knees, Val listens to Dream's lullaby, a soft, sunlit melody that does not suit the nightmares he now knows are spilling out of him. Oh, that's right. If Hunter falls asleep, Val should stay close by, so he doesn't wake up from a bad dream all alone. Popping back up, Val jogs to his tent with marbles in his stomach. The lamp that he and the hatchling found has become a beacon for every moth in the surrounding area, dimming the light as if the bulb were dying.

Val tries not to make any noise as he slips back into the tent to sit on his sleeping bag. Against the further wall, Hunter lays on their side, facing away from Val. When Val listens to them, he receives the smallest bit of feedback from Hunter's presence, like someone whispering two rooms away. It doesn't feel like sleep, but it doesn't feel like anger or fear either, which is better than he hoped for.

As he takes his socks and shoes off again, pulling his legs up onto the wooden bed frame, his gaze hinges on the tallest point of Hunter's shoulder, not entirely unlike the mountain they're camped out at the base of.

"Val."

He goes stock still, breath held.

"The insects inside Innovation."

Val starts to breathe again.

"Are they hiding from humans?"

Confusion pries Val's mouth open as he frowns. "What do you mean?"

Hunter turns onto their back, winding their arms underneath their head to stare at the top of the tent. "You said being around living things makes you want to understand them."

Val's face burns as he hears words that now sound like a drunken confession.

"Are they scared of us?" Hunter asks. "Of the things we make them feel?"

Gaze dropping to his knees, Val lets himself remember Knives. *Names are for humans, or those who wish to pretend.*

"Knives, the Cardinal Major," Val starts, his mouth drying up like the title itself is soaking up his spit. "I think he hates humans. He finds them irrational. I tried to give him a name, so we could talk easier. He was very cross with me for that. Said that spending time with humans makes you useless."

Hunter turns onto their side, looking at Val like an owl in the dim light. "I keep wondering why the insects aren't more of a constant problem. Why they aren't roaming around and killing people at will. Maybe it's because the spiders are bringing them to Innovation as soon as they can, so they're away from human influence."

Val's mouth opens and shuts. He puts his hand over his chest, finding the exact two ribs that Knives slipped a blade between. "He wasn't supposed to stop. Knives was on his way back to Innovation, but he pulled me aside to talk to me. His assistant was complaining about it. I think I distracted him. Maybe this is why . . ."

Hunter hums. "Not even the Cardinal Major is immune to you."

Val's gaze darts over to them, but Hunter turns onto their back again, eyes closed. "What do you mean by that?"

With a huff that's stumbling on its way to laughter, Hunter just says, "Thank you for telling me you want me to live."

Val straightens up like he's been electrocuted, gripping his sleeping bag as he leans toward Hunter.

"Even if you did say it in the strangest way possible," Hunter mutters, and Val bites his lip to counteract the goofy grin trying to take hold of his face. "Can't say anyone's ever told me they want to put their hands in my organs. Flattering . . . in its own way."

Val feels something buzzing inside him from the soles of his feet to the crown of his head. He's staring so hard at Hunter's face—their eyes closed, their cheek resting in the crook of their own arm, curtain of black hair like ink spilled over their shoulder—he's certain Hunter must know how intensely Val is studying them. There is no single coherent thought in Val's mind, just a swarm of sense memories crowding in and flooding his nerves. Touching would be nice, but he'd settle for less. Much as he wants the heat again, he wants expressions more. Even while his pulse rushes to his clit, Val thinks he'd be happy enough if Hunter simply let Val look at them, at the scars and the metal and the layering of muscle under skin and all the ways their face has yet to emote in front of him.

As soon as the hornet's nest of Val's mind settles on a question, he slowly rises up to his feet. The words pour into the hollows of his teeth as he crosses the space between them, step by aching step. Val isn't even sure he's breathing as he finds himself standing beside Hunter, hip to hip, and he watches as if from outside his own body as the very tips of his fingers brush over black fabric. Their pulse—Hunter's pulse is so pretty, a deep drum echoing in Val's skull and ricocheting up his arm until all the empty spaces inside him are filled up.

Val meets Hunter's wild-eyed gaze with his hand easing over their cock.

"Do we have to wait for another nightmare?"

Hunter's breath rattles out of their chest, but the sound is lost to the hatchling as they let out a scream that rips into the air with the violence of bones cracking in half.

Hunter bolts to their feet, already slinging their things back onto their body, and Val turns toward the sound as a liquid, perfect resonance grips him by the brain.

"Knives," Val breathes.

Hunter looks at him. "Fuck."

11

Knives is a meat grinder standing at the edge of the campground. Val and Hunter both go bolting out of the tent, but as soon as he's on his feet and ready to run, Val feels himself pulled in the direction of the churning magnetism coming off of Knives. There's a fishhook in his chest and he's being reeled in by hands much stronger than his own. Val may not be able to stop Knives, but he can at least put an obstacle in the Major's path, and that's better than nothing. It's what Val *should* do.

"You get to Dream, I'll go to stop Knives," Val says, but his head spins as Hunter wheels Val around to grab his face in both hands, as if they mean to crush Val's skull. At least that's what the black fire in Hunter's eyes seems to suggest they want.

"Absolutely the fuck not," Hunter says. "*You* go to Dream. I'll get the hatchling. We're not fighting tonight. We're running."

Val's mouth opens, wanting to say something useful to Hunter, but he can feel the moment that Knives steps into his bubble of awareness, graceful in its precision, stomping any words back down Val's throat. Knives is as calm as ever, and Val's heart is going to burst.

"I can distract him long enough that you and Dream—" Val's voice is cut off as Hunter squeezes Val's head between their hands, drawing Val's gaze back to an expression of pure, molten anger, a look Val has never seen on Hunter before. It's almost enough to block Knives from his mind, the realization that Val has been gifted another new thing from this person. Hunter is shaking mad, a slight tremor in their arms as they hold Val by the face and stare him down like they hope to press sensibility directly into his empty head. This is fury—as beautiful as a building collapsing around Val.

"*I'm not done with you.*"

Hunter's voice comes out of their mouth like a thunderstorm, unseen pressure sending snaps of electricity through every word. Val almost doesn't hear them over the strange awe of watching Hunter feel something so powerful. When they speak again, their fingers press into Val's cheeks and temples hard enough to bruise, and Val can't look at anything else.

"If all you want to do is get yourself killed, then you should at least *let me be the one who kills you.*"

Hunter wrenches their hands off Val's face so hard that their nails slice into Val's cheeks. Maybe it's the pain that clears his head, or maybe just the thrill of knowing that he put such a blistering emotion inside Hunter, but Val nods, breathless, as warm blood beads across his face.

"I'll save your fucking hatchling," Hunter says. "Take Dream and don't look back."

Of course, Val can't very well argue with the trail of dust Hunter leaves as they sprint out of sight on quiet steps. There's no time to even be angry at the fact that Hunter is apparently reading Val's mind. Ignoring the heavy confidence of Knives's boot steps is a bit like turning his cheek from an earthquake, but Val forces himself to follow Dream's lullaby instead, running toward the feeling of Dream rustling back to consciousness.

When Val gets there, Dream throws open his tent with the revolver in his hand. "What is it?"

"Knives."

"Son of a—" Dream clamps his teeth down. "Let's get the fuck out of here. Where's Hunter?"

"Getting the hatchling."

"We're running in the opposite direction, *now*," Dream commands, pointing away from the beautifully smooth sound of Knives in the distance—a piece of metal ringing in Val's head, threatening to ruin everything.

It is all the more disorienting to turn and see, right where Dream's hand is pointed, the familiar shape of the centipede doctor that accompanied Knives at Southern Truth. Val was so fixed on Knives, he didn't even notice the other hatchling approaching.

"Disgraceful larvae," the doctor hisses, poison already dripping from their teeth.

Dream turns his body to aim with the revolver, and the doctor scurries forward with alarming speed. Val sprints for Dream, taking the two wooden steps up to shove his back against Dream's chest. If it weren't for the ill-fitting white lab coat, Val might not have been able to keep his eye on the doctor's body, but he catches the unnatural streak of color. Val braces himself to stop the doctor's teeth with his own skin if he has to, while Dream slips his empty hand around Val's chest, holding them together as he points the revolver out into the forest. The doctor circles the tent with the parading steps of countless legs, and Val can feel every movement like a snare drum drawing his eye. The doctor is no strategist, and the moment they slip through the back of the tent to try and surprise them, Dream spins Val and himself around like they're dancing, and without hesitation, shoots the doctor once in the head and once through the pack of medical supplies hanging from their waist.

The doctor's massive body collapses into a twitching heap, half concealed by the ruined tent, but their face is already regrowing. White bone begins to spiral up from the open wound like a fresh sprout, muscle spiderwebbing across the growth. This doesn't seem to concern Dream as he reaches into the folds of his coat for a glass bottle and his lighter.

"This one's a problem," Dream mutters, dumping something across the prone body of the centipede and the wreckage of the tent. Val grits his teeth as the lighter sparks, wondering if this doctor would also enjoy having their hair stroked like his hatchling, or Hunter. They probably hate it out here, but Dream is right. Their speed is an issue so long as they're following Knives's orders.

The fire is brilliant and the smell is horrific.

"We have to go!" Dream barks, shoving Val forward.

Another gunshot rings out south of them, and Val grinds his teeth down around his own heart.

"Have some faith in Hunter," Dream says, already jogging away. "We don't have time to worry."

Fear explodes through Val's blood with gasoline quickness, erasing everything useful from his mind until there's nothing but old impulse that guides him into position directly behind Dream. If he can't do anything else, he'll at least be able to take a bullet for their pillar. *This is the job. Hunter would do the same.*

Dream keeps going without looking back, and Val has to force himself forward, grabbing the back of Dream's coat to make sure he stays in place. Maybe it's the sting of burning flesh in the air, but Val's eyes are watering up. His own panic makes it impossible to sort through the chaos and isolate Hunter, or their hatchling, or Knives, so he shifts all his focus into making sure he won't trip and slow down Dream.

At least Dream is running now. Val didn't know he could. He might be opening his wound to do it, but they're moving at a good clip. Further and further away from everyone and everything. Val isn't even sure if he managed to get all of his things out of the tent. He has a backpack on, yes, good, and Dream has his bag jostling around his shoulder. Val should probably take that from him, to ease the weight.

"Shouldn't we wait?" Val suddenly asks.

"*You* can," Dream calls. "I'm not stopping."

Val grips his coat tighter, worrying his teeth in frustration as his feet refuse to stop running. He never got his socks back on. They're jammed into his pockets in little balls, and his shoes are now cutting into the skin of his ankles. *Hunter would do the same. Hunter would do the same.*

It feels terrible to leave, and it's all he can do.

They run until their footsteps chase the moon away. They don't speak another word either, Dream just comes to a suspiciously abrupt halt hours later, setting his cane back onto the dirt like he intends to turn a key in a lock. When he looks back at Val, Dream's face streaked with sweat and etched with exhaustion and unconcealed pain, his eyes suddenly pop open.

"You're crying."

Val sniffs, his breath leaving him in short bursts like carbonation. The stop in motion is apparently permission for a horrible stream of tears to start burning out of his eyes.

"It's nothing personal, I just sort of hate you right now," Val says through stuttered breaths.

Dream heaves a sigh. "Yeah, me too, kid. Sorry."

Val can't imagine just how pathetic he must look in that moment, enough to make Dream sweep him into an almost painfully awkward hug. With his face mashed into the front of Dream's stiff jacket, Val lets himself cry for long enough that the anger at having to keep moving melts into an aching sadness at not knowing what happened to the others. He still can't sense Hunter or their hatchling, but he can't sense Knives either, and the uncertainty is a slow poison.

"We should—" Val tries to speak through weird hiccups. "Get to a—town. Somewhere with hu-humans."

"Why?" Dream asks.

"The h-hatchlings don't like humans," Val gets out, fingers digging into Dream's coat. "We can hide easier. H-H-Hunter knows. We talked about it."

"Okay," Dream says, holding the back of Val's head. "Makes sense."

"Why is crying so uncomfortable?" Val whines, his voice tightening into an unrecognizable octave.

"Just get it out," Dream says, his thumb brushing through Val's hair. "Gotta catch my breath anyway."

Ignoring the fact that neither of them breathe like humans, Val falls silent, to compose himself once more.

"Are you hurt?" Val asks, forcing himself to push away from Dream. "Your hip, is it alright?"

"It'll get us to a town," Dream says. "Let's go. No time to wait."

Feeling like a swollen rag, Val follows after Dream as he creaks back into motion. Val can't sense anything as they walk, only able to trust that Dream knows where he's going. This isn't the companionable silence of Hunter and Dream focused on a task. This is fear and tension sapping away all the sound from the air.

The warmth of the sun has chased the chill of the night away by the time Dream speaks again.

"If I were Hunter," Dream starts. "I'd know that the only way to buy us time would be to slow down or distract Knives. And the only way to slow down a spider like that is to force them to spend a lot of time healing. Assuming our new chatty friend is doing alright, Hunter has access to enough acid to at least make things difficult for the Major. He's gotta time it right, but . . ."

"But Hunter's good," Val finishes.

"So that's that," Dream says. "We'll meet them at the next town. End of discussion."

"Yes, sir," Val answers automatically, but his voice is cracked.

It takes half the day, but Dream guides them to a small, cramped town that smells like cobwebs and wood rot. They have to walk by a graveyard to make it to the main road, and when they do, Val can feel the residents staring at them. None of them are out on the streets of course—a real street too, paved and all—but they swarm behind closed windows and doors, like nocturnal creatures afraid of the daylight. Val's stomach is beginning to gnaw at itself as he realizes he hasn't had much food since healing up all the acid wounds, but all of that vanishes as they pass by the hulking carcass of a train. Val's fingers tighten in Dream's coat reflexively, on guard at the inexplicable feeling that this massive thing may get up at any moment and resume its barreling course off track.

"The plan was to connect this place to Innovation," Dream explains in a whisper. "Insect wrecked the station on one of the first trial runs."

The engine car is on its side, a shattered headlight staring at Val as they walk past. Two cars down, the metal on the sides of the train have burst outward like a bomb went off inside. Toward the tail end of the train's shell lies what used to be a station, though half of it is in ruin from the momentum of a train that didn't pull its brake in time. There's a small mountain of shattered stone that has sat so long, an entire ecosystem has grown around it. The longer he looks, Val starts to see a tree growing from inside a passenger car. It must have pushed up through the ruined floor at some point.

This nest of death and life woven together so tightly brings Hunter's voice back to Val's mind, and he remembers that he might have just made another promise. He's been doing that a lot lately. Val touches his cheek, flakes of dried blood peeling off from where Hunter's nails cut him. Of course, there's no mark left, but what else is an agreement to let someone kill you if not a wound that has yet to bleed.

Past the wreckage of the station lies rings of buildings, a few prominent blocky structures at the very center advertising goods and services, flanked by rows of shorter, narrower structures like shark's teeth. The central plaza might have been impressive if it weren't held in the grip of decay, but most of these shops look like they are clinging to their structure out of spite more than care. Dream stops in front of a long dried-up fountain, admiring the mildew and rust coating it, and lets his breath out.

"Welcome to Respite," Dream says, his own voice sagging like bloated wood.

"Does this town belong to a pillar?" Val asks.

Dream meets his gaze, tired and soaked through with pain, and Val already knows what he'll say.

"Yeah."

Dream and Val check into a bed and breakfast that is more dust than matter, and Val inhales a stack of pancakes prepared by the pigeon-esque, terrified man who appears to be running this entire operation by himself. With his energy back, Val bullies Dream into allowing Val to look at his hip.

"You're not a fuckin' doctor, what are you gonna do?" Dream asks, but Val gives him the lightest shove and Dream crumples onto the stiff bed with a grimace that looks like it traveled up from his toes all the way to his teeth.

"You're in pain," Val says. "Stop moving for one minute. And *feed* for heaven's sake. Take your coat off, I'll clean the wound."

With a not insignificant amount of muttered cursing, Dream takes his coat off, passing the shockingly heavy burden of old leather to Val to drape on an armchair. Val pauses briefly at the solid *thunk* the coat makes when he sets it down. Washing his hands is more for the joy of cleaning his skin than Dream's safety, and Val takes his time scraping under every nail before joining Dream again. Sitting on a bed beside the pillar might have given Val shivers a short while ago, but now Val is holding a bottle of antiseptic and he can't really remember why he was ever nervous around this man.

Dream's frown is bone deep while he untucks his shirt. "Be gentle, alright? It's not as bad as it looks."

"Unbutton your damn shirt," Val says and Dream scoffs.

Val was expecting a thin, brittle body, but he is more than a little shocked to see that Dream is completely solid. He doesn't have nearly the same bulk as Hunter, but he isn't fragile like Val expected, save for the dirty bandage plastered to his side. Val peels up the barely held-together tape and makes a face at the ice cream scoop of flesh missing from Dream's hip.

"Ouch," Val says, staring at the gouge mark, all pink and raw.

"The real kick in the teeth is that it wasn't this bad before they pulled the bullet out, but we weren't careful. We thought I'd heal. Should've seen their faces when it didn't close up." Dream gives a sandpaper laugh as Val douses a cloth in antiseptic.

"Who pulled the bullet out?" Val asks.

"Remi," Dream says, then clarifies. "Remembrance. She was here with Sig. The two of them traveled a lot because Remi liked to write everything down, little histories, ya know? Ah—"

Dream sucks in air as Val starts to wipe the cloth against angry red skin. It doesn't bleed the way Val would have expected. It's less an open wound and more of a *frozen* one.

"I wish I had her journals," Dream goes on. "Remi's, they probably have the most comprehensive account of my family. She wrote everything matter-of-fact. Exactly what happened and nothing more. Talking to her was always strange. Couldn't help but think, *how are you gonna write about this later?*"

"What happened to her journals?" Val asks, setting the soiled cloth aside and getting a new one. When he presses his fingers against raw flesh, he flinches automatically as he thinks about trying to run with a wound like this. Dream must have spent years hardening himself to the pain of it. That must be how he got so strong.

"Whoever killed her took 'em," Dream says. "Mare didn't pull the trigger that time, but I have a feeling he might have told someone about where she liked to write. Now her books are gone, books full of our lives."

"Do you think it was this Queen of Innovation?"

"Yeah. If not by her hand, then by her order," Dream says.

Val sets his hand over the empty space where muscle and skin should be, feeling warmth pouring through the cloth and out of Dream's body. "How much time do you think we have in this town before Knives chases us out again?"

"Mm, I give it a day at most," Dream says. "Which means we can give Hunter about half that time before we gotta keep moving."

"He'll be exhausted," Val says. "We'll need to let him rest before we move on."

"Or . . ." Dream licks his lips. "We tell him to stay here so he can heal, and we don't let a fucking human follow us into a war zone."

"You know he won't do that," Val says, prepping another bandage. Dream's small pouch of medical supplies was mostly crushed into the bottom of his pack and there is a huge crease across the absorbent pad that Val sets down. "You can tell Hunter to stay, but if he can tell himself that you're releasing him from the job, you know he'll just follow after you like he used to. The only difference will be that you won't be able to see him."

Dream reaches up to rub at his eyes. "You two are so fucking annoying."

"You're a real charmer yourself," Val says, flattening the bandage to Dream's wound and passing him the roll of medical tape, rife with fibers clinging to the edges. "Rip some pieces off for me."

Dream does, passing Val several lengths of tape until the bandage is in place again.

"Did you grow up here then?" Val asks, looking at him.

Dream shakes his head. "Mare and I grew up by the northwestern coast. A farmer raised us up, Harlyn. She was a good person. Loved us both, even when we made no sense. She always said, *I'm no good with kids, I only do plants.* But we definitely weren't kids. Respite is the place we hit when things started making sense to us, about what we were, and what we could do. We stayed here for a while, long enough for people to start spreading rumors about how you could come here to get the best rest of your life. 'Course they didn't know we were stealing their dreams. They thought it was the water, and then thought maybe it was the food, or the beds, or the hospitality. We had to leave before anyone caught on to us not aging, but those were good years. I always looked forward to stopping here on our way in and out of Innovation. Like an oasis just for Mare and I . . . we spent a lot of time here."

Dream closes his eyes, and Val begins to button his shirt back up for him, wondering what the younger version of Dream looked like, the one before the scars, before the weight of death sloped his shoulders and steeled his eyes.

"You started hunting insects because you wanted to free Mare of them, right?" Val asks.

Dream nods.

"You taught others to hunt with you, to thin out the problem."

"But the thing about humans," Dream says, "is they're real good at dying. Not me, I should've died decades ago. But I lived, and got bitter, and humans thought it was so fucking romantic. So they died when I couldn't. Kids. Kids with dreams. Pretty dreams, Val, beautiful dreams. They gave them to me without knowing it and now I'm full of 'em. Too many dead kids with lovely dreams. They wanted so many things, and all I could give them were weapons."

Val pushes the hair off of Dream's forehead, wishing he could see those dreams too.

"I think maybe the worst part about this whole damn thing is that I finally understand what the fuck Mare was talking about," Dream says. "I get it now. The silence. Talking to someone and not know-ing what they're thinking, not getting glimpses into their heads, or stealing their dreams, or accidentally winding up on their pedestals. Talking to you must be how Mare felt when he started talking to the spider in Innovation. It really is incredible. To get to know someone the slow way."

Val runs his fingers down the side of Dream's face, to the zipper of scar tissue where Mare pushed him away, the person who knew him better than anyone. "You allowed me into your company for my silence and here I am, talking your ear off every day. No wonder you asked me to keep my mouth shut so many times."

Dream exhales through his nose, and Val feels it on the side of his hand. "It's not so bad . . . when you talk."

"I talk too much," Val tells him. "Much too much. Before we were chased out of camp, I even told Hunter that I wanted to feel his organs because I couldn't shut up."

A tired laugh rattles out of Dream's throat. "Well that's a fucked up thing to say to someone."

"I know," Val says, face burning at the memory. "I forgot myself. I do that a lot when I know someone's listening. It's exciting, you know? Being heard. Must be very annoying for the both of you. And I'm sorry, but I . . . I'll have to annoy you at least one more time."

Dream opens his eyes in confusion.

"You can't see my dreams," Val whispers to him. "But I'm going to tell you anyway."

For a moment, Dream looks much younger, like his concern is shaving years off his face. Val smiles at him, holding Dream's cheek with his thumb resting in the valley of scar tissue.

"I would like to destroy Innovation," Val says. "If I understand the hatchlings and the spiders the way I think I do, then it's nothing more than a hiding place for them. Humans make them feel emotions, and emotions complicate their lives. They want to keep things simple, but when I asked our hatchling what they wanted more than anything, they told me they wanted to be held one more time."

Dream's eyes slide shut with a mournful sigh.

"The only memory they had before Innovation was a vague feeling of someone's arms around them. I think that's the difference between the hatchlings and the spiders. The hatchlings may just be one gesture of kindness away from humanity. It's the spiders who are telling them they don't need it. And this Queen is telling the spiders how to live without mercy."

"No wonder they hate us," Dream says. "My family. We're nothing *but* emotion. Must feel awful to them."

"I want to help the hatchlings," Val tells him. "But I'm not human either. I gave our hatchling permission, but I think it was yours and Hunter's presence that got to them. You softened them, and I pushed, that's all. I bet that's why Moon is doing so well. He's surrounded by humans every day in Indulgence. You wouldn't even know he used to be something else. Imagine if all the others could live like that."

"Now you're trying to rope me into a fucking city-wide rescue mission." Dream sighs. "You're nothing but trouble, Val."

Val smiles, though it stings the back of his throat. "I can't make you do anything. I just wanted you to know what I see when I close my eyes. I want everyone to walk away from that place. That includes you and Mare."

Dream goes slack against the bed, eyes closed, arms laid out beside him. "Kids like you always have the nicest dreams. Bloody on the outside, candy underneath."

Val feels him falling into his stasis like fabric sinking through water. One more sweep of his fingers over Dream's forehead brings fresh anger that Val can't see inside there. He wants to understand the weight; he wants to shoulder some of the burden so Hunter doesn't have to do it alone; he wants to be given the chance to be selfish and ask whether or not Dream thinks about Val in his sleep.

But Val is locked out, same as he always was. Leaning down closer, Val presses a kiss between Dream's brows. On some subconscious, automatic response, Dream's hand finds Val's back and presses them together. Val's heart thumps loudly enough that he's surprised it doesn't wake Dream, but this is some long buried routine, one that lives in Dream's muscles, like breathing or walking.

Dream holds Val against him, turning onto his side so they're facing each other. Eyes still closed, effortless in his sleep, Dream pushes his forehead to Val's and tucks his nose in until all Val can see is a blur of warm, sun-soaked skin. Val is shivering in Dream's heavy grip, utterly terrified to risk the fallout from Dream waking up and realizing what he's doing. So Val lays there, trembling, as Dream gives him a kiss meant for Mare.

It's so soft, it makes Val want to cry all over again. Dream kisses him with the gentle, graceless motion of someone who only cares to be close. This is a kiss for someone who knows Dream loves them, loves them enough that he doesn't need to impress them. A kiss that says, *I'll see you in the morning*, because he knows he can do better tomorrow.

A kiss from a man with endless time and endless chances.

Val holds his breath, the only thing keeping him from making some animal howl of grief. It's too heavy. He can't stand it—knowing with absolute certainty that this is how nice people kiss, and that it isn't at all what Val wants. It takes Val an embarrassingly long time to extricate himself from Dream's arms when every inch he pulls further away from the man is like removing a blade from his guts. When Val finally gets to his feet, looking down at the sleeping pillar with his face at ease, Val starts crying for the second time that day.

"Of course people think it's romantic," Val mutters, too shaken and frantic to keep his thoughts inside his head. "You're in love."

⬻

Taking a bath feels like a selfish thing, but Val does it anyway, just for some space between himself and Dream. He's preparing not to be crushed by the thought of moving on from this town without Hunter and their hatchling. Much as he wants to tell himself that maybe Hunter found a new spark for life away from dangerous people like Dream and Val, he knows it's not as simple as that.

For a moment though, he allows himself a brief fantasy of Hunter and their hatchling living like normal people, or, as normal as they can be. Maybe Matthew will join them, with Liz and her sister. Maybe Hunter will find a new calling in keeping hatchlings out of trouble, and they'll run their fingers through each other's hair. Maybe Hunter will finally find a name that isn't stained with blood.

Val starts laughing in the tub at the image of this family made of mismatched puzzle pieces. As he dries off, standing amid a mobile of freshly cleaned clothes he set out to dry, he remembers the feeling of Matthew's hard shell, and the softness of the wings Moon never unfurled. He puts his hands onto his chest, finding the place where Knives pierced him, and tells himself it's time. He can't now, not on his own, not on the run, but after. He's pretty sure he has enough people to ask for help.

Later. He'll get the scalpel out later.

Val lays down on the other twin bed in their cramped shared room and lets himself take a strange, weightless nap. He jerks awake as if no time has passed at all, save for the lack of sunlight. Dream is up as well, staring out into the darkened town through the filmy window.

"Something doesn't feel right," Dream says.

Val sits up, startling as he realizes he's only in his towel.

"The people here. I don't know if we can afford to stay," Dream says. "Let's pack up and move. We can wait outside town limits for a little longer, but I might have made a mistake."

Val bolts into the bathroom, putting still-damp clothes onto his body. "What do you mean you made a mistake?"

Dream is grumbling quietly as he watches. The only light is in the bathroom, and Val wonders if Dream's trying to hide them from sight.

"They might have been warned about us," Dream says. "I didn't think about it. Knives didn't exactly do a good job of chasing us, huh?"

Val turns the light off and starts repacking. "Are you saying he *wanted* us to come here?"

"No," Dream says. "I think he knows better than I do that this place is hostile. This is the closest town outside Innovation, and they might be on the lookout for strangers like me. Hell, for all I know, they might have gotten word from the last place I bought cigarettes from. Might not even have anything to do with the spiders."

"Well, I suppose that's a guarantee that Knives won't come here," Val says.

"It also might mean losing a limb before we escape."

"I *just* got my hand back," Val mutters. "Can we hide?"

"C'mon, the station's our best bet. Don't do anything weird while we're walking."

Dream and Val leave the bed and breakfast together with the gaze of the same pigeon-eyed proprietor on their backs the whole time. Val makes sure to stop and put a hand on Dream's shoulder to ask, "Is your hip alright?"

And Dream just says, "Stop worrying. It won't kill me."

As soon as they're outside, Dream picks his cane up and walks twice as fast toward the wreckage of the train station. Val tries to follow as quietly as he can, wishing they could do something about the street lamps dotting the road like orange stars. He can feel the residents watching them, their gazes burning from inside every building they pass.

"Do you think maybe leaving in the dead of night was actually a worse idea?" Val asks in a whisper.

"Shh, I know what I'm doing," Dream says.

Everywhere they step, tension follows them in a bubble as they enter someone else's gaze. It's the smell of sweat beading along someone's hairline as they wait to see what will happen. Val links his arm with Dream's just to stay level with him, searching as vigilantly as he can for the feeling of someone reaching for a gun.

The husk of the broken train is a welcome sight as they turn to walk the length of it. As soon as they break line of sight from the nearest window, Val thought it would make him feel better, but his own anxiety only ramps up as he loses track of the other people. Dream at least looks calm as he guides them toward one of the passenger cars that's still standing on its wheels. He points to a shattered, open window.

"Get in there and see if you can unlock the main door."

Val starts scrabbling up the side of the train, and Dream shoves him up by the seat of his pants, sending Val spilling into the car and onto a bench that's covered in rust and dead leaves. He gets back to his feet in a tomb of decay and new growth, stepping on old wood and new vines as he makes his way toward the front of the car. Dream knocks on the door and Val meets him on the other side, searching for a lock to flip. After finding a lever and accidentally ripping it from the wall in a shower of rust, the two of them shove the door open, and Dream joins him inside.

"Alright, just keep an eye out," Dream says while he gets a cigarette. "This is gonna take some focus. I won't be able to see anything coming. I'm counting on you, alright?"

Dream sits on the nearest bench with his hands folded over his cane, and Val perches across from him with his breath held. Val's eyes are getting better at seeing through darkness, but everything is indistinct. He has to rely on all of his senses to get a picture of this mausoleum of a train car, and Dream beginning to blend into the plant growth around him while he lights his cigarette.

It's like watching a tree blossom before his eyes. Something shifts in the air, heavy pollen, or swirling ozone. Dream's body is still enough to feign death, but something like life is pouring out of him. Val can't help but picture a dandelion sending seeds flying through the air as

Dream tips his head back and exhales a cloud of thick, white smoke. It's much more than it should be, and it fills the air with a sweet scent as it floods out of the windows of the train car. As Val sits there, he remembers his first meeting with Dream and Hunter. The euphoria that gripped Hunter, rendering them completely useless while Dream held them in it.

Dream smokes two cigarettes down to the filter before he opens his eyes again. "It's easier when they can't see me. More natural. If I hold it 'til the morning, they'll forget we scared them."

"Will you be alright?" Val asks. "Do you need food?"

"I'll get it in the morning," Dream says. "It's fine. Haven't . . . done it quite like this in a while, but I'll be fine."

He settles onto the bench, leaning his head back and hiking his foot up next to Val's knee. It's not like his sleep-stasis. It's much *dreamier* than that, the heaviness of his body and the relaxed set of his face as he puts an entire town under a spell. There's a beauty to him that Val might have easily gotten swept up by if he didn't know more about this man, but now it only seems to make Dream all the more untouchable. Even knowing how much space there is between them, Val still wants to help him. He tries to tell himself how wrong it is that Dream is so clearly in love with his own brother, but he can't make the feeling stick. It rolls off of Val, leaving only the sadness of seeing Dream fight so hard to get back to this person.

Brother is a human word, and neither Dream nor Val are bound by those rules. The thing that truly astounds Val is the thought of walking with the same man for hundreds of years and still loving every inch of him. Val isn't sure he wants to live that long, doesn't even know if he's capable of love in the same way, but there is something awesome in that thought. As Dream shifts around, his shoulders slumping as he gives himself over to this other state, Val once again finds himself wondering what it would be like if Hunter actually killed him. Not out of anger or some kind of predator-prey drive, but out of kindness. What emotion allows you to say, *I won't make you walk alone for centuries?*

Is that what Mare tried, and failed, to do?

Dream looks sort of drunk, lost and glazed in the throes of this euphoric magic, and Val drops his gaze like he's walked in on someone naked. Trying to focus on their surroundings is less about safety and more about *not* looking at Dream, or the column of his throat while he breathes deep, sighing breaths. How many times has Mare seen this? Val can't imagine they touch each other the way Hunter or Knives has touched him, but then again, he doesn't know Mare at all. He has no idea what happens when euphoria and despair undress each other. Maybe it's the messiest thing in the world. Val can't imagine being disgusted by anything as soft as that sleepy, directionless kiss was.

Val swallows, closing his eyes with his fingers bunched into the front of his trousers. He tries to clear his mind, but he can't stop himself from picturing Hunter in Dream's place, sitting in front of Val in complete relaxation. It would make him stupid to see Hunter truly defenseless like this. He can't even picture what Hunter's face would do with nothing to think about, how their expression would shift as they relaxed, but Val is pretty sure he would go through the pain of regrowing both his hands for the chance to find out. If Hunter ever willingly bared his throat to Val the way Dream is right now, Val knows *he'd* be the animal. It makes his teeth chatter to think about it.

Sweat on his palms, Val exits the train car to sit outside instead, needing to put some space between himself and Dream's spell. The crisp night air reminds him that he's supposed to keep watch, and with a pinch of his own cheek, Val turns his attention to the town, waiting to see if another knife will find them before sunrise.

Spending the night seesawing between imagining Knives brutally killing Hunter and his hatchling, and fantasizing about Hunter undressing for Val, leaves him feeling dizzy and half-hollow. Dream, on the other hand, steps out of the train car like a new man. He somehow looks rested and healthier than ever, which puts a scowl on Val's face.

"I take it no one came for us," Dream says.

Val shakes his head. "The town feels different too. Do you think they forgot about us?"

"Hope so," Dream says, rolling his shoulders. "Man, I haven't done that in a while. Feels good to get it all out."

He whistles, and Val pushes himself up like a jagged twig beside Dream.

"Do we have to . . . I haven't felt Hunter or the hatchling," Val says.

Dream frowns at him. "Sorry, kid. We can't risk Knives getting to us first."

Val feels himself deflating, glancing behind him at the town. "Can't we at least leave a message or something? In case they come through here."

"Sure." Dream nods. "Just don't say anything weird. Don't want to upset anyone after all the work I just did."

Val starts walking back toward the center of Respite with a painful tightness over his skin, like it'll start peeling away at any moment. Reminding himself over and over and over again that Hunter isn't dumb enough to get themself killed so easily, Val tries to string together a useful message to leave for his friends, but all he can think about is Hunter growling at him, *I'm not done with you.*

I'm not either. When he finds himself standing in front of the same grimy fountain from the day before, Val does a double take. This is not the same rusty town they walked through. People are walking around, talking to each other, cleaning up windows and *laughing.* Val is dumbstruck as he realizes what Dream did to them. The tension has been scrubbed out of the air and replaced with life.

"You looking for something, kid?" a woman walks up to Val, sleeves rolled up to her elbows. "New here?"

Val stumbles back to reality. "Uh, yes, I'm so sorry to bother you. Is there anywhere I could leave a message for someone? Unfortunately, I'm on my way out of here, but I suspect a friend of mine might show up soon. I wanted to let them know where I was headed."

"Well if they're staying at the bed and breakfast, you can leave something with the owner. That way if your friend's name pops up, he can pass it on."

Val claps his hands together. "Thank you so much!"

She gives him a funny look and just shakes her head. "It's nothing."

Running back to the bed and breakfast, Val pushes the doors open, half-expecting to get greeted with twitchy hostility from the man who checked them in half a day ago, but Val finds him cheerily dusting all the surfaces behind the front desk.

"Well hello young man," he says. "You leave something behind?"

Ignoring the surreality of this town breaking through its own shell of decay, Val explains himself to the owner of the inn.

"Well sure, son, if you leave a note addressed to the right name, I can pass it along to him if he shows up in the next couple of days."

Val thanks him over and over as the man produces a piece of paper and a pencil. Sensing the ticking of the clock that is Knives, Val tries not to think too hard as he scribbles out a note for *Hunter & Hatchling*. His throat is tight, and he knows Dream has already allowed them to stay here too long, so he licks the envelope with shaking hands, sealing it to leave behind.

"Come back anytime," the innkeeper says. "You'll get the best night's sleep of your life in Respite."

Part III

THE UNKNOWN

12

A little bit of sense returns to Val as he stops on his way out of Respite to buy himself some food with the spare coins fished from the bottom of his pack. It's the last of any currency he has squirreled away, but the woman running the general store gives him an extra orange, probably because he looks so pathetic.

In the bright light of day, Val can feel the tendrils of grief and anger hanging off of him so much clearer. When he gets back to the train station, Dream has used one of his own knives to carve an arrow into the side of the train pointing down the tracks.

TO INNOVATION →

Val gives him a weak smile. "Thank you."

"Let's go."

He spends the next hour of their time walking alongside the overgrown train tracks, pushing his own senses to their absolute limit in a desperate attempt to sense either Hunter or the hatchling. He can feel Respite slipping out of his grasp, his own body getting clumsy as he tries to reach further away from them, until he finally trips on nothing and Dream has to straighten him up and tell him to keep his eyes forward.

"They'll find you," Dream says. "We gotta watch ahead of us, not behind."

Val grinds a complaint up in his teeth and starts watching the tracks instead. They go on for so long, he can't see where the railroad begins or ends, but when he lifts his head up, he can start to make out the edges of a city. It's faint, like a specter in the distance, just the mere suggestion of dark shapes.

It fills him with dread.

"What happens when a pillar rots?" Val asks.

"We fall apart," Dream says. "Physically or mentally or both. Like regressing into some base part of our beings."

Val holds his tongue, afraid to ask what might become of the embodiment of a nightmare with nothing but raw instinct to guide him.

"Let's hope they've kept Mare well fed," Val mutters.

Again, Val notices that Dream isn't using his cane nearly as often, but he can't bring himself to ask about it. For some reason, the thought of conversation is like nails on a chalkboard to him. So they walk in silence, burning up the daylight as they follow the fossil of a railroad. Val isn't sure when he starts to feel tired, but the ache and the dull anger catches up to him when the sun is beginning to dip below the tree tops in the distance. They still have a ways to go before they're back in the safety of a forest, and Val has been telling himself that as soon as they're in it, he's going to sleep again. The need for it doesn't quite fit him right, his body completely unused to this sagging feeling pulling him closer to the earth, but they're far too exposed to set up camp now.

He wants nothing more than to put up his tent and burrow into his sleeping bag and maybe try crying a little more. Emotion has welled up behind his eyes like a stopped drain and it, too, is making him heavy. Everything is heavy. Everything hurts. And all he can do is aim his body toward the approaching woods like a puppet steered by a bored child.

Val thinks he would do just about anything to go back to when his primary concern was wondering if he was pissing off Hunter and Dream with his babbling. Just as the ache hits him to go back to that time, he stumbles on the sensation of metal in the distance. Grabbing Dream, Val puts himself back in front of the pillar as Knives's presence grates against Val's.

Dream already has his revolver out, touching Val's shoulder with one hand and aiming with the other at the black silhouette of Knives's coat as he walks calmly from the other direction of the train tracks.

"You must be tired, Spiderling," Knives calls. "You hardly noticed me."

"Stop," Dream snarls, already pulling the trigger enough that the slightest twitch will fire it. "Unless you want to spend a week regrowing your entire body."

Knives holds his gloved hands up and open. "You have the advantage. I only came to talk to my younger brother."

Val feels his jaw trembling, his vision cracking like glass around the sight of Knives, and no one else. *All alone. No one else.*

"Where is your doctor?" Val asks. "I can't feel them."

"I'm afraid they've reached the end of their usefulness," Knives answers.

"You abandoned a wounded friend?" Val spits back.

Knives lowers his hands, tucking them neatly behind his back. The sun is caught in his pommels, and the glare is blinding for a moment as he tilts his head. "There is no point in carrying a broken shield. Your master knows this better than you do. You've shed the dead weight from your own company and bother to ask me why I've done the same."

All Val hears is *dead* before a high pitched ringing deafens him to anything else. His backpack slides off his shoulders, the wind is in his face, and Hunter's knife is in his hand. He can see in painstaking clarity as Knives reaches for his own weapons on the inside of his coat. There's no sound when the gun goes off, but Val watches as a bullet from Dream's revolver shatters Knives's right elbow, ripping through fabric and muscle and bone. The pain doesn't stop him of course, and Knives twists out of the way of Dream's second shot, but at least Knives only has one gun instead of two. Not that Val cares. He wouldn't have stopped running either way, and he doesn't feel it at all as a bullet rips clean through his shoulder. He doesn't feel anything until he's barreling directly into Knives's chest, knocking him to the grass with enough force to make Val's teeth snap shut around his own tongue. The world is red and metal as he stabs Hunter's knife through the Major's flawless throat, and Val eats another bullet straight through his chest.

Blood pours out of him and onto Knives's face as he grabs one of those silver pommels, pulling as hard as he can while Knives deigns to show Val his own snarling mouth. It isn't pain that's slowing Val, but his strength leaving him with every ounce of blood soaking through his clothes. The damn knife is lodged so deep, Val didn't think about how it might very well be fused into the skull itself until Knives is pressing the barrel of his gun to Val's forehead. Val dies perched atop the Cardinal Major's chest before he can even ask the question searing his mind into a rabid frenzy.

What did you do to Hunter?

Val jostles awake in Dream's arms. They're running. With a gasp from freshly rebuilt lungs, Val clings to Dream's coat. They've made it to the treeline but Val can't see the train tracks.

"You awake, you fucking maniac?" Dream snaps.

"Yes, yes, I'm sorry."

Dream unceremoniously drops Val onto the ground, hardly stopping to make sure Val is upright before he starts running again.

"What happened?" Val asks, tearing after Dream.

"Killed him," Dream says. "Took your cue and pulled both the knives out of his face. Hopefully that'll slow him—"

There is a sound that Val didn't know a living thing could make.

He remembers when the kids at the orphanage found out that there was supposedly a person who could sing a note to shatter glass, all them trying and failing to replicate it. That's what it makes Val think of—violence itself packed into a scream so loud that animals are fleeing alongside Dream and Val as they weave through the forest. The trees may just uproot themselves to get away from the sound of Knives howling at his own revival. It's pain and grief and anger and confusion resonating with each other so horribly, Val is sure that if he put his hand over top of Knives's mouth, it would rip his arm to shreds.

A newborn screaming with brand new eyes.

"Go!" Dream shoves Val's shoulder to keep him moving.

"Are you alright to run?" Val asks, panting alongside Dream.

"Yes! Shut up!"

Val follows the order, his hands still ringing from the metal of the knife he tried to remove.

They run until they can't anymore, stopping only when Dream nearly buckles over and he has to hold himself up against a tree so he can press a hand into his hip. Val doesn't need to ask what they're doing. He can feel Knives following them. The Cardinal Major's presence has gone from a clean, beautiful cut to broken, bloody glass, and he has not stopped moving since he woke back up. It's like running from the edges of a tornado, and all Val can do is shove some food into his mouth and wait for Dream to keep moving.

They don't stop to talk or sleep or even look around. They only go from *running* to *limping*, back and forth like a heartbeat as Knives relentlessly presses after them, a wolf nipping at their heels.

"I can feel him pushing us off course," Dream mutters at one point. "We've lost the train tracks because he's forcing us north just so we don't risk running into him. I can't waste any more bullets on him and he knows it."

"Where are we headed right now?" Val asks, voice hoarse as he tries to stop himself from healing anything unnecessary. All he cares is that his body can move. He doesn't need anything else. Speaking, breathing, and feeling are all optional as long as Dream can lead.

"Toward the deadlands," Dream answers. "If we turn back now, he'll catch us. He's keeping us from cutting closer to Innovation. We lost our chance to get to Inspiration after the campgrounds, but now, the only option is to keep going this way, or to take the *very* long way back toward Respite."

"Are there any other towns between here and Innovation?"

"No," Dream says. "At this point, if we want to avoid Knives, we have to cross through the deadlands."

Val nods, the only thought in his mind that as long as Knives is chasing *them*, he won't hurt anyone else. If Hunter and their hatchling decide to go to Innovation as well, Val would rather keep the train tracks clear for them.

"Then let's go," Val says.

They don't stop, and neither does Knives. Val feels the muscles in his legs tearing and healing as he commands himself to keep moving at all costs. And they're still not fast enough. Despite their best efforts, Knives continually closes the gap between them, the chaotic noise of his presence growing like a horde of locusts buzzing just behind them. It's nighttime when Val realizes they're going to lose this race, casting Dream a questioning glance, trying to ask without asking if this is the time to use himself as an obstacle for Knives, but the pillar only shoves him again.

"*Go.*"

It's morning when they break through the forest, and Knives is close enough that Val can feel the vibrations in his own mouth like bits of sand as he sees the deadlands in all their ashen glory. The earth turns a dehydrated brown beneath their feet, and there aren't trees so much as there are skeletons, mere echoes of plant life that used to be here centuries ago. As soon as Val is past the deadened edges, his shoes meeting dried, cracked ground beneath them, he stumbles over the complete lack of sensation.

It's like the caves where the pillars hide, only worse. Val has to grab onto Dream's coat again just to keep himself upright as his senses dull down into utter silence. He can't feel Knives, he can't feel Dream, he can hardly even feel his own body as they run further from the living earth. Dizziness sweeps over him, sweat breaking over his brow, but Dream dutifully pulls Val alongside him, turning back only once before giving a haggard laugh. Nausea churns in Val's gut as he turns to see Knives standing at the edge of the forest, teeth bared, refusing to set foot on the dead ground. His eyes are hidden once more by the pommels of his knives, but Val can see two tracks of dried blood connecting his eye sockets to his neck.

He put them back in himself . . .

Knives takes one shot at them, a bullet grazing Val's bicep with searing heat, before the white trees make it impossible to aim.

"Why isn't he following us?" Val asks, panic bursting behind his eyes. "Dream, what's out here?"

"Nothing," Dream answers, his hand firm around Val's arm. "Absolutely nothing."

It's a ruin. Val looks behind them again but Knives is gone from sight, hidden by a ghastly forest of dead trees. Another shot now would be useless, but when Val faces forward, he doesn't feel any safer. Bone white trunks spread out before them, growing more and more sparse against an empty landscape. They look like skeletal fingers reaching up out of the dirt to try and snare weary travelers just like Val and Dream.

Val feels sick, like his lack of senses has somehow poisoned him. They slow their walking pace, the only thing keeping Val on his feet while he adjusts to the awful void. It feels as though the ground itself is moving underneath him, pitching him off balance.

"Hey, hey, hey."

Val blinks up at Dream, realizing he tripped and Dream caught him.

"You here?" Dream asks.

Val pulls himself up and shakes his head. "I'm sorry. This place is . . . unsettling me."

Brows furrowed, Dream kneels down on the hard earth, guiding Val with him.

"He's not coming in here. Just get your head on straight."

Val leans his forehead against Dream's chest and closes his eyes to keep the world from spinning.

"What did you all do to this place? I've never felt something so . . . empty. Does this happen every time people fight?"

Dream puts his hand on Val's back. "Yeah, something like that."

"No." Val weakly slaps the front of Dream's coat, feeling a hard outline of something he's got tucked behind the leather. "No more fake answers. Tell me what really happened."

Dream grumbles quietly. "I'd love to tell you all the bloody details, Val, but the honest truth is that I barely remember it. It was so long ago. The world was a different place back then. My family is about the only thing that *hasn't* changed."

"Then tell me what you think happened," Val says. "Just talk, it's . . . it's helping me feel less dizzy."

With a sigh, Dream runs his hand up and down Val's back. "It's kind of embarrassing. We didn't even know what we were yet, let alone what the humans wanted from us. We were young. Like you. When a bunch of humans came to us for help, we said yes. We fed off of them, and we didn't want them dying out. Just pure selfishness. A competition, really, to see who got to keep feeding off the humans longer."

Val swallows through a dry throat, the nausea slowly settling into something else as Dream talks.

"Mare and I knew that these monsters were causing a lot more nightmares than good dreams. And those old monsters, they were something else. They didn't even try to act human. Made it easy. My siblings and I weren't even fully formed back then, so we didn't think much about killing these things that terrified humans. They came to us in despair. The fuck else were we gonna do?"

Dream pauses for long enough that Val lifts his head to see the look on his face. He almost startles, thinking for a moment that it isn't Dream at all, until he figures it must just be the angle and his own dizziness making Dream look like a different, younger man.

"Those creatures were drawn to the scent of blood. They were dumb. Vicious, but dumb. The same trap worked over and over again. Just had to cover it with enough human blood and keep going. They'd come here looking for food, and Mare and I would put them to sleep. The rest was just weaponry. We lived here for years, Mare and I, spilling blood into the ground that whole time. There was a group of humans who made themselves stay with us, because *we* needed food, and blood for the trap, but they took to covering their eyes so they wouldn't have to look at any of it. It wasn't earth when we were done. It was just . . ."

Val can feel it under his knees as he sits there. The complete absence of life.

"We wiped out an entire species and I didn't think twice while we were doing it," Dream says. "That whole time, those humans were so damn stubborn about making themselves hang around us, and then after, they were so grateful. They treated us like heroes for soaking the ground so full of blood that nothing will ever grow here."

Val pushes himself back to see if the world is less disorienting, finding Dream staring out at the dead earth with the blank-faced confusion of a child.

"Were those humans where the Eyes come from?" Val asks, a fluttering feeling in his chest.

Dream huffs, confusion turning to petulance. "Yeah."

Val gives a dusty laugh as he reorients himself. "No wonder you hated Hunter at first."

Frowning, Dream gestures out at the wasteland in front of them. "This is what we taught them. How am I supposed to react to that? They revere us for what was ultimately a bunch of teenagers shooting fish in a barrel. Bloodthirsty fish, but still. I can barely remember what they even looked like. And the Eyes think *we* need protection."

Val braces his hands on Dream's shoulder and rises back to his feet, finally feeling steady enough to try walking again. "Maybe the reverence isn't for you killing monsters so much as it is for the fact that you came from humans. They're responsible for you, in a way. They think they made you, so of course they want to look out for you. But they're probably scared of you too. You're capable of things humans can't do. Only reasonable that you two have a complicated relationship. You only need each other for the worst things."

Dream picks himself up, righting his cane to lean on it. "There you go saying reasonable shit again. I still don't like it."

"You don't have to," Val says. "I don't think that's the point."

"Why are you smiling like that?" Dream asks, eyes narrowed.

Val shrugs, walking toward the hulking outline of Innovation, steadiness coming back to him in drips. It's much more distinct now: a real city, the biggest Val has ever seen by far. It puts Foundation and Indulgence to shame. Something this big wouldn't surprise Val to see it start shifting and rustling to life at any moment. There's no way such a massive thing was made by hands the same size as his.

"I guess it just occurred to me that your family led to the start of the Eyes, which means it's *really* your fault that Hunter is here at all. This is where they started too. You probably knew their great-great-great-great—"

Dream smacks Val's back with his cane. "I get it."

"I guess I'm saying thank you," Val says. "I'm glad I met you both."

"Mercy, don't start with that shit." Dream shakes his head as he catches up to Val. "We're not done yet. If we waste too much time out here, Knives is going to set his own trap at the end of the deadlands."

"Will you be alright with no one to feed on?" Val asks. "There won't be any where we're going either."

"We're close enough now, I'll be fine," Dream says. "Our detour at Respite will keep me going for long enough. Besides . . ."

Dream is looking at it too, terrifyingly huge spires bursting out of the horizon like cold, metal arms reaching toward the sky.

"I can feel Mare," Dream says. "He's alive. I know it. Something's pointing me right to him."

Val nods. "Lead the way, Professor."

Dream rolls his eyes. "Smart ass."

That time, the silence is easier. All they can do is keep walking, passing by the occasional bizarre skeletal tree, not a trace of color to its bark. Their shape is a lot more blunt than any tree Val has ever seen, and there are no places where he can envision leaves sprouting. They really are more like finger bones than anything else, and Val gets a chill as he tries to imagine what those old extinct monsters might have looked like.

Hours pass, and the air grows chilly and bitter as the moon rises. Val's mouth falls open as he realizes he left his backpack behind when he attacked Knives.

"Shoot."

"Yeah, sorry, didn't exactly have it together to go fetch your dead body *and* your shit," Dream mutters.

"I really am an idiot," Val says. "Did I eat all the food in your bag?"

"Yeah," Dream says, stopping to rustle through his own supplies. "It's uh, mostly bullets and cigarettes in here by now."

"Lovely," Val says.

"Do you need to stop for the night?" Dream asks.

Shaking his head, Val takes Dream's bag from him. "No point in stopping. We're too close."

"What do you have left in your pockets?" Dream asks.

"My scalpel," Val answers.

Dream gives a scoff. "Even worse off than when I met you. Well, let's be honest. You're much better with your words anyway. Still can't believe you talked a hatchling onto our side."

Val puffs up his chest. "I am quite convincing when I want to be."

"You're a damn weirdo is what you are," Dream says. "But, luckily for all of us, you're more interested in making friends than killing people. What do you think happened with the hatchling anyway? There's no tool in them, right? That means they pulled it out already."

"If I had to guess, the Queen removed their tool and did something to make them forget their life as a human. If our hatchling hurt people before ever meeting the spiders, they probably *wanted* to forget. I'm sure that's what would have happened to Matthew if he'd gone to Innovation like he was supposed to."

"So they let the hatchlings cause enough destruction that it becomes the better option to just forget," Dream says.

Val lets his breath out slowly, more and more grateful that he was able to get through to Matthew and their hatchling, but they're not the only ones by far. "Do you think the gunsmith in Prosperity is still there?"

With a heavy sigh, Dream gives a big shrug. "Fuck, Val, I have no clue."

"Maybe after we wrap this up, I can go check on him," Val announces. "You should come with me. It could be cathartic. Maybe the house you were squatting in is still empty. Do you think Mare would like it up there?"

"No, but, long as we're being honest, Mare's kinda hard to please," Dream says.

"Really?" Val asks. "In what way?"

"Every way," Dream answers. "He likes what he likes, and isn't interested in anything else. I once tried to convince him to take a trip up north with me to see snow again. We spent so much time on the southern coast, I forgot what it felt like, so I needled him for ten years straight until he finally agreed to go with me."

"And?" Val prompts.

Dream starts laughing. "He fucking hated it, except for the fireplace in our room. Said he liked tending the fire. He was hypnotized by it. I told him, 'hey maybe you like the fire so much because the cold makes you appreciate the warmth for once.' He looked like he wanted to kill me."

The expression on Dream's face is harder to read by moonlight alone, but Val can still see the affection plain as day in the lines of his mouth. An easy smile, the kind that happens without thought.

"I still think about that trip," Dream admits. "How good he was just because he knew I wanted to be there. That's the thing about him. He might complain, or drag his feet for ten years, but he never says *no*. Not when he knows it's something you really want. He let me pull him all over the world just so I wouldn't be there alone."

"Is that . . ." Val's mouth is dry as he tries to get the word up. "Is that what it means to love someone?"

"I don't know," Dream says. "Love is a human word. Humans are more adaptable than we are. I think most of them probably would have taken the fucking hint after they got shot and stabbed by the same man."

Val laughs. "I'm not sure that's true. Humans are also stubborn. Look at Hunter."

"Point taken."

"You've been with them the longest, but you barely understand people," Val says. "Kind of funny."

Dream frowns at the barren landscape, the strange white trees that seem to glow in the moonlight. "I have to stay away from them, or I risk changing them."

Val starts laughing harder. "You're such an old man sometimes."

"The fuck does that mean?" Dream snaps.

Val hitches his pack higher onto his shoulders, adjusting the straps to fit his arms a little more comfortably. "I'll tell you when you're even older."

"I'm gonna kill you, I swear to god. You say one clever thing and it goes right to your fuckin' head."

Dream swats at him, but Val ducks out of the way, walking on with his gaze set on the massive glittering shell of Innovation. There are a few lights dotted throughout the structures that make up the city, a series of windows lit up from within like artificial stars. The tallest tower in the city disappears into the darkness of the night sky, but Val can see light reflecting off of the glass like a cluster of glistening eyes. If he'd seen this place a month ago, it might have terrified him in its grandness, but now all he can think is that this is an impressive web for the spiders to hide in.

"Do you think Hunter would like snow?" Val asks.

"I don't fuckin' know," Dream says, then sighs. "Maybe. Seems like he could probably make it work anywhere."

"You've seen his dreams by now, haven't you?" Val turns to him.

Dream doesn't say anything for a minute, his cane hooked over his shoulder. He looks like he does when he wants a cigarette, reaching in his mind for something a little too far away.

"You care about 'em, right?" Dream asks.

Val nods. "I think so."

Dream gives a brusque laugh. "Trust me, kid, you don't stab a man in the throat for a person you *don't* care about."

Val's face heats up.

"Here's a lesson, then," Dream says. "Haven't given you one in a while, so listen close. Not being able to see inside someone's head is a good thing. I could tell you what Hunter dreams about, but you'll like the answer better in his words."

Val drops his gaze, hot from head to toe. "Right."

"Get to know 'em the slow way," Dream says. "Like a human."

Val nods, letting his mind wander as he steeps in this fragile warmth. He builds a picture in his head of a house sitting on a lawn of snow. It looks sort of like the one he met Dream in, and sort of like the orphanage he grew up in. He thinks that Matthew would probably not much like the snow, a bit too uncertain for his legs as they are, but if he had a path to walk, he would be faster than anyone else. Moon would probably thrive in it, but Moon would do well just about anywhere. He might not like to have to dress for the cold though, so comfortable with his skin out. The hatchling wouldn't like the chill, but Val is sure they would enjoy the warmth of a house full of people. He can't quite picture Dream enjoying the snow-covered earth the way the boys at the orphanage once did, but Val can easily imagine him smoking in front of a hearth, and well, now he knows Mare would sit with him, as long as there was a fire to tend.

When he tries to put Hunter into the picture, Val can't decide where to put them. Would Hunter like the snow, the quiet crunch of it as they left a trail of boot prints wherever they walked? Would they like to be by a fire, slowly thawing after staying out for so long that their ears turned red? Their piercings would grow cold while they were outside, but the warmth of their breath would turn to steam in the air. Val almost trips again while he thinks about it. Touching the chilled bits of metal in their face, standing close enough to feel the heat coming off their body, watching the tip of their nose turn pink.

Val feels an ache in his hands at the near painful desire to make this image real. He wants to see Hunter with nothing better to think about than the cold. How pretty they would look without their guard up . . . fragile, even. Val's jaw hurts as he holds the image in his head. He's not sure he could ever say it aloud, but it's intoxicating to think about Hunter showing Val the vulnerable parts of him, the way Val wants to bite as badly as he wants to soothe.

Would Hunter even let him? The chance to give back some of those perfect clean cuts or the heated, messy press of their teeth in the dark makes Val's head buzz. If he's ever allowed to touch Hunter the way he wants to, he'll do it in the middle of the day when the sun is at its brightest, so Hunter has nowhere to hide. He'll turn every light on if he has to. There's no way Val would miss the chance to watch every inch of Hunter reacting to him. It makes Val's mouth water, hoping to turn Hunter *soft*.

He'll have to try later, after he severs the leash that keeps Hunter so ready to kill.

Val's list of *laters* is growing longer by the day.

It might be the utter silence of the deadlands at night, but Dream and Val don't talk again as they walk through the moonlight. Only with the warmth of the morning sun pressing into his back does Val even think about asking Dream what their plan is. Getting to the border is one thing, but there's bound to be a horde of hatchlings ready to stop anyone approaching the city.

Val is getting ready to broach the subject, his mouth dry from the hours and hours of walking, when Dream stops short, staring hard at something in the distance. Val follows Dream's line of sight to the shape of a person amid the bony trees. With his senses so muted, Val completely missed their presence. Fear of Knives sends a cold sweat dotting over the back of his neck, but, no, this person is wearing something completely different. They aren't as massive as Knives either, standing in what looks like a tattered old dress, a braid of steel-wool hair hanging between their shoulders.

"... Sig?" Dream's voice is much too quiet for a human to hear, but they turn to face him.

Raising a hand up to their mouth, they hush Dream. As they walk closer, carefully, like the ground is littered with shards of glass, Val can see their body is perfectly in line with one of those white trees. It halos them in a skeletal silhouette.

Sig is very clearly wearing a dress that was not made for their body. The straps don't quite sit right on their shoulders, the fabric shaped to hug a full chest that Sig does not have, and the hem clings awkwardly to their thighs. Their shoes are nothing but skin tight slippers and Val wonders if they're trying not to leave any footprints.

"Sig, fuck, is that really you?" Dream reaches for them, his voice still a harrowed whisper.

Sig gives a smile with the very corner of their mouth. "Took you long enough."

Dream lurches forward and pulls Sig into a hug, his cane sliding off his shoulder, which Val scrabbles to catch.

"Careful," Sig says, patting Dream on the back. "We're right on the edge of their sight lines. No sharp movements out here, alright?"

Dream pulls back from them, his own smile tinged with disbelief. "Look at you. Shit. How long have you been out here?"

"I'm not sure," Sig answers. They look almost as old as Dream, or maybe just more exhausted. Val has noticed the way Dream's skin has changed from the pallid hermit he met in Prosperity to a man who drinks in sunlight, like a tree regrowing its bark. If Dream is new growth, then Sig is storm-weathered—soft cracks splintered over their cheeks, and shoulders, and arms.

"It's been too long," Dream says, reaching up to touch their chin. Sig is only an inch or two shorter than Dream, but the delicate look of them makes Val feel like *he* has more solid mass than they do. "Thought you made friends with humans, huh? You gotta go feed, Sig. You'll rot out here."

They nod, laying their hands on the front of Dream's coat. "I will. I just couldn't risk missing you." Sig smooths their hands over Dream's shoulders, as if to convince themself that he's real. "Is it time? Are you going to bring our brother home?"

Dream's expression collapses as he makes a sound halfway between a laugh and a sob. "Yeah, I'm gonna bring him home."

"I knew that you'd try again," Sig says. "I came out here to start planning, you know? To help. I'm not sure wh . . . when that was, but I think I've gotten it down to the most likely scenarios."

Dream shakes his head. "Should've known you'd be holed up somewhere over-thinking."

"You can see the city from here," Sig says, turning and pointing at the metal and glass in the distance. "But they can see us too. The deadlands are good and bad, you know? The insects, they won't come out here, but they know that we might, so they've got someone up there with a rifle. Whoever it is has *very* good eyes."

"A rifle? Fuck, I didn't think about that," Dream says. "They'll have perfect visibility out here. They'll see us immediately."

"That's what I've been thinking about," Sig tells him. "If you want to move around the city, you have to deal with them first."

"We gotta circle back around." Dream shakes his head. "Maybe go north and then cut back to avoid the open area."

Sig turns to Val, big ashen eyes taking him in. "Hostage or partner?"

"Shield," Val says.

Sig's brows jump up. "Even better."

"Oh, yeah, Sig, this is Val. He's uh, he's with me."

"This is good." Sig starts nodding. "Yes, good. You'll definitely get into the city easier like this. Good, good, good, this moves plan D up to plan A."

"How many plans did you come up with?" Dream asks.

Sig just turns away and starts walking northward, the shiny fabric of their violet dress shifting like water against their back. "It's been dry out here, they should all still work . . ."

Val passes Dream's cane back over to him, and Dream takes it with one last shake of his head. "Val, meet my younger sibling, Foresight."

Sig leads them to a lopsided house, or what might have been a house if anyone else had built it. For Sig it appears to be more of a glorified storage shed, and when they shove open the door from a frame that isn't cut right, the entire inside of the building is stacked floor to ceiling with *things*. What visible walls there are have been plastered with pieces of paper covered in drawings and plans and lists. Sig steps around everything like a minefield they memorized long ago, but Dream and Val just hover by the door, boxed in on all sides. It smells like wax from a small graveyard of candles that have been burned down to puddles.

"Shit, you've been working hard." Dream looks around the room, lit only by sunlight streaming in through the cracks in the walls, and one makeshift window. "You've been out here planning and forgot to eat, didn't you?"

Sig gives a rusty laugh. "Guilty. But you're the one who waited as long as you did. Daydreaming again?"

"Yeah, well." Dream's voice comes out in a huff and he grimaces at the ceiling. "I'm a coward, alright?"

Sig starts moving boxes, trying to unearth a crate currently acting as a load bearing weight for a precarious tower of books. "You have every reason to be. But I'm sure Mare will be happy to see you this time."

"Come on, then, give me your best estimation of what's going on with him," Dream says. "You think he wanted distance? Does he want to hurt us? Is he trying to . . . rot where we can't see?"

Sig finally gets to the right crate, kneeling down and taking stock of whatever's inside while quietly counting. Turning to Dream, they set their hands over their knees, crouched up in the corner of a house they must have built themself. "I think that fifty years of solitude is enough to make anyone regret their mistakes."

Val can see Dream chewing on the inside of his lip.

"Does it really matter why he left?" Sig asks. "You'll go to him no matter the answer. So why bother asking?"

Dream's fingers tighten over the handle of his cane, and Val leans forward into his line of sight. "Weren't you just telling me not to go cheating for answers you can get yourself?"

Dream's eyes narrow to slits. "You're on thin ice with me, boy."

Val grins at him. "I'll take that promotion to manager now."

Dream mouths *kill you* as Sig walks up behind Val.

"Here." They pass over a box of bullets. "Do you still have Mare's revolver?"

Dream snatches the box from their hands with a scowl. "'Course I do."

Sig nods again. "Why don't you two wait here? I have to go check a few things, and it's best if you're not causing too much commotion in the daylight. It'll be harder for the marksman to see you at night anyway. I'm sorry I don't have any food for your shield, but at least you won't sweat yourself to death in here. There might . . . be a bottle of water . . . somewhere."

"Hey, are you really okay with this?" Dream catches Sig's arm, staring hard at their face. "You and I both know how bad he fucked up."

Sig nods, no hesitation. "I don't ever want to willingly let one of my siblings go. I can't get Remi back, but you can still get Mare. So you make sure he knows that I want to see him, alright? He's still my big brother."

Dream lets Sig go and nods. "Yeah I'll tell him. *After* I strangle him."

Sig chuckles, a little more life in their eyes. "You couldn't hurt him even if you wanted to. I'll be back. Val, you make sure my brother doesn't do anything rash."

Sig winks at Val, and Val grins back at them. "Been my full time job for a while now."

With a pat on Val's head, Sig slips back outside, and Dream starts shoving a path clear so he can sit on some of the sturdier looking crates.

"Water's over here," he says, reaching behind him. "C'mere. Give me my bag."

Val slings his pack around and Dream fishes out one of the pieces of gauze from his medical supplies. With a metal canteen from Sig's boxes, Dream starts wiping all the dried blood from Val's face and neck.

"Thank you," Val says.

Dream just shakes his head, the gauze a little scratchy on Val's throat.

"You should sleep," Val says. "Save your energy while we're stuck here. The last thing you need is to start feeling weak while we're inside Innovation."

"Yeah, maybe you're right," Dream says. "You too, then. No need to risk your body healing anything you don't need while we got no food."

"Okay."

Glancing around the room, Val scratches the back of his neck. "I'm not sure I'll fit though . . ."

Dream shifts on the crate, pushing his back to the wall and setting his cane aside. "Sorry, just gonna have to make it work."

Val sits down between his knees, not wanting to impose, but Dream only pulls Val closer by the waist.

"Lean on me, shit, I'm trying to help you."

"Oh." Val starts laughing, letting his back rest against Dream's chest. "Will you be able to sleep like this?"

"Of course," Dream grumbles. "I can sleep anywhere. You're the one I'm worried about falling over and cracking your skull on one of these crates."

Val shuts his eyes, trying to settle his head, but it *thunks* into something on the inside of Dream's coat.

"Shit, sorry." Dream pushes whatever it is to the side.

"Is your coat just lined with weapons?" Val asks.

"Mostly," Dream says.

"What else is there?" Val asks, his body finally going slack after so many hours of nonstop movement. It's easier than he expected to start slipping further toward sleep.

Dream sort of sighs, sort of grumbles, and folds his arms against Val's stomach like a seat belt. "Took some of Mare's stuff with me . . ."

"What did you bring?" Val asks.

Dream exhales, and Val feels it on the top of his head as a few strands of his hair flutter out of place. "He, uh, had a pair of gloves. *Has*, he has a pair of gloves. He got it in his head that if he could avoid touching humans, he'd have fewer nightmares, so he took to wearing them. Not sure it actually worked, but it made him feel better."

"I'm sure he'll be glad to have them back," Val murmurs, his body growing heavier.

He sags against Dream, mind full of syrup as he thinks he missed a golden opportunity to lay in a hammock with Hunter while they were in the woods. That would have been nice. No space *not* to touch.

"You remember that dream I made you have back in Prosperity?" Dream asks.

"Mm."

"That's the only time I've ever been able to look in your head," Dream says. "I spent a while trying to figure out which part of that was good for you. Figured you just hadn't woken up to whatever piece of your insect brain was waiting to try to kill me."

Val can barely hear him over the scent of old wood and sweetness.

"I guess maybe I let you come with me because I was waiting for it, ya know? Someone to finally do it."

Dream hardly even smells like cigarettes anymore. His scent, his *real* scent, the one he keeps buried under booze and tobacco and oil, it's faint and soft and sweet. Not sugar sweet, not like the powerful candy shop scent of the hatchlings with their tools, but something more natural than that. Something earthy and precious.

"All this talk of humans and spiders and pillars. I think I figured it out."

Val feels like he's being cradled in the shell of a pumpkin, sinking into soft pulp.

"I asked you for a good dream, and I watched you killing me."

When Val wakes up, he'll have seeds in his hair.

"That was *my* dream. Sorry, kid. I won't make you do that again."

Sig wakes them while the sky is still steeping with darkness. Soft candlelight breathes through the lopsided house, bringing Sig's cracked face into view.

"It's almost time," they say, gently shaking Dream's shoulder. "Everything's in place. The rest is up to you following my lead."

Dream pops awake like he was never asleep. "I never fuck up your plans."

Sig smiles. "You *are* much better at seeing them through than I am. You would have built a better house as well."

Val feels heavy as he slides off the crate and back onto his feet. "You don't . . . have anything edible here, do you?"

"Here." Sig offers up an apple. "You're in luck. I went far enough north that I could steal one for you."

Val eats the whole thing down to the core. "*Thank you.*"

With a tired smile, Sig puts their hand on Val's head. "I would never know you weren't a human."

Val almost drops the apple onto the floor. "Really?"

"Mm. You have a nice scent. You know, underneath the blood."

Val turns to Dream with a breathless grin. "Let's go. We don't want to waste any more time."

"God, turning the fucking lights down a bit, you're blinding me." Dream stands up, rustling through his coat for Mare's revolver, and begins to reload it. "Sig, you promise me on Remi's name that as soon as you're done helping us, you're getting your ass back to the nearest human town."

"Well I can't say no to my older brother, now can I?" Sig says. "You'll meet me there, right?"

Dream scoffs, though his lips are just slightly curved into a smile. "You tell me where to meet you, kid."

When Sig smiles again, it's like all of the cracks and wrinkles in their skin disappear under the warmth they must feel at seeing Dream do something familiar.

"Bring Mare to Good Fortune. If he can make it all the way up that lift, I'll know he's really back."

Dream tucks the gun away and pushes Val toward the door. "You heard 'em. We got plans now."

Sig pads quietly after them. "And make sure to bring Curiosity and Mischief a souvenir."

"From that shithole?" Dream points at Innovation, once again reduced to a series of reflections cast on glass windows. "Ozzi's got better taste than that."

"Then I'll ask Val to bring one."

Val nods at them. "I'll keep my eye out."

"That's a nice boy you have with you," Sig says. "Make sure he stays that way."

"Yeah, yeah." Dream looks back at the city, narrowing his eyes. "How do you plan on distracting that rifle?"

"I've been setting up a network of . . ." Sig clears their throat and shakes their head. "No time to explain. Let's just say I have a lot of fireworks and I'll send you on your way."

"Works for me," Dream says. "Let's go."

"Oh, wait, I wanted to ask you something." Val jogs up to Sig, heart pounding as he realizes they're about to careen past the point of no return. "This feels like a silly question what with everything else going on, but did you make a deck of sight seal cards for someone in Good Fortune?"

Sig blinks at him, brows slowly lifting higher. "Yes, yes I did. H-How is the Lady Violet? I owe them a visit . . ."

"They're good," Val says. "They did a reading for me, it was lovely. There's just something I needed to know. There's a card in there with a drawing of a human hand in the clouds."

"Is that how it looks to you?" Sig gives a clipped laugh. "I was thinking about fog when I drew it . . . Good Fortune gets very foggy in the harvest season, reaching all the way up your chest. People get lost in it sometimes."

"Oh . . ." Val's head cocks to the side.

Sig gives a gentle smile. "Not the answer you wanted?"

Rubbing the back of his neck, Val realizes he forgot what Lady Violet said of the card in the first place. *You won't be satisfied with someone else's words.*

"No, I'm just getting ahead of myself is all." Val straightens up and sticks his hand out. "Thank you for your help. I, uhm, I like your dress."

Sig smiles back, returning the handshake like a steady metronome. "Thank you. It was Remi's favorite."

It takes about thirty minutes for them to reach a white tree with a ribbon tied around it, Sig's marker to determine the very edges of the line of sight from Innovation. Dream and Val huddle there, waiting for Sig to set off whatever light show they have promised.

"You ready to run?"

"Yes, sir. Are you?"

"Yeah. I'm stronger than ever."

"You're a bad liar too, you know that?"

"I think it depends who you ask."

"Is it because we're getting closer to Mare that you're getting more annoying?"

Dream laughs, and the sound is immediately drowned out by a burst of crackling fire exploding from somewhere behind them. The two of them are already sprinting when they hear an accompanying gunshot piercing through the cacophony. Val flinches at the force behind a bullet that can travel so far and still scream.

It's a simple plan, really. Sig sets off enough noise and light to distract someone watching from the scope of a rifle. The sound and light come in waves, never settling long enough for anyone's eyes or ears to adjust. Sig promised they would be far enough away not to risk getting shot at themselves, which only puts Dream and Val in danger. Val's biggest concern is his own dampened senses. He's just as distracted by the deafening sounds and the gaudy lights sprinkling through the air.

He wonders if it's a spider or a hatchling behind that rifle. Probably a spider, up there in some metal tower without a single soul around to distract them from their job. It must be infuriating to have Sig screwing with their performance. If this spider is anything like Knives, this is exactly what they'd hate.

Commanding his body to stop caring about *breathing*, Val huddles behind a dead tree, and Dream comes crashing into him, squishing Val up against the bark. Sig said there would be a pause in the show, and for them to lie low for it. With his cheek pressed up against bone-white bark, Val goes still as he feels the barest pulse underneath his own. Reaching with his fingers, he touches the trunk of the tree, shocked by how soft it is, like the velvet on a deer's antlers. Dream grabs Val's fingers, stopping him from moving, and Val remembers that they can't afford a mistake right now.

As a new set of achingly bright light tears through the sky, they break back into a sprint. In the glow of fireworks exploding above them, Val can see the edges of the forest that surrounds Innovation, which will shelter them directly into the city limits. With every step across the dry, hardened ground, there is a flicker of excitement growing steadily through Val's chest. This place isn't dead at all. It's just *new*.

The last stretch of land is the most exposed, and Val isn't at all surprised when the rifle gets a clean shot straight through his chest. As he bleeds out into the hungry earth, he can see Dream crouched behind the nearest tree, eyes fixed on the windows of the closest tower in Innovation.

When we're close enough, just let them shoot me. You can figure out where they are.

Asking me to kill you again, huh?

Val shuts down while Dream takes aim.

Almost there.

⸺

Waking up and seeing Dream's head turned to the sky and artificial light struggling through lush tree branches is just as much of a relief as his senses rushing back to him. Val can feel Dream's lullaby again.

"Made it?"

"Made it," Dream says, nodding at Val. "I know where they are. Let's go."

They walk slower through these trees, hoping to go unseen as Sig's show reaches its most disorienting climax. An artificial rainbow goes screaming overhead as Dream and Val discover another paved road cutting through the perfectly straight rows of trees, beckoning them into the streets of Innovation. It's there that Val feels the wall. He'd almost forgotten about it, so long since he'd even considered the reason why they started out on this journey.

It's not a solid wall, hardly visible at all in the darkness, but when he reaches out to touch it, it's as heavy as brick passing over his skin.

Pushing through it takes effort, like walking under a waterfall, actively trying to force him away. Despite the fact that there is no physical presence whatsoever, Val braces himself under the impossible weight of what he is sure is Mare's presence, distilled into a curtain of iron.

Shuddering, Val turns to offer a hand to Dream. The pillar looks starstruck, shaking his head as he lets Val pull him forward through the wall.

"Is this like what you did to Respite?" Val asks, shivering as a chill seeps into his skin.

Dream's jaw clenches shut as his body passes through it. He lets his breath out through his nose, one of his eyes twitching slightly when he's clear of it. "This is worse."

"Rifle first, Mare next." Val says, tugging on Dream's arm.

"Right, right." Dream's voice comes out a hush of steam, his eyes unfocused as he lets Nightmare's presence wash over him for the first time in decades.

They press on underneath the tight row of trees toward the closest building, but Val is leading Dream by the hand through the streets of his brother's hollow city. With his senses back to their fullest, Val can feel the shivering heartbeats of at least a hundred hatchlings pulsing in front of them, their hackles raised from Sig's display. Val wonders if they can all hear Dream approaching them, or if Nightmare's veil is so strong that it can even eclipse Dream from their sight. Val has never felt someone so *loud*.

In the distance, Val can feel one of those glass buildings buzzing so frantically, he knows with absolute certainty that it is where all of them must live. A hive for the hatchlings, the spiders, their Queen, and at the center of it all, Nightmare is singing a lullaby that pours through the city like blood from an open wound.

13

They're outside in the middle of the night with cool air on their faces, but the sound is like they're walking through some cavernous cathedral as Mare's lullaby fills the whole space. They move through his song just as much as they move through the city. For the first time, Dream truly looks lost, and Val has to pull him under the shade of a tree and grab his face.

"Where is the rifle?"

Dream stares at him for a full three seconds before light comes back to his eyes. "Right, sorry. There."

He points out the nearest towering structure with a perfect vantage point into the deadlands, and Val stares at it, throwing out his own senses like a blanket on a fire. He knows exactly what he's looking for. It's bound to be a spider, one of the sentinels that Hunter told them about. They won't be as stainless steel as Knives, but they'll be different from the hatchlings. He's not looking for a pistol either, but a rifle.

The spider pings on his radar, a piece of stained glass amid a clear pane. Val can feel hands layered over his own, fingers longer than his carefully and efficiently taking apart the pieces of a large gun. The spider may work quickly, but Val can feel a mothwing sadness in the spider's chest at having to treat this piece of equipment in a manner that isn't *proper*. The spider is muttering an apology as she dismantles her favorite gun.

"Found her."

"*What?*" Dream stares at him, but Val only grabs Dream's hand and starts running.

"She's packing up," he says without looking back. "We have to get her before she finds another perch."

"Did you always know how to do that?" Dream asks, but Val is losing the ability to talk as he tells his legs to go faster.

Talking is unnecessary, hearing optional, sight selective. He can figure out where to run as long as he has a mental hook on the spider with the rifle. Dream will catch up. No time, no time, no time. If anything diverts Val now, if they get intercepted or captured or distracted, the spider will go back to monitoring the borders, looking to shoot anyone who approaches the city.

Now that they're inside the wall, Val notices a few stray pulses that aren't contained in the hive building. The spider with the rifle is one of them, two hatchlings are patrolling far enough north that they won't be an issue. From the center of the city though, angry metal is taking shape once more as Knives begins to move toward them. Val can feel him like a cold breath gathering in his lungs.

Val stops dead in the middle of a street that's so wide, he can't image what kind of vehicle needs this much space. Turning to Dream, Val gives him a polite smile and lets go of his hand.

"Knives is coming. I can get to the spider with the rifle before he finds me."

"If I'm not slowing you down," Dream finishes. "I hear you."

"I think he'll care more about me than you anyway," Val says. "Sort of seems like now's the perfect time for you to disappear and do what you came here to do."

"Does, doesn't it." Dream nods, opening his coat and peering at the handles of a staggering number of guns and knives he has haphazardly arranged into hand-sewn pockets and straps lining the interior. "You want one?"

Val shakes his head. "You said yourself that I'm better with words."

Dream gives a closed mouth laugh.

"I . . . I got you into the city. Does this mean." The words fall apart in Val's mouth as he starts blinking through a painful sheen of water in his eyes.

Dream lifts Val's chin up with the side of his hand, and brushes Val's bangs back from his face with a whisper of his fingertips against skin. "Yeah. Job's over. You can do whatever you want now."

Val takes a deep breath that seems to fill his entire body with air.

"Just, uh, maybe do me a favor," Dream says, pulling out the engraved revolver and fastening his coat back up. "Next time you see Hunter, fire 'em for me. I have a feeling you two will find each other before I see you again."

Smiling, Val nods. "I would love to."

"Good luck, Val."

"Thank you, Dream."

As soon as Dream begins to turn away, Val doesn't waste a second watching him go. Running full tilt in the direction of the spider, he shuts Dream out of his own awareness, refusing to let himself worry.

Looking ahead, not behind.

They'll meet up later.

There's so much left to do. Val couldn't carry any extra weapons even if he wanted to. His hands are already full with all these plans for *later*.

He hardly spares a single second's glance at this towering city as he runs through it. His vision is narrowing into a series of vibrations, warning him what's in his path and where not to step and how far he is from any of the spiders or hatchlings. When he shuts himself down to his barest components, he runs so much faster. Flying down these yawning streets, Val doesn't stop until he's at the base of the building where the new spider is. He doesn't think twice about the smashed windows, just vaults through the first opening he sees and takes his shoes off before tearing up the nearest flight of stairs.

If Hunter can make himself unnoticeable, maybe Val can too, just for a little while. He asks his heart to stop pounding, tells his skin to stop sweating, begs his mind and body to stay completely silent as he flattens himself to the wall next to the door to the roof of this bizarre sculpture of a building. The spider took her time, and Val thinks that she might be waiting for someone to come to her so she can snipe whoever opens the door, knowing her allies would heal from it. Her own vibrations are calm as compared to Knives, and Val guesses she's very good at waiting. Maybe she knows Knives is on his way, and figures it's best to stay here where she has the advantage of a single door. She's standing there with her rifle broken down inside its case, but she undoubtedly has other weapons. All Val has to do is stop breathing until she decides it's safe to find a new roost.

"Ma'am?"

She's talking to someone. Val commands himself to stay still through the shock. She must have some kind of radio with her.

"I can't sense or see anything useful from here, but that display was obviously a smoke screen for something. Should I move or wait?"

Val's head is starting to get spotty after several minutes of his body holding itself in utter and complete stillness.

"Yes, ma'am, you're right."

She pockets whatever device she was likely speaking through and starts heading for the door. Val's got pins and needles in his fingertips as each soft step of her boots draws closer and closer. Gripping his scalpel in his right hand, Val lets his body turn back on as the door bursts open with a rusty screech. The spider puts one foot on the stairs as Val throws himself at her. He drags the blade across her throat as she jabs her own knife into Val's flank. With a grunt, Val screams in his head that he's not allowed to feel pain right now, and the left side of his body floods with numbness while he tries to bleed the spider dry.

"I'm sorry!" he shouts, using his own wrist like a horse's bit in her mouth to pull her head back.

She stabs him again before stumbling into the wall, the hard shell case dropping to the concrete stairs with a deafening clatter. She coughs, her third attempt with the knife falling short as the blood loss starts to weaken her grip. Slumping forward, Val feels her heartbeat growing faint as she collapses into a heap.

Val leaps off of her, tearing through the contents of her coat—the same heavy black coat that Knives wears, only smaller—taking several packs of dusty crackers that he swallows the contents of without chewing, and then ridding her of a small pistol, her knife covered in Val's blood, the thing she was speaking into, and her rifle's case.

The spider waves a hand at Val in a weak attempt to stop him as he throws open the heavy door to the roof. He tosses the pistol and the weird radio over the edge without a second thought, the drop too far down to even hear when they shatter, but he opens the case, pulls out the biggest piece of the rifle, and holds it over the edge of the building. It takes one full minute for the spider to heal, her heart restarting in a manic flurry. She shoves open the door with blood stuck to her neck, staring at Val with an open mouth.

"Don't."

Her voice is small, her right eye wide and shiny with the abject fear of losing something precious. Her left eye is not an eye at all, but a glass lens set into a metal scope jutting out of the socket.

"Please," she adds, a breathlessness that strikes Val in the chest. His body has already sewn itself back together, but he feels that sadness like a cut between his fingers.

"I have a problem," Val says to her, heart racing. "There's nothing I can do to stop you. You'll heal from any wound, or your Queen will fix you up again. But I have to do something, because I told my friends to come to this place, and I can't have you shooting them. One of them can't heal like we can. At least if I break your gun, I might be able to get them here safely."

Her hand is held out uselessly between them, her right eye darting between Val and the gun.

Val's teeth start to chatter. "I'm sorry I hurt you. I don't really want to. But do you see the complication?"

She nods. "If I let you bind my hands, will you give it back? I can't very well ignore my Queen, but . . . I can't help it if you waste my time while someone walks through the border."

Val hugs the piece of the rifle to his chest. "You mean it?"

"You're one of us," she says, her shoulders sloping from relief with her gun a little closer to safety. "Harder to lie to you."

"I'm helping the pillars. Working with humans," Val says to her. "Aren't you supposed to hate me?"

"I would hate you more if you broke my gun," she says, back straightening.

Val pulls her knife out of the waist of his pants and holds it out toward her. "Will you make yourself pass out so I can tie you up?"

She juts her chin out. "No need for that. Just give me the bolt handle so I know you're serious."

"The . . . the what?" Val asks.

She takes a short breath and closes her eyes. "Just pass me a piece of my gun, *please*."

"Oh." Val gives a laugh, picking a tiny piece of metal at random from all the little indents in the rifle case and tosses it to the spider. "May I ask your name?"

She catches the shiny piece and holds it to her chest, letting a breath out as her eye slides shut. "We've all been warned about you, you know. The rogue spider who loves names."

"I'm not surprised," Val says.

"The Cardinal Major was furious that you titled him. He said to call him Knives was a mockery."

As she speaks, Val can feel her body shifting internally, certain processes slowing down while others speed up.

"It was the first time I'd ever seen him *angry*," she says. "I was told that spiders are better than that."

Lifting her head up, the glass lens is pointed up at the very first bits of sunlight spilling into the night sky. She's shorter than Val was expecting, hardly any bigger than he is. The metal in her left eye sits coldly against the deep brown of her face, but she must have the most beautiful view from this height.

Slowly but surely, her heartbeat is slowing down all on its own.

"I didn't say so, but I kept wondering what name you would come up with for me if we ever met. Another thoughtless name, like *rifle*. You lack creativity, you know that?"

Val nods, speechless.

"I spent so much time trying to name myself in preparation for your visit, it started feeling . . . exciting."

The sky is getting fuller as the morning approaches, and the spider lets out a sigh at the empty sky above them.

"I can't see the hand anymore."

Val feels a fist around his heart and he, too, looks up to start scanning the sky. This is often the best time to see it, when the sky feels thinner somehow, like the change from night to day allows for a clearer glimpse at these things that don't belong in their world. As if those hands are holding the curtain of nighttime away for the sunlight to reach them.

But that day, it's just wisps of cloud over a hollow pink sunrise.

The girl sighs, letting her head droop to the side as she starts to lose consciousness. "I'm the North Sentinel of Innovation, and I'm the best shot in this entire city. Better even than your half-dead Pillar."

Her voice grows to a sleepy mumble as her presence begins to turn to pure radio static. "But you may have the honor of calling me Arum."

"Nice to meet you, Arum," Val says.

Arum slips the piece of metal from her gun into her own mouth before she crumples to the ground in a heap of black fabric. Val bolts over to her, pulling the heavy coat from her shoulder and hurriedly cutting strips of fabric off to bind her wrists and ankles together. It takes much too long, but he hauls her unconscious body over to the edge of the roof, propping her up against the concrete wall beside her rifle case before he fits all the pieces he took back into place.

Val pricks her finger with the knife, and Arum jolts back awake with a frown, holding the little piece of metal like chewing gum in her mouth. "I thought you'd leave me unconscious. Knives is almost here."

"Is this all the ammo?" he asks, holding a box out to her.

She holds his gaze for a moment, her mouth a hard, thin line, and then she sighs. "There are bullets in the magazine."

"Which part is that?" he asks blankly.

"The curved bit there! Just toss it with the clip you have," she grumbles.

Val plays hot and cold until she confirms which part is safe to throw over the edge of the roof, and then he sits down in front of Arum, who staunchly ignores his gaze with her right eye.

"I don't mind if you tell Knives it's all my fault—"

"It *is* your fault," she mutters.

"Well, I won't tell him how quickly you agreed to my terms," Val says. "I'm sure he's going to untie you and get you more bullets and let you perch somewhere else. So, when you get there, maybe you can just . . ."

Val's chest tightens as he pictures Hunter and their hatchling wandering unknowingly into Arum's perfect sight. They would never know. Her vision would outreach their senses, and Hunter would be dead before he knew it was even a risk.

"Just please don't kill my friends." Val's voice cracks as his damn tears start up again. He throws his arms around Arum's neck and squeezes her much too tight, his body moving on some fresh grown instinct that he has yet to put words to. "You'll know them when you see them. They're very distinct. Our hatchling hasn't picked a name yet but they have very thin fly's wings and two eyes in each socket."

Arum's body stiffens under Val's awkward hug, her heart rate suddenly spiking, but Val just keeps babbling.

"And Hunter, you'll know them as soon as you see them, they're very big and they have black jewelry all over their face and the prettiest hair, just please don't hurt them. I don't care what else you do, but Hunter is good and he needs to live for a very long time because he hasn't figured out how to smile yet."

Val jerks away from Arum as Knives cuts his way into Val's awareness, his boots stomping up the stairs with absolutely no care for stealth. When Val turns back to Arum, her face is awash with profound discomfort, physically shying away from Val's words and his tears like a stain.

"You're such a mess," she mutters. "Do you really think giving me perfect descriptions of your weaknesses is a good idea?"

Val sniffs, trying to shove the sadness back down so he can ready himself for Knives, but his eyes are still running.

Arum heaves a sigh. "Is this what we all have to look forward to? Groveling and tears?"

"There's lots of good stuff too," Val says, Knives's echoing steps rising up beneath him at purely inhuman speed. Val pulls Arum's knife back out, holding it just so Knives sees it first. "It's not as scary as you think. Emotions."

She *hmphs* and tilts her chin up. "Be careful, *Val*. My brother doesn't like it when his family is threatened. He might go overboard when he sees this."

"Thank you for worrying." Val flashes her a small smile and sets the tip of the knife to her throat. "You're very nice, Arum."

"I know," she says, straightening her shoulders as much as she can in spite of the restraints. "I've been practicing."

The door to the roof opens once more with a *boom* as Knives throws it hard enough to put a dent in the wall behind it. Val doesn't even have time to pretend to be threatening before Knives has a gloved hand in his hair, dragging him across the concrete roof. Val drops the knife, a yelp escaping his throat as Knives tosses him against the wall, knocking the wind out of him. Before Val can try to get his breath back, Knives puts a hand around Val's throat. All Val can see is his mouth ripped into snarl.

"Killing you a thousand times wouldn't be enough."

It isn't a bullet or a knife that meets Val's head, but Knives's own closed fist.

A series of fresh concussions keeps Val utterly disoriented for the length of time it takes Knives to carry him away from Arum's roost. When he is finally allowed to wake up again, his body is laid up on a stiff cot underneath harsh, buzzing lights. It is nothing less than a full system shock to see a familiar face leaning over him.

The centipede doctor glares at Val, brushing back their curtain of shoulder-length hair. "Finally. I was beginning to think he altered you."

"You're alive," Val says.

"Obviously." The doctor waves a hand and darts over to the other side of the room. "Despite your wretched Pillar setting me on fire, I'm fine. The Cardinal Major had to send me home though, which I *do not* appreciate."

They spit the words at Val, lower lip fixed in a pout, but when they see him grinning back, they lose their grip on their own annoyance.

"S-stop looking at me like that," they mutter. "I'll knock you out again."

"He lied, you know," Val says. "Knives said you'd reached the end of your usefulness. He made me think he'd killed you, but all he did was bring you to safety."

The doctor looks around the room, worrying at their own hands as redness blooms under their cheeks. "I . . . I'm sure he was saying that to confuse you." They fold their arms, raising their chin with a haughty smile, despite the blush still clinging to their face. "And you fell for it. That's why he's the Major. He's very smart."

"Does that mean my friends are alive too?" Val asks, sitting up in his cot.

Shoulders hunched, the doctor points at him. "You're trying to get in my head. He warned me you would do that."

"I'm just talking," Val says.

"Your words are poisonous and stupid," the doctor snaps. "I have to go and it has nothing to do with you."

They fly out of the room in a flurry of limbs, and the door locks behind them with the decisive *thunk* of a deadbolt. As his senses readjust to being awake, Val feels something tied to his ankle and lifts the sheets to see that he is leashed to the metal frame of the cot. His old clothes are in a pile on the table across the room, his scalpel folded neatly on top. Pulling an IV out of his arm, Val tests the length of the restraint, unable to reach anything useful. All he's wearing are a pair of thin pants.

This room at least appears safe. It's some kind of infirmary with an unsettlingly clinical feel to it that Val has never encountered before. Everything is so terribly clean and white. Sitting down on the end of the bed, he closes his eyes and lets in the cacophony of living things filling the building all around him. Hatchlings on every side, pulsing with life, roaming the halls of their hive and waiting for orders. Most of them still have their tools—little beacons tucked away inside the flesh of all of these creatures, keeping them tuned to a miserable frequency.

Beneath them all, Mare's singing is so loud, it feels like it could reach through the floor and slice Val apart. Maybe that's why the hatchlings still have their tools inside of them. Mare's singing is enough to keep anyone on the edge of despair, and the tools would only keep them hating it more.

Nestled in beside Mare's presence, there is another that sits like an island in the middle of a great, churning river. Mare's song doesn't touch this empty space, merely diverts around it, and there is no doubt in Val's mind that this is the Queen, keeping herself close to her engine.

Knives is much closer though, and the moment Val tries to tune into him the way he did with Arum, there is a sharp sting like noisy feedback directly in his head as Knives swats Val away. Val doesn't have time to search for Hunter or Dream before Knives comes kicking down his door.

Val smiles at him and all his anger, and Knives lets a stuttering breath out through clenched teeth.

"Your scalpel worked after all," Val tells him. "The one you put in my ribs back at Southern Truth. I can see and move much better now."

Val can practically hear Knives clenching his fists.

"I didn't realize how badly you were broken," Knives says.

Val shrugs. "I stopped being scared of you, and it really opened my eyes."

Knives hasn't moved an inch from in front of the door.

"Do I scare you, Knives?" Val asks.

He turns his cheek just a few degrees. "You make the most horrendous sounds."

"But I bet your Queen is completely silent," Val says. "Right?"

Knives swallows, the muscles in his throat rippling underneath his skin.

"She's had a lot of time to purge herself of anything human," Val goes on. "I just wonder how you all deal with Nightmare?"

"What do you mean?" Knives asks.

Val's head tilts. "You think *I'm* loud. Mare has been crying for, what, fifty years straight? Can you not hear that?"

Knives goes stock still again and Val gets a jolt of realization like a lightning bolt.

"Is that how it works?" Val asks. "Your Queen has been telling you that you don't feel emotions while you live inside the saddest sound I've ever heard? I suppose it would be preferable to cut out the part of you that could feel what Mare's feeling. I'd have lost my mind years ago."

"Then I was right to bring you here," Knives says. "In enough time, you'll also choose to mute yourself."

Val studies the resolute look on Knives's face, completely at odds with his tensed body and clenched fists.

"You're such a fake," Val says, starting to laugh. "You're seriously going to keep telling me that you don't feel anything? Like you didn't throw a tantrum in the woods because we pulled your knives out? Like you didn't lie your face off pretending that you so coldly left your assistant behind when you probably couldn't stand the thought of losing them? Look, you're too scared to even get near me."

In a blink, Knives crosses the room to pin Val to the cot by the neck, and only then does Val process that he's not wearing his gloves. Knives holds him down, skin to skin, baring his teeth again.

"You . . . want to touch me . . ." Val squeezes the words out past Knives's fist. "I bet . . . that's against the rules. Is that why you had to do it in the chur—"

Knives crushes harder until Val's words sputter into useless coughs.

"You have no idea how horrible it is to go out there time and again," Knives speaks through a clenched jaw. "I'm the only one she trusts to send into the world of humans and still come home. We've lost two of our sentinels to the *noise* you all make, and now even my sister has begun to whisper. You and your humans make horrid, awful sounds. From your mouth and your body and your brain. They stick to me even after they've stopped. How can sound cling to an object? It makes no sense, but I am covered in cobwebs."

He swallows as Val tells his body to stop breathing again.

"If I can just force myself to get *closer*." Knives's fingers tense as he says it. "If I can understand how humans work, then I can figure out how to stop them. I can keep them from corrupting my family. I'll get your awful noise off of my sister."

Val can't speak to tell him that he and the pillars really have more in common than they realize, but Knives seems to hear what he's said and bucks off of Val like he's been burned.

Coughing his way back to speech, Val pulls himself upright. "Why can't you just admit that you're lonely?"

Knives checks over his own hands like Val may have left a rash on his skin. "I don't have to listen to someone who would choose humans over their own."

"Oh, hush," Val says, wheezing as his throat rebuilds itself. "I didn't *choose* humans. I like pillars *and* humans *and* spiders *and* hatchlings. I like all of you! Even when you're miserable and confusing and stabbing me, I like you. We're *family*, you idiot, you said it yourself. If you want to pick your own damn name, then by all means. You don't have to take the one I gave you."

Knives turns his head from Val, like something unseen has caught his eye.

"Why do you care so much about names?" he grumbles.

"I'm not very well going to call you *Cardinal Major* for the rest of our interminable lives," Val spits back at him.

Knives huffs through his nose. "You certainly have a human's hubris."

"Yeah, I've learned a lot from them," Val says. "Wonderful things, like humor, and being slightly less insufferable all the time."

Knives faces him again, his composure returning to him in inches. "You really believe that humans would fully welcome you into their ranks?"

"Of course not," Val says. "I know for a fact that they won't. I don't need them to. As long as I'm being honest, there's really only *one* human I care about accepting me anymore. As long as he does, the rest is just time. And I happen to have that in excess."

Knives tilts his head. "You willingly put yourself into a very precarious position. To give one person that much power over you."

Val folds his legs back onto the bed, shrugging with a lot less fervor. "I have friends. I know they're not going anywhere. It's not that I need Hunter's *approval*, I just . . . want him to think I'm nice."

"And what happens when this hunter realizes you aren't?" Knives asks.

"I told Hunter they're allowed to kill me," Val answers. "They'll figure it out."

"A very imbalanced proposition," Knives remarks with a scoff.

"Yes, well, how is this any different than you and your Queen?" Val asks. "You do anything she asks even when it drives you crazy. Hunter hardly asks for anything and he still makes me feel nice. I bet your Queen doesn't even touch you. Has she ever shown you kindness?"

"She doesn't need to," Knives says. "I earned her trust already. And before you go demanding proof, I'll tell you. I know she trusts me, because she already told me that when she leaves Innovation to find a new home, I and I alone, will be accompanying her to her new hive."

"W . . . what?" Val's brows furrow, the lights in the room feeling twice as bright as they were a moment ago. "You're leaving?"

"Yes," Knives says. "She has already deemed Innovation a failure and has decided to liquidate our hive so we can relocate and start somewhere else."

"Liquidate?" Val echoes, his vision tunneling as he stares at the pommels in Knives's face. "What does that mean?"

Knives gives him a polite smile. "All of the hatchlings inside the city will be destroyed, along with the rotten Pillar of Nightmares. They've come to end of their—"

"*Shut up!*" Val barely hears himself shouting. "She can't just kill everyone. There's at least a hundred people here!"

Knives folds his arms behind his back. "I wonder what you'll do about that, Spider."

Val doesn't hear anything over the sound of every single hatchling's heartbeat pulsing inside his own chest. He can't let them die. He can't let them stay here without even knowing that they could just leave. That it's okay if bad things happen, because someone might just be able to shoulder that with them. He can't. He can't. His head hurts and his chest is full to bursting and he *can't just do nothing.*

Knives's mouth is moving, but all that goes away when Val sees his own reflection in the pommels of those silver eyes.

14

The great city of Innovation is nothing but a ruin. Hunter has been watching it reveal itself with increasing clarity as they walk the path to its borders. What was probably once a beautiful sight has been reduced to a cracked, rusted version of itself. It is a shell that has already hatched whatever was growing inside it, and now nothing but scavengers are left to crawl among the wreckage.

Hunter can't sense the hatchlings or spiders, but they can feel the wall, like atmospheric pressure bearing down on their sinuses—Nightmare calling out to anyone who will listen.

No, that's not true. Hunter knows damn well who he's calling out to.

"So strange to be coming back," the hatchling mutters, their arms tightening around Hunter's neck.

Hunter adjusts the hatchling's body in their arms, hoisting them up higher on their back. "Are you scared?"

"Yes, I think so," the hatchling admits with a laugh like a bird's chirp. "But I'm more scared for Mister Val. I don't think anyone here will be very happy to see him."

"Mm." Hunter doesn't want to scare them any more, so they leave it at that.

"Thank you for carrying me while my legs regrow," the hatchling adds in a nervous flood. "I'm sorry it's taken so long."

"It's fine," Hunter says.

"The food you made was very good too," the hatchling adds, jostling around on Hunter's back. "I've never had someone cook for me."

"You can stop with that," Hunter says to them. "I'm not mad at you."

"Are you sure?" The hatchling lowers their face to Hunter's hair. "I thought for sure you were upset with me for forcing us to separate from Mister Val and Mister Dream. You looked very unhappy when you realized we had to go away from them."

"Alright, I was a little mad," Hunter says through a sigh. "But I promised Val I'd keep you safe. And he promised me he wouldn't die. So everything's fine."

"Good," the hatchling says, perking back up. "I'm excited to see Mister Val again."

"Yeah, you can stop telling me that."

"Ah, I'm sorry."

Hunter tries not to roll their eyes, taking a deep breath instead. "It's fine. I'm sorry, too. I'm just . . . preparing."

The hatchling's wings make a soft rustling sound as they flap, a thing Hunter has noticed happens when they're unsure of their words.

"The closer we get . . . the worse I feel," they say.

"Yeah." Hunter holds their legs tighter. "Me too."

Hunter has known about the wall their whole life, something all the Eyes are made aware of. They say it feels akin to getting sick, and to never wander close to it or it might take you off a job. The two of them have been steadily approaching the wall for hours and, despite the clear sunny day, it casts a dark sheen over the city, slowly turning it more foreboding as they get nearer. There is no comfort in approaching a labyrinth of shattered glass and corroding metal, but turning back isn't an option either.

Knowing it's Mare is just enough of a lifeline for Hunter to keep themself walking. Clinging to the hatchling helps a little as well, but

Hunter's mind keeps spiraling into moments of anger, disappointment, fear, and defeat, like every off-beat of their heart is one inverse.

There is a slight tremor in the hatchling's arms, and Hunter yells at them in their mind to calm down and stop twitching. If they hadn't tried to fight someone as dangerous as Knives, they wouldn't have gotten hurt, and Hunter could have met up with the others. *You've been nothing but trouble and now Val could be in danger and Dream could be dead. We never should have taken you. I never should have hunted Val. I don't deserve these eyes.*

"I—I think my toes grew back," the hatchling says. "If you want me to walk on my own."

Hunter blinks, resurfacing from the pull of the Mare's presence, like shaking ice cold hands off their throat.

"No," Hunter says. "Listen. When we're through that wall, I don't know what will happen to me, so I might need you to guide me. Can you do that?"

"Oh!" The hatchling swallows, setting their chin on top of Hunter's head, redoubling their grip on Hunter's body. "Yes, I can show you where the hive is. I'm certain that's where Mister Val will be too."

Hunter nods, steeling themself to the sight of what looks like an oil slick staining the air. The wasteland of Innovation sings a warning to them with the scent of decay and the sound of Mare's voice. Closing their eyes, Hunter tries to find the part of them that Val called *strong and capable* while Mare whispers into Hunter's ear, *if you crawl into an open grave, you can't blame anyone but yourself for getting buried.*

The hatchling's heartbeat is faster than a human's, pounding softly against Hunter's back as they stand at the wall beside a long overgrown railroad.

"Have you picked a name yet?" Hunter asks.

"Uhm, well, I was thinking about what Mister Val—"

"Just say it."

"Nora."

Hunter almost laughs, already sure that they were remembering Val calling them *No* as a tease.

"Alright, Nora. Get ready."

Hunter breathes in deep, and a second later, Nora does the same. This air is practically rotten, leaving the taste of rust in Hunter's mouth as they try to stabilize themself. They need every bit of calm and focus they can scrape up out of their own blood for this, no room now to be anything other than an animal. They'll have time later to figure out how to put it away, but for now, he'll be whatever he needs to be to get this done.

Hunter steps through the wall with Nora clinging to him like a child, and searing cold panic drills through his spine.

You shouldn't have come here.

Hunter's breathing stalls, every hair on his body standing on end. It's as if Mare himself is pushing on Hunter's chest to get him to turn around.

You couldn't kill Knives before. What could you possibly do to him now?

"That was . . . different," Hunter says aloud.

"Hunter?" Nora squeezes his head, but Hunter can't hear them—not with Mare taking shape in front of him, flesh and all.

He is so clearly Dream's twin. The same nose, the same mouth, only Mare's eyes are wider, his face perfectly smooth, easily ten or twenty years younger, and his hair is long enough to be half pulled off his face. His clothes are completely unrecognizable to Hunter, some sleek style that must have been in fashion when Innovation was in full swing. There is an elegance to him that doesn't quite fit right over the unyielding pressure of his presence—as if Hunter is only seeing a fraction of something much larger.

"How many failures do you need under your belt before you stop trying?" Mare asks, calm, almost merciful in his diagnosis.

There's ice in his throat, keeping Hunter from speaking.

"If you come here, you'll only hurt them worse," Mare explains. "What do you think will happen to Val if he loses you? He's still fresh. He can't handle that kind of loss. It might seem dignified now to die at the hands of someone stronger, but what will that matter when you make a monster out of him?"

Hunter feels Mare's voice chipping away at him like nails scraping up his skin. It *would* be awful. To make Val as ruthless as Knives.

"He'd kill Dream," Mare goes on. "*Really* kill him. And you know Dream would let him do it. That man is holding on by a thread as it is, and if Val can blame him for your death . . ."

Mare mimes a pair of scissors snapping shut, and Hunter starts choking.

"The real question is: how badly do you want to fuck this up?" Mare asks, nothing but sympathy in his gray eyes. "They will forgive you for turning back. But no one will be left to even try if you get yourself killed."

Is he right? Hunter is drowning in worst case scenarios. He already screwed up, it's true. He got caught by Dream outside the Dueling Cities, he failed to protect Val at Southern Truth, he let them all get caught by the hatchling when he succumbed to panic with Val in that tent, and he failed to keep them all together when Knives came to the campgrounds.

He can still hear Nora's screams echoing in his skull as Knives took a butcher's blade to their legs. The two of them barely got out of that as it is.

What the fuck is he doing here?

"Hunter!"

He startles at Nora tilting his head back, forcing his gaze onto their split eyes.

"We need to go!" They're pleading with him, anxiety pinching their face. "I can feel Val!"

Hunter takes a sharp breath, his mind and his body rattling back to the present moment as he remembers why he came here.

"Cover my eyes," Hunter says.

Nora's brows jump up. "But don't humans—"

"Just do it!" Hunter snaps, shutting his eyes first while Mare shakes his head like a disappointed teacher.

Nora fits their hands over Hunter's face, and he lets his body take over, breaking into a sprint to get free of the specter of Nightmare. Running toward buildings as gigantic as these ones strikes Hunter with an instinctive fear, but he tries to remind himself that this place isn't alive anymore. He knows exactly what he has to worry about, and it isn't these rusted shells.

Knives is waiting.

Thinking about him in this sea of despair is like ripping open a scab. Hunter had no intention of even trying to fight Knives back at the campground. All he wanted was to pull Nora away, make Knives bleed just enough to force him into healing, and double back to Val. He wasn't expecting the greeting.

As soon as Hunter was close enough to hear, Knives addressed him. "Val."

Hunter had stopped dead. He could sense Nora already pinned underneath Knives's boot, struggling ineffectually.

"That *is* the name you want to be called, isn't it?"

Every one of Hunter's lessons on patience were eroding on the edge of Knives's voice as he realized that Knives could smell Val on him.

"Oh?" With a petulant stomp of his heel, Knives broke Nora's neck under his boot, crushing Nora's presence down to a pilot light as their body set about rebuilding, and Knives began walking in a straight line toward Hunter. "You're not my spider."

Those four words said so much. They said everything, really.

Stringing together snippets of old conversations, a shadow that

Hunter had been avoiding finally took shape as he realized what Val and Knives really were. Sort of like the Pillars, but not. Using the same tools in different ways. Yes, they were like brothers, and also something else. Something more. Something jagged that wants to hurt just as much as it wants to heal. Like Dream's hands on Mare's body, and Mare's bullet in Dream's hip.

Hunter had left Val to this once before, and there it was again, threatening to drag Val back. So Hunter tried to stop it, telling himself as he prepared to sprint that if he could hurt this thing just once, maybe it wouldn't matter that he and Val weren't the same kind of broken. But Knives doesn't feel pain like a human, and even with two of Hunter's daggers sheathed to the hilt in Knives's torso, Hunter wasn't good enough to stop him. It was only by Nora launching themself at Knives to bite acid into his neck that Knives missed his shot at killing Hunter. And Knives repaid the favor by hacking into Nora's legs while the acid ate into his throat. It was lucky that Nora had the use of their hands and a full supply in their stomach.

They got away by the skin of their teeth, but Hunter hasn't shaken that interaction from his mind. The moment that Knives realized he wasn't speaking to Val, but to someone wearing Val's scent, was like cutting himself on a piece of glass he'd just been admiring. Knives was *angry*, and Hunter was jealous.

"This way, this way!"

Hunter readjusts as Nora steers him away from one street to another.

"We're getting closer, do you feel it?"

He does. Heartbeats are crowding his senses, a whole cluster of them in the distance, and two more, much closer than that. Hatchlings must be coming to investigate the intrusion, and Hunter is sure he doesn't have the wherewithal to fight like he normally does, so he bolts for the nearest building. Nora spots a smashed window and Hunter carries them inside.

"If you stay still, I can go talk to them," Nora whispers. "It's probably me they felt. Since you're so quiet."

"Don't be long," Hunter mutters, fishing out the wrap for his eyes.

Nora climbs off his back, dashing through bits of broken glass and scattered objects that Hunter doesn't recognize by sound alone. He tightens the fabric at the back of his head and finds a wall to huddle against. The Tongues used to tell stories about Innovation, a city dedicated to technological advances. It was meant to be a new foundation for the blend of human will and the strength of the Pillars. People had even begun to research whether it was possible to reverse the spread of the deadlands. Nearly every advancement made in the other towns originated here, but it also meant that some of the settlements staunchly refused the influence of such a strange city. Sitting in its rotted husk, Hunter can understand why people were afraid of this place.

He can't imagine living in a city so massive that it feels like one mistake could crush everyone inside of it. The desire to look at the wreckage is powerful. Hunter wants to know this place that Dream had at one point been so proud of, but the moment he pulls the wrap down from his eyes, Mare's cold steel is staring back at him.

"Did you send the hatchling away to get killed?"

"No."

Hunter covers his eyes again, pushing the heels of his hands over the fabric just to be safe.

"Is that the plan, then? No one would blame you if you said your friend got killed while you were fighting through the city. They'd probably believe you if you said Knives did it." Again, Mare sounds so *understanding*, like he's been here too, so jealous and petty.

Hunter grits his teeth. "Nora's fine."

"Mm, maybe you should kill Dream while you're at it," Mare says. "Val looks up to him so much. They'll be hardly any room in his heart for a useless human when they're through with this mission. Those two will be as close as, well, brothers."

"Shut up." Hunter feels for his closest dagger, gripping it like he means to break it.

"That's what drives you crazy, isn't it?" Mare's breath is hot on Hunter's ear, his presence like a cold spot crouched against Hunter's side. "They both have something you can't touch. It's not for humans. Maybe you can scratch an itch, but they'll never love you like they do their own family."

Fingers press into the front of his clothes, right over Hunter's heart as Mare puts an arm around his shoulders, like he truly means to comfort Hunter.

"It's not that it disgusts you either," Mare says, pity dripping from his voice. "You already tried that and it didn't work. No, you want the same thing. You want to be protector, and friend, and family, and lover. You want to be everything, but you can't manage any of it properly."

Mare is cradling Hunter against his chest while Hunter struggles to breathe. Mare's arms are thinner than Dream's, but he holds with the iron grip of a thousand miserable hands.

"It's alright," Mare soothes. "If you came here to die, it'll be over soon. Maybe you'll find some peace if Val cries over you."

The sound of a shoe on broken glass has Hunter pulling out the dagger, but it's only Nora saying, "All the hatchlings have been called back to the hive. They said something bad is happening. They were afraid."

Hunter sheaths the blade on his thigh and gets back to his feet. "Then we should go faster."

"What if it's too dangerous for us?" Nora asks, approaching him with the frantic pulse of a hummingbird.

"Then we'll have to be more dangerous," Hunter says. "Let's go."

Hunter doesn't wait, just scoops Nora up so he can run easier. They cling to his neck with a yelp.

"I-I shouldn't be so close!" Nora tries to argue. "Val won't like it!"

"He'll like it less if we get hurt," Hunter says.

He doesn't have time to unpack what the fuck Nora means. Val can't be *that* jealous. They're not even really together, they don't owe each other anything. It's just . . .

"It's nothing," Mare purrs, his voice clinging to Hunter like frostbite. "You made a mistake, not a promise. Why else would he keep looking for Knives when you're right next to him?"

Nora's arms cinch around Hunter, their body going stiff as they both feel a convergence of living creatures. Hunter knows the smell of a fight, and blood is thick in the air around them.

"It's straight ahead," Nora says, though their voice flutters with fear. "There's another hatchling coming!"

"I know."

Hunter slows, drops Nora onto their feet, and sprints. This hatchling doesn't smell like poison or acid, but they're covered in blood, he can tell that much. Their movements are frantic, careless even, but Hunter can pick up another scent mixed into theirs like paint. A much too clean, distilled scent of untouched *something*. It makes no sense, the way Val smells like he's never been outside, but Hunter knows he's gone places no one else could.

Val's blood is spattered on this hatchling's face.

"There you are," Mare sings.

Hunter zeros in on the hatchling, listening to the sound of their body. Two human legs, two human arms, four additional legs jutting out of their back. Nothing about their pace suggests they're armed, and their breathing even sounds a little panicked. They're not coming out to stop Hunter, they're running from whatever tore open their chest. The wound itself is still healing, creating flashes along their pulse as their body shifts around.

They try to pivot out of Hunter's way, and he catches their ankle, sending them sprawling face first onto the road. Stepping onto their back to keep their extra legs flattened, Hunter's grabs their wrists in one hand, and yanks their head back with the other.

"Why are you running?" he asks.

"T-there's a spider on a rampage." The hatchling sounds as scared as Nora, their body trembling. "It's not safe!"

Hunter steps off of them, pulling the wrap from his eyes. "Do you still have your tool inside you?"

The hatchling shies away, shoulders up to their ears as they shake their head.

"Hide," Hunter says. "*Now.*"

The hatchling sputters back to life, stumbling to their feet without a second glance. Mare is left standing in their wake, solemnly admiring the bloodstain on the pavement.

"You let them go?" Nora asks, panting as they catch up.

"Something's not right," Hunter says, grabbing their hand and running in the direction of the hive. "If a spider is attacking the hatchlings, there's going to be chaos. You should help them get away from here."

"*What?*" Nora balks, their hand sweaty in Hunter's grip.

With his eyes open again, Hunter can plainly see the strange architecture of this city, and the fact that only one building in this entire place has been maintained in the slightest. They're coming up to its front doors, a single strip of shiny metal in a field of rust.

Another hatchling comes bursting outside, clutching a broken human arm to their chest.

Hunter stops and wheels around to grab Nora's shoulders. "This is what Val wanted. For the hatchlings to get away from this place. I'm going inside to find him, but I need you to help the ones that are fleeing. I'm not asking. You can do this."

Nora's eyes are watery, each of their four pupils dilated, and their heart is beating like a rabbit's, but they nod.

"We'll meet up with you later," Hunter says.

Their wings buzz. "Okay!"

Running for the doors to the hive building, Hunter sidesteps another limping hatchling with a bloodstain slashed over their back and shoves his way inside a hallway that smells of antiseptic, sweat, plaster, and blood. A chorus of noise hits him square in the chest, screams echoing from a great distance and footsteps thundering all around him, carried through this great structure in metal veins.

The building itself is not the largest in this city by a long shot, but Hunter is struck by a dizzying awe as he realizes how deep below the earth it goes. It's not dissimilar from standing in Modesty and feeling the rumblings of Indulgence far beneath the road, only this city doesn't vibrate with life.

Val is the sound of cracking glass several floors below. There's a trail of bleeding hatchlings like guide posts directing Hunter toward a massive stairwell. He runs by indiscernible shapes with mostly human faces, catching beetle shells, and butterfly wings, and compound eyes. At one point, Hunter has to flatten himself to the wall to avoid getting trampled by another centaur-esque hatchling with the body of a millipede.

None of them care about Hunter. They only care to get away from whatever is happening below them.

"Yes, I suppose it is best for you to look this in the eye." Nightmare hangs off Hunter's shoulders like a spectral scarf. "You've already turned your back on the people who raised you. No need to pretend now."

Hunter wheels around, slashing at the illusion with a dagger, and Mare simply vanishes. Panting, Hunter swallows through a dry throat and faces a door broken off its hinges, leading onto one of the basement floors. There's blood on the frame, probably from a hatchling bracing themself. Here, Val's song is loudest, almost loud enough to drown out Mare.

Stepping over another puddle of blood, Hunter keeps his dagger out, slowing his pace to take stock of whatever it is he's walking into. It's harder to tell while he's stuck in between Mare's keening, and the hatchling's howling, and Val calling to him like an oasis at the center of it all. He's slowly making his way down a stark white hallway, unnatural lighting buzzing overhead and illuminating a sign that advertises

CAFETERIA →

← *RESIDENTIAL FLOOR 3*

along with something else that's been scratched off. The sign itself has an archipelago of blood spatter across it.

At the sound of footsteps, Hunter picks up his pace.

A hatchling hisses, "*Stay away!*"

A thunder of metal and plastic pushes Hunter into a sprint. Val is definitely fighting with a hatchling, he'd know that ringing-glass heartbeat anywhere. As he shoulders open two swinging doors, the smell of blood hits him like a bolt of lightning. This room was clearly some communal dining area at some point, but now it is nothing but wreckage. Tables and chairs are upturned and scattered, half the room is dyed red, and there is a mess of human and insect offal strewn about the room.

The hatchling he'd heard earlier is pinned to the floor underneath a blood soaked body. Hunter's eyes are telling him that this person turned red is a stranger, but the sound, and the smell, and the *feeling* are all Val's. He's straddling the hatchling's chest, a pair of papery moth wings crushed beneath them. In one hand, Val holds his scalpel, and in the other, a dagger that Hunter doesn't recognize.

"So sorry," Val says. "Yours is in a bad spot."

All the fear Hunter had felt for Val's safety evaporates as he watches Val cut into the hatchling's throat. Some long buried instinct tells him to look away when Val reaches with his fingers for the open wound. The hatchling can only gurgle and cough while Val removes their tool from inside their neck.

"There you are," Val coos, and Hunter looks back to see a short needle in his hand, the kind you might use to stitch up a wound.

Satisfied with his work, Val breathes a sigh of relief before he brings the needle to his own stomach. Hunter didn't even realize he wasn't wearing a shirt until Val pierces his own skin, his eyes wide, his breathing not just held, but *stopped*. It's like his body has frozen still while he pushes the needle inside himself, covering the wound with both hands while it bleeds through his fingers.

Val's shoulders shudder as Hunter realizes what he's been doing. Pulling as many of the hatchling's tools out as he can, and using his own body like a living pin cushion to keep anyone else from getting to them. How many pieces of metal must be inside him by now? With a groan, Val hunches forward like he might vomit, but he grits his teeth and, breath by breath, relaxes once again.

His hands fall away from his now-healed stomach, and only then does he notice Hunter staring at him. The sound Val makes as he meets Hunter's gaze is impossibly soft. Only half a breath, but the look in his eyes is a mile deep. He stumbles back to his feet, the dagger and the scalpel back in his hands, and Val takes a few staggering steps in Hunter's direction.

"You're alive."

Val is stained from head to toe, his body practically singing from god only knows how many fights and impromptu surgeries he just went through, but his eyes are watering up.

"You're really alive."

The hatchling on the ground sparks back to life with a gasp, and they both turn to watch them scrabble on hands and knees, wings fluttering frantically, until they're back on their feet and running as fast as they can for the exit. Val stares at the double doors swinging shut, and then looks down at himself, and the tools in his hands.

"Oh . . . oh I really didn't want you to have to see me like this," he says, his voice stuck in a hoarse whisper. Looking around at the room, Val gives a laugh held short by nerves. "I've made a terrible mess." He turns back to Hunter and offers a bloody, dimpled smile. "I'm sorry."

Hunter puts his own dagger away before reaching for Val's hand with both of his. Val's breath starts to shorten up as Hunter cups Val's fist and slowly begins to loosen his blood-slicked fingers from the handle of the blade.

"I was scared," Val says, sounding just as confused as he is upset by the concept. "I don't think I like being scared."

Hunter pries the dagger away from him, replacing one of his own missing weapons against his bicep.

With a sniff, Val's breath hitches and his voice cracks in half as he asks, "Are you really here?"

Hunter puts his hands around Val's head, feeling the soft shell of his ears, and the heat coming off his cheeks. He's actually crying, tears tracking through the blood stains, shoulders shaking. Hunter presses his face to Val's hair, brushing his mouth across Val's forehead with no care as to whatever stains might be on his skin.

Hunter tells him, "I got your note in Respite."

Val claps his free hand over top of Hunter's, pulling Hunter's palm over his mouth to rest chattering teeth against Hunter's skin. He doesn't bite, just steadies himself as he licks the heel of Hunter's hand.

Hunter can't bring himself to speak louder than a pin drop with Val's tongue and teeth pressed harmlessly against him. "What did you mean when you said I smell like a river?"

Val flattens Hunter's fingers to his own face, breathing in deep through his nose. "I meant that I like it."

Val's presence settles around Hunter like a blanket secured around his shoulders, and he finally exhales a single sigh of relief at the thought that they're going to be okay. Val is still Val, and some part of Hunter is convinced that as long as that's true, they'll be able to get out of anything.

Partway through his nibbling on Hunter's hand, Val licks and nips his way into an actual kiss nestled into Hunter's palm. Staring at Val through his own fingers, Hunter feels himself leaning closer, drawn in by how softly this bloodied boy touches him. Maybe it's because Hunter knows exactly how sharp he really is, that at this very moment he is full of metal ripped from other people's wounds and still he gives Hunter a smile like powdered sugar.

It would be nothing at all for Val to kill Hunter, but it's Val who offered his life. The thought of Hunter offering his own body to Val in return grips him with a fist in his chest. What would it be like if Hunter let Val do whatever he wanted? Would there be metal, or would it all be skin?

How does a spider kiss?

"Aren't you two supposed to be trying to kill each other?"

The two of them jump away from the sound of an even-toned voice. Val shoves his back against Hunter's chest, holding the scalpel out in front of him with both hands as they look at the face of what must be the Queen of Innovation.

There isn't just a lack of presence to her. There is *nothing* to her. No scent, no song, no vibration, no feeling, and yet, there she stands, in a much plainer version of what Mare was wearing—white shirt tucked into gray trousers which are tucked into black boots. She looks like she was cut from stone, with cheekbones to match and not a single hair out of place in the ponytail it's tied up in. She touches her chin, leaning toward Val with wide, curious eyes.

"I thought for sure that seeing such a violent display would turn the human on you, but that's what research is for, isn't it?" she asks.

Val is pushing into Hunter, forcing him to back away inch by inch. "Leave us alone."

"I can't quite do that," she says. "You have a lot of valuable information in that head of yours. And besides. You took something from your brother. He'd like it back."

Hunter puts his hand over Val's chest as Knives enters the room from the other side of the cafeteria. He's no longer wearing his coat, a sleek black uniform hugging his body, and one of his hands is clasped over his right eye. His face is fixed in a snarl as he comes to stand beside the hollow Queen.

"Come on, now." The Queen's voice is that of an endlessly patient mother. "I know you have it."

Hunter is sure now that the dagger strapped to his bicep is one stolen from Knives.

"I gave it to one of the hatchlings," Val lies without hesitance. "They're long gone by now."

With a soft sigh, the Queen turns to Knives and holds her hand out. "I'm sorry, sweet thing. We'll have to use a spare for now."

Knives reaches into his jacket with a frown, producing a much less ornate dagger by the hilt. "As long as you do it . . ."

"Of course," she soothes, wrapping her hand around Knives's to hold the dagger with him.

Knives pulls his hand away from his eye, and the Queen and he raise the dagger together. Hunter starts pulling Val further away from this strange display, waiting for the bloodiest moment to urge them both to run, but the Queen points at them.

"Ah, ah, ah, you're my guest," she says. "I can't have you running away before I've shown you to your room. Don't worry."

To his credit, Knives doesn't scream when the blade slides home, instead sinking to his knees to grab the Queen's waist. His mouth is open but no sound comes out, and the Queen puts her hand onto the back of his head.

"He'll play nice while I talk to you," she assures them. "Allow me to have a word, little spider, and I promise your human won't be killed."

Val's heart is pounding under Hunter's fingers, and Hunter can practically hear his mind racing, but he already knows they have no choice.

"Fine," Hunter says.

"Wait, no." Val turns to him, but Hunter drops his hand to Val's waist.

"I can't outrun a gun, Val. Besides, we're not done yet."

Val looks like he's got something stuck in his throat, but he turns back toward the two spiders with his scalpel, pointing at Knives with it.

"If you do anything to him, I'll—"

"Spare me," Knives spits back at him, pulling himself back up to his feet. Tears and blood and fluid coat his face, not entirely unlike Val's. "She said I won't kill him, so I won't."

"Thank you, dear." The Queen pats Knives's cheek. "Will you take him to one of our suddenly quite empty rooms?"

He bows his head. "Yes, ma'am."

The hollow Queen looks right at Val. "Come along, now."

Still he hesitates, so Hunter pinches Val's hip. "I'll meet you with our friend."

Val gives him one more glance, his anxiety melting and reforming into resolve. "Promise?"

Hunter nods. "Promise."

⌁

Walking away from Val hurts less when Hunter knows that both of them have already decided that they're definitely getting out of here. Dream is still out there somewhere, and there's no point in dying now while Mare is trapped inside this place. That doesn't mean Hunter enjoys the notion of being alone with Knives. As soon as the spider walks past Hunter with his chin held high and a scowl on his face, Hunter feels ice water creeping back into his hands.

He doesn't need Mare's whispers to feel the ire.

Glaring at the back of Knives's head, Hunter takes stock of his own weapons—only a few blades left, but he still has his rope, and the tranquilizer they took from Nora. Seems like that was years ago now.

The air is thinning the longer he has to look at Knives. The two of them are nearly the same height, which shouldn't piss off Hunter, but it does. Knives has a pistol strapped to his thigh, the butcher's blade nestled against his back, and at least one other visible blade on his belt. That's not even counting the scalpel pieces Val said were sewn on the inside of his jacket.

As soon as Knives starts leading him down the stairs, Hunter knows they're not going where they're supposed to. He follows anyway, because it's closer to Mare, and he knew damn well how this was going to go the second it was clear that Val wasn't coming with them.

Knives takes him three more floors below the cafeteria before guiding Hunter into a narrow hall. The lights down here are even dimmer than upstairs, most of the bulbs already dead or dying. Ceiling tiles are waterlogged, and the floor is warped and uneven as they tread further and further from anything Hunter recognizes.

"This place is falling apart," Hunter says as they pass by a dusty sign whose only legible direction reads *Containment*.

"Yes, that's why we're moving," Knives responds with a sneer in his voice. "The Pillar is drying up, and so are all the resources of this city."

"What have you been feeding him, if you have no emotion to give?" Hunter asks, keeping his gaze fixed on the center of Knives's back, in case he reaches for a weapon.

"Memories," Knives answers. "It's not quite enough to stave off the rot, but it's kept him going this long."

"The hatchlings," Hunter clarifies. "Right."

"Without proper food, the Pillars take whatever they can, even if it's not sufficient. They really are little parasites."

The hall veers left, widening into a long passage with a window spanning the length of the wall. More harsh light bleeds in through the glass, but Hunter doesn't dare take his eyes off Knives, his fingertips brushing the handle of the dagger on his thigh. Hunter doesn't need to look as it is. He can sense exactly who's down here.

"Those daggers in your face," Hunter says. "They make up for your shit senses?"

Knives comes to a stop, and Hunter does too, a few paces away.

"Yes, as a matter of fact, they do," Knives says. "My Queen has spent a long time perfecting me to make up for natural disadvantages. Like broken humans who have no presence and can only pick up the scent of the nearest stronger creature."

"How many bullets you got left in that gun?" Hunter asks.

"Only takes one to kill a human."

"Then what are you waiting for?"

Knives lets his breath out slowly, still refusing to look at Hunter. "You know, when I had Val on a table at Southern Truth, I could already smell the infection. Human all over him. But he still came to me willingly. He let me touch him even when he thought I was an enemy."

Even if some part of him knew this already, hearing Knives gloating about it puts a scowl on Hunter's face, and a hard stone of determination in his gut.

"Killing you now would only upset him," Knives says. "I'll outlive you no matter what happens. All I have to do is wait."

It's only two full strides to close the distance between them. Knives feels the movement first, already starting to twist away from Hunter. In a perfectly smooth arc, Knives turns to his right, just like he did before when Hunter tried to get the jump on him. Only this time, there is a single moment of hesitation as Knives first reaches for his gun before he redirects his hand to the blade strapped to his back.

Hunter meets Knives's hand with his own dagger, slicing through Knives's palm and grabbing the handle of the butcher blade. With a growl, Knives wheels around, letting Hunter take the knife just to backhand Hunter with his fist. Hunter's head rattles on the impact, but he steps back as Knives grabs the other blade on his hip, facing Hunter with his lip curled. The mismatched handles jutting out of his face are like a distortion in Hunter's vision, so he drops his gaze to the pale skin of Knives's throat.

Hunter barely stops himself from smiling. "That's a lot of words to say you have no bullets."

If a taunt doesn't get him to fire the gun, there must be nothing left in the chamber. Knives isn't perfectly ambidextrous, but he isn't useless either as he slashes at Hunter with his off hand while the right one heals. It's a wide, angry strike that Hunter slips inside of, jamming the decorative dagger into the soft hollow at the base of Knives's throat. Hunter shoves with all his weight behind it until Knives slams into the glass window with a shivering *crack*. Knives grunts through the impact, blood pouring down his neck as he tries to bury his other dagger into Hunter's thigh. The blade cuts into his muscle while Hunter catches Knives's wrist so he can stab the tranquilizer through Knives's bare hand.

Knives drops the dagger, maybe in pain or maybe in shock, reeling his other fist back to clip the side of Hunter's head. Stars explode over Hunter's vision, but he can feel those blades like magnets guiding the heel of his hand up to knock the pommel of one of the daggers sticking out of the spider's eyes.

Knives screams the moment the metal loosens. Hunter twists the handle, shoves the dagger in as hard as he can, and the spider goes slack like a puppet with its strings cut.

15

Val is shivering slightly as he follows the Queen of Innovation out of the cafeteria and into a cramped hallway. She's about Dream's height, though she's thinner and her body is shaped like an arrow.

She doesn't have a heartbeat, only static. It terrifies Val.

"What do you want from me?" Val asks, voice small.

"You have very important data I need," she says. "Observations that I haven't had access to."

"Are you really going to kill all the hatchlings?"

She pauses in front of a door, turning to Val, her thick eyebrows knit in a mild frown. "Who on earth told you that?"

Val's mouth falls open. "Knives."

Her head cocks. "It's like you speak another language. Come inside already, I don't have time for your rambling. This place is falling apart at the seams."

She opens the door and Val follows after her, keeping distance between them at all times for fear of getting too close to her silence. It fills him with anxiety and dread even more than Mare's grief. Sadness he understands, but what can he do about *nothing*?

The room itself appears to be some kind of office, with more buzzing fixtures filling the space with harsh white light. The whole place is muted, and it would be utterly forgettable, save for the two bodies that are pinned to the wall next to each other, like human-sized dolls. Each one is stuck through with knives in symmetrical placements. The Queen takes a seat at a desk across from the macabre display, offering no comment as she pulls herself up in front of some kind of glowing screen with words displayed on it, resting her fingers onto a pad of keys.

"Sit."

Her voice is even, but rushed, and she points to a metal chair with a dull, blue cushion on it that's next to her desk. Val startles at her command, slinking over to sit down and try to subtly push the chair back from her for a few more inches of safety.

"What . . . are you?" he asks.

"I *was* Nightmare's spider," she answers, her fingers flying across the keys. Val finds himself staring at the screen as more words pop up at dizzying speeds.

"When the hatchlings wanted guidance, I became a king," she says, her posture beginning to hunch. "And when I needed more soldiers, I made myself a queen."

Val blinks, prying his gaze off the screen and onto the side of her face. "Dream said the person who took Mare away from him was a man."

"Mm." She nods, pulling a hand up to lean her cheek against it. "I've been all sorts of human shapes by now."

"Did you shape *yourself*?" Val asks, unable to help the note of awe slipping into his voice.

"Of course," she answers, face cast in the artificial glow. "I'm sure you've noticed by now how malleable our bodies really are. It's not that we resist change, it's that it has to be done with intention. You have to want it."

Val's mouth hangs open. "I could just change myself whenever I want?"

She shrugs, gesturing blandly at him without turning her head. "You already did. You still have some organs suited to bear children, but your chest isn't designed for breastfeeding. I'm guessing you didn't have the data available to finish the shift."

Val glances down at his own body. "I thought I was just strange."

"You are, by human standards," she says, pulling at her own bottom lip and letting it flick back into place before she turns to Val again. Her eyes are like gazing at the full moon only to realize that it's hollow inside. "Their rules don't apply to us."

Val is frozen in her line of sight, heart threatening to break through his ribs.

"At first, I thought we were meant to feed on the Pillars, an expansion of the food chain. That would have been more logical. But we can eat anything: flesh, plant matter, chemicals." She raises her brows. "So where do we fit in?"

There's three feet of space between them, but there's pressure on Val's chest like she's squeezing the air out of his lungs by hand. He can't bring himself to look at the bodies hanging on the wall, but it's like they, too, are staring at him. "I don't know, but I feel better when I'm with them."

"Pillars or humans?" she asks, an ember of curiosity burning in her gaze.

Val swallows. "I-I don't know, both. Aren't the pillars just . . . denser humans?"

"Fascinating," she mutters, her fingers picking up again. She must be transcribing their conversation. "The Pillars wiped out the last type of creature that fed on humans and effectively became a species of passive apex predator. Supposedly, they came from plants. Nightmare claims he and his brother were found inside of a pumpkin. Quaint, isn't it? Humans nurtured them into existence—harvested the Pillars from their own desires."

Val shrinks away from her bizarre language and her unblinking eyes. She can type without even looking at her hands.

"Our kind hatch from *within* humans, like cocoons. The objects inside us are like conduits that alter our bodies. It forces metamorphosis. Coming into contact with a Pillar sets off the shedding, followed by a phase of mindless feeding, and only one of our own can stabilize them into a more sociable state. Unless, of course, we pull the object out ourselves."

"You're . . . very smart," Val says, his voice barely audible.

She turns to her screen again, voice dropping back to a monotone. "I've been told."

The only sound in the room is from her fingers pecking at those weird keys, and Val's own pulse.

"Where do the objects come from?" Val asks.

"I don't know," she says. "I stopped trying to figure that out after Nightmare fell into a coma. More pressing matters at hand. It could be some kind of natural process, like bone calcifying, or cysts forming. Some of the spiders are fond of the notion that some god or something put those tools inside us, but I don't particularly see the benefit in that. The only thing I know is that this world produces predators automatically. That 'why' is someone else's egg to crack."

Val's head feels like it's swelling up. "B-but what about the hand? In the sky?"

"This one?" the Queen asks, bored. She turns to him, mimicking the shape of the half curled fingers with perfect accuracy. There's the slightest bit of anger tucked into the lines around her eyes as she says, "You started seeing it after you pulled your tool out, right?"

Val nods with a lump in his throat. Holding his gaze once more, the Queen moves her fingers achingly slow and smooth, until she finishes the gesture.

Pointing to the empty space between her fingers, she says. "It's how you might hold a scalpel while performing surgery to keep even pressure on the blade."

Val can see it clearly in the space of her hand. He's never actually seen a surgeon work in real life, but now it's like the metal is right there in her grip.

And then she shakes her hand out, as if to flick water from her skin, and places it back on the keys. "I'm sure the real reason you see it is that pulling your tool out killed you several times over, and there was lingering psychological trauma from the incident, resulting in an afterimage on your brain. It's usually the first time we die. Of course there's an effect."

Folding her arms against her chest, she regards her own work with a mild pout, and Val can't explain why he feels like he's being shamed.

"Neither Pillars nor spiders can have children of their own," the Queen goes on, more to herself than Val. "We do resemble each other in some ways. Dense humans . . . that is an interesting turn of phrase. If they are dense, then are we . . . but, no."

Staring at her screen, it's like she's forgotten Val is even in the room.

"What do you want from me?" Val squeaks out.

"Yes, right." She reaches for a set of black shelves on the desk and removes a small device, not unlike the radio that Arum was speaking into. She does something, its lights changing color, and sets it on the edge of her desk before turning her chair to look at Val once more.

Val can't help but startle at her full attention.

"You have information on Nightmare's brother. I need it."

Swallowing through a swollen throat, Val grips the edges of his chair. "What information?"

She weaves her fingers together over her lap. "Years ago, I began an experiment involving a pair of Pillar twins. Pillars are not nearly as self-sufficient as we are, they function as two halves of a whole. I wanted to know what, if anything, could drive them apart, and if the separation itself would have side effects. I have *half* of the data. I don't imagine the man himself would be willing to sit down with me, but you may have a more objective view on Dream's state of mind anyway."

She speaks so fast, Val almost doesn't hear everything, but it comes through on a delay.

"You made them fight on purpose?" Val asks.

She nods. "Back then, I was shaped more like you. Nightmare has a preference for men, and a weakness for anything he thinks is vulnerable. In this case, he thought my kind needed help, and when he realized we didn't, he feared for another massacre on humans. His willingness to jump to the worst conclusion worked in my favor."

"Their entire argument was fake?" Val feels himself pulling away from her even when he has nowhere to go.

The Queen quirks her eyebrow. "It depends on how you define fake. The tension was already there. I only pushed on it. Nightmare was worried about Dream self-destructing. He came to his own conclusion that separation was the only thing that would keep Dream safe from his own influence."

Because you lied to him, Val doesn't say. He can't bring himself to give sound to words that resemble an accusation when he's sitting in the presence of something that turns his stomach in fear.

"You're . . . not a spider anymore?" Val asks.

She taps the desk without breaking eye contact, *tap tap*. "Focus."

Val shrinks in on himself.

"When you met Dream, had he already decided to come here?"

Trying to remember how to speak normally, Val reaches back in his memories. "I . . . I think I made him realize that he should try."

"Was he scared of you?"

Val can't look at her huge, empty eyes, dropping his gaze to his blood-covered knees instead. "He knew I was dangerous, but he let me come along. I think he figured that he was either going to get to Mare, or die trying."

"Suicide," she says with a sigh of exasperation. Gesturing at the wall where the two bodies are pinned up like a museum display, she tells him, "I've a strong distaste for it, personally. I've lost two spiders to attempted self-destruction just because they spent too much time with humans. A miserable affair."

Val spares a glance toward the two people hanging there, seeing with a pinch of nausea that they are dressed just like Arum and Knives in crisp black uniforms.

"West and east sentinels?" Val guesses.

"Failures," she corrects.

Wetting his rapidly drying lips, Val manages to ask her, "Maybe it wasn't humans, but because you forced them to live inside someone else's nightmare?"

In an aching silence, Val watches the Queen's expression drain of any light, settling into a perfect carving of distaste as her brows and lips thin, and her eyes grow dark.

"You can hear him?"

Val is a mouse in her gaze. "Yes."

Her top lip twitches. "You're supposed to be immune to the influence of Pillars."

"I'm not," Val says.

She touches her front teeth together with a soft *snap*. "This . . . explains a lot. I must be the only one who doesn't hear him anymore." Whipping back toward her screen, she starts typing twice as fast, one incisor pulling at her bottom lip.

"Sneaky. Little. Pumpkin."

She says each word like a curse.

Val has no idea what he's supposed to do, but the single-minded anger radiating off of her keeps him pinned just like the dead spiders on the wall. With a furious *click* of a button, she spins around and gets out of her chair.

"Come along, stray," she says, patting her hip. "We're going to have a talk with Nightmare."

Val can do nothing but follow the Queen on stiff legs, wondering what it would even do to attack this person. His scalpel would surely have no effect on someone who's had this long to numb themself to anything they wanted. A person who changes their shape, not for their own sake, but for the integrity of an experiment.

"Are you a man or a woman?" Val asks.

"I cut out any of those organs decades ago," they respond, sounding utterly tired of the implication. "Unnecessary weight."

"Why don't you feel like the other spiders?" Val watches their back, the way their clothes hardly move while they walk. Nothing touches them at all.

The Queen of pure nothingness turns on their heel to look down the length of their nose at Val. It's not that their eyes are bright, it's that everything around them looks dull. Val's gaze is magnetized to theirs.

"You are annoying me," they say, and their voice is somehow inside Val's head, echoing against his skull, like Mare's song. "No more questions or I take the larynx."

Val drops his gaze to their shiny boots, waiting for them to resume their walk. They lead him down a staircase much narrower than the one he took to get to the cafeteria, descending a few spirals in utter silence before stepping into a wide hallway. The Queen's footsteps click like the tongue of a disappointed teacher as they pass by an operating room that is dizzyingly familiar.

He's seeing double at the arrangement of instruments, tables, lights and a stretcher for a patient. Almost like he's been in this room hundreds of times.

The Queen doesn't spare a glance, walking with undiluted focus past the surgical tools, and what must be some kind of decontamination chamber, and finally emerges into a cavernous room full of incomprehensible wires and tubes and tanks. It takes much too long for Val to notice the three other bodies in this room, so overwhelming is the Queen's silence. In the dead center of this underground laboratory, held in what looks like a coffin of glass, Nightmare is deeply asleep. There's some kind of hose snaking out of his mouth, an IV in his arm, and hundreds of bandages wound over his body. Val knows it's him, not just by his lullaby filling the room, but because Hunter is sitting on the floor beside his bed.

Hunter takes one look at the Queen and pulls themself up, backing away from the Queen's impatient stride. When Hunter winces at their right foot hitting the ground, Val sees strips of fabric tied around Hunter's thigh to staunch blood flow, and his stomach drops. The Queen pays Hunter no mind, but they do pause to look at Knives tied up and gagged, struggling against ropes that Val is sure are Hunter's doing. There a few more knife handles sticking out of his chest, but apparently he's already healed around them.

"Children are such a bother," the Queen says, turning away from him.

Val hurries as quietly as he can to stand at Hunter's right side, and Hunter immediately braces a hand on Val's shoulder to take the weight off their leg. Looking up at Hunter's bloodied face, Val catches their eye so he can mouth, *Dream?*

Hunter puts their finger to their lips, before they slide their hand down from Val's shoulder to his waist.

The Queen slaps both their hands onto the glass above Nightmare's face, their eyes wide as their own silence crashes into Mare's singing.

"Wake up." They don't shout, but their voice has force behind it, like a train barreling off its tracks, or a bullet ripping through skin.

Hunter's hand drops to Val's hips, their fingers slipping into the pocket where Val's scalpel is.

Watching Mare open his eyes makes Val tired just to see. The effort is so clear, like each lid weighs a ton. As soon as Mare sees who it is that's woken him up, his face turns from smooth, flawless clay to veined, craggy rock. It looks like he's biting the hose in his mouth as he glares from inside his case with enough fury that Val's surprised the glass doesn't splinter from the hatred pouring off of them both.

"What did you do to me, Nightmare?" the Queen demands, wide eyes boring into him. "Toxins from the rot? Do Pillars become venomous when they're dying? What is it?"

Mare's hands are slowly curling into fists as Hunter pulls the scalpel from Val's pocket. They lean down to Val's ear, whispering in a breath, "Distract her," before inching away from Val.

With an icy startle, Val looks at Knives on the ground beside them, gnawing at the ropes between his teeth.

"I know you can still communicate." The Queen slaps the glass as Val kneels at Knives's chest.

Loosening one of the blades stuck inside Knives's torso takes a bit of effort, and Knives gives a muffled groan as it slides free of his body, trying to squirm away from Val. Taking the knife to the ropes around Knives's face, Val doesn't bother to be careful as he cuts through the gag around Knives's mouth, drawing a little blood from his cheek.

"What are you doing?" Knives snaps.

"Sorry," Val says, wrapping both hands around the grip of the newest blade sticking out of Knives's face.

Pulling this one free is a lot easier now than it was back when they fought beside the train tracks. It's barely had time to heal inside his head, and when Val rips it free, Knives howls. Shying away from the sound, Val clutches both of the stained blades to his chest as Knives writhes on the ground, his pained screaming melting into something closer to sobbing.

Val feels a flicker of pity in his stomach as he thinks about trying to comfort this person, but no sooner does the thought enter his brain than he feels the Queen's hand on the back of his neck.

"You should be nicer to your brother."

Being enveloped in a complete absence of sensation nearly stops Val's heart from the chill. Knives is crying and shouting inches away from him, but it may as well be miles away for all Val can hear of it. At that moment, it's just him and the hand on his neck.

The Queen sighs.

"It's been years since he cried this much. He came to me like this. Nothing but tears and trembling shoulders. He wanted a family, so I gave him one. What good has that done?"

"He still . . ." Speaking now is like spitting up glass, but Val does his best. "He still has a sister."

"Ah, the north sentinel never took to me the way he did."

Knives is glaring at Val now with one regrown eye burning into him. His iris is green. Nothing special about it really, the green of the grass growing up through the broken train tracks. It even has a little spot of brown in it to mimic the rust, and Val tells himself he should remember that color.

"Maybe you should try talking to her more," Val says, looking at that eye. "She's a nice person. I bet she'd help you if you asked."

"All that one wants is her rifle and a tall perch," the Queen responds. "Where we're going isn't nearly so vertical. She'll break faster."

Knives pants through clenched teeth, shoulders straining against the ropes. The Queen pinches Val's neck, their nails digging into his skin.

"Done crying then?" they ask.

"Yes, ma'am," Knives answers.

"Good. You know I hate that sound."

"Sorry, ma'am."

They tug Val up to his feet by the neck, turning him around to see Hunter sliding their arm underneath Mare's back to hoist him out of bed. There's a mess of bloodied wires sitting on the white sheets, Val's scalpel turned red once more, and the hose dangling off the side of the cot.

"I forgot about you," the Queen says, nails finally piercing Val's skin like push pins. "You're barely human as it is. It's a clever trick. Who taught you that?"

Hunter swallows, keeping their mouth clenched shut. Finally free of the hose in his throat, Mare wheezes at the Queen, "You look different than when you tried to eat me."

"Yes, I'm beginning to regret that," they respond. "Is that why you've been so quiet for the last couple decades?"

"You poison me, I poison you." Mare gives a weak wave of his hand, head heavy against Hunter's chest. "You make me shoot my brother. I drive your spiders crazy."

"Mm, what a nice, even exchange," the Queen mutters.

"Thought you'd like it," Mare says, eyes sliding shut again.

The Queen takes a step closer, and Hunter hauls Mare all the way out of bed, backing away with pink tinged bandages hanging off Mare like ribbons. He looks like he weighs all of five pounds, but Hunter's pant leg is shiny and wet with blood.

"Oh, that's right. You're human."

The Queen sounds genuinely surprised, looking at Hunter like they've only just fully seen the person standing across the room from them. Val is sure they're realizing now what he's been coming to terms with since Indulgence—how easily Hunter pries up the lid on emotions Val didn't know he had access to. Perhaps that's why the Queen is so quick to anger now. The second Hunter stepped into Innovation must have been like a whisper to every hatchling and spider in the entire city. Which also means the Queen must know how much damage Hunter could cause just by being here.

Ignoring every instinct he has screaming out not to hurt this person, Val holds his breath, and jams the knife he took from his brother straight into the Queen's stomach.

"I'm sorry, I'm sorry, I'm sorry." The words spill out of him for reasons he can't explain as lukewarm blood spills between his fingers. It feels as bad as if he'd stabbed himself, like his mind can't tell the difference between their bodies. Pulling the knife free, Val slips away from the hand on his neck, the Queen's nails scraping him like thorns as he turns around to see what he's done. The Queen's brows knit together, staring at Val in disbelief. It's not even anger, just plain confusion.

"That hurts."

They lift their shirt up to watch the wound bleed, touching the edges with their fingers as more blood pours out in an even spill, no heart or pulse to guide the flow. Turning their impatient gaze back to Mare, they sigh.

"One wasn't enough, hm? You're going to drive another species to extinction before you finally rot."

Val's arms are trembling from gripping his knives and fighting off some primal urge to help the bleeding creature in front of him. *It's me, that thing is me, that's where I started, or what I could become.*

Tears he can't feel streak down his face as the Queen snatches the blade out of Val's hand, turning toward a panting Knives. As soon as he realizes they're going to untie him, Val throws himself at the Queen, wrapping his arms around them to try and pull them away.

"No, no, he's not ready." His hands press into their wound, no body heat in their skin.

They look over their shoulder at him, eyes huge, and Val feels the first stir inside their chest as he squeezes tighter.

"Please," he says, not even really sure anymore what he's begging for.

He can feel something waking up inside them, old routines attempting to resume, only to be denied by sheer force of will and layers upon layers of rust. They're keeping their own body frozen with hands too numb to care. Their heart doesn't beat, their lungs don't breathe, their blood pours out of them like an upended bottle, and their eyes don't blink as they glare at Val.

"You are so noisy," they tell him.

When the knife slides into his flank—cleanly, right below the ribs, no bone in the way, deep, deep, deep—it hurts a lot more than a knife should. It hurts more like a bullet, or he thinks possibly like a broken heart. There's a sound in his head like shattering glass and he doesn't know why this time of all times, he is afraid he won't wake up again. He's terrified, really. He's got too many plans. He can't die now. He hasn't even fired Hunter for Dream.

Val slides off the Queen, crumpling onto the ground to meet that green eye again. Knives is looking between Val and the Queen, and Val can't tell if Knives is afraid for them, or of them.

At least he feels *something*.

❦

The moment Hunter puts his arms around Mare, the feeding starts in earnest. It's heavy, grasping to fill a fifty-year void, and Hunter almost buckles under the weight of it, but he manages to pull Mare away from that bed and toward the other side of the room. He doesn't stay standing for very long, sinking to the floor the moment his back hits the wall.

"Sorry."

Mare's voice is pure exhaustion.

"Can't . . . turn it off."

"It's fine," Hunter whispers back, propping Mare against his chest so he can re-tighten the makeshift tourniquet he tied around his thigh. Mare is so thin, he feels hollow like a bird against Hunter's chest, but despite how frail he is, how his hair has gone silver, and his muscles atrophied, his face is still the younger version of Dream's.

Hunter hears Val apologizing, watches blood soaking through the hollow queen's shirt. She takes the knife from Val, and Hunter has to fight to keep his eyes open. Mare's fingers may as well be inside his head, taking so greedily from the first proper source of food in years that Hunter's vision is swimming.

She's stabbing Val, *fuck*, but he'll be okay. Val's always okay. This'll be the last time though. Hunter will make sure of that. They don't need to keep doing this. So many better things to be doing with their bodies than handling knives.

Hunter hears glass shattering before his mind catches up. He's so heavy, it's hard to focus, but that's right, the same window he shoved Knives into is broken. There's glass spilling all over the floor now. It's sort of pretty, like water, or ice. Did he push Knives *that* hard? No. No, someone else is there. He can see the barrel of their gun.

Mare's fog begins to clear as soon as Dream hops over the ledge of the window, landing with a *crunch* in the mess of broken glass. The clarity is like pulling his head out of water, and Hunter looks over to see Val crumpled on the ground and the queen looking rather annoyed at the bullet hole in her stomach.

"Brittle, huh?" Dream says, reloading his revolver.

"Apparently," the queen answers, her voice starting to show the strain.

Dream walks over to them, his cane haphazardly strapped to his back, and grabs Val's arm to haul him across the floor toward Hunter and Mare.

"Stay the fuck away from my family," Dream says.

"I believe that one's mine." The queen puts her hands on her stomach, her face beginning to crumple as pain registers in her system for what Hunter thinks might be the first time in her entire life. Her presence feels sort of like when Val is healing, only it's not pops and crackles of life, but tears and fissures splintering through rock.

Dream sets Val's head on Hunter's good thigh before pointing the revolver back at her.

"No he's not. I don't give a fuck about that one." Dream gestures at Knives. "But these three are mine."

With both Nightmare and Dream in the room with him, Hunter takes a deep breath, focus coming back to him like fresh rain. He can feel Val quietly rebuilding, Mare beginning to shake the dust off, Dream's hand trembling ever so slightly on the handle of the revolver,

Knives in some kind of stunned silence, and the queen's body softly crumpling as fifty years of held breath collapse inside her chest.

"One more shot should do it," Hunter tells Dream. "She's brittle, like you said. I don't know if she can even heal anymore."

"Really thought it'd be harder to kill you," Dream says, exhaling as it becomes clear that this spider has been dying just as long as Mare has. The queen sinks to her knees at that, folding in to hold the two wounds, and Dream *tsks*. "Kinda leaves a bad taste to kill a wounded thing like this."

"I'll do it," Hunter says.

Dream turns to him, brows raised. "Do you even know how to use a gun?"

"She's ten feet away, I can do it." Hunter holds his hand out. "Take Mare, give me the gun. If we don't, Val's gonna spend the rest of his fucking life wondering if she's alive, or if she can change. It's not worth it to let this haunt him."

The look in Dream's eye is something Hunter has only seen in those nightmares he was never meant to have—a look of resignation as all that self-forged strength slips away. He looks upset, and he looks young, and he looks *lost*.

"Honestly, Dream . . ."

Hunter startles as Nightmare begins to push himself up off the floor. Dream lurches forward, catching his hand, and Hunter pushes him by the hip until Mare's got an arm slung around Dream's shoulder. He's not wearing clothes, just a network of tightly woven bandages that are probably keeping his body from falling apart after rotting here for so long. Dream looks like he's scared to touch, like he might accidentally hurt Mare worse while his expression is shredding on an emotion he can't run from anymore. Dream's breath shortens up as he stands face to face with Mare, like a mirror cracked on one side, tarnished on the other.

"We're supposed to protect humans," Mare says, putting his hand around Dream's on the revolver. "Don't make him do that."

Dream nods. "I know, fuck, I know."

"This is mine, isn't it?" Mare asks, pulling the gun out of Dream's hand to look at the engravings. "Kept it for me, hm? Thanks. This place is running out of everything, you know?"

Val gasps awake on Hunter's legs, but the sound is drowned out by Nightmare firing the revolver at the queen, stopping her with her fingers on the pommel of Knives's remaining metal eye. Val bolts upright, but Hunter grabs him by the shoulders and twists him around to push his face into Hunter's chest. It only takes a moment before Val's breath starts to hiccup, no doubt sensing the lack of a sixth working body in the room. He hugs Hunter back, curling up as a tremor rocks through his legs and his shoulders and his arms, the queen's held-breath silence finally breaking open.

Mare drops the empty gun in a clatter of metal, turns back to put his hand on Dream's face, and kisses him like he wants to fall inside Dream's body. Dream puts his shaking hands on Mare's back, opening his mouth like nothing would make him happier than to swallow Mare whole.

Hunter drops his gaze, fingers tightening around Val, but he hears Mare's tired whisper. "You're no killer. Don't start pretending now. You're supposed to be soft. I like when you're soft . . ."

Dream hoists a limp Mare up into his arms and turns to catch Hunter's eye again. "We gotta get out of here. He's gonna start losing pieces if I can't get him to a town quick enough."

"We should trade," Hunter says. "He can feed on me while we walk."

"I, uh." Dream glances at Mare, head propped on Dream's shoulder, eyes shut again. "No offense, but I don't want anyone else touching him."

Hunter almost laughs, nodding instead as he braces himself to stand.

"What should we do about the other one?" Dream looks back at Knives, who's got a twisted up face like his own anger has robbed him of the ability to talk, tears streaming out of his one good eye again. The queen's body lays prone behind him, nothing now but a machine without fuel.

Val doesn't pick his head up, just speaks, muffled, into Hunter's chest. "Leave him for Arum."

"Who the fuck is—never mind. Whatever. I'm leaving," Dream says, carrying Mare back through the broken window, but when Hunter goes after him, Val pops back up.

"You're hurt! Put me down."

Hunter tightens his grip and steps through the broken window. "It's fine."

Val grabs Hunter's face in both hands and Hunter's mind replays Mare kissing Dream as Val demands with a pout, "Let *me* help *you*."

"Oh . . . kay . . ."

Hunter sets him down, bare feet and all, and Val immediately puts Hunter's arm around his shoulder.

"Lean on me."

Hunter does, letting himself ease the pain in his right leg with Val's help as they begin the long walk back up and out of this miserable place. They're about halfway up the stairs when clumsy footsteps begin thundering down toward them. Nora shrieks when they see Val, throwing themself at him to rub their cheek against his.

"Mister Val, I missed you very much!"

Val grabs the back of Hunter's shirt to stay standing, giving them a one-armed hug and a tired laugh. "I missed you too. Can you help me get Hunter out of here? He's bleeding."

"Yes!" Nora peels off of him with a smile, their front now stained pink from dried blood. "Would you like me to ask one of the others to carry him? I think he would fit on one of the beetle shells."

Hunter is ready to give a firm *no thanks*, but Val's face breaks into a grin and he starts nodding with visible relief in his eyes, and Hunter swallows his refusal.

"Isn't that great?" Val asks as Nora goes running back up the steps. "There's someone big enough to carry you too. I wish I could . . . I'll have to get stronger."

Hunter opens his mouth to say something like *I'm not sure you can put on that much muscle mass*, but then a million other things that are much tougher to say pile in after, and he simply closes his mouth again.

The awkwardness of accepting a ride from a hatchling with the hard shell of a cockroach is easier to handle when Val looks so happy about it, and Hunter distracts himself by looking at the knife wound. Not pretty, but not fatal either. He starts pushing the fabric aside while Val passes the disinfectant to him, hugging one of Hunter's black pouches to his chest. The sting of the alcohol is enough of a burn to fight the embarrassment of Val thanking the hatchling profusely for carrying Hunter out of here.

"It's nothing," the hatchling says.

"I owe you," Val tells them. "Hunter is important to me, so I really appreciate it. And I'm sorry for hurting you earlier."

The hatchling looks as uncomfortable as Hunter feels, shaking their head without looking at Val. "It . . . needed to be done. This place is not so scary anymore."

Nora comes back with another hatchling twice their size with legs a perfect stem colored green, and approaches Dream with their shoulders up to their ears.

"Would you like a hand? Pillar, sir?"

Dream is leaning up against the wall, catching his breath with Mare still clutched against his chest.

"Don't hurt yourself," Mare mumbles. "If they wanted to kill me, they've had plenty of chances."

With a grumble, Dream lets the hatchling take Mare, but not before he puts his own coat around Mare's shoulders. "Just . . . let me keep an eye on him."

The second they make it up all those stairs, Hunter slides off the beetle shell and catches himself on the wall. "Thank you."

Val slips back under his arm in a heartbeat, like that's where he's always been. "So stubborn . . ."

A minute of walking in relative silence to the tune of so many mismatched footsteps, Hunter realizes there's no more song. The air is truly quiet again now that Mare is awake, save for the shuffle of bodies.

Val, though, he buzzes like one of those artificial lights, so many things tucked away inside him that he hasn't had the time to figure out yet.

"Are you okay?" Hunter asks. "You put all those tools inside you."

Val smiles at him, dimpled, bloody, blindingly bright. "You know me. I heal from anything."

"Do you want them out of you?" Hunter asks, limping resolutely toward the busted open doors of the hive.

Val has timed their footsteps so he can take Hunter's weight whenever Hunter leans onto his right leg.

"I haven't decided yet."

"You let me know," Hunter says. "I'll do what I can."

Val laughs. "If you tell me something you like, I'll let you pull some metal out of me, how about that?"

Hunter almost laughs. "You think I'm itching to cut you open?"

Val blinks up at him, expectant, and Hunter tries to imagine putting his hands inside Val the way Val did for the hatchlings. Hunter's no stranger to blood, but what if Val gave him one of those sparkling smiles when Hunter had his hands inside Val's stomach? For some reason, his mind once again replays Mare and Dream's hungry kiss, and Hunter gets goosebumps shooting down his spine.

"I'll think about it . . ."

Val smiles, squeezing Hunter's hip.

Stepping outside to a full crowd of hatchlings is overwhelming, from the sight, to the sound, to the scent in the air. Most of them shy away as Val, Hunter, and Dream walk further outside, but they don't look afraid, not exactly—more nervous than that, and maybe a little confused. Hunter feels like he's shriveling up with that many eyes on him.

"We didn't know where to go," Nora explains. "And I was worried about you."

Val grins at them. "We need to get to the closest town, but it would be nice to find some water on the way, so let's start with that."

Nora looks over-the-moon, flitting over to direct the other hatchlings. Their enthusiasm alone seems to make the others willing to listen. Hunter's just glad they're not looking at him anymore.

"Should we stitch up your leg now before we start walking?" Val asks.

"Yeah."

Val looks entirely too happy to help Hunter find a place to sit down across the street from the hive, digging through one of Hunter's packs for a needle.

"Would you like me to do it? You must be tired."

"Val your hands are disgusting."

Val's shoulders startle up to his ears as he remembers. "Oh. Right. Oops."

"Nora," Hunter waves them over. "Think you can find some water or something? Just to clean Val's hands off so he can stitch my leg."

"I'll get the doctor," Nora calls and goes running back into the crowd.

"Is there a doctor?" Hunter asks.

Val frowns, pushing closer to Hunter's side. "I forgot."

When Nora comes back practically dragging a massive centipede hatchling by the hand, Val's frown deepens. The hatchling wears a lab coat over their human torso, and their face is bright red at the coaxing.

"I'm surprised you didn't stay behind with Knives," Val says, voice losing the shine it usually has when he speaks to Hunter.

"Yes, well, I think . . . living is nice," the doctor sputters. "The Major would understand . . . probably."

"Can you stitch wounds?" Val asks.

"Obviously," the doctor sneers.

"Then fix Hunter's leg. If you do anything weird—"

"Yes, yes, you're very scary, we all know," the doctor snaps.

They sink down lower, poking around in their own coat and at a small pack hanging awkwardly from their shoulder. They smell like fear and antiseptic.

"I can do it," Hunter mumbles.

"Please, you both have filthy hands," the doctor says, snapping a pair of pale gloves on. As they come closer, their presence rings with anxiety, and Hunter thinks it must be from Val looking at them with such scrutiny, but the moment their gloved fingers brush Hunter's skin, it rings louder.

"I'm sorry I ca-can't numb you," the doctor says, hesitating with the needle and thread.

"I've had worse, I promise," Hunter says.

Hunter puts his hand in Val's hair just to touch something familiar while the doctor sews the knife wound shut, their hands trembling all the while.

"Humans are so . . . fragile," they mutter, face going pale.

"You have terrible bedside manner," Val says.

"You're making this worse," they snap, pulling the thread tight. "All your *concern*. It's making me nervous."

"Oh." Val shrinks down lower. "Sorry."

Tying off a knot, the doctor snips the thread short and smooths a bandage down over it, taping it off quickly and efficiently, probably just to stop looking at it.

"Maybe you can help with Dream's hip later," Val says, voice much quieter. "You're much better at this than I was . . ."

"Of course I am." The doctor zips away from them with a *hmph*, but their face is beet red once more.

With a sigh, Val whispers, "I wanted to be the one to stitch you up . . ."

Hunter wants to laugh, his breath bubbling up in an approximation, but it doesn't quite show on his mouth as he remembers the hundred eyes just a few steps away. Val pouts at Hunter's swallowed amusement.

"Am I being weird again?"

"No. Well, maybe," Hunter says, brushing his fingers against Val's hip, now tacky with dried blood. "I'm just getting used to how you show . . ." *affection* is the word he wants to say, but he doesn't know what Val would call it. "Concern. That's all."

"Get your ass in gear," Dream barks from a few paces away. "Mare's gonna die before we leave the city borders at this rate."

Val helps Hunter back up again, falling into step with him automatically as they approach Dream leaning on his cane next to the hatchling holding Mare like a bundle of bandaged kindling.

"He's not dying anymore," Hunter says as they walk over. "He's feeding on me, you know. Both of you are."

Dream lifts his chin with a grumble. "Yeah, well. Sorry. I guess."

From the arms of the hatchling, Mare gives a laugh strained through a cough, still too tired to open his eyes. "You call that an apology?"

"It's been a fucked up month!" Dream snaps. "And *you* have no business giving advice to anyone."

Mare's entire body shakes as he laughs, a leaf barely hanging onto its branch, and Dream puts his free hand onto Mare's back as they walk.

"Once we're safe again, I'll go back to find Arum," Val says. "I think she'll want to make sure Knives doesn't rot down there. She's probably the only person who could keep him contained right now. Later though," he adds, and Hunter thinks he's probably just voicing this for himself. "You and Dream and Mare come first. And I want to make sure Sig made it back to Good Fortune. Oh, and Matthew, I hope he's still with Liz. I hope they found Patience. Moon might want to know we're safe as well. Yes, Knives can wait a little longer."

Slowly, their parade of bodies begins moving in the direction of the abandoned train tracks, the fastest route back to town. Nora sends some of the quickest hatchlings to look for fresh water, running back up to Val and Hunter to check on them every other minute, doing a terrible job of hiding their concern, but Hunter doesn't mind so much when it's just their familiar eyes.

Val's hand cinches in Hunter's shirt as they pass the skeleton of another staggeringly tall building. "The queen really died, right?"

"Yes," Hunter says, touching Val's hand on his waist. "Mare made sure of it."

"Do you think . . ." Val loosens his grip, letting Hunter's fingers slide in between his. "Do you think if I spend the rest of my life with humans, I'll be able to die like one too?"

Hunter feels like he pulled a muscle as Val looks up at him with honest to god hope in his eyes. It's hard to meet his gaze like that, and Hunter breaks eye contact, squeezing Val's hand and shoulder instead.

"If that's what you want, then I hope so."

Val shifts toward him, and Hunter reaches to steady him on instinct, but Val only puts his arms around Hunter's stomach, burying his face against Hunter's chest again. Hunter startles at the sudden hug, heat flooding his face as he feels a couple of the hatchlings turning to stare at them.

"It's okay," Hunter mumbles, touching the back of Val's head and neck.

Val nods a couple times before he pulls away, pawing at his cheeks with the back of his hand. "Dream is right. It really has been a . . . fucked up month. We were just walking around, how did so many tasks manage to pile up? I'll need years to see this all through."

Laughing, Val wipes a streak of red off his face, still somehow smiling like a light bulb, and Hunter's lips start to curve up.

"I don't know if I've heard you curse before," Hunter says.

Val grins around the red. "You and Dream have been terrible influences on me, you know? I used to be a proper boy."

"No you didn't," Hunter says, smiling. "Nice try though."

The rest of the group is steadily pulling further ahead of them, though Hunter can see out of the corner of his eye as someone turns to look. It's Nora again, he can hear their wings, but just as he's about to assure them not to worry, Val puts his hands on Hunter's stomach, his fingers curling up in the fabric, and Hunter *can't* turn his head from him. Not from Val, not from such a beautiful, blood-soaked thing.

The same pull he felt down in the depths of the hive finds him again, steadily pushing Hunter closer to Val and his red lips and diamond eyes. When Hunter touches Val's wrist and feels a pulse hammering under his fingers, he knows he doesn't care enough about someone else's blood not to get closer. He'd swallow it all if he had to, as long as Val was underneath.

A third heartbeat slides between theirs, drawing both their gazes to the erratic sensation of Knives careening toward them. He comes bursting out of the hive doors, his butcher's blade in one hand and a dagger in the other. Val's face bursts into an angry frown, once again moving to stand in front of Hunter. Hunter is about to call to Dream to get his gun out, but when he opens his mouth, someone beats him to it.

Hunter hasn't heard the sound of a long distance rifle in a very long time, and it cracks like a whip through the air. Knives crumples onto the pavement without so much as breathing their air.

"This that sister you were talking about?" Hunter asks.

Val beams, raising his hand to wave at something in the distance. Hunter follows his gaze to a small dark shape emerging from the second floor of one of the buildings they already passed by. A woman jumps out of the window, gracefully catching herself in a roll, and pops back up to sprint toward Knives. Something metal glints in her hand, and Hunter thinks for a moment that someone else is about to stab Knives, but she claps one end of a pair of handcuffs onto Knives's wrist, and closes the other around her own.

"*Val*!" she yells.

He goes running toward her, and before Hunter can make the decision whether or not to limp after them, the smell of smoke wafts over him, and Dream steps up beside Hunter, lit cigarette between his fingers.

"Let 'em have a second," Dream says. "He'll be right back."

Hunter nods, watching as the other spider—he's pretty sure her name is Arum—passes Val the butcher's knife, the dagger, and something that might be a spyglass. Val holds the objects against his chest, nodding repeatedly as the woman speaks to him. Val points at the remaining knife in their brother's eye, and Arum has an impossible look on her face. Hauling Knives up against her, back to chest, all she does is shrug back at Val.

After a moment, Val leans down and kisses her forehead, and her whole body scrunches up for a single second, like she expected something else. Val comes jogging back to them, and Hunter watches Arum cradle Knives like a baby, both of her eyes open wide.

"Need a hand?" Dream asks, pointing at Val's new bounty.

"Yes, please," Val says, passing a blood-flecked rifle scope to Dream, which he shoves into his pocket. Hunter takes the blades from him, securing them against his thighs before the three of them start walking back toward the soft murmur of the crowd ahead, and Nora waiting expectantly.

When Knives wakes up again a few seconds later, it isn't with a scream of anger like Hunter expected, but with a pained sob. He's crying so loud, the entire crowd of hatchlings shudders in response, like an icy wind is tearing through the city.

Val freezes up, shoulders hiked, breath held, lips in a thin line.

Before he can even try to turn around, Dream puts a hand on the back of Val's head, and Hunter puts his on the small of Val's back.

"Not yet," Dream says.

"Later," Hunter reminds.

Val nods, his breath coming back in little puffs as he starts walking again.

"Can I lean on you?" Hunter asks.

Val jolts toward him, pulling Hunter's arm up around his own shoulder again, and slipping his other around Hunter's waist, and he's gripping so tight, it's not really helping Hunter walk, but it is helping something.

"Thank you," Hunter says.

Val doesn't stop squeezing him until the sound of crying fades into the ruins behind them.

Got rid of the queen, huh?" Arum clearly already knew the answer, *but saying it aloud was different. It put a new color in her eyes.*

"Yeah," Val said. "I'm sorry."

"I'm not," she said back.

Val pointed at the knife sticking out of their brother's eye. "Should I take that too?"

"I think he should do it himself," she'd said.

"What if he doesn't want to?" Val asked her. "What if he's too scared?"

She'd shrugged at him, and Val could see her working out the different possibilities in her head, the chance that he would refuse, or that he simply couldn't, or that he did and it still didn't change him.

Pulling Knives's back against her chest, she told Val, "I'll just have to wait until he's ready."

"I want to help," he'd said to her, sadness beginning to thread through his skin.

"You did," she replied with a sudden fierceness. "Now it's my turn."

Val knew they were running out of time, and he didn't have the space to say, thank you for not killing my friends, for trusting me, for trying at all. I'm sorry about the queen, and Knives, and I don't know what it would look like, but maybe one day I can be a real brother to you. *So he kissed her forehead instead and whispered, "I'll see you later."*

There's an invisible line that they cross, somewhere after they walk by the overgrown hollows of the Innovation train station, when the hatchlings begin to murmur louder and louder until they're talking amongst themselves almost like a regular crowd. Val, Hunter, and Dream are mostly quiet as the hatchlings surround them in a ring of warm noise. Val doesn't feel much like talking anyway. He's too busy listening to the others.

It doesn't quite feel like time is actually passing until their hatchling comes running up to him with Val's backpack in their hands.

"Hunter found this," they say, four pupils fixed on Val. "So we hid it for you."

Val breathes a sigh. "Thank goodness. I have clothes after all."

He reaches to take it from them, but their fingers tighten on the straps, face flushing pink. "Uhm, Mister Val, I picked a name. It's Nora."

"Oh!" Val smiles. "I'm so happy to hear that."

"Also, I think I would like to be a girl. If that's okay."

Val lets go of the bag to hug Nora instead. "It's nice to meet you again, Nora."

She drops the bag and crushes her arms around Val's back, wings buzzing frantically. Just as quickly though, she jumps away, puts Val's backpack into his arms, and drops her head to say, "I'm sorry."

Val frowns. "For what? You've been great."

Her eyes go shiny at the compliment, but then she mutters, "My legs got hurt and Hunter had to carry me for a very long time. They also made me lots of food, so I could keep healing. I know they're your important human, so I'm sorry for taking so much of their time."

Val turns toward Hunter with a smile, and Hunter gives a microscopic startle that Val feels more than sees.

"You took care of Nora."

Hunter's gaze skitters away, his shoulders barely twitching into a shrug. "Told you I would."

His embarrassment makes Val's heart race, and he turns back to grin at Nora. "Don't worry, I'm just glad you were able to help each other. All's forgiven."

She sighs with relief. "Good. I found you some water too, so you can clean all this blood off. Here, I'll show you."

She takes his hand, and Val reaches back to take Hunter's.

"Oh, uh." Hunter lets himself get pulled along.

"I guess that means we're stopping," Dream announces before Nora pulls them too far away to hear.

The trees out here aren't nearly as tall as the ones near Good Fortune. They stand just big enough for Hunter to walk underneath of them without brushing his head against the leaves, like a series of umbrellas spread wide open to catch the sky. It's brighter here too, and the ground is warm on Val's bare feet from all the sunlight soaking into the grass.

Nora proudly presents a swath of shallow river stretched several yards out in front of them. It doesn't look any deeper than a foot at most, but Hunter looks visibly relieved at the chance to stop walking.

"Nora." Hunter unhooks the large pouch from his back and holds it out to her. "Can you bring this to Dream? So Mare doesn't have to sleep on the ground."

"Yes!" She takes it from him and goes jogging back toward the noise of the others.

"Giving up your hammock?" Val asks.

Hunter starts easing himself down onto the grass, and Val sets his backpack aside before joining him.

"He needs it more than me," Hunter says, trying to pull his boots off with a grimace as he reaches for his right foot.

"Let me." Val pushes Hunter's hands off so he can do it instead.

Hunter just pulls back without a word as Val loosens the laces.

Tugging Hunter's boot free, Val glances up as Hunter unpins the lengths of excess fabric that cover his arms and chest. There's a staggering number of empty straps bound to him, ghosts of all the weapons he's given up along the way here. He unhooks another thin length of rope from his waist, and then unravels the loose fabric from his legs as well, revealing yet more holsters segmented down each thigh, and the two weapons they took from Knives. When Hunter nudges his other boot off, he upends it, dropping a small switchblade onto the grass.

Val can't look away while Hunter slowly disarms himself, methodically pulling every weapon and holster and spare bit of weight off his body. There are two thin leather straps tucked under his arms that Val never even knew were there, and Hunter reaches back with a shrug to pull a knot loose and they, too, fall away. He must have had every single defense up for Innovation, and here they all sit, in a useless pile.

Finally, Hunter peels off his actual shirt, and Val holds his breath while Hunter lets his go. Loosening the small tie, Hunter shakes his hair free and leans back on both hands with his eyes closed.

All Val can feel is his own racing heart as Hunter fills his lungs with nothing in the way. Val didn't know that something as simple as breathing could look so handsome, or that he'd ever be so excited to see someone else's exhaustion worn plainly on their body. There are cuts on Hunter's face, bruises splotching over his ribs, a network of red indentations all over his skin, and the bandage stained pink on his thigh, but Val is vibrating at the thought that, soon enough, Hunter will have nothing better to do than to sit still and let this heal.

"Will you sleep with me tonight?" Val blurts out, gripping Hunter's knee because he can't stand not to be touching him again.

Hunter's eyes pop open, that calm momentarily turning to glass as he stares at Val.

"In my tent," Val adds, face burning. "Since you gave your hammock away. I only have the one sleeping bag but I think you could mostly fit."

Hunter blinks at Val, then drops his head and breathes a laugh that's almost too quiet to hear over the soft sound of the river behind them. "Yeah, Val, I'll share your tent. Now will you wash all that blood off?"

Val jumps back to his feet, heat in his face as he realizes he completely forgot about how disgusting he is *again*. "Sorry!"

He doesn't think twice before shucking off his bloodstained pants and splashing into the river. The chill isn't nearly as bad as the last time they washed off like this, and he sinks down onto his knees in a patch of waning sunlight to start scrubbing his hands under the water.

"I wasn't thinking," Val starts saying. "Knives told me that all the hatchlings were going to be killed and I just got so upset."

Hunter steps in after him, only wearing his shorts and his jewelry and nothing else.

"Now I don't even think there was any danger, he just wanted to shake me," Val says.

Val runs his nails underneath each other, desperately trying to make sure his hands are clean, as Hunter sinks down across from him, feet planted on either side of Val's folded legs.

"I guess we both sort of fell apart there," Val says, rubbing at a particularly stubborn spot of blood on the back of his hand that refuses to scrape up. "When the queen got annoyed with the spiders that disobeyed, they hung their bodies up on the wall like a reminder. I guess when Knives gets annoyed, he just tries to make you more annoyed than he is."

Hunter reaches in to scoop Val's hands up out of the water, bringing them up to his face so he can run his tongue over the dot of blood before showing it to Val. "It's a freckle."

Val's breath leaves him. "Oh."

Hunter looks back at the little mark, head tilted. "Didn't know you had those."

"I . . . didn't either," Val admits, looking at it closer, a rogue bit of pigment toward the crease of his thumb. "I guess I haven't looked at my hands in a while."

Hunter cups his hands together to pour water down Val's arm, smoothing his fingers over to wash more of the blood off. "As much as I might hate Knives right now, if you want to try and get something a little less murderous out of him, I think you of all people could manage it."

Val stares at the restrained expression on Hunter's face while he runs his hands down each of Val's arms, clearing a little more blood off each time.

"You really hate him?" Val asks.

Hunter lets his breath out in a short huff, dipping his hands back into the river before wiping them over Val's face.

"No, not really. Or, I don't know, I do hate him right now, but I think that'll probably go away eventually." He pushes clean water over Val's forehead, cold droplets running down Val's nose and cheeks. Something twists up Hunter's mouth, his eyes going dull, and it makes Val worry at his own hands, like he's about to get bad news.

Hunter rests his hands on Val's shoulders, his thumb brushing up and down the slope of Val's neck.

"He's got a connection to you. And he didn't fucking earn it."

The anger of those words doesn't quite match up to the whisper of Hunter's voice as he says them. Val inches up a little closer, trying to get a good look while Hunter turns his face away.

"Could it be that maybe, just maybe, you're a teeny tiny bit jealous?" Val asks, pinching his thumb and forefinger together.

With a sigh, Hunter looks Val in the eye again, brows knit, mouth thin, and it's a relief, really, to see the real anger.

"How could I not be?" Hunter asks, voice climbing up in volume. "The Pillars, the spiders, the hatchlings, you all have something I can't touch. It's like you can talk without speaking. Half of you have tried to kill each other, and at the end of it, you're still bonded."

Hunter breathes through his nose, fingers pressing harder into Val's shoulders. "When you were unconscious in the hive, and Dream had a gun to the queen, he called us all family. You and me and Mare."

"Really?" Val asks, chest tight.

"Yeah." Hunter nods. "I'd be lying if I said it didn't make me happy, but I don't know if I really can be."

Val's shoulders are slowly bruising under Hunter's fingers, and Val lets him, the feeling like lit matches underneath his skin.

"I *shouldn't* be," Hunter corrects himself. "I shouldn't be like Knives. I shouldn't *want* to be like him at all. All he's done is hurt you, so why the fuck am I jealous?"

When he pulls his hands off and sees little red fingerprints in Val's skin, he sighs. "Fuck, I'm sorry."

Val shakes his head, feeling like he's got the moon in his eyes. "I'm not."

Hunter meets his gaze like he's been snared by it.

"You and I had a pretty rocky start too," Val says.

Hunter's lips part, giving a nod in millimeters. "I remember."

"You know, right after he got me away from you that first time, Dream said that if anyone had the right to kill me, it was you." Val can feel that he's not blinking, but he doesn't want to risk missing an instant of whatever this expression is that's steeping on Hunter's face. "You were the first person to leave a mark on me. Do you have any idea what you've done to me?"

Val smiles as his heart kicks up his throat, and he pushes himself up on his knees to look at Hunter eye to eye. "If you want to be family, we can be family. If you want to be coworkers, we can do that too. We could be friends, we could be partners, we can—we can do whatever you want. I know I'm not truly human, but I've gotten very selfish about you."

With fresh, cold water rolling over his legs, slipping his hands around Hunter's face is the warmest thing.

"The fact that I know you could kill me makes me feel more alive than anything else in the world," Val tells him. "You're my Hunter. You're *my hunter*. Right?"

Hunter's fingers slide over Val's waist, his arms slowly circling to pull Val's chest against his, and Val is utterly entranced by the awe strung through Hunter's eyes as he answers, "Yes."

"Then give me as many titles as you can," Val says. "I want all of them."

Hunter puts a hand on the back of Val's head, almost sort of smiling again, and even that slight fracture in the calm is enough to make Val's pulse roar.

"Should have known it wouldn't bother you," Hunter murmurs.

"Not many things do." Val is suddenly breathless, possibly running on adrenaline alone. "Is there still blood on my face? I've been hoping you'd kiss me all day."

Hunter's eyes flash and he drops his gaze again. Val nearly dissolves as a blush begins to creep over Hunter's cheeks. "Almost got it all. C'mere."

Guiding Val's face in closer, Hunter licks the corner of Val's mouth, hesitant and slow and warm. Val starts to melt as Hunter tilts his face and licks the fullest part of Val's cheek, and right above Val's eye, and the edge of his jaw. Heat swells through Val's hips and he pushes forward to return the favor and run his tongue over Hunter's bottom lip, and over the knuckle shaped bruises forming on his temple, and when Hunter leans his head back, Val tastes the column of his throat, from the hollow at the base all the way up to the point of his chin.

"Is that everything?" Val asks him, face to face once more.

Hunter's gaze sweeps over Val's skin, gripping tighter as he studies. "A little more . . ."

Val shivers as Hunter paints Val's parted lips with his tongue. If it means the chance for Hunter to clean him up like this, Val happily swallows the lie of blood he knows isn't there anymore. Dirty, clean, he'll be whatever Hunter likes best.

Touching his finger to his own cheek, Val asks in a whisper, "What about here?"

And Hunter nudges his hand aside to lick that too.

"Here?" Val asks, tapping his shoulder.

And Hunter follows his lead, sinking down to fit his mouth to the place Val touched. Sliding his fingers through Hunter's hair, Val can hardly breathe as he pushes Hunter's face in closer until he feels teeth. The increasing pressure of Hunter biting harder, harder, *harder* into Val's skin wrests a noise out of him—like his lungs have decided that he needs air to live after all. Maybe he always did, and he just forgot. It's hard to think of anything else when his heart is beating inside Hunter's mouth.

It's only Val's teeth beginning to chatter from being nearly naked in the water that forces them out of the river and onto the bank to dry off and redress. Hunter leaves the weapons off, and they find a good place to set up the tent, nestled in the middle of a ring of murmuring hatchlings. They seem to be keeping their distance for now, none of the hatchlings visible to Val as he goes about building his tent. Val wonders if they need the space, or if they're generously granting it to Hunter and Val, but he doesn't mind either way.

Hunter sits down inside the tent, digging out the disinfectant once more, but Val says, "I'm going to check on Dream and Mare. Rest your leg, alright?"

"Fine," Hunter says, and Val wants to bathe in the barest hint of brightness in his eyes.

In a new set of old clothes and a long buried pair of nearly ruined rubber-soled shoes that had been pressed to the bottom of Val's backpack, he follows the sound of Dream's concern until he finds the black hammock strung up and swaying gently between two trees. Dream stands beside it, staring at Mare tucked away in the fabric, like he's only a hair away from crumbling apart. Val hangs back for a minute as Dream lifts his hand, hesitating all the way down while he slowly reaches for Mare. It's like watching the bark of an old oak tree peel away into something fresh and soft and scared. Dream looks at Mare like his eyes were made for it, and Val is ready to pretend he never saw something so tender, until he catches a brilliant red stain on the front of Dream's shirt.

"Your hip!" Val goes sprinting over to him, and Dream jostles out of his trance, glancing down at himself.

"Oh, shit."

"Sit down," Val urges, gently pushing Dream toward one of the trees that's holding Mare up. "You went running without your cane too much, didn't you?"

Dream braces himself on the tree trunk, sliding down until he's sitting in the roots. "It's not *that* bad."

"It's bled through the bandage, so it's not good," Val snaps back, lifting the edge of Dream's shirt up. Fresh blood threatens to drip down Dream's stomach, and Val quickly reaches out with his senses for the pulse of the nearest hatchling, like he's casting a fishing line.

"Come here, come here, come here," he mutters, right until Nora comes bounding up to them.

Her eyes fly open at the blood and she doesn't even ask before taking off running. "I'll get the doctor!"

"You're panicking for nothing," Dream says, leaning his head back against the tree. "It's just . . . waking up, that's all."

Val meets his gaze. "What do you mean?"

Dream waves his hand, setting his cane down onto the grass. "I, uh, I guess that spider wasn't the only one going brittle."

"Are you telling me that you've been keeping this from bleeding just by sheer force of will?" Val asks, voice rising.

Dream shrugs, exhaustion flooding into his face as he sighs. "Can't hold my breath around him."

Val scrubs his hands over his hair. "You're really something else."

"Back at ya, kid."

The doctor returns in a flurry of feigned annoyance, and Nora leans her hands on Val's shoulders so they can both watch the doctor work. Val touches Nora's fingers in a silent *thanks* for the pressure. Cleaning and redressing the wound is simple enough, and the doctor finishes in a few minutes, rising up taller than everyone else so they can fold their arms.

"You have to change that bandage every few hours, you know? It'll get infected."

Dream nods. "Don't worry, doc, I got three fucking nurses following me around now."

"Is he going to be alright?" Val asks.

The doctor flicks their hair aside. "Yes, as long as he's not stubborn about it. Which, as far as I understand it, is not a Pillar's strong suit. Now, may I sleep? Or are any more of you about to start losing pieces?"

Val feels a swell of dizzy relief. "I think that's the last of it, thank you."

"Well. If you need me. Just please politely wake me up," the doctor says. "I'll be right over there. But only for emergencies, yes?"

Nora starts leading them away with a, "Yes, doctor. Do you have an extra lab coat somewhere? I think I'd like to learn more."

Head spinning in nearly every direction, Val reaches his hand out and flattens his palm to the top of Dream's head. "I can't actually bring myself to do it, but just imagine for a moment that I could shake you senseless."

Dream smirks, picking up his cane and using the handle to nudge the edge of Val's shirt collar aside. "You could at least pretend to have a little shame, ya know? I could have died out here."

Val pushes the cane away, covering the bite mark on his shoulder. "Says the man lording his mortality over me."

With a tired laugh, Dream drops the cane again. "I'm starting to think you learned a little too much following me around."

"And now you're going to take credit for my wit," Val says, easing his way back into a smile.

"That's my right as your teacher," Dream responds, eyes sliding shut. "That's the real reason anyone becomes a professor. So their students make 'em feel smart for the rest of their lives."

"Didn't you say I was the worst student you've ever had?" Val asks.

"That was, uh, last term," Dream says, nodding as if he's just decided, his body starting to relax with the pull of impending sleep. "We're on a new term now. Different class."

Val wants to wake him back up and ask approximately one thousand questions. He wants to wake Mare up while he's at it and wring every last detail out of them both, but then it occurs to him that Dream has just given him permission to stick around for another "term."

"We'll talk later then," Val says, rising up to his feet, and brushing Dream's bangs off his forehead.

When he gets back to the tent, Val claps his hands together and says, "I have a favor to ask."

Hunter sits up to look at him. "Anything."

Val whispers about a hundred apologies while Hunter kneels down to pick Dream up off the ground. Hunter keeps his weight on his good leg, and turns to the hammock where Val does his best to nudge Mare aside to make room. As gently as he can, Hunter eases Dream in beside Mare, and the hammock sways with the extra weight, the trees softly groaning before they settle again.

Instinct—or whatever it is that makes flowers turn toward the sun—takes over as Dream slowly winds his arms like vines around Mare's back, and in tandem, Nightmare twines his legs with Dream's.

Their faces slot in together, forehead to forehead, nose beside nose, and two different lullabies begin to harmonize as the twins breathe each other in.

⎯◆⎯

Val and Hunter sit side by side in the tent with the afterimage of Mare and Dream clinging to each other burning the back of Val's eyelids every time he blinks. Val hasn't even bothered unraveling his sleeping bag, the two of them just sat down in silence and haven't moved since.

Val exhales. "They're really . . ."

"Intense," Hunter says.

"Yeah."

Val's face is burning from the picture of tenderness. It makes his chest ache to think about knowing a person so well that your arms may as well have been carved to hold them.

"Sorta scary," Val says with a clipped laugh.

"Yeah."

Val can feel Hunter again, their body humming beside Val's as they stare at nothing. It's not dark out yet, and the tent itself is full of orange light from the slowly setting sun. Val never noticed the hole in the side of the canvas until he sees the extra beam of light on Hunter's torso out of the corner of his eye.

Hunter's hand is braced on the ground beside themself, and their fingers are a beacon in Val's vision. Whatever this strange intensity in the air is, Val feels like he'll snap if he doesn't move through it. He doesn't remember until he's trying to discreetly slide his own hand over toward Hunter's that, of course, Hunter can feel Val much better than Val can feel them. There is no *discreet* when it comes to Hunter, so Val turns to put both his hands on top of theirs.

Hunter startles, their eyes open wide as they glance at Val and back to nothing, but they let Val take their hand. They let him inch up closer on his knees. They turn their head toward him without looking him in the eye as Val crawls into their lap, starts pawing at their shirt, his breath coming faster and faster.

"I just want to look at you." Val hears his voice turning to a whine as he slides his hands up Hunter's chest, over skin and scar tissues and jewelry and muscle.

Hunter pulls their shirt off for him, and Val leans his weight onto Hunter's chest until they spill onto their back. Swallowing a knot of panic he doesn't really understand, Val pulls Hunter's hair down again, combing his fingers through it while Hunter eases their hands around Val's waist like they're worried he'll take off running if they don't hold him still.

"You okay?" Hunter asks.

"Dream told me to fire you," Val says in a rush. "So you don't have to watch out for him anymore, unless it's what you want to do. You-you can do whatever you want now."

"Oh." Hunter's voice is hardly sound at all as they stare back at him.

Val puts his fingers over Hunter's open mouth, their breath catching on his fingers. Sliding his hands down lightly over Hunter's neck, he touches their pulse, their muscles gliding as they swallow against his skin. Val's panting as thinks about feeding himself to Hunter, sliding down their throat, letting pieces of himself become part of their body.

"Val?"

They're worried again. It's in their expression, and the strength of their grip on his waist. Val gives a quiet moan through closed lips as his clit starts to ache like someone's pinching him. He shifts his hips further down Hunter's stomach, smoothing his hands over the jewelry in Hunter's nipples, and Val arches his feet at the sound of Hunter's breath stuttering past their lips.

The forest isn't quiet. It's full to the brim with the sound and the scent of life in every direction, so Val tells his body to shut it out. All he wants is Hunter, the blown-out look of their eyes, the soft snares in their voice when Val sets the pad of his finger on their piercing, their hands carelessly digging into Val's hips as they nudge him back just enough for Val to feel them getting hard through their clothes. With that heat pressing between his thighs, Val folds forward to drag his tongue over the metal ornaments in Hunter's chest.

Hunter moans from the bottom of their stomach when Val nudges the jewelry with his tongue. They're pulling on Val's hips, pushing up with their own, and Val can feel the strain in their breath like it's coming from his own chest—*not close enough*—as Val presses his lips to their nipple.

"I want—" Hunter loses their words in Val's mouth as impulse takes over and Val sucks skin and jewelry onto his tongue. Slipping their fingers down the back of Val's pants, Hunter tries again with a shredded version of their voice. "Wanna take care of you."

Val picks his head up, sees the flush spreading over Hunter's body, their head tipped back, eyes shut tight; he feels their nails digging in harder as they try to rub their cock against Val through too many layers of fabric. This must be what they've been hiding: waiting for darkness and wielding a knife just to keep Val from seeing the way they *want*. More desperate than Val ever thought Hunter capable of, but so much prettier too.

Another gift for Val to unwrap as he unbuttons his pants. The two of them wrestle Val's clothes off, but before Val can even try to get Hunter fully undressed, hot skin presses into his clit, and Val's hands go weak. It doesn't matter if it's not *this*. Eyes sliding shut, Val picks his hips up, a smile stealing his whole face as he slides his own ache against the length of Hunter's cock.

When a smooth bit of metal catches Val's clit, he makes a noise somewhere between a moan and a yelp, his eyes flying open to see two demure dots of silver in Hunter's skin.

"I didn't—know you had that," Val squeaks out through halted breaths.

Hunter pants at him. "We had sex before, you didn't feel it?"

"It was dark," Val shoots back, cheeks burning. "And I was tired, and worried about you, and I just . . . thought you were very good. I haven't really slept with a lot of people, I don't exactly know the difference!"

Even with a bruised and blushed face, Hunter actually looks a little smug at hearing that, five percent of a smile lifting their mouth. Val sparks right back to needy at the sight of it, reaching underneath himself to steady Hunter's cock against his slit.

Hunter curses from the first press into Val's cunt, their legs bending up as Val leans his hands on Hunter's chest to stay in place. There was a small part of Val that worried it wouldn't be as good the second time, but some physical instinct is already overwhelming him, his body pushing him all its own to take more. Val can't imagine a greed this deep will ever go away.

Hunter's hands guide Val with bruising tightness all the way down until their hips are flush and Val almost yelps again, not from any pain, but the fullness of finally getting what he's been drowning about for days on end. Holding himself up over Hunter, Val wants to pay attention to figure out exactly what it is that they like, but the answer seems to be *everything that's happening*, and pretty soon, Val can only try to keep himself together through the urge to melt every time Hunter slides all the way inside of him.

Last time they did this, it was hardly about them at all, and the difference is winter and summer. Even with Val's senses going haywire from his own body, he can feel Hunter underneath him, their heart pounding underneath Val's hands, their breath shaking in their throat, their hips pushing up to meet Val's. Their presence sings too—not like Dream's or Nightmare's, much softer than that, but thick like blood, and deep like a drum. If Val could crawl inside that song, he would. He wants to slip the sound between his ribs so he can fill his lungs with it.

They are both alive. They are both skin and metal, and when Val sees what pleasure does to Hunter's face, he thinks he can understand spending ten years just to convince one person to come and see snow with him.

When Hunter comes, they keep pushing Val's hips down into their own, as if they could possibly get any closer. Val squeezes their waist, waiting patiently for the fire to burn out. He doesn't need more, not with Hunter wounded and a hundred or so other bodies in the woods, but he stays seated on top of them, taking every second he can get to look at this person before the night can steal the light away.

In the last minutes of sun, Val leans down to whisper in their ear, "Next time, let me take all of your clothes off."

Hunter touches Val's thighs. "Sorry. Just didn't want you thinking about my stitches."

"Oh no, did they rip?" Val tries to reach for their thigh, but Hunter snatches his hand, bringing it back to their cheek.

"All good."

Val stares at Hunter, the soft set of their face as they breathe against Val's skin, and Val can't stop himself from touching with both his hands. He cups Hunter's face and sets his thumbs on the corners of Hunter's mouth, gently pulling at their skin.

"What are you doing?" Hunter asks, quiet laughter slipping through their voice.

"You almost gave me a real smile in the city," Val says, nudging their lips up again. "I'm just helping you along."

Hunter starts laughing, and Val slides his fingers out of the way to watch it bloom. A careless, simple joy that fits right in with the rest of their jewelry. Val wants to drink up the soft brightness of it, marveling at the way a few little changes—nothing but angles and lines and sounds—can turn a person from stone to moonlight.

"It's not fair, you can't do this right when it's nighttime," Val says, gripping Hunter's face tighter as it gets harder to see. "Teach me how to use my eyes in the dark!"

Hunter runs their hands up Val's arms, the tent finally succumbing to darkness around them. "Later."

Val folds forward against them, resting his forehead against Hunter's. "Promise?"

"Promise."

It takes another two nights to get through the woods. Hunter allows Val to hold his hand sometimes, when no one else can see, but if any of the others get too close, something makes him snap his hand back. When they're near enough to see Respite at the end of the railroad, the hatchlings decide to hang back in the safety of the woods. Revealing themselves all at once to an entire town of humans may not be the right decision just yet, but Nora excitedly tells Val, "We've been talking, and I think now that Mr. Nightmare is awake, we might be able to salvage some nice things from Innovation."

"Be careful," Val tells her with another hug. "If you see Arum, please tell her I hope she's alright. If she needs help with Knives, I'll try my best."

Nora squeezes him back with shocking tightness. "If he turns out anything like you, I'll be happy."

Val just laughs, wondering if that's possible. After this entire journey, he supposes he should know by now that nothing is impossible, but he can't help but hope that Knives will be someone new, not just *someone like Val.*

When he picks a new name, Val will know that it's time to talk.

They only get a few words out of Nightmare each day, and he's barely able to hobble along with help from Dream and Hunter so that the four of them can book a room at the bed and breakfast in Respite without causing complete alarm.

"He fucked up his leg," Dream explains while Val fills out the guest book. "While we were hiking."

"Even the most prepared hiker can slip," the owner responds with a sagely nod. "The doctor's office opens tomorrow at eight A.M. sharp if you need her."

Hunter and Val share a room across from Dream and Mare, and the first thing Val does is beg Hunter to take a bath with him. A bit of reluctance sneaks into Hunter's *sure* but that doesn't deter Val from dragging him to wash off under running hot water for the first time in much too long. Even though Hunter looks somewhat like he's been cornered by a bear, he lets Val scrub soap into his skin for several minutes, taking note of every dip, divot, scar, bump, and burn on his body.

Once they're both in a tub of hot water, Hunter ties his hair back up, his gaze locked on the wall, and Val reaches out to touch his cheek.

"I didn't realize you were so shy," Val says with a smile.

"I . . ." Hunter's eyes dart up and down, but he tugs Val's wrist closer. "I'm not used to this."

"Which part?" Val asks, brushing aside a stray hair from Hunter's temple.

"Being looked at."

Val's eyes flash, and a wave of embarrassment hits him as he remembers what Hunter was doing before he joined up with them.

"I went from years of hiding specifically from people like you to . . . sitting in a bathtub with you," Hunter finishes with a mumble.

"I'm sorry," Val says automatically.

Hunter shakes his head, touching the back of Val's hand to keep it on his face. "I just need to get used to it. You got a heavier gaze than most."

"Close your eyes then, I want to stare at you," Val says.

He does, lids sliding shut as his mouth threatens to pull into a smile. Val holds his face, counting Hunter's piercings in silence—a hoop through his right eyebrow, a bar through the left, a loop around his septum, a stud in the left nostril, two dots on the bridge of his nose between his eyes, and one on the valley of skin right above his top lip. There's too many to count on each ear, and Val doesn't even try, just takes the moment of calm to press his lips to Hunter's, delighting in the brief jolt of surprise that dissolves on Hunter's tongue as he opens his mouth.

Bit by bit. That's all Val needs.

"If you ever want to pick your own name," Val starts to say.

Hunter pulls Val back for a much rougher kiss that Val can feel all the way down to his toes before Hunter tells him in a whisper, "I want the name *you* gave me."

Val sighs as he realizes that words can taste as good as food.

It takes forty-eight hours of rest at the center of a human town for Nightmare to truly wake up again. When Dream knocks on their door one morning looking sheepish, Val already knows what he'll say. He felt the pillar stirring sometime in the night. It was subtle, but Hunter and Val both woke up at the change, listening in awed silence as Mare's presence blossomed into something a little more familiar.

It's lighter when they're together, Hunter had whispered, and Val nodded against him. As natural as the oxygen in the air.

"Mare's awake, right?" Val asks as he stares at Dream the morning of.

Dream scrubs at the back of his neck while Hunter shuffles up beside Val. Dream's gray eyes are swollen, rimmed in red, and Val is sure that he and Mare have already been talking for hours.

"Yeah, he's up. Talking more. I figured of all people, you two probably earned at least a couple questions, if you want 'em."

"Are you okay?" Val asks quietly.

Dream looks like Val pulled a gun on him for the animal look of panic in his face. He swallows once, his fingers rolling over the handle of the cane, and he exhales.

"We're not done talking. Probably won't be for a while, but."

He freezes, every other process halting as his eyes start to water up in front of them. Hunter's pulse spikes from behind Val, and he opens the door wider while Val reaches out to pull on Dream's sleeve.

"Come inside and sit for a second," Val says.

"I-I shouldn't be away for too long," Dream says, turning his head back toward Mare, but he doesn't resist as the two of them herd him into their room to sit him on the arm chair nestled in the corner. Hunter perches on the windowsill beside Dream, and Val lowers himself onto the floor to sit between their feet.

"What happened?" Val asks.

Dream takes the biggest breath Val has ever seen him take.

"Just the dumbest goddamn thing," Dream says. He leans his cane against the wall and runs his fingers through his hair, startling midway through when the cane slides down and the metal handle smacks into the wall. "Fuck."

He's as thin as a sheet. Val puts his hands around Dream's calf, just to make sure he's really there, and Dream sighs into his fingers.

"You'd think we'd be better at talking after this long, but so much of our time is spent just feeling the space around each other, sometimes just fucking speaking is harder than anything else," Dream says, giving a wry laugh. "We just started doing things to try and help the other, until we weren't even aware of it. Taught myself how to like alcohol just so he wouldn't see what I was dreaming. Did a lot of things just so he wouldn't have to think about me. But he was always thinking about me. Muting myself like that only scared him until he thought the only way to fix it was to push me away. We thought we were helping each other, and by the time we'd both gone too far, there were too many other problems. When his spider said he wanted a city free of humans, Mare was so relieved that they weren't planning a massacre, he let them use him to build that wall, but it drained him so fast, he couldn't stay awake."

Leaning his forearms on his knees, Dream stares at the patterns in the faded carpet.

"As soon as Mare shut down, the spider tried to preserve him, like suspending him between sleeping and waking. Tried to pull things out of him while he was dreaming. The tech inside Innovation is a lot better than it is anywhere else, so he had a lot of tools to force feed Mare to keep him going. The queen saw Mare's dreams of our brothers, Curiosity and Mischief. Mis got himself hurt trying to help with one of the hatchlings, and while he was dying, Ozzi . . . consumed him. To keep him alive. And now they share a body. Like a peach with two pits."

Dream gives a soft smile as Val remembers Ozzi's impossibly bright eyes.

"The spider got the idea about sharing with Mare, but after a few bites didn't make him feel any different, he gave up. But, well, you know already. It did change him. Started numbing him to Mare's dreams. The spider was too pissed at Mare being useless, he started changing himself around so Mare wouldn't want to talk to him anymore. So Mare talked to his sentinels instead. We're all kind of petty in the end, huh?"

Val plucks Dream's pant leg with a smile. "Seems like it."

"Does this mean you two are okay?" Hunter asks.

Dream glances at both of them and leans back to stretch his shoulders against the chair. "I have a feeling we could talk for another hundred years and we'd still have things to figure out, but maybe it's not so bad if we breathe different air every once in a while."

Head tipped back, Dream closes his eyes. "I'll take you to see him, just . . . give me a minute."

Neither of them need to say, *take as much time as you need*. Val gets up to sit beside Hunter on the windowsill, turning over Hunter's hand to trace the lines on his palm while Dream takes a nap in their room.

About an hour later, Dream stands with his hand on the doorknob to his and Mare's room, glaring at Hunter and Val.

"Don't push him too hard. He's still healing."

Nodding, Val looks back at Hunter and then to Dream, and then down at his old clothes. "I feel like I'm not dressed nicely enough."

"The fuck you need to dress up for?" Dream asks. "Had to buy Mare shorts for a child with the money Nora swiped from Innovation, you think he cares what you're wearing?"

Val concedes with a laugh, and the three of them step into the other room. There's a smell in the air like ripening fruit as Dream walks over to the bed where Nightmare is propped up. Dream hooks his cane onto the headboard and sits down on the edge of the mattress, looking all the world like an over-doting parent.

It feels like walking too fast will somehow hurt Mare, so Val slowly approaches the bed with his fingers in a tangle. Hunter doesn't make a sound, just shadows Val as they come to stand in front of what looks like Dream's younger, frailer ghost, with tendrils of limp silver hair hanging over the heavily veined skin of his shoulders. He's still bandaged up in places, but Val can see what looks like a seam along his bicep, almost like a scar, but not quite the same.

Nightmare turns heavily lidded, pale gray eyes to Val and Hunter, offering the best version of a welcoming smile that a nearly dead man can give.

"I know I owe you two a rather generous apology," he says with cracked lips. "Perhaps we can get that on credit while I crawl out of the grave?"

His voice is poked through with exhaustion, but underneath that is an old charm that makes Val laugh at the joke even with its limping delivery.

"Plenty of time for that," Val says with a shake of his head. "I actually wanted to ask you about the queen, if that's alright?"

Dream looks poised to step in and kick them out at a moment's notice, but Mare licks his lips and nods. "When I first met him, he went by Raleigh, but I guess he shed that too."

"Were you around to meet any of the other spiders?" Val asks.

Mare gives a sheepish frown. "Sorry. I was asleep for this whole *queen at arms* business, and the only way I could communicate with the spiders was through their nightmares. I can't say we had very nice conversations. I'm afraid I am partially to blame for the ones that died. I know they saw Raleigh like a parent of sorts, and since I couldn't hurt him, I pushed on any weak link I could. East self-destructed, but West tried to take me with him, so Raleigh stopped him. South offered herself to Raleigh after he failed to gain anything from eating me, and Raleigh didn't leave any trace behind. He always seemed so interested in the way the pillars came in pairs. He really thought it meant something important. Never bothered to notice how his own family was clinging to the ghosts of their own humanity."

"Did they all like each other?" Val asks.

Mare nods, half a smile on. "I really do feel quite bad about what I did to them. They were terrified of humans even while they imitated them, and Raleigh couldn't comfort them even if he'd wanted to. He didn't even try. That wasn't the progress he was interested in."

Mare leans his head back to take a deep breath, and Dream touches his shoulder.

"Thank you for keeping my idiot brother alive," Mare says.

Val smiles and glances behind him at Hunter, who looks about ready to put his hands over his eyes again, but he holds still, bunching up the back of Val's shirt instead.

"Anytime," Val says. "If you need to hire us again though, I might ask for money next time."

Mare gives a wheezing laugh, eyelids drooping shut. "You're telling me Dream dragged you two across the world, nearly got you both killed, and didn't even pay you? My god, that's bleak."

"I paid for room and board. Sorta," Dream mumbles.

"Mercy, we'll be in their pockets for a hundred years on that debt." When Mare opens his eyes again, he looks right at Hunter, a spectral smile clinging to his mouth. "You're one of those specialized humans, right? The group that split off centuries ago?"

Hunter swallows. "Formerly."

"Quit then? Ah." Mare nods. "I suppose that means all my thanks goes solely to you, instead of the organization. And my sincerest apologies to you as well. I don't love that a human was put at risk. Sort of antithetical to the whole . . . pillar thing."

Hunter's hand is a fist in the back of Val's shirt. "It's nothing."

"It's a pretty big something by my count," Mare says back. "I just wanted to say that I'm very sorry for what I said to you in Innovation. That was the rot talking, not me. It would have happened to any human who stepped through the wall."

Hunter nods, muscling through the discomfort of sitting under this magnifying glass. "I know. Wouldn't hold it against you."

Mare's head lolls toward Dream and he says, "What a nice couple of boys you've managed to steal."

Dream scoffs. "You just haven't been around Val long enough to hear him say something weird. Don't worry, give it time. He's creepier than you."

"Something to look forward to," Mare breathes back.

"Anything else you want to ask before he passes out?" Dream turns to Val again.

Val can feel Hunter on the brink of bolting, so he shakes his head. "Nothing I can't ask later."

Dream nods, turning back to Mare to brush his hair aside. Val is prepared to leave them, knowing that Dream needs these waking moments with Mare *much* more than he or Hunter does, but he stops mid-turn and faces Dream again.

"Actually, I think Hunter and I recently became homeless, do you happen to have any suggestions of where we could stay? I'm a bit low on cash."

Dream barks out a laugh. "Shit. I don't think anyone would mind if you borrowed the family hideout for a while. Though I'm sure Rez would be happy to take you in for a bit too. And there's always Patience, since no one's using it. We got time, we can find something."

"It is quite literally the least you could do for these two," Mare wheezes at him.

"Okay, okay, yeah, I'll figure it out, promise. Long as you don't mind walking at our pace for a little while?"

Dream meets Val's gaze again.

"We could use the extra help," Dream adds. "If you're not busy."

Val looks to Hunter first, getting a slight nod out of him before grinning back at Dream.

"We'll help each other. That's what families do, right?"

Dream starts laughing again, looking over at Mare as he steadily sinks toward sleep, and back to Val and Hunter to give them a shrug and a smirk.

"I have no fucking clue, Val. But if you want into this one, we always got room."

Hunter smooths his hand up Val's back, relaxing in degrees behind him, and Val grins.

"Yes, please."

The end.

A NEW SEASON

When Hunter told Val that he had to go back home, he was worried for a lot of reasons. Mostly he was worried that Val would become distressed at the same realization that Hunter had been simmering in ever since they left Innovation. He had no idea how many Eyes were still active, and none of them were aware that the hatchlings are just . . . hatchlings. The Eyes would have more luck saving people by brushing the hatchling's hair than they ever would with knives, but who would be able to tell them that?

"I have to track down the Tongues," Hunter said to Val in their shared room at the Hollow Inn on the night of their arrival. He'd been sitting in the windowsill when Val came to ask him why Hunter looked so upset. They'd finally made it with Mare and Dream back to the sleepy town where they were meant to meet up with Sig, but Hunter couldn't relax.

"I need to tell them what I've learned," Hunter told Val. "I keep thinking about how awful it would be for any of the Eyes to stumble on the hatchlings you left behind outside the city and accidentally start a real war."

Val's eyes went wide, and he crawled into Hunter's lap to put his hands around Hunter's face. Hunter barely withstood the concern in Val's eyes, close enough to cut him.

"What if they hurt you?" Val had asked.

Hunter felt Val's fear crushing into his shoulders.

"You worried about me?" Hunter asked in quiet disbelief.

"Of *course* I am," Val whined, and it was as distressing as it was lovely to hear.

"They won't," Hunter told him. "We don't actually blind each other, Val. We just let people think that so they stay away. I couldn't bring myself to correct Dream when I still felt like one of them but . . . I'm not anymore. Don't worry, they're not going to hurt me."

Val let his breath out, his head falling heavily onto Hunter's chest. "Can I come with you?"

Hunter had touched the back of Val's head, wondering how such a little thing as him could be so heavy.

"I've thought about this a lot," Hunter said. "Best case scenario, you come along and the others feel you from miles away and move too quickly for us to catch up. Worst case scenario, they think you're using me to find them, and decide to do something about it. They won't hurt me, but they'll hurt you without a thought. I can't have that."

Val's hands tightened into fists, concern pouring off of him like steam. Hunter could feel the heat of it as he put his hands on Val's back.

He clung to Hunter for the rest of the night, through their check in with Dream and Mare, and through dinner while Hunter ate more than the two pillars and spider combined. Hunter has never been more conscious of his own humanity, especially when Val is wound around his back, listening to Hunter's heartbeat through the palms of his hands.

It was Dream who told Hunter that he had the right idea going back to the Tongues. With Mare back on his feet, and Val as strong as he'd ever been, Dream told Hunter he had nothing to worry about.

"No offense to you and Mare, but I'm not worried about you two anymore," Hunter had said to him.

Dream had laughed and nodded his head. "I'll keep the kid out of trouble, alright? If we stay at Indulgence, he'll be too busy for it between Lux and Rez. Just don't be long. Don't know if I can handle it if he starts getting weepy about you."

He was only sort of joking, but Hunter could see all too clearly the moment Dream and he came to the same question.

What does a spider do when he's sad?

That night, the answer was to not give Hunter any space. Hunter practically wore Val like clothing while Val processed the impending distance. Through a bath and into bed, Val had his nose pressed to Hunter's neck.

"What if I forget what you smell like?" Val asked. "It's so subtle . . ."

Hunter let Val lay on top of him, sliding his hand up the back of Val's shirt. "Then you'll remember when I come back."

Val's arms cinched tighter. "Be quick."

"I'll try."

Val had been holding himself back while Hunter's thigh healed, and they had hardly any space from Dream and Mare, but when Val stole a kiss along Hunter's throat, like he thought he might not get away with it, Hunter could feel Val's need to connect. Hunter felt it himself, completely at Val's mercy.

This is what Hunter thinks about most as he begins to track down the Tongues. The feeling of holding onto Val's thin body and trying, trying, *trying* to figure out what this thing is that makes Hunter want to give Val whatever he wants, to bite him and kiss him and not let anyone else near him. It's almost like panic, except it feels too good to be that. The warmth that Val puts in Hunter's chest is so unfamiliar, so strange and so deep, Hunter has no clue how to resolve it. He's pretty sure he never learned the words for something like this.

While he's crossing through forests day in and day out, Hunter lives in the memories of Val's tent, and that bed in Good Fortune. Hunter doesn't recognize his own voice when he's saying Val's name.

That was never part of the deal. Paying people made it easy. Money bought him rules, but Val doesn't come with those, and he's still figuring out how to speak to someone who will remember all the things that he says.

The night he told Val that he was leaving was a little better. Separation was looming around the corner and he used that to get his body to move when his mouth wouldn't make any sound. He pulled Val closer and held on tighter until Val was the one to ask him.

Will you touch inside me again?

His voice was so quiet, like it was all a big secret. Nothing Hunter ever paid for in Indulgence felt as dirty as pushing his hand past Val's underwear to touch his slit. It wasn't just the fact that Val still had his clothes on, or how wet Val had gotten just from thinking about this. It was the impossibly soft noise that Val made, like he'd been dreaming about Hunter's fingers for months.

It made him feel guilty for not having touched Val sooner. But as soon as Hunter thought *I should be paying more attention to you*, the immediate feedback of *don't spend your waking hours with your mind in Val's cunt* left him dizzy. Of course, he stopped spiraling when Val asked for more with his hands curled in Hunter's hair.

In the woods somewhere north of the deadlands and west of Foundation, where the trees grow thicker and heavier, like massive ropes yanked up from deep in the ground, Hunter pulls out the note that Val wrote to him in Respite and puts the paper to his nose to try and catch the scent of Val. He reads the words Val wrote to him, afraid to touch the letters in case they wear off.

> *Hunter,*
>
> *We're moving on from Respite. Dream said we need to keep moving and I know that you'd do the same and that's the only reason I haven't fought Dream to go*

back. I can't stand thinking about you hurt, so I can only act as though you're okay. You'll be meeting us inside Innovation. You'll help me get the hatchlings to safety. I need you to be there so we can finally help Dream get back to Mare.

When we finish this job, I would very much like to spend more time with you. This whole trip, I thought you didn't have a scent, but that's not true. It's just soft and quiet and it moves. You have a scent like a river.

Val

With his tongue on the seal of the envelope, Hunter licks what Val once licked while he jerks off with a fervor he's wholly unfamiliar with. The queen of Innovation gave herself nothing, and she grew frail and bitter over time. What would happen if Hunter spoiled his spider instead?

In northern plains far above Foundation, Hunter pulls his own hair with his mind on Val's hands. When they were in that bed in Good Fortune, Val kept squeezing his leg into Hunter's thigh, right into the place where his freshly removed stitches had been. Hunter knew it was an accident, but something about feeling the sting of his own wounds with Val coming on his hand pierced him like one his own needles. He's craved pain before, but Val gives it new depth.

The mountains on the northeastern coast have never been more miserable. Finally pinning down the Tongues is the only relief in those dry, cold cliffs, and Hunter has to remember through the impatience that he only has one chance to do this right.

He'll give them his story, he'll do everything he can to convince them that he's telling the truth, and then he'll come home. He's so close. So close.

He's

almost

home.

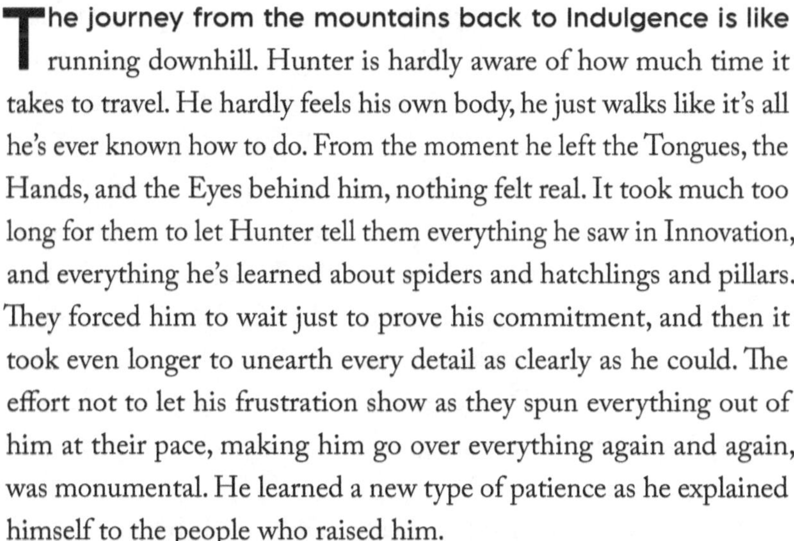

The journey from the mountains back to Indulgence is like running downhill. Hunter is hardly aware of how much time it takes to travel. He hardly feels his own body, he just walks like it's all he's ever known how to do. From the moment he left the Tongues, the Hands, and the Eyes behind him, nothing felt real. It took much too long for them to let Hunter tell them everything he saw in Innovation, and everything he's learned about spiders and hatchlings and pillars. They forced him to wait just to prove his commitment, and then it took even longer to unearth every detail as clearly as he could. The effort not to let his frustration show as they spun everything out of him at their pace, making him go over everything again and again, was monumental. He learned a new type of patience as he explained himself to the people who raised him.

When he did lose his grip for one second, it wasn't with an angry outburst.

"I'm . . . caring for one of the spiders."

"You're caring for one of them?"

"Yes."

"How?"

"I'll figure out what he needs, so he never winds up like that queen. And as soon as we're done talking, I'm going back to him. I can't be your Eye

anymore. I have a name now. If I hunt again, it won't be for you. It'll be for the family that took me in."

Walking among his former community with eyes firmly bound, Hunter didn't feel the urge to sit and talk with anyone. He didn't want to sharpen his knives, he didn't want to ask how the Hands were doing. There was no draw to rekindle a connection, and that was really how he knew.

From now on, Hunter is only Hunter. The further he gets from the mountains, the lighter he feels. He took all of his weapons with him when he left to find the Tongues, and it's only on the way back that he realizes how heavy they all are. It's not as though he expected to have to fight his way up there, but the pressing fear of that conversation drove him to arm himself. Now that he's only headed toward Val, he doesn't need to wear these. They're only slowing him down.

When the silhouette of Modesty shows itself in the distance, Hunter almost breaks into a sprint, but he doesn't want to scare anyone in the city. Forcing himself to take the road at a regular pace, he removes the knives from his arms and stuffs them into the packs strapped to his hips instead. It's mid-morning when Hunter steps back onto the roads of Modesty, and he makes an impulsive decision for a quick detour before taking the lifts down to Indulgence with a waxy paper bag in his hand.

Maybe it's the fact that he's finally standing still, but as he slowly sinks below the surface, anxiety crawls up Hunter's throat. What is he supposed to say? As far as he knows, Val has been staying with the pillars here, Lux and Rez. Is he just going to knock on their door and ask if Val is home? What if he *isn't*? What if one of the gems recognizes Hunter as a former customer? What if Val has already talked to them about Hunter? It's not like Eyes come through here all the time, they'd know exactly who he was.

Fuck.

Hunter almost wraps his eyes as he walks out of the lift, but the dizzying feel of coming back to this bustling city forces him to keep going with his eyes open. He slinks through the crowd, skulking toward the neighborhood that surrounds the underground lake with pebbles dropping into his stomach every step of the way.

Dream said Lux's house is the biggest one, and Hunter doesn't need heightened senses to find it, but he has to force himself up the wooden steps to get to the door with every bit of strength he has, and there he stops.

Val is inside the house. Among the cluster of heartbeats and footsteps and voices and scents carrying through from the other side of the door, Val is the only weapon in a peaceful house of gems. Hunter doesn't even know how long he's been gone, but Val is just as shiny and sharp as he was the moment Hunter said, *I'll meet you in Indulgence.*

Val had told Hunter, *please run as fast as you can, so I can't follow you.*

Hunter had kissed Val just so Val would close his eyes, and Hunter could take the moment to disappear as quickly as he could.

And now he is back, with absolutely no clue how to say hello.

It isn't Val who opens the door, but one of the pillars, a short man with perfect hair and cutting eyes, who startles at the sight of Hunter standing on his porch.

"Oh. Are you the one we've been expecting?"

Hunter reflexively backs away from him—this must be Rez—and gives a sputtering response. "I think so, yes. Probably. U-unless you're expecting someone else. I'm . . . here for Val."

Hunter's shoulders sag, and Rez's lips quirk into a smile. Turning his head, he calls over his shoulder, "Val, there's a very large person at the door asking for you."

There's a sound like something heavy getting dropped, and laughter floats through the house, not Val's, but someone else saying, "I'll get it, go!"

"I'm sorry!" That's Val, shouting as he's running on bare feet that thump quietly across the house.

Hunter stands there like he's waiting to catch a bullet with his bare hands. Rez politely steps aside, holding the door open with an expectant look as Val comes hurtling around the corner.

"I don't usually tolerate running in my house, but this is a special occasion," Rez says pleasantly.

Val doesn't stop until his toes are just shy of the doormat, staring up at Hunter with the biggest eyes—light reflecting off water, blindingly bright. He looks exactly the same, save for the nicer clothes. His sleeves are rolled up to his elbows, hands slightly pink and damp, and Hunter thinks he must have been washing dishes or something. Val smells like soap and fresh laundry and polished metal.

"You have to take your boots off." Val's voice rushes out of him in a single breath, and he points to a rack of shoes right inside the door. He's bouncing on the balls of his feet.

"Oh, sorry." Hunter steps into the house, and Val lifts his hands, only for his fingers to curl tightly into fists as he waits for Hunter to kneel down, set the bag aside, and undo his laces.

"I have errands to run, Val. I'll trust the house to you while I'm gone."

Rez slips outside, and the door closes with the click of a lock. Hunter hears Val take a sharp breath only inches away, and Hunter's hand slips off his boot and onto Val's calf. Squeezing Val's leg through the fabric of his trousers empties Hunter's head of whatever had him hesitating on the porch. He's here, he made it. There's nowhere left to travel. His whole body rings with the ache of nonstop weeks of walking, and now it's over. Looking up at Val, Hunter blinks as a sudden emptiness yawns around him, only to snap back around Val and his cut glass smile.

"Hey," Hunter says, hardly any sound behind his voice.

Val bites his lips, his whole body leaning forward an inch at a time, like he's worried he'll get scolded, until Hunter tugs on his leg, and then Val latches onto Hunter's shoulders.

"Hey," Hunter says it again as he skims his hand up to Val's waist. "I'm back."

Val crumples, sinking to the floor with his knees between Hunter's legs, his arms locking around Hunter's neck, face pressed to the side of Hunter's head. Shaking ever so slightly, Val hugs like he means to force all the air from Hunter's chest.

"No more trips," Val says, not really yelling so much as losing control of the pitch of his voice.

Hunter winds his arms around Val. "Okay."

"I mean it, I really missed you," Val goes on.

"Okay." Hunter nods, feeling his mouth trying to twist into a smile. "Missed you too."

"Bring me with you next time," Val says, his voice turning to steam as he braces his feet on the floor to try and push himself even closer.

"Okay." Hunter puts his hand on the back of Val's head, brushing over Val's hair. "Were you good while I was gone?"

"Yes, I was *perfect*, just ask Dream."

Val sounds like he's about to shatter, so Hunter keeps his hand anchored to Val's back while he picks at the laces on his boots. When they're loose enough, Hunter hoists Val up with him when he stands, and he nudges his boots off his feet one at a time with Val clinging to his chest.

"Hey." Hunter can't bring himself to speak above a whisper, and he doesn't know if it's because he's hardly spoken over the course of the trip home, or if he's just too focused trying to listen to Val. "It's good to see you again."

Val makes a soft sound, almost like a gasp, and he pulls back just to press his mouth to Hunter's and steal his breath instead.

Oh, right. This. Val's hands are small against Hunter's face as he gives a kiss that could almost be *demure*, if it weren't the two of them. Just as quickly, Val drops his head back down and mumbles, "I'm sorry. Don't say nice things if you don't want me to kiss you."

Hunter feels like he's been shaken awake from sleep right on the brink of a dream. He was so much hungrier than he realized, and his lips go dry the second Val pulls away. He likes Val's mouth. Val might be half Hunter's size, but everything he does is done with intent, and even a simple kiss from him has a beginning, a middle, and an end to get lost in.

Remembering they're in someone's entryway, Hunter tucks his face toward Val to speak lower. "Where can I take you?"

Val's hands bunch up the back of Hunter's shirt. "My room is upstairs."

Hunter starts walking toward a large staircase, feeling the other bodies in the house shifting in response to his movements. He passes an open archway, and a few people go scurrying away. As he carries Val up a large staircase, another trio skitters out of sight on the second floor. Taking the cue, Hunter turns in the opposite direction of the curious strangers, passing by a few closed doors before Val points out the right one.

His bedroom inside Lux's home is lovely, yet oddly barren. Val's things are all contained around a bench pushed against the end of the large bed, and judging by the empty closet in the corner, Hunter guesses none of the drawers in this place have anything of Val's in them.

Hunter sets Val down on the edge of the plush, blue bedspread, and kneels in front of Val to gingerly rest his head on Val's chest.

"I should . . . wash up," Hunter mumbles, fingertips resting on Val's thighs. "You look all clean and nice."

Val slides his hand down Hunter's back, around the pack with his hammock rolled up inside. "Let's get these off of you."

Hunter nods as Val starts searching for a knot to untie. The weight of knowing he doesn't have to walk anymore is settling over him, and Hunter's hands feel clumsy as he tries to get the rope off his waist. Val, on the other hand, deftly plucks the pack free from Hunter's back, and starts unwinding the extra fabric from Hunter's torso so he can wrestle off all the extra sheaths.

With all the straps off his chest, Hunter closes his eyes to breathe without the constriction. Across from him, Val goes perfectly still, and Hunter knows Val must be staring again. His hands slip back around Hunter's face, but Val holds himself a breath away to ask, "May I?"

"Yeah," Hunter answers.

Val kisses him again, his heart pounding softly through his lips. Hunter opens his mouth, half expecting to taste blood on Val's tongue for the way Val's body crackles beside his.

Pulling away with a shaky laugh, Val holds their foreheads together. "Sorry. I'm just so excited to see you again. And feel you. And smell you. And listen to you."

Hunter's shoulders tick up higher, stiffness threatening to pull him away, but he holds onto Val's thighs to keep still. Already he's completely submerged in Val's attention, and it's just as overwhelming as it ever was, but the sound of anticipation bleeding into Val's voice is worth it.

"Don't apologize," Hunter mumbles, and fuck him, the burning in his face just never gets better. "It's okay if it's you."

Hunter can hear Val's restraint splintering, too much weight on too little wood.

"I thought about you so much," Val says, his fingers tensing around Hunter's face. "I couldn't *stop* thinking about you actually. Sometimes I'd be doing chores for Rez and my hands would just take over so I could think more clearly, and then minutes would go by and everything would be done while I wasn't looking."

"Wait, really?" Hunter asks.

"Yes, is that bad?" Val's breathing is quickening by the second, his body poised like he's about to use all his weight to shove Hunter to the ground.

Hunter can picture it: Val's hands simply working on their own without instruction while he lets his mind wander somewhere else entirely. It seems like something a spider could do—no connection needed between the brain and the body.

Hunter starts to shake his head. "I don't know what's good or bad. I just want to know what's happening with you."

"Don't go away again," Val says, quieter. "I don't like when I can't feel you."

Hunter wraps his hands around Val's waist, almost—sort of—maybe—trying, trying, *trying* to smile for Val.

"I don't like it either."

Val pulls Hunter in by the face to kiss him again, his thighs squeezing into Hunter's sides. The way Val can draw Hunter toward him with hardly any effort still confuses him. Val has the subtle sweetness of a pitcher plant, his open mouth so bright and so obvious, it still sends goosebumps down Hunter's arms and legs as his body begs him to run. *This pretty thing will hurt you. Even if he lets you pin him down, even if you're the one inside him, it's because he* let *you.*

Fingers trembling, the two of them half spilled over the bed, Hunter rips the collar of Val's shirt open for a glimpse of that spider-silk skin. Fitting his own chattering teeth down onto Val's shoulder, Hunter bites as hard as he can, shivering at the breathy gasp Val gives before winding his arms and legs around Hunter. Val keeps him there while Hunter tries to fix an ache that's been in his mouth for weeks.

A knock at the door sends Hunter reeling back, so absorbed in the taste of a bruise forming and healing underneath Val's skin that he didn't even notice someone else coming. The ice in his throat immediately starts to melt when he sees the look on Val's face.

"Hey, Valley, did you two leave this bag by the door?"

Val's cheeks are flushed, his eyelids heavy over dilated pupils, his mouth open for every rabbit breath he takes. A few of the little red scores in his shoulder have pin drops of blood from Hunter's teeth. When Val smiles at him, Hunter feels a knife at his throat as blood rushes to his cock.

"Oh shit, sorry, did I interrupt?" the voice in the hall asks.

Hunter bolts for the open door to the bathroom, shutting himself inside so he can remember how to breathe while Val talks to whoever that was. Probably the boy named Moon. Val talked about him a little before Hunter left, the hatchling who works for Lux. Val said they were friends. Apparently friends enough to call him *Valley*.

"Sorry, I wasn't paying attention." Val's voice is muffled on the other side of the door.

"No you certainly weren't," comes the teasing reply. "Don't worry about it, I'll put it in the kitchen. Where's the hunk? I want to meet them."

"Hunter's a little shy with new people," Val answers quieter. "I'll try to bring them down later, but no promises."

"Alright, alright," the person sounds like they're smiling. "I'll allow it."

"Ever so generous, Moon," Val says back before the door shuts again.

Heaving a sigh, Hunter sinks down in front of a tub, fiddling with the knobs like he's actually made a decision about taking a shower. Val doesn't knock, just slips into the bathroom on light feet.

"Did you bring something?" Val asks.

Hunter looks over his shoulder and back at the empty tub. "Yeah."

With a soft laugh, Val crosses over to kneel behind Hunter and set his chin on Hunter's shoulder. "This place is so nice, there's a separate shower and tub."

Hunter blinks, turning to see that, yes, there is a standing shower in the corner. "Don't know if I've ever stayed somewhere like this."

Val's arms slip around Hunter's waist. "Time to wash up?"

Hunter just nods, far too choked to speak aloud. Val presses a kiss to the back of Hunter's neck, between his hair and his shirt, before he goes to turn the water on, and Hunter forces himself back to his feet, hot and cold all over. Angling away from Val, Hunter starts pulling the last of the weapons from his legs, setting them beside the sink, along with his undershirt.

Unfortunately he's in front of a mirror, and that's not any better, so he turns his back to it just as Val returns to press his face to Hunter's chest. Startling stiff, Hunter grips the countertop as Val hugs tight, speaking into Hunter's skin.

"Can I come with you?"

"Yeah," Hunter mumbles, the only sound he can get out. He's certainly not about to give the full answer of, *I can't say no to you when you ask like that so just spare me from asking at all.*

Val immediately starts shedding his clothes with a smile, leaving a minefield of fabric in his wake before taking Hunter's hand to drag him to the shower. Hunter barely shrugs out of his pants without getting them wet as Val keeps tugging him toward the warm water, but it is sublime to feel the endless nights of travel beginning to melt off of him. Hunter finally plucks the tie from his hair to stand directly under the spout, and his eyes close automatically.

Val's hands blend with the water as he starts to rub soap over Hunter, and that time, Hunter is too tired to feel embarrassed. While Val is focused on running his hands over Hunter's arm, Hunter steals a glance at the bite mark, more pleased than he means to be that it's still visible. It probably should have healed by now, but maybe Val is tired too. Or maybe he just wants to wear it.

"Is that better?" Val asks, his voice echoing off the tile.

Hunter leans his shoulder on the wall and nods. "Yeah."

"If you sit down, I can wash your hair," Val offers.

Warm from his head to his toes, Hunter just lets Val nudge him into kneeling so Val can gather up all his hair. The feeling of Val's fingers rubbing along his head is too good for words, so Hunter doesn't bother.

"You look like you're going to fall asleep," Val says.

"Sorry." Hunter puts his hand out, touching Val's stomach, the water collected in his navel.

"You've earned it," Val says, moving aside so he can rinse the suds from Hunter's hair.

Val adds something else that helps loosen all the tangles, and Hunter starts to wake up again, eyes peeling back open. He's face to face with Val's belly, the soft press of his hip bones, and the slight indent of his waist. Val has a small, dark patch of hair between his legs, but there's barely any other hair on his body, aside from his head. He's so soft. Hunter can almost forget that he's full of metal.

Tracing his fingers over Val's skin, from his ribs to his hairline, Hunter asks, "You still have all those tools in you?"

Val catches his eye and smiles. "I don't even feel them anymore."

Leaning forward, Hunter rests his face on Val's stomach. "I'm glad you're okay."

Val gives a fluttering laugh that Hunter feels on his cheek. "We should get you to bed before you fall asleep in here."

He turns the water off before Hunter can bother assuring Val that he's not going to sleep until Val is, but Val is already passing him a towel.

"Maybe you need two, for your hair," Val starts muttering as he opens a cabinet under the sink. "Oh! Your clothes . . ."

He turns to Hunter with his eyes wide. "You only have the one outfit. I should ask if they'll wash it for you. Maybe Rez has clothes you could borrow. Or, well, you won't fit anyone's here but . . ."

"It's fine," Hunter says, cinching the towel around his waist. "I can figure it out."

Val flits around, still naked and damp, picking Hunter's clothes up to put into a basket and rescuing his own to put back on. Watching him scrub his towel over his hair in front of Hunter without thinking twice is oddly soothing. Hunter slinks over to lay his hand over Val's back, studying the way his fingers span across a huge swath of Val's skin, the bumps of both his shoulder blades and his spine.

Val turns to him with a smile and starts patting Hunter's chest and shoulders with his own towel. "You're not supposed to walk around wet, right? You could get a cold or something."

They're in front of the mirror, and Val's body is entirely contained within the frame of Hunter's own.

With a start, Val pulls away. "I'm sorry, I'm being pushy, aren't I? I know this is still new for you. I should let you dry off in peace."

He puts the towel around his shoulders, and picks up his clothes and the basket with Hunter's to take into the other room. Hunter finishes drying off with his back to the mirror, wondering if that was Val's self-consciousness or his own. Val moves so quickly sometimes, it's hard for Hunter to keep up when he doesn't know how he's supposed to react. No job means no rules. Striking *coworkers* from their list of connections brings all those other titles front and center. Family, friend, something more. Is he meant to change between them? Or is it everything at once?

Hunter shuffles out of the bathroom with the towel tied off around his hips, frowning mildly at the basket with all of his clothing in it sitting by the bedroom door. Val is perched on the bed, expectant, like he's ready to read Hunter a story and put him to bed. Crossing in front of a large window with all of the lights of Indulgence caught in it is a little like passing in front of the scope of a rifle but Hunter walks over to Val with goosebumps over his arms.

"I can just wash my clothes."

Val shakes his head. "It's alright, I'll get them washed while you rest. We should find you some new clothes anyway. You don't need to dress for weapons, right?"

The way he asks it—hesitant, unsure—pierces Hunter's gut.

Hunter nods. "Right."

Val smiles and pats the bed behind him. "So, just rest for a minute, okay? I'll take care of it."

With another nod, Hunter sits down and Val gives him room to get under the covers. He takes the damp towel away, but Hunter takes Val's wrist before he can go anywhere.

"I'm sorry for leaving," Hunter says, bracing himself to meet Val's gaze again.

Val goes perfectly still, eyes caught wide open, his body turning to air. "It's okay."

"I didn't want to go," Hunter says to him. "But I had to. I had to be careful. I don't even know how long I was gone, because I tried not to think about it. Figured if I wasn't focused on doing it right, I'd just get distracted."

Val's pulse beats frantically in his wrist, pressed softly against Hunter's hand. His mouth opens slowly, like he's working up a question and waiting for the sound to catch.

"Were you tempted at all . . . to stay with them?" Val's voice is quiet and cold, wind slipping under an old door.

Hunter looks at Val, hearing the voices of the Tongues in his head as they made him an offer to return home, an offer that he was surprised to feel absolutely nothing in response to. He thought it might have been something like shock that left him numb over it, but hearing Val ask him again makes the absence so much clearer.

"No," Hunter says. "I don't have anything left there. I guess part of me wondered if I should have spent more time with them to make sure they understood every possible thing, but I was too impatient. I tried, you know? I tried to do it your way, just by talking. But it was hard enough when half my brain was busy trying to figure out what the fuck I was going to say to you when I got back here. Just didn't want to be there any longer."

Hunter gives a hushed laugh. "Thank god Dream didn't answer the door today. If he'd made fun of me, I might have lost my nerve from all that thinking."

Val's face breaks into a red-faced grin and he laughs too, dropping the towel to the floor just to put his hands on Hunter's chest. His gaze wanders as he brushes his fingers over Hunter's skin, as if to sweep something away. Like the hands of a clock ticking second by second, Hunter watches Val's face turn from beaming relief to a panicked sadness. His smile collapses as his lips thin into a line, his breath shortens up into puffs, and his wide open eyes well up as his hands clamp down onto Hunter's shoulders.

Val's voice comes out rusted, like all the metal he swallowed is stuck through his throat. "I was scared you were gone for so long because you wanted to stay with your old family."

Hunter's hands sear with heat like he's caught a dagger by the blade. Val's crying again. Fuck. It's the worst thing in the world. Hunter's body acts first, arms clamping around Val and hauling him down to the sheets like he's trying to hide them both from sight. And then his own panic kicks in as he processes that this isn't a fight. This isn't even an argument.

"I made you cry," Hunter says, cradling Val's head against his chest. "I'm sorry, fuck, I'm sorry. Let me fix it."

Val's body is stiff as he curls up tighter, and Hunter has to walk himself back from the urge to find a fucking knife to deal with someone's tears. He doesn't need weapons. He needs to make Val warm again, the way he's supposed to be.

Hunter wrests the covers up from underneath Val just to pull them both under. Trying to keep his grip soft, Hunter wraps himself around Val and brings their faces together to lick some of the salt from Val's cheeks.

"I'm sorry," he says again, kissing Val's temple. "I'm not going anywhere, okay? You and Dream, you're my family. I want to be with you."

Val's hands slowly loosen their grip on Hunter's shoulders. "You mean it?"

"Yeah." Hunter presses his mouth to Val's closed eye. "They asked me to stay, Val. I already turned them down."

Val lets out a sigh from a chest wound so tight, he shudders against Hunter as he lets himself breathe again.

"I like being your family," Val says, voice in a quiet squeak as his arms snake around Hunter's neck.

When Hunter feels his lips trying to smile again, he kisses it to Val's mouth instead, trying to see how many it will take to scrub the fear out of Val's voice. Two more gets Val's breathing to space back into something that sounds a little more like anticipation. The third dredges Hunter's name up out of his belly. He stops counting after four, when Val runs his hands over Hunter's chest, his fingers skimming down to touch the metal in his nipples.

Hunter can't stop himself from groaning quietly against Val's lips, not entirely sure if Val meant to do that, but the relief from soothing Val only makes it spear that much deeper to be touched like that.

"I-I'm sorry, you're tired, I should let you rest," Val starts.

"Don't care," Hunter mumbles, pressing on the small of Val's back to get them closer.

Finally, Val smiles again, fingertips grazing over skin and jewelry. "It's been a while since . . ."

His face is steeping red again, a much prettier color when it's not from sadness. Hunter's breath catches in his throat when Val nudges the metal.

"I missed you," Val whispers, pressing his mouth to Hunter's jaw. "A lot. I thought about you all the time. I wanted to touch you so bad."

Hunter's fingers dig into Val's hips as Val pulls on his nipple. "Fuck." His voice is barely audible, but he can see Val grinning out of the corner of his eye.

"I didn't know how bad it could get, wanting someone who's far away." Val sounds like he's losing his breath. "I touched myself a lot. Sorry."

Val laughs softly, dragging his palms over Hunter's piercings as molten heat pours down Hunter's spine. *Don't make me say it.* Hunter slides his hand over Val's ass and between his legs, hoping his body can talk for him. It's been god only knows how long since they fucked and Hunter's barely had time to do anything for himself while traveling, and now Val's talking about jerking off while thinking about Hunter. Hunter is helpless now.

"I'm here." Hunter presses into the fabric of Val's pants, searching for a reaction as he draws his fingers with muscle memory toward Val's clit. "If you want something, let me give it to you."

Val's hands twitch over Hunter's chest when Hunter finds the swell under his clothes. Shifting his legs out of the way, Val presses his body even closer against Hunter's. "Let me look at your face this time."

Those words may as well be hands around Hunter's throat. He knows Val doesn't mean it like that, but the strange spark of fear flares down his thighs alongside the desperate need to be inside Val again. He wants it bad enough to ignore everything else as he starts pulling Val's clothes off for the second time that day.

If this is what Val wants, Hunter will just have to learn how to be looked at.

It's not *just* Val. At least he knows that. Hunter has always preferred things in the dark, or at times with his eyes bound. But no one's ever looked at him the way Val does. And only Val would ever crawl into his bed in the middle of the night to try and satisfy him. Thinking about that now—the first time they were in Good Fortune; it feels like years ago—Hunter knew what Val wanted. He could practically taste the arousal coming off Val's body while he slipped out of his clothes in the dark of that room.

If it weren't for Val's own boldness, Hunter might have given in a lot faster, but Val isn't the type to take something and let it go. No, he wants to study it, breathe it in, touch and taste and smell until he understands how it works. It used to piss Hunter off, how fearlessly curious Val was. Val's own fear of Hunter lasted all of one day before that, too, became rabid curiosity that Hunter felt like sights on his back every waking moment.

He was so hard cleaning Val's blood up after every cut of his knife. Seeing and feeling how badly Val wanted to be touched by him was as thrilling as it was terrifying. That Val saw something desirable enough in Hunter that he would be so fucking reckless with his own body. Stupid, but it made Hunter curious too. That's when it really became clear to him. Hunter was going to follow these two bizarre creatures wherever they went because he'd already been changed beyond recognition.

He knows now that he and Val are two of a kind in that regard— changing each other even when they don't mean to. Pushing Val onto his back in the bright light of this room, Hunter feels that change on full display as he submits himself to be stared at. When Val's pupils dilate, it's almost like the black is overtaking the white, like the pupils themselves are growing larger. He looks like he'll swallow Hunter whole as he lays on the bed with no clothes on, his thighs parted around Hunter's hips. When Hunter meets a gaze like that, with the weight of the entire fucking night sky behind it, there is no amount of muscle that would make him feel strong enough to hold that up.

Maybe Hunter should just stop trying to be strong. What does strength matter when he's already painfully hard and two inches away from fucking Val again? Is that what Val's hoping to see? How bad Hunter wants this? Fine. *Fine.* If he can't say it, he should at least show it.

Hunter shoves the bed sheets away and grabs Val's thighs, bending his legs back to get their hips closer together. Val gasps, and Hunter shivers at the sound that he *knows* means Val is paying attention with every one of his senses, human or otherwise. Hunter holds Val by the waist, his cock resting taut against Val's stomach, and he can feel the heat of Val's blood rushing to his clit. Even touching Val just like this, nothing but surface tension between them, makes Hunter feel like Val can see every inch of him—every major artery, every joint, every soft spot, pulsing for Val. Hunter is sure that one false move will cut him open.

Val's gaze flicks between Hunter's face and the head of his cock, and a grin spreads over his mouth.

"Do you want me?" Val asks.

Hunter can only nod, what with Val looking so *delighted*. Desperation he can handle, but Val is far from mindless. He looks like he knows exactly what he wants, reaching with hand outstretched to lay his fingertip on the metal nestled tight in Hunter's skin.

Hunter doesn't hear his own voice, just feels his mouth move as he curses. The jolt of sensation zipping from his cock right up to the back of his head almost makes him forget that Val is studying him.

Val. There's an almost childish joy in his face, even with his tongue pressing into his incisor like he's thinking about eating Hunter. He probably is. It is only at that moment, with Val painting a line over Hunter's slit to touch both ends of the metal bar, that Hunter realizes he has no idea what a spider needs to feel satisfied. Hunter can barely breathe with the pad of Val's finger gently pressing into him while a sort of drunken confidence seeps into Val's expression.

"You can have me now," Val says, his smile searing so brightly in Hunter's vision, it's bound to leave a ghost behind after he closes his eyes.

Hunter's never put his dick in someone so fast. He has half a mind to ask if it hurt, but Val gives a gasping laugh and the thought leaves just as quickly as it came. It's Val. He'll stop Hunter if he needs to. Val may not always know what he's doing, but at least he knows what he likes. He does, doesn't he?

Fuck, it's good. Hunter didn't forget, but distance and time turn memories into movies that don't exactly line up with the reality of burying himself inside someone who can rearrange their own body at will. Someone who sheathes knives in his own skin won't care if Hunter moves a little roughly. It's only because he wants this so bad. He should try to temper himself, to give Val more of his time. He was gone for so long, it's only fair that he pay attention to Val now that he's back, but he can't think about anything except how perfect the pressure of Val's cunt is.

Val still looks like he's figuring out where he's going to start eating Hunter, and it becomes so crystal clear how lost Hunter is inside this boy. It doesn't matter that Hunter is used to doing the work, that he likes to push himself, to feel his own body inside someone else's. Val's expression pierces him like every piece of jewelry that's ever been put in his skin. Hunter wanted to be the strong one, like he had something to prove about earning the right to be the one who fucks Val, but it's always better when someone else holds the needle.

Val looks like he adores whatever it is he's watching. Is that expression for Hunter? Is this what he looks like when Hunter closes his eyes? Fuck. As dizzying and grand as those buildings that scrape the sky in Innovation.

Hunter's fingers are going numb on Val's hips. It's hard to pay attention to the details of Val's face when Hunter's trying to be good and not come immediately, but it's been too long and he missed Val more than he can admit. Every time they do this, it feels like Val is shaping himself to take Hunter deeper. There's no other way it could feel so fucking good.

Did he say that out loud?

"You like it that much?" Val asks, his voice pressed through quiet panting breaths.

Hunter shuts his eyes again as the embarrassment of losing control of himself melts against the bone-deep pleasure of giving Val what he wants. When Val reaches out to touch Hunter's chest, soft fingers and spider-silk wrapping around the metal of his nipples, everything else splits apart. Hunter has no idea where he is, whose bed they're in, if it's night or day, or if anyone else can hear them. His face is pressed to sheets that smell like Val who smells like soap and hot iron and Hunter is moaning with his cock shoved to the base inside Val. His skin is vibrating around all the metal, both his and Val's. Maybe if he fucks Val hard enough, he'll feel one of the tools Val pierced himself with so long ago.

This wasn't supposed to happen.

"Can I come in you?" Whose voice is that? They're pleading.

Val's cunt tightens around Hunter like a fist, his palms warm as he flattens them to Hunter's chest.

"Yes, please."

Hunter isn't human again until they fuck themself empty. Val's legs are holding Hunter's body together as they forget whatever they agreed to before they started. There are more important things, like Val's little pleased breaths as he squeezes his thighs into Hunter's hips. Hunter's arms are shaking by the time they remember they were supposed to let Val look at them, and they struggle to hold their body back over Val's when their balls finally stop aching.

"S-sorry," Hunter mumbles, out of breath, barely able to keep their eyes open.

"For what?" Val asks. His gaze is vivid electricity and Hunter shakes their head.

"I-I don't know." They drop their face back down to the sheets with a hushed laugh before the rest of their body follows in a heap. "I'm . . . tired."

Val wriggles out from underneath them, wrapping his arms around Hunter's head and tucking his face in close until Hunter can feel his breath. He's too close to see but Val is buzzing in their arms.

"Close your eyes," Val says.

Hunter does, gratefully.

"I'm so glad I have you back."

He does have Hunter, doesn't he? Thoroughly. Shamelessly. Hunter starts to sink through the bed, but Val's warmth follows them down, tied around each one of Hunter's fingers.

"I won't let you go again."

***

Hunter's dreams are predictable, and that's why they hate them so much. If they were more of a surprise, maybe Hunter wouldn't crumble so quickly, but no matter how many times they feel someone ripping Val away from them, it doesn't get easier. Not to see Val getting hurt, and not to have Dream put a hand on Hunter's shoulder and say, "It was only a matter of time. You knew that."

They didn't know that. They *don't* know that. They wake up every time full of anger and guilt and fear like an open wound, ready to shout at Dream not to give up so fucking easily. Val is right there, why won't Dream do something?

Only this time, Hunter wakes up in a bed they've never slept in, in a room they don't recognize, and they can't cauterize the wound in time to keep the panic down. Lurching upright, Hunter catches Val's scent first, their arms snapping around Val's body where he sits at Hunter's hip.

"Hunter?"

They crush Val against their chest as they remember where they are. Val's arms wind around Hunter's back, fingertips pressing into their shoulders.

"Another nightmare?" Val asks.

Hunter nods.

"You're safe now," Val says, voice bright, cheek to Hunter's chest. "Dream and Mare will be home soon, and I have some clothes for you to try. I don't know what size you wear, so they might look a little strange on you, but it's just for a little while."

Hunter lets their breath out, this utterly normal conversation grating against the bloody visions from their dreams, but they squeeze Val tighter.

"I've never worn clothes like yours."

Val pops up with a smile. "Really?"

Slowly, Val coaxes them back to reality. After some trial and error with the clothes that mostly don't fit, Hunter winds up in a thin white shirt that makes them want to steal their wrap back from wherever their clothes are getting washed, and a pair of gray pants that might have sat looser on someone else, but the material is soft enough to forgive the tight fit.

Val takes Hunter's hand to lead them out of the bedroom and back into the house. Hunter isn't sure what burns more: Val leading them like a lost child through a house full of strangers, or the fact that Val is the first person to hold Hunter's hand like this.

"What did you bring home?" Val asks as they take the stairs back onto the first floor. "It smelled good."

He pulls Hunter into a kitchen where three other people are eating at the end of a long counter. They wave at Val as he goes by, and Val gives them each a vivid smile before he picks up the little bag that Hunter brought.

"It's, uh, pastries," Hunter tells him, voice muted automatically as they angle away from the other people in the room, shadowing Val against the counter. "Before you and Dream showed up, I only went inside the city for a couple of reasons. One of them was for this bakery in Modesty, the kind of place that just closes up when it runs out of stuff. They keep weird hours, so I missed it a lot, but I kept coming back to see if they had these."

Val peers inside to see the two snowball-sized pastries covered in sugar.

"They're better when they're fresh," Hunter mumbles as Val pulls one up. "But they're still good. Really sweet though. The first time I had one, it made me sick."

Val pauses, giving Hunter a look as bright as a sunburst. "It made you sick?"

Hunter glances away with a shrug, another wave of embarrassment threatening to push them over. "I don't eat things like that very often. All that sugar and oil, it's not something I can make in the woods. And I ate it too quickly . . ."

Val raises his hand up to cover his mouth, but Hunter doesn't miss the dimple forming as Val tries not to laugh. "I'm sorry, I'm sorry, it's just that you're the strongest person I've ever met and you're telling me you ate a sweet so fast it made you throw up." His shoulders shake as some laughter drifts through his fingers. "That's the cutest thing I've ever heard."

Hunter really wishes they were wearing their old clothes as heat sweeps down their back from the flashes of Val's giggling—light piercing through holes in a curtain.

"Does that count?" Hunter asks, hooking a finger through a loop on the waist of Val's pants in lieu of looking at him. They hear themself whispering, but they can't help it. "You told me to tell you something I liked."

"Yes!" Val immediately rushes to answer, eyes wide. "Can I try one?"

"I brought them for you," Hunter says, focusing on the fabric of the belt loop pressing into their skin.

Val takes a huge bite out of the sweet, sugar scattering back into the bag and some sticking to his face as he holds it in his mouth for a few seconds before he swallows.

"You like cinnamon? And sugar? And vanilla? Fried dough?"

Hunter nods. "Guess so."

"It's good," Val says, finishing it off in a few more bites like he's only just remembered that he's hungry.

Hunter wants to lick the sugar from Val's lips, but the three people behind them are like weights on their back, so they settle for pressing some into the pad of their finger to put in their mouth. Val beams back at them, the bag clutched in his hands, still more crystals stuck to his face.

"Do you want the other one?" Val asks.

Hunter starts shaking their head as they touch Val's lips. "You're a mess."

Val has a certain kind of smile that blacks out the rest of the room he's standing in, whether it's a kitchen or a bedroom or the entire forest. It's the kind of look that yanks Hunter closer, like rope around their waist. Every time Hunter sees that smile, they see the person that Val could have been if he hadn't wound up right here. The Val who could have eaten Dream. The Val that Hunter would have fought instead of protected.

There's a version of that smile that's a weapon, not a gift. Knowing it makes Hunter want to kiss Val just to try to get some of their gratitude out. They think so hard about it, they can already feel Val's warmth pressed against their body. Hunter brushes their thumb over Val's lips, tipping forward just an inch before one of the people behind them pushes their chair out, and Hunter startles so bad, they see their hand twitch on Val's face.

"I probably shouldn't eat that as my first meal," Hunter says, shoving their hands into their pockets. "Been on the road too long. Stomach's not used to it."

Val nods. "Later then."

The two of them both turn toward the mingled presence of Dream and Nightmare at the same time. It's like the hush of a rainstorm drifting toward the house. Hunter isn't sure why they have the urge to put their hair back up into a bun, but they find their fingers working automatically while Val smiles.

"The two of them have been working with someone Lux employs while they recover. Doesn't Mare feel so much stronger than before?"

Hunter nods. It's unmistakable. Dream and Mare have both regrown a few layers since Hunter last saw them, and their conjoined aura is stronger than anything Hunter's ever felt. The rainstorm is a hurricane by the time Dream is throwing open the front door. Val takes Hunter's wrist instead of their hand as he walks toward them, another big smile on.

"Dream! Look who I found!"

Warm rain while the sun is still shining. That's what it is to stand under the same roof as Dream and Mare.

"Fucking finally," Dream says. "No more staring out the window, you hear me? You looked like a ghost."

Val gives a laugh, his shoulders shrugging up to his ears. Dream nudges his boots off with the end of his cane while Mare hangs a jacket up on a coat rack by the door. Mare has his own cane, but he stands a lot taller now than he did before. Judging by the way Dream holds his weight, he hardly needs his anymore. His wound must have finally closed up while Hunter was gone.

Dream is also wearing new clothes, *nice* clothes. He's cleaned up, or at least as much as he cares to, and Hunter is very glad that this is not the pillar they met in the woods on the day that they fucked up with Val. With Mare standing behind him, Dream has never looked bigger. He smiles with his whole face, and without that bulky coat weighing him down, Hunter can see how solid the man is, and how much wider than Mare he is.

"Took you long enough," Dream says. "Was starting to think you got lost."

Hunter shakes their head. "Just talking to stubborn people."

Dream smirks. "We all know what that's like. C'mon, let's sit down. Tell us how it went."

The four of them drift into some kind of parlor with a bay window looking out onto the underground lake. Dream and Mare sit side by side on a long couch facing the window, and Val guides Hunter to the cushion on the windowsill to sit across from them. Dropping their gaze to their knees, Hunter starts to explain in more detail the conversation they had with the Tongues.

"It's not that they're unreasonable," Hunter starts to say. "I just don't know if they're ready to accept that the situation is so complicated. I hate to say it, but I think you know exactly what would change their minds a lot faster."

Glancing up at Dream, Hunter expects the dour expression on his face. "Mm."

Mare turns to Dream. "Is this not the closure you've wanted with these people? I think it would do you well to tell them yourself that there's no more war to fight."

Dream turns his scowl to the ceiling. "I'll think about it."

"I'm pretty sure I haven't made them *more* aggressive in the meantime," Hunter says. "But as it stands, it makes sense for Val and I to be closer to Innovation. Just in case one of the working Eyes finds a community of stray hatchlings and decides to get heroic about it."

Val grabs Hunter's sleeves. "Are we going back?"

Hunter looks at him, the stars in his eyes, and they can almost hear the word Val didn't say.

Are we going home?

"Wouldn't you rather be closer to them?" Hunter asks.

Val nods immediately, and Hunter has no idea what the tightness in their chest is.

"Where does that leave us?" Mare asks, patting Dream's knee. "The kids are going to fly away."

Laughing, Val looks over at the couch. "I don't think we're kids. Hunter definitely isn't."

Mare gives Val a smile that lands somewhere between *pet* and *student* in its simple warmth. "Everyone under a century is a child to me. Sorry, I don't make the rules."

Val just laughs again while Dream leans his arms onto the back of the couch. "Shit, I don't know. Should we go back to Respite? They haven't had a one of us stay with them in a long time. It shows."

Mare catches his eye, silver brow quirked. "Is that where you would like to be?"

"Maybe," Dream says, face pulling into a smile. "But it can wait if you're not ready to be near Innovation again."

Mare shakes his head. "I'm not scared of that place, if that's what you're asking. And besides, I owe the other spiders an apology one day. I shouldn't make them come to me for it."

"Well then." Dream gives Hunter and Val an expectant look. "You up for another trip?"

"We should let Hunter rest for a little," Val starts. "He only just got back. He hasn't even eaten dinner yet."

"How long's he been here?" Dream gestures at Hunter. "Get 'em some food, what are you doing?"

Val turns back to Hunter with wide eyes. "I'm sorry, you must be starving! I'll go see what's here."

He takes off like a bullet and Dream shakes his head. "Idiot got distracted again."

Hunter shrugs. "I did too. You, uh, you look well. Both of you."

"Thanks," Dream says with a smirk. He leans over to tug on Mare's perfectly buttoned up collar to show the very edge of one of the seams of scar tissue that now line his body. "Everything's healing up pretty nice."

Mare pushes his hand away with the look of a man who is far too used to being fawned over or shown off. "Forgive my bluntness Hunter, but you look like you haven't slept in months."

Hunter's mouth opens slowly. "Uh. Well. I sleep. I just don't always get much out of it."

"That's definitely not our fault this time, right?" Dream asks.

"No, no." Hunter smooths their palms over their thighs. "This is just me."

"Nightmares?" Mare asks.

Hunter can't hold his gaze for more than a millisecond. "Sorry. Guess you're probably going to see those."

"Don't think about it," Mare says. "I promise you, I've seen much worse."

"You really okay with leaving all of them behind?" Dream asks, pointing vaguely behind him, as if the Tongues are just in the other room.

Hunter nods. "Yes."

Dream seems satisfied with that. "Take your time."

"How . . ." Hunter takes a breath, listening for the sound of Val's carefree footsteps in the kitchen as he rustles up some food. "How is he?"

Dream doesn't need any more clarification, giving Hunter a pointed look before he nods. "He's good. Sturdy."

"Hardly been weird at all," Mare adds. "I'm almost disappointed by how normal he is."

"That's because he wants you to like him," Dream explains. "He's extra nice around you because he's worried you'll think about him like another Raleigh."

Mare's brows furrow. "Oh. What a silly thing to think. They're nothing alike."

"Really?" Hunter asks, more urgency than they meant to put into their voice.

Mare gives an elegant shrug. "Raleigh wore masks and costumes. I never knew who he really was underneath the experiment. Your Val, on the other hand, I don't think I've met anyone less interested in lying. Besides, how could I be scared of the puppy waiting in the window for his human to come home?"

Hunter sits there, speechless, while all the air in their chest gets squeezed out.

"It was kinda funny," Dream says, pushing himself up to his feet. He holds his hand out to Mare, who eyes Dream, and then his own cane.

"I happen to have a device for this," Mare says, lowering his voice.

"This one?" Dream snatches up Mare's cane and hooks it over his shoulder before offering his hand again.

"Oh, thank you, I didn't realize it was broken," Mare says with no inflection, allowing Dream to help him off the couch.

"Gotta keep a close eye on these things," Dream says, marching Mare out of the room like a proud peacock. "Don't worry, that's what I'm here for."

Val comes bounding back up to Hunter to ask if he prefers vegetables or meat, so Hunter goes with him into the kitchen. Apparently, Val has been learning to cook. According to Moon, a beautiful man in a skirt with a bit of shimmery makeup lining his eyes, it has been going *okay*.

"Not everyone can eat raw meat," Moon says, patting Val's head. "Let's stick to vegetables tonight."

Val is full of determination, staring down a cutting board like it's a complex mathematic equation, and Hunter finds a corner to stick to so they're out of the way. They watch Val trying to cook with Moon gently herding him like a very tall sheepdog, listening to the sounds of a hatchling heartbeat harmonizing with Val's. It was like that with Nora too, but now Hunter isn't so jealous to hear the way they complement each other.

Waiting in the window for his human to come home.

Hunter is the one that this doesn't occur naturally for, but Hunter is also the one that Val waited for.

"This one?" Val asks, reaching for a thin glass bottle of spice in a pale rack.

"No, Valley, that's cinnamon."

"Whoops."

"Just a little, okay?"

"Yes, sir."

Moon gives him a smile and a shake of his head. As Hunter watches them, they realize that they don't really know what brothers or friends or lovers are supposed to act like. There's familiarity between Moon and Val, decidedly different from the familiarity that exists between Dream and Val, or Dream and Mare, or Hunter and Val, but Hunter recognizes chords in every one of these songs.

Hunter starts fading as the kitchen warms up, eyelids getting heavier, muscles pulsing with a dull ache from weeks of travel. They're barely awake when Val proudly presents a bowl of seared vegetables that Hunter savors like it's the only thing they've eaten in months. Warm food made just for them . . .

"Thank you," they say.

Val looks like he's glowing as he holds a smile back. "Should I get you to bed?"

Hunter nods. "Sorry. Kinda looking forward to a dreamless sleep."

"It's okay."

Val really does look pleased enough just to have Hunter here with him. After a mumbled apology to Moon about how tired they are, Val takes Hunter back to his bedroom, waiting until Hunter is back under the covers to ask if he can sit with them for a little while. When Hunter says yes, Val crawls into bed with them to hug their middle with his face pressed over Hunter's heart.

Hunter is about ready to drift off when Val speaks again.

"Thank you for earlier."

Peeling their lids open, Hunter sees Val's serene expression, a blush cresting over the tops of his cheeks as he nestles closer.

"Sorry for pushing you when you're tired, but I really like making you feel good. I don't really know what I'm doing, but I hope it wasn't a burden to let me see you like that."

Hunter's face burns as Val winds one of his legs between Hunter's. This isn't something Hunter ever thought they'd have to explain to someone who isn't already versed in this language, let alone to someone Hunter plans on seeing again and again and again.

"It wasn't . . ." Hunter gives a short whisper of a laugh. "Fucking you isn't a burden, Val."

Val tips his head back to smile at Hunter. "So it was all good?"

Hunter pushes Val's face back down against their chest to get out of that spotlight gaze. "Yes."

Val hugs them tighter. "I'll get even better, I promise."

Hunter lets their breath out, too tired to dissect what exactly Val means. As long as they're back together, that's what matters. They can figure anything out without distance bleeding them dry.

Waking up from a dreamless sleep with Val curled up at Hunter's side is a world of difference. The peaceful look on Val's face is enough to prepare Hunter to walk across the world again. When the Tongues asked Hunter how to temper a spider, Hunter didn't have an honest answer. It wouldn't have done any good to say that Hunter didn't fully understand the spiders, and that the price for Val's endless appetite was Knives's blistering jealousy, but Hunter doesn't exactly understand themself very well either.

Watching Val like a chemical reaction as Hunter gives and takes different things, studying everything it yields—this isn't like any relationship that Hunter is aware of, but they're no authority on how to care for someone, and neither are the people who raised them. None of them know what it means to have someone fight for them, nor would they understand how exhilarating it is to try and figure out what Val wants. Will a kiss turn him soft? Will a bite warm him up? Will Hunter melt in that heat?

They have time to find out.

Hunter almost feels normal with a good night's rest under their belt, until Val holds their hand under the table while they're eating breakfast, and then they feel the magnifying glass of Val's focus warming their skin.

"You really are the worst kind of brother," Rez is saying to Dream from his perch on the armrest of Lux's chair. "Do you know how much money a house is these days?"

"Respite is dirt cheap right now," Dream says to him. "You kidding? No one wants to get near Innovation, not yet. They'll be glad for anything we offer, I promise."

Hunter doesn't have room to be overwhelmed by the presence of the four pillars in the room while Val is sliding his fingers between Hunter's like the webbing on their hand isn't suitable for polite company. He makes every gesture feel heated.

"He's got a point, love," Lux says to Rez. "And besides, they're family. I'm not about to let family go hungry."

Rez fixes her with a pointed stare. "If I turn my back for one moment, you'll buy the biggest house in Respite."

Lux smiles back at him. "What if we want to visit? I'm sure the twins understand that if they're accepting help from us to get a place to stay, it has to be big enough to fit any of our family who wants to drop in. Why do you think we have *this* house?"

Rez doesn't blink. "Because you wanted the biggest one."

Val's fingertips are velvet on Hunter's palm, tracing the lines that cross over their skin. It's washing Hunter's appetite away as they stop listening to the conversation. Val touches them so confidently, appreciation in every brush of his fingers. When Hunter finally gets a mind to tell Dream that they can head back out whenever he wants,

Dream actually looks excited to travel again, immediately turning his smile toward Mare, who's listening patiently to Lux.

Hunter spends the day assuming they're going to take the road on foot again, venturing out into the Dueling Cities with Val to find a few more articles of clothing to take along with them this time. The two of them are packed again by the end of the day, so Val brings Hunter to the edge of the lake to get away from everyone for a little while.

"Are you really okay to go back there?" Val asks.

Hunter nods, sitting next to Val on a stone bench overlooking the black water painted with reflections. They're technically still on Lux's property, right on the edge of a long walking path that surrounds the huge lake. Somewhere in the distance is the sound of rushing water.

"Arum wrote me a letter," Val says. "Two of the hatchlings came all the way out here to give it to me. I felt them pawing around on the surface and went to meet them in the woods."

Hunter turns to him, brows furrowed. "What did she say?"

Val pulls his feet up to sit cross-legged, one knee resting on Hunter's thigh. "She said that our brother hasn't picked a new name yet, but he's not using *Knives* anymore either. She just calls him brother or eldest. But, listen!"

Val grabs Hunter's arm, eyes no different from the vast lake with light caught in the surface.

"The other spiders aren't really dead. The queen was just keeping them in some kind of stasis. Arum and he, they were able to undo what the queen did, and now there's four of them. They're all trying to help each other. Isn't that nice? East and West are still healing, but Arum sounded so happy to have them back. I think they'll be able to move on together a lot easier. Still, I hope Knives isn't ignoring Arum."

Hunter puts their hand on Val's back. "Do you want to be with them too?"

Val's face slips out of the excitement, sinking into something a little more confused. "I don't know. I mean, I want them to be okay. And I want to meet them all. But I wasn't part of that life. I worry I'd feel like an intruder if I tried to spend too much time with them now. Especially when everything's so fresh."

He leans his head against Hunter's chest, and Hunter pulls him closer by the hip.

"It's so weird. I know I'm like them, that our bodies work the same, but I don't have the connection they all share. I'm still an outsider."

Hunter slides their fingers up Val's spine. "That's how it felt going back home. I could walk with them and talk with them, but it wasn't the same. Even normal conversations didn't feel normal anymore."

Val nods against them. "I like talking with you."

Hunter laughs, trying not to fight the way their lips keep pulling into a smile around Val. "I like when you talk to me."

"Even when I say strange things?" Val asks.

Hunter pauses, remembering the embarrassment on Val's face back at the campground when he realized he'd said something extreme. It's not often that Hunter actually feels fierce, but the sharp urge to protect Val in that moment can't be anything else. Hunter pulls Val against themself, not even thinking to check if anyone else can see them as Val breathes against Hunter's shirt.

"I don't need you to pretend you're human, Val."

Val nods again, relaxing into Hunter's grip.

"I'm trying to stop hiding from you," Hunter tells him. "Don't start hiding from me now."

Val presses his face to Hunter's neck. "Right."

"You're not going to scare me off," Hunter says.

Val laughs, mothwing breath fluttering over Hunter's throat. "I know."

Val sighs, and Hunter finally feels like they're back on solid ground. As long as Val trusts them, they'll be fine.

"Are you sure you're ready to travel again so soon?" Val asks.

"Yeah. This isn't our home anyway."

Val looks entirely too pleased to hear that, and Hunter almost laughs at the ecstatic expression on his face.

"You want your hatchlings back," Hunter says, brushing their fingers over Val's forehead.

Val presses Hunter's hand to his cheek with a soft smile. "I already have my favorite one."

Hunter's breath slowly leaves their chest as they look at Val's happiness. Maybe *spider* isn't just a name. With Val sitting on their lap, half Hunter's size and an expression of impossibly innocent satisfaction, Hunter can feel the web. It's stuck to every inch of Hunter's body. Val opens his mouth to slip Hunter's thumb onto his tongue, and goosebumps ripple up their arms at the wet warmth and the feel of a presence so much bigger than their own wrapping around them. They very well could be sitting in the shadow of eight extra legs as they weave silk around Hunter's body, but all Hunter can feel now is the harmless press of Val's teeth on their hand.

Is it possible for the two of them to raise each other? Hunter has been so focused on figuring out how to give Val what he needs, but Val still thinks about Hunter as a hatchling. Maybe they're both pulling shell from each other's hair. Maybe that's what it means to be a family. Dream set them both on this path, but Dream already has his other half.

Hunter presses on Val's tongue, and Val swallows around their thumb.

"Val?"

His eyes open wider, black and white and full of light. Hunter's lips part to tell him something, anything, a gesture of honesty to make things clearer, to strengthen whatever this thing is that they're building. But by the time the words take shape, Hunter has already started dissolving on Val's tongue.

"You're so warm inside," Hunter mutters.

Val's breath leaves him in a rush against Hunter's hand. When he smiles again, it is not quite so innocent, or maybe Hunter is just feeling the venom from a bite Val never gave him. Val pulls Hunter's thumb from his mouth so he can nuzzle his face to Hunter's cheek.

"Then touch me," Val says.

Hunter pulls Val's hips closer, heat pouring through them as they tug Val's shirt up from the waist of his pants.

"I like when you want me." Val's voice is soothing in Hunter's ear, to counteract their roaring pulse as they try to slip their hand down the back of Val's pants.

"When you stop thinking about everything else," Val whispers as he reaches between the two of them to undo his button and zipper. "I've never felt anything so nice."

Hunter tries not to make a sound as they push past fabric and press through folds of slick skin. Val gives a dreamy sigh, kissing the side of Hunter's face with their fingers burning up inside him.

"I meant what I said back at the campgrounds," Val says quietly, almost shy. "You can touch anything inside me. Whatever you want. I'll heal."

With Val straddling their hips, Hunter can feel their own cock aching through their clothes as Val tightens around their fingers

"Do you think we could be like the pillars?" Val asks, and his voice is just starting to reveal the steam underneath while Hunter tries to fit more of their hand inside.

Hunter can barely breathe. They can't see, or feel, or hear, or smell anything that isn't Val, his metal and his blood and his jagged glass and his soft silk.

"Like twins?" Val asks.

Hunter grits their teeth to keep from moaning, turning their face toward Val's as if that will keep this from spiraling out of control. To think of Val needing Hunter the way Dream needs Mare is almost too much to take.

Val runs his hands through Hunter's hair, the slightest tremor in his legs as he clenches around Hunter's knuckles.

"Let me take you inside," Hunter breathes. "Please."

Val's *yes* sparks all the way down Hunter's throat.

They quickly make their way back to the house, and Hunter quiets their presence on instinct, hoping no one notices them or their fingers wet with Val. These new clothes sit much tighter than Hunter is used to, and they can't exactly calm down when Val keeps squeezing the hand Hunter just had inside him.

The moment they're back in Val's room, he boxes Hunter up against the bed, eyes wide, face flushed, and asks, "Will you take your clothes off?"

Hunter exhales their relief at the clear direction, reaching for the edge of their shirt. It'll always feel somewhat like trusting a loaded gun, but Val's hands are still soft when he touches Hunter's chest. He waits with a bitten lip for Hunter to get their pants off before sliding up between their thighs to grab Hunter's waist.

It looks like Val is debating whether or not to ask something, his eyes shining with whatever it is he's thinking about. Hunter almost thanks him when he decides not to say anything and just smooths his hands over Hunter's torso, like he's getting the wrinkles out of his favorite shirt. It's not really fair how gentle Val is with the presence of a hungry predator, but he only touches with his fingertips and Hunter starts fading.

There's no moment between Hunter's hands gripping the bed-sheets, and gripping Val's hips instead. The fabric becomes skin while Val plays with Hunter's jewelry. It seems like that's all Val wants to do, pressing his thumb and his lips and his tongue to the metal threaded through Hunter's skin. He opens his mouth and Hunter's eyes snap shut when Val starts to suck on their skin.

Pulling on Val, Hunter tries to get their bodies closer but their mind is in Val's throat and all they're doing is getting the front of

Val's pants wet. When Val's fingers drift down Hunter's stomach, they give a soft moan at the rush of blood as they wait to be touched. Val's palm is searing hot on the skin of their cock and Hunter's hips twitch automatically.

Lifting his mouth up with another kiss, Val asks Hunter with a reddened face, "Will you lay down for me?"

Hunter almost doesn't hear him, as if there's a deafening sound coming from Val's fingertips as he finds the two ends of the metal piercing in their cock. It's certainly the only thing they can see, Val's slender fingers passing over the drops of silver in their reddened skin. There's a soft, teasing laugh, and Val lifts his hand to press on Hunter's sternum, asking in a firmer voice.

"Lay down."

That time Hunter actually hears him and slides back onto the bed with Val watching like a perked daisy. When he crawls up over Hunter's legs, he's much more solid, a sweet haze in his eyes as he says, "It seems like it's better when I don't ask."

Hunter doesn't really know how to listen when Val puts his hand back against their pulse to hold them still. Val opens his mouth, little red tongue painting over metal and fluid, and Hunter pushes their hands over their face. Every inch of Hunter's body is aching to get inside Val, but fuck it's good to be swallowed. Some base pleasure unfurls in Hunter's spine at the thought of feeding Val like this, and the satisfaction rattles out of their throat while Val tastes them deeper.

Val makes a noise to echo Hunter's, and pops his mouth off to start taking his own clothes off. Hunter tries to help, but Val doesn't really need it as he kicks his pants off the bed. The smile on Val's face as he lowers himself onto Hunter's cock is too much, like he's eating something sweet that he knows he shouldn't, but he's this far, so what's the point in stopping?

He's *cute*. It's the first time Hunter has let themself think that. The dimpled smile and the slender body and the way he carries himself might all be part of what he is—a pretty veil over the sharp teeth—but Hunter realizes that they don't really care. They look liking at Val, even when the weight of his gaze is a little too much.

Once he's seated on Hunter's hips, Val places his hands back onto their chest, and Hunter's mind scatters again.

"You're so pretty," Val says.

Hunter lets their eyes slide shut when Val tenses his cunt, his fingers already playing with the jewelry in their chest again. Breath shaking in their lungs, Hunter grabs Val's waist and lets him satisfy his curiosity while Hunter can stand it. They have no clue how much time has passed by the time they *can't* stand it, drowning in steam as Val studies them for a reaction.

"I didn't know this could have such an effect on you . . ." Val plucks on one of their piercings and Hunter's hips jump underneath Val, a strangled moan wresting out of them.

When Val gives a startled laugh, woven through with breathless excitement, Hunter tries to move Val's body for him. Sparks pour through them as they finally get a little movement inside Val, and Val's teasing expression melts into something hungrier. Looking at Val while he arches his back, eyes out of focus, shifting his legs to let Hunter push up into him, all Hunter wants to do is feed him.

This boy, this spider, this growing reaction is Hunter's responsibility. Even when Hunter's patience snaps and they beg Val to *let me fuck you, please*, and Val is on his back with bruises blooming underneath Hunter's fingers, Val is smiling like this is what he hoped for all along. Hunter is somehow the kind one for letting Val play with Hunter until the only thing they could respond with were bruises and bites. It's all food for Val, and Hunter can't stand how good it feels to be part of the meal.

Val gasps when Hunter comes, like he can feel it all with perfect clarity, and fuck, maybe he can. Maybe he feels everything, Hunter's skin and cum and metal filling him. The blatant excitement in

Val's breath makes Hunter's face burn, but before they can even think about hiding from Val, he touches Hunter's throat to feel Hunter catching their breath. Val smiles again, soft, sweet, the pad of his fingertip resting on the bump of Hunter's larynx as they swallow.

"I like your body," Val says absently, his gaze scanning heavily over Hunter. "Sometimes I wish I could crawl inside you."

Hunter's eyes peel open, breath constricting, and they sink down to bury their face in the covers beside Val's.

Val combs his fingers through Hunter's hair, turning toward them like the needle of a compass. "Too much? Sorry. You just taste so nice."

Hunter shakes their head, no words good enough to respond with, so they just slip their hands between Val's legs and hope he understands. Val immediately clings to Hunter, shifting over so he can close his mouth back over Hunter's chest, moaning happily into skin where there will surely be broken blood vessels tomorrow.

I would carry you inside me if I could.

When Hunter and Val meet Dream and Mare in the morning with all their things, the four of them take the lift to Modesty. Hunter knows damn well he didn't get enough sleep, but Val is once again standing perfectly straight—a strand of taut silk beside him. Once he opened the door to try and find Val's personal limit on physical pleasure last night, he realized he was consigning himself to not nearly enough rest before a day of travel, but he can't very well say no to Val when he starts talking like that.

I can hear your blood. It sounds excited.

The sense memory of Val coming on Hunter's skin is so vivid, he keeps brushing his palms over his clothes, like his hands are still wet.

Bracing himself for a day on autopilot, he is more than a little surprised to see Dream pull a key ring out of his pocket as he guides them toward a car.

"Wait . . . are we . . . driving?" Hunter asks.

Dream gives Hunter a wild look. "Of course we're driving, you think I want to walk that far ever again? No fucking thank you. We don't have to hide anymore. Far as I'm concerned, we're just normal people now. So we're gonna drive."

Dream throws his and Mare's things into the trunk, and Hunter almost sags with relief.

"Not everything has to be done the hard way," Dream says, throwing Hunter a smirk before he gets into the driver's seat.

Leaving all his things in the trunk does feel a little dangerous, but as soon as Hunter and Val are seated in the back and the car is bouncing along a dirt road away from the Dueling Cities, his eyelids grow heavier and heavier until Val touches Hunter's cheek.

"Lay down," Val says, patting his own legs. "We'll be driving a while."

Folding onto Val's lap is a lot more comfortable than Hunter expected. Maybe it's just from Val petting his hair, or the smell of Val's clothes, or the way he so easily says *we*.

"I'll wake you up if we need you," Val says.

He pulls the tie from Hunter's hair, and smooths his hand down Hunter's shoulder. Hunter is light and shapeless with Val watching over him. He knows he won't have nightmares with Dream and Mare in the front seat. It's only sleep now, in the adoring grip of his spider and all his silk.

It doesn't matter where they go.

THE HOUSE THAT DREAM AND NIGHTMARE KEEP

Respite may be a dehydrated version of itself, but something about that immediately endears Nightmare to it. He, too, needs a little work. Watching the people of the town slowly but surely chipping away at half a century of decay makes Mare feel comfortable. Well, he feels comfortable observing from a distance. He still has little to no interest in leaving the house that Dream bought for them.

He didn't say it at the time, but Mare was beyond grateful that there wasn't a conversation needed about Val and Hunter living apart from Mare and Dream. He did have a small freezing fear that Dream would also want to be alone, or to stay with the others, but everyone seemed satisfied with the arrangement. After a vaguely threatening conversation with a salesman in Respite about the fact that no one in this entire world wanted to buy land there, he sold them an abandoned house on the outskirts of town for dirt cheap, and agreed to help organize the construction of another house in the woods beyond the destroyed train station. Privacy for the spider and the hunter to create a way-point between Respite and Innovation.

Mare threw himself into the task of cleaning the new-old house, while Dream tackled the problem of how the fuck they planned on making money again. His words. The two of them have held nearly every job in their time in various cities, and even though they both know that Lux would not allow her brothers to languish, neither of them wanted to be dead weight in her pocket.

"There's always teaching," Mare said to him one early night. "People love to learn from you."

Dream groaned. "I'm sick of teaching. I want to do something easy for once."

Mare nodded, refraining from telling him that, no, Dream rarely wanted easy things, but it was okay to be tired.

It was after one of the hatchlings brought Val a trinket from Innovation that Dream got the idea to open a shop. Everything else was just setup. Mare watched him with fractions of his old verve as he put everything together. He used the kids of course, the three of them cobbling together a storefront at shocking speed, and before he knew it, Mare was spending most of his time in the house while Dream was out overseeing his new shop.

It's been weeks, and Dream and Mare have not touched each other in private. Val and Hunter had to stay with them before the other home was livable, and it was easier to slip into old habits around the two of them, fixing the collar of Dream's shirt, patting his knee, accepting his hand when getting back to his feet. But the moment Val and Hunter were able to move into the other place, the house turned on Mare.

The first couple of nights with the shop, Dream exhausted himself so much that it was easy just to send him to bed. A few more after that, Mare joked to him at the table they don't need to eat at, "Is your new baby doing well?"

"You can come out with me, you know?" Dream said, resting his hands on the empty table. "You don't have to work, but if you want a change of scenery."

"Oh, no, it's alright." Mare waved his hand. "There's so much to do here. Plus if you're out of the house, you can't argue with me about paint colors."

"Alright," Dream said.

Every time silence threatened between them, the house always gave a creaking whisper, and it felt like nails in Mare's spine.

"Just . . . don't work too hard," Mare found himself saying just to talk over the sound.

Dream shook his head. "I just want to set us all up. Make sure we don't have to worry."

"Of course."

"You need something, you tell me."

This fierceness is new, and Mare isn't quite sure how to handle it. Dream always did his best to stand up for Mare, to keep him from having to see any more unpleasantness than he already had to, but Dream was also the one who would threaten a person with tears in his eyes. Dream was the first to cry while they talked in that inn, and also the first to laugh, and the first to say he was sorry with his face pressed to Mare's stomach.

That was the most they've touched, aside from waking up in a haze in that hammock to find himself tangled up with Dream. Mare had held his breath when he realized that Dream was with him, went utterly and completely still so he could try to feel everything that was different about Dream before he inevitably woke up with the fear of hurting Mare. He pretended to be asleep while Dream kissed Mare on the forehead and got back to his feet.

There is armor around Dream now, and maybe that's why Mare doesn't know how to touch him. A month of burying themselves in work leads to Mare having more conversations with the house than with Dream. He talks to the walls while he paints them, explaining why this shade of green reminds him of the garden they were raised in on the northern coast, or how this frankly tacky painting of Foundation is endearing when he remembers the years Mare spent pretending to be a university student there.

When Dream sleeps, Mare stays awake, just in case.

And a month later, he is exhausted.

Dream finds Mare staring out a window one morning, sunrise still pushing its way through the night sky, and he puts a blanket around Mare's shoulders.

"You're not feeding."

Mare doesn't want to look away from the window.

"What if something happens while we're both asleep?"

Dream squeezes his shoulders, sighing from behind him.

"You sure you're not just trying to keep your nightmares from me?"

Mare shrugs, feeling the strength of Dream's fingers through the blanket.

"There's that too."

Dream turns Mare around to look him in the eye and say, "I stopped drinking, okay?"

Mare blinks, his own apathy going brittle at the anger and the shine in Dream's eyes.

"So, go to bed," Dream demands.

Mare stares at the drop welling up in the corner of Dream's left eye and nods. "Alright . . ."

Dream's arms fall to the side and he sighs. "Thank you."

Mare follows Dream away from the window, and pads down the hall toward the bedroom that Dream is always flitting in and out of. Mare doesn't realize until he's sitting on the edge of the bed that he has been thinking about this as Dream's room, not his, not theirs.

It smells like him. Mare starts to wilt in the direction of the pillows. They used to share a bed. They used to be inseparable. Was it a spider that got in the way? Or just time? Mare touches the tip of his nose to Dream's pillow and shivers at the familiar earthy-sweet scent. That's his. That's Dream. He looks different, but he smells the same. His brother, his only good dream.

Mare presses his face to the pillow as heat and guilt wash over him.

His perfect brother that Mare himself cracked open and bled.

What in the world does Mare think he's doing, trying to play house like nothing happened? Even now, he's frightening Dream without even meaning to. Mare is actually going to kill Dream at this rate. And then he'll have nothing left but to ask Val to kill him too. At least he already has such a polite worst case scenario waiting for him.

Curling up in Dream's bed, Mare pulls the blanket tighter around his shoulders and waits for the wretched orchestra. The people of Respite tend to have nightmares about the deadlands, or Innovation, or monsters lurking in the woods. Relatively tame, all things considered. The nightmares in Indulgence are a bit more colorful, so Mare knows he's getting the easier deal here, even if he gets a little less food out of it.

He isn't expecting to wake up as Dream is getting home from the shop. The sound of something heavy *thunking* down onto a table propels Mare out into the kitchen to see Dream giving a worried look to a record player. Mare slept all the sunlight away.

"Fuck, I hope I didn't break it," Dream says. "Should've let Hunter bring it in for me."

Mare slows to a shuffle as he sees, swallowing to fix his dry throat. "Is this for your shop?"

"No, it's for you," Dream says. "This house is too fuckin' quiet. Unless it's settling. Then it's way too fuckin' loud."

Mare tugs the blanket around himself, sweaty and cold at the same time. "Read my mind."

Dream smirks at him, mostly with the right side of his face thanks to that scar. It's *that* smile that Mares knows best, and even that is now irrevocably changed thanks to Mare's cowardice. His eyes though, they're the same. A familiar sky seen through a different window.

"Thank you," Mare says, his voice still creaking back to normal.

Dream puts his hands around the base of the record player. "Where do you want it?"

Nightmare lurches forward, losing the blanket to the floor so he can help carry the hulking thing into the living room. It winds up on an end table beside a couch that neither of them have sat in at the same time since they moved here.

"My god, is it full of sand?" Mare asks, feeling his arms ache from the short trip.

Dream laughs. "Pretty sure it was an antique even in Innovation."

"Do you have records for it?"

Dream scratches his chin. "Not yet. There's a music shop in town. Hardly has anything, but I might be able to pick up a few. What do you, uh, want to listen to?"

Mare meets his gaze, maybe just the slightest bit of hope in Dream's eyes as he waits for an answer.

"I'd rather it be something you like," Mare tells him. "So you can come home to something nice."

Dream's expression turns sideways and his mouth does something more confused than a smile. "I already come home to you."

Mare's lips part, just barely catching himself from arguing that he's far from nice.

Dream pats the side of the record player. "I'll just get everything they have."

"Sure," Mare says with a nod.

The house is clean but the two of them are still coated in dust.

"Mind if I smoke?" Dream asks. "I can go outside but—"

"No, no, it's fine." Mare waves his hand.

Dream actually sits down on the couch and digs through his jacket for his matches and cigarettes.

"I try not to smoke around Hunter as much, ya know?"

Watching him strike a match, the glow on his face briefly turning his eyes molten before he breathes all that fire into his lungs—this, too, is new. He shakes the match out, and pale smoke drifts up from the cigarette, and the blackened edge of the match, and his own opened mouth.

"Not used to keeping house with humans," Dream says.

He glances around, realizes there's nowhere to put the match, and laughs to himself.

Mare holds his hand out for it. "They're a different kind of fragile."

Dream gives him a plaintive look, holding both his hands up, unsure which one Mare wants.

Plucking the burnt match from his fingers, Mare adds, "A different kind of strong as well, I suppose."

"Yeah." Dream laughs. "Hard to think of Hunter as fragile when I know how vicious he and Val can both be. Val's only ever snapped for him."

His eyes are warm now, like the smoke is filling his whole body. Mare can feel his own heart, the places where his scars pull against the softer skin, fresh growth replacing the rot. He can feel Dream's heart too. His beats when Mare's rests, leaving no empty air between them.

"You gonna keep your hair long like that?" Dream asks.

Mare glances at the silver hanging over his shoulders and shrugs. "Should I?"

Dream puts the cigarette in his mouth and reaches up to touch the ends of it. Careful, so careful, hardly touching Mare's collarbone.

"More to play with."

"For you or me?"

As soon as Mare says it, he wants to swallow the words back. Too much too soon, they're not ready for that kind of talk. Pushing them back to some kind of normalcy now will only lead them over the same cliff later.

Dream pulls his hand away to hold his cigarette as smoke languidly spills from his parted lips.

"I will if you let me," Dream says.

His voice never used to sound like this. Mare's heart leaps up his throat as all the decades of isolation begin to stack up on the couch in the shape of his twin. How strange that the *old* Dream looked younger, less sure of himself. The old Dream was so full of hope, it got him into trouble when he met people who didn't want all that light in their eyes.

This is a new Dream, tamped and packed into a shell. The edges are hard, the light filtered, the core completely solid. He no longer looks at Mare with questions in his eyes. This Dream has been walking in the same direction for long enough that now he knows exactly where he's going.

He used to be shy.

Mare swallows. "Would you even know what to do with it?"

Dream smirks at him. "I'll figure it out."

Mare didn't mean to give him innuendo but all he can think about then is showing Dream his own strange, new body and nothing about that is safe.

"How often do you eat human food?" Mare asks, desperate for a subject change.

Dream shrugs. "I eat at the shop sometimes. Hunter always has food."

Mare crushes the burnt match in his palm. "I'll cook tomorrow."

Dream's smile lingers until he brings the cigarette back to his lips for another drag. "Sounds good to me. You want me to get you anything?"

"Just tell me where to go. I'll do it."

"You sure? I can always make Val go for you," Dream says.

Mare shakes his head. "I don't want to keep asking them for things."

"You know you don't have to be scared of him, right?" Dream asks. He sinks back onto the couch, going slack with his head tipped back. "I wouldn't blame you if you were, but Val's fine."

Mare turns away to go get rid of the match. "I just don't like debts. They fester."

"You think everything festers," Dream says with a laugh, and Mare feels warm water dripping down his spine at the fondness in Dream's voice. No fear at all, only patience.

"Everything *does* fester," Mare calls from the kitchen as he brushes char off his palm.

Except you, apparently.

Mare puts his gloves on to go to the market. During their stay with Lux and Rez, he was rarely alone. Dream would hardly let him out of his sight. Here though, things aren't as overwhelming, which Mare tells him before Dream goes out to the shop.

"I'm serious, I'll happily go get your shit for you," Dream says when he sees Mare preparing to go out—gloves, cane, jacket.

"Honestly, Dream, I'm fine," Mare tells him. "It's not like I'm buying enough for a feast. We eat like birds as it is."

"Let me at least walk out with you," Dream says. "Do you even know where the market is?"

Mare allows this, something stirring in his mind as Dream puts his jacket on, and stuffs his keys into his pocket.

"The scars have sealed," Mare tells him. "You don't have to worry so much."

"Alright, alright, c'mon." Dream lets them out of the house and locks the door behind them. "How're the nightmares out here?"

Mare shrugs, righting his cane on the sidewalk. "Rather unremarkable, all things considered. Half of them are afraid of the stagnation returning. The others are scared that restoring the town will cause more problems. Everyone is scared of the woods."

"The woods?" Dream asks, walking up beside him and offering his arm for support.

Mare looks at his cane, and then at Dream, the offered contact yet again in the safety of the public eye. Wrapping his gloved hand around Dream's bicep, Mare feels how solid he's become. The two of them set off, only briefly negotiating the shifting of their steps and their weight before they're walking in sync.

"I'm guessing something in the woods has upset them," Mare says. "A lot of them are having nightmares about gunshots."

"Oh." Dream gives a low laugh. "That was probably our fault. Had a bit of a disagreement with the Major a few miles outside of town. I bet they heard the shots."

"It feels like cheating for us to be the cause of their dreams," Mare says. Another prickle of embarrassment sweeps down from his neck to the base of his spine at the sound of his own voice trying to joke, but Dream only laughs back.

"Blame it on the spiders. They're the ones who started it."

Dream smirks, glancing at Mare only for a moment before looking ahead again. The old Dream used to grin with his entire face, but the scar Mare cut into him has changed the very shape of his smile. It's less bright, but it's got something else to it. Something that Mare can't look directly at.

When they reach the center of town, Dream points out the market, and Mare slides his arm free.

"I'll see you at home," Mare starts.

"Hey."

Mare turns to Dream, head tilted.

Dream sticks his hands into his pockets. Even when he looks tired, his gaze doesn't spare an inch as it passes over Mare.

"It's building up again. Be careful."

Mare's lids tick open wider. "Did you only offer your arm so you could look inside me?"

Dream looks him dead in the eye. "Yes."

It's not the admission that unbalances Mare, but the surefire way he says it. He doesn't even look guilty, and Mare turns on his heel just so he doesn't have to keep looking at this stone version of his twin.

"I'll see you at home." Mare snaps the words this time without looking.

"I'll be there," Dream calls back.

Mare walks through the market, fuming. *Of course it's all building up.* He picks through every single apple looking for the most perfect one as he shouts at Dream in his head that there has never been, nor will there ever be, a safe place to let that out. It's been months since Dream came here with Val and let out his own euphoria, and Mare can still taste it on the air—sweet flowers blooming in his throat. It tickles him with every breath.

As Nightmare weaves between aisles of food and goods, every person he passes flickers in the corners of his vision. They are cloaked in glitches of their own fears, and Nightmare does not look at them, to spare himself the moment where their despair cracks through the mask and bleeds out of their mouth.

Until he runs into Hunter.

Blinking out of his haze, Mare straightens himself up as Hunter keeps their gaze on the floor.

"Do you need a hand?" Hunter asks with that thunder-on-the-way voice.

Mare gives a pinched frown. "Be honest, did Dream tell you to come here?"

Hunter's brows furrow. "No, I was on my way to the shop, and you still have a cane. I can hold your bag if you want."

Hunter knows better than to look a pillar in the eye, and Mare is grateful for the small buffer, even if he already has intimate knowledge of what Hunter is afraid of. Their nightmares are tangled in their eyes and their hands—dreams of losing the family they just earned. It's so honest, it's almost sweet. A pup's fears in the heart of a wolf.

"Fine." Mare holds out the bag. "I admit I'm not doing the best job this morning."

Hunter takes it with a nod. "Is this the first time you've gone out on your own?"

"That makes me sound like a recluse," Mare mutters as they start back through an aisle that Mare is certain he already blindly walked through once.

"Are you healing?"

"Yes."

"Do the hatchlings bother you?"

"No, no, they're fine."

"Do Val and I bother you?"

Mare takes a breath as he examines a can of very nearly expired tomatoes. "Why would you bother me?"

Hunter stands beside Mare, eyes on the shelf across from them. "Do you want me to list every possible reason? Nothing would surprise me, but I'd rather know outright."

Mare plucks the can up and places it into the bag. "This may come as a surprise, but between Dream and I, I'm not the jealous one. I'm not particularly scared of Val as it is, and, well, no offense, but you are far too caring to ever concern me."

Hunter's gaze drops away from Mare's again.

"I'm not scared of what could happen, Hunter," Mare says as they cross the aisle. "The problem is that fifty years have already passed, and I am the only one out of the loop. I have a lot to catch up on. It's overwhelming."

Hunter gives a whisper of a laugh. "That I do understand. I've never . . . lived in a town before."

Mare looks over them, at their shrugged shoulders and their skittering gaze and the way they carry themself like they are half their size.

"Ah, you'll get the hang of it," Mare says. "What you lack in knowledge, I'm sure Val will make up for in boldness."

Hunter's lips twitch as they consider a smile. "Fair enough."

Hunter is thankfully silent for the rest of the walk through the market, and Mare watches them head off toward the shop that Dream runs, shrouded in a mist that only Mare can see. No, there is no fearing a person so hopelessly clinging to the life around them.

The earnestness of it almost makes Mare forget that Dream has been sneaking glances into the glass of Mare's own emotions. He takes his annoyance out on the furniture as he shoves another room around to realign the feeling of it. His arms have a pleasant ache as he starts to wash and chop ingredients for dinner. Every snap and crunch of the knife through a vegetable is a human's dream of breaking a bone or hurting a loved one or ripping the walls of their own house apart.

What did Dream see while Mare was asleep yesterday?

When Dream comes home, Mare is seated at the table with two plates of food sitting out. Dream looks like he's walking into a trap as he slowly approaches.

"Damn, you really cooked," he says, eyeing the full plate in front of the empty chair.

"You have to be careful with that hip of yours." Mare speaks into the glass he's holding. "Making sure it never opens up again will mean steady fuel for a while. Don't get complacent."

Dream sits down adjacent to Mare, looking over at him. "So I'm not eating enough food, and you're not eating enough dreams?"

"Embarrassing, isn't it?" Mare asks, swirling his glass. "I'm having wine. Don't be mad."

"Can't be," Dream says. "Look, I'm sorry. I could feel it on you, that's all. It was too much time in Indulgence. You filled up too fast. It's an easy fix."

Mare sets the glass down. "We're trying to make a good impression here."

"They won't know it's us," Dream says back.

"We're the only new people in town," Mare replies. "You know how this works."

Dream raises his hands up. "Alright. I'll stop."

He picks up his silverware and Mare waits for him to take a bite before he does the same.

"It's good," Dream says. "You and Rez swap recipes?"

"He doesn't use enough spices," Mare replies.

Dream eats with a smirk, and Mare fights the pull of selfish pride at putting that look on Dream's face.

"I got some records," Dream says. "Try them out when we're done."

"Sure."

Mare can feel every bite of food that Dream swallows. There's a pocket of warmth sliding down his own throat before he gets to his own. He can taste tomato on the tip of Dream's tongue, so he chases it with a drink of wine that he holds in his mouth for much too long. It mixes together between Dream's teeth.

***

The records range from tinny reproductions of Foundation orchestras from two hundred years ago, to utterly tasteless and nevertheless nostalgic albums from Innovation only a few years before the wall went up. Mare scans the backs of all the albums, and begins to listen to them, one per day.

The first record is the kind of music Mare used to complain about to Dream in the apartment they shared in Innovation. More noise than instrumentation, but now Mare finds himself wondering why he was so harsh on it. The sounds themselves aren't all that different from the sounds of walking down the crowded city streets, or taking the train, or sitting on the roof and listening to the machinery of a building groan.

When Dream comes home and hears it blaring through the house, he laughs as he sets his things down.

"Still can't dance to this shit," he says.

Mare points at the newly assembled coat rack by the door right before Dream drapes his jacket onto the back of the couch.

"You got a coat rack?" Dream asks, brows pinched.

"I got a coat rack."

"You went out?"

"And I got a coat rack, yes."

Dream hangs his jacket up on it, giving it a shake before taking a seat on the couch. Mare turns back to the picture frame he's been trying to fix, laid out on the coffee table on a bed of old newspapers.

"You're not overworking yourself, right?" Dream asks, rolling up his sleeves.

"No," Mare answers, watching out of the corner of his eye as Dream lights a cigarette. This time, Mare feels the heat in his mouth and the smoke filling his lungs as Dream breathes. "Are you?"

"Course not," Dream says, waving the match out. He startles as he sees the new ash tray on the coffee table, quirks an eyebrow, and puts the match onto it. "You've been busy."

"We're supposed to live here, right?" Mare peels off an uneven splinter of wood from the frame. He knees are beginning to ache from his place on the hardwood floor. "We should act like it."

Dream is staring at him, breathing smoke out of the corner of his mouth away from Mare. He loosens the top button of his white shirt, scrubs his free hand over his scar, and leans back onto the couch until his head is facing the ceiling.

"You think you'll take up singing again?" Dream asks. "Won't get as many noise complaints in our own house."

Mare immediately gets a shiver of gooseflesh down his spine, and he doesn't know if it's his or Dream's.

"Only if you're the one playing," Mare says, setting sanding paper over the divot he just made.

"Fuck, I haven't touched a guitar in sixty years."

Smoke pours off of him like a steam engine. Mare runs his tongue over each of his teeth until he figures out what kind of tobacco Dream's smoking.

"You gonna go to bed at a normal hour tonight?" Dream asks.

Mare has already sanded too much off the frame. "If you insist."

"I want you to feed, for fuck's sake," Dream says. "Got me worried."

Mare's gaze is drawn to him, his body sprawled over the couch, arms stretched over the back, legs kicked apart, cigarette burning from his right hand.

"Worried?" Mare repeats, pressing his thumb against the edge of the frame.

Dream brings his hand back over to his mouth, but stops short before he can take another drag.

"Unless you're saving it up for me," Dream mumbles. It's hard to tell from where Mare is sitting on the floor, but it looks like Dream is smirking.

Mare's lips part as he stares at the cigarette, his own mouth watering up as he waits to feel the heat again.

"Guess I deserve it," Dream says, looking at the filter between his fingers. "Maybe it's time to quit this too."

Mare snaps his mouth shut when Dream stubs out the cigarette.

"You need anything before I throw you into bed?"

Mare blinks as a sliver of wood pierces the pad of his thumb. Dream flinches.

"If you're tired enough to get splinters, you're tired enough to sleep," he scolds, cupping Mare's hand in his to look at the skin of Mare's thumb.

Mare glances at Dream's face while he stares at the splinter. It's not often Mare can study him without risk of Dream looking back. It's too much when they lock eyes, but there is still so much for Mare to see. So many little differences in Dream's face and body and voice and mannerisms and the way he tells Mare what to do without an ounce of hesitation.

"Ouch." Mare's voice is a whisper as Dream pulls the splinter out.

"Got it," Dream says, placing it on the table before gripping Mare's hand. He looks Mare dead in the eye. "Go to bed. I'll be a little longer."

Mare nods, sliding his hand free.

Dream's skin feels like fresh soil. Mare picks himself off the floor and takes his pounding heart to Dream's room. He changes quickly, not so fond of sleeping in long sleeved shirts and pants, but he can't very well make Dream look at his seams. He slides under the covers of Dream's bed as chills sweep over him. Wrapping himself up, Mare shivers as the missed connection sinks into his skin.

He wants to burrow into Dream, drink the smoke out of his lungs, bury himself in warm dirt.

When he wakes up with Dream lying, blanket-less, on the other side of the bed, Mare pulls the covers over him, careful not to touch.

⌁

The second album is full of the verve of Indulgence. Horns and electric guitar fill the house while Nightmare cooks dinner for Dream. He *could* dance to this, but he doesn't. They could see a band just like this play live if they ever had the patience.

Which is exactly what Dream says over a bowl full of artichoke hearts. "I'm sure Lux knows where five bands just like this play."

Mare nods. "That would involve standing in a club with much younger humans."

Dream laughs. "Records are just fine."

It's easy. Familiar. Not *their* music, but nice enough to work to. Mare even manages to ask if Dream has an opinion on the arrangement of the furniture in the sitting room as he stands in the center of it, doubting.

"Looks good to me," Dream says, his cheek propped against his fist as he sinks into the couch.

Mare knows he's not looking at the room. "You won't mind if I turn everything upside down?"

"'Course not," Dream says.

"I've been thinking of starting a fire in the bedroom."

"Gets pretty cold in there."

"Do you think the neighbors will hear if I take a hammer to the walls?"

"What are they gonna do? It's your house."

Mare puts his hands on his hips while Dream plays with the stubble on his own chin. *His* house? Certainly not. Dream looks like he's feeling each individual hair flicking against his fingernail as he looks at Mare. His gaze is still weighted with fifty tons of absence, so Mare stalks over to Dream's jacket, finds his cigarettes and matches for him, and comes back to place one in Dream's mouth.

"Smoke if you want it so bad," Mare says, striking a match for him. "There aren't any humans here. And I hate seeing you fidget like that."

Dream meets him in the offered flame, and Mare holds his breath just to feel Dream inhale, hold, exhale.

"You want one?" Dream asks.

Mare shakes his head, his gaze snagging on the scar across Dream's cheek. He hasn't allowed himself to really look at it, for the memories that always worm their way up when he does, but that night, he finally touches it with Dream's smoke curling around him. A rigid, deep red line cut into the brown of his face, a monument to Mare's frustration.

"I really didn't know what it was," Mare says.

Dream looks up at him, his eyes the same gray as the smoke he breathes.

"I know."

He puts his hand on Mare's hip, slowly, easing around the thinner shape of him.

"I lost weight . . . in the coma."

"I know. It's alright."

Mare licks his rapidly drying lips as a horrid thought takes root in his mind, his fingers straying from scar tissue to crow's feet. His chest feels like it's caving in so he covers it with a breathy laugh.

"We're hardly even twins anymore."

Dream's eyes widen, and Mare feels sick to his stomach at the fear bleeding into Dream's face. Mare's entire body jolts as the match in his hand finally burns its way up to his skin. He flinches, dropping the charred wood, which Dream catches and crushes in his palm without a second thought.

"Sorry," Mare breathes, stumbling away from him.

Dream stands up, his hand tightening on Mare's waist to keep him still. They're still the exact same height, but Dream's eyes have gone fierce again.

"Like it or not, I'm still your brother. You're not gettin' out of that so easily."

Mare swallows, his skin regrowing over the burn, and Dream leaves to go brush the ash from his palms.

Dream goes to bed first, and Mare waits until he's asleep before Mare crawls in after him. Lying in the dark with Dream's heavy breathing beside him, Nightmare feels the glass in his chest beginning to crack.

When they carried him out of Innovation, he was completely empty. No dreams of his own, or of human beings. He didn't even have any despair left inside him, so unbearably hollow he was. To haul himself up out of the rot, he's had to feed so greedily, he's already full to the brim. Shadows are slipping out from the seams in his skin.

Dream is right, because of course he's right. The only safe way to feed is through give and take. If all Mare does is drink in bad dreams and never lets anything out, he'll just get sick. He's been in that place before, he's seen what it does to Dream, and to any human who comes into contact with him. He'll also have Val's ire if he accidentally upsets Hunter in his own imbalance.

He shouldn't have said that they don't look like twins. It's not what he meant, not really. But even after, Dream still touched him, still insisted, still called him brother.

Thank god.

⬦

In his sleep, Dream shows Mare the most sickly sweet image of a family reunion at Lux's home, with Hunter and Val in tow. There's no sound, just heat flowing through a house full of their siblings. He still dreams about Mis and Ozzi as two separate boys. He dreams about Sig wound around Remi like sweet vines. He dreams about Hunter carrying Val on his back. And he dreams about Nightmare, stealing him away from everyone else to kiss him in the gardens.

Mare wakes up from Dream's vision with a light sheen of sweat over his skin. It's been so long since he watched himself from Dream's eyes, but Mare looks different now. The Mare in his dreams doesn't have scars or silver hair.

He called Mare *pumpkin* with his hands reaching out.

Mare showers until he stops feeling so clammy.

That day, when Mare puts on the next record, he only gets about a minute into the first song before he rips it off the player. He stands there in the ringing silence with the vinyl in his hands as the echo of velvety guitar whines in his head. It sounded just like how Dream used to play. It sounded like soft nights on the southern coast when they had nothing better to do than write music. It sounded like Dream's hands peeling apart Mare's body.

Before he knew it, Mare had broken the vinyl in half, his hands gripping the edges tight enough to cut himself. When reality slips back in, he puts the broken pieces into their case and walks it to a public trash bin before coming back home to lie in bed with his hands clasped to his forehead.

The glass is shattering. He can't keep it together. With shadows clawing out of his eyes, Mare watches the walls of the house start to rot, the ceiling bloating as water begins to drip through the wood. The foundations shiver as the earth churns beneath him, threatening to swallow the entire house with Mare inside it. He can't move of course, he's covered in spider bites, poison coating his blood and weighing his limbs down like lead. People are banging on the door. He can smell gunpowder and hatred. They'll tear the walls down, and then they'll tear Nightmare limb from limb.

When Dream comes home that day, he takes a seat at the table with Mare. "No music?"

Mare sips a glass of water. "I had a headache."

"Sorry to hear it," Dream says back. "Early night tonight?"

"I think that's best."

"You need anything?"

"I already ate."

"Do you *want* anything?"

Mare forces himself to look at his brother and all his concern. It hangs off of him like dew drops ready to spill.

"What have my dreams been like?" Mare asks him.

Dream puts his arms on the table, gaze softening around Mare. "Last night, you couldn't speak. No tongue. I was with Val and Hunter while we all ignored you sinking into the ground."

"Did I cry?"

"Buckets," Dream says, a hint of a smile. "You that jealous?"

Mare shrugs. "In the grand scheme of our lives, you've spent a comparative minute with those two, and you've brought them into the family. How could I not be?"

Dream picks his fork and knife up, looking satisfied.

"Not as jealous as you, of course," Mare goes on. "Even in your good dreams, you're always stealing me away from everyone else. It's like you think someone will swoop in the moment you're out of the room."

"Someone did," Dream says, pointing at Mare with his fork.

Mare tilts his head. "I didn't sleep with Raleigh."

"I . . . I know," Dream sputters. "I still don't like it."

He starts eating with renewed vigor and Mare's mouth begins to pull into a smile. "I never made him dinner either."

Dream looks up at him and back at the food. "Good."

Weaving his fingers back together, Mare sets his chin on his hands, his gaze wandering toward the walls. "I never touched him. I never wanted to. The only time we ever did get close to each other was when he took a bite out of my leg. And I was half-asleep for that. I'd have shot him a lot sooner if I'd been able. His hands were cold. Bloodless. Even if I'd given him the chance, he wouldn't have known what to do."

Dream is staring at Mare as he slips into a poisonous haze, and Mare is about to cough out an apology, but Dream spears a piece of broccoli like he's trying not to smile. He looks for all the world like he's gloating over Mare's vengeful whispers, and fuck, it's a good look on him. Everything is a good look on Dream when he wears it so easily. There's hardly any hesitance left in him now and this confidence is going to pull every one of Mare's stitches out.

They go to bed at the same time that night, and Mare winds up changing his clothes in the bathroom before sliding into bed.

"Need any help getting to sleep?" Dream asks. He's sitting on the edge, undoing all the buttons on his shirt.

"Sure," Mare answers, watching the fabric peel off his back. Were his shoulders always so broad, or has Mare just gotten that much thinner?

The change is immediate—pollen in the air, wind in the branches. Mare sinks into the pillow, gaze fixed on the skin of Dream's back. He looks warm. He always looks so warm. His Dream grew so strong while Mare was asleep. Maybe all of Mare's yearning fed him over the years. Maybe that's why Mare is still so hollow.

Dream places his hand on the bed between them, catching Mare's eye with a smile.

"Go to sleep."

Mare paws at the sheets while his eyes slide shut.

"Sweet Dream . . ."

—▼—

Mare knows the shape of this heat. He's seen this dream countless times, like an old play. He's a child again, seen through Dream's eyes, and Dream has his hand clenched in Mare's shirt. They are sitting behind the house of the woman who raised them, under the shade of an oak tree.

"I like you . . ."

Mare can still remember when Dream really said those words to him, and Mare's own confused response.

"You say you love me all the time. Why do you always gets so shy when you say *like* instead?"

It's not fair, really, that Mare can only see this memory from Dream's eyes and not his own.

"Well, I know I love you! You're my brother. But I also . . . like you . . . you know, like how other people like each other . . ."

Only Mare knows how fragile Dream looked while he said that. Watching himself through Dream, he always sounds so much crueler than he meant to.

"What, like you want to kiss me or something?"

He feels Dream's shoulders tick up, his whole body warm from head to toe, and he turns his face toward the ground to nod. His fingers were practically ripping Mare's shirt.

"Okay."

Dream's head whips back up, eyes wide. "Really?"

The young version of Mare shrugs, but the look on his face does not relay the way Mare's heart was pounding. "Why not?"

He really hadn't thought about it up until that moment. Mare always knew he and Dream weren't like other people, but no part of him had ever considered intimacy as anything other than his brother comforting him after another nightmare. But when the nightmares became easier and Mare no longer needed the same soothing, Dream still offered it. It took no time at all for Mare to feel like he was the one taking care of Dream.

But this was different. This felt selfish and warm and new and utterly intoxicating. Kissing Dream felt entirely too good to be allowed, and maybe that's why, even centuries later, the mere thought of it makes Mare dizzy. If he doesn't apply restraint, it'll be the only thing he ever does until he dies.

When Dream kisses Mare in the depths of his sleep, the dream shifts. It loses shape, slowly melting over the heat of the memory until there's nothing to be seen, just glimpses of skin and the feeling of Mare's hair tickling his own shoulders and molten gold boiling in his hips until Mare finally wakes up with his heart pounding and his legs bent up around nothing.

He immediately checks to make sure that Dream is still asleep, then slowly straightens his legs back out. A chill sweeps up his skin as the sweat cools and Mare pulls the covers up. Dream is utterly and completely still beside him, and Mare wonders what terrible thing he gifted to Dream while Mare was getting spoiled by sweet memories.

Pulling himself out of bed, Mare feels heavy like he's soaking wet.

It takes all morning to feel any kind of steady, Dream long gone by the time Mare remembers to eat something. The house lets out a miserable creaking whine, reminding Mare to cover the silence with another record.

This one he also recognizes. It's the Foundation String Orchestra. They've heard iterations of this music countless times over the years. Mare turns the volume up, letting it fill the house as he takes stock of every room, tapping out the rhythm with his fingers. Today, the house is not nearly so hostile. The furniture almost looks settled, the colors a little more permanent than he remembers. Maybe it's the tempo of the music encouraging him to move faster, but there's hardly reason to rearrange that day.

Mare cooks too much food, his hands slipping into autopilot as if they still live with a house full of people. He can give the rest to Val and Hunter. What does it matter anyway?

When Dream comes home and Mare is still at the stove, he isn't sure if Dream left early, or if Mare lost track of time and started late.

"Sounds like a party in here," Dream says, walking up behind Mare with a smirk. "The kind with stiff clothes and everyone watching a little too closely."

Mare smiles at the stock pot. "How many daughters did we have to dance with while living in Foundation?"

"Too fucking many," Dream says, leaning up against the fridge with a laugh. "Got pretty good at it, though. Dancing, I mean."

"Yes, because I could see exactly where you were fumbling steps while you were dancing with others. It made it easy to correct you later."

"Yeah, thanks for that," Dream says. His voice is as warm as the heat pouring off the stove.

"Of course, the better you were at dancing, the more people wanted to dance with you," Mare notes.

"And I didn't have the heart to tell them that you were the best dancing partner in the whole city."

"They were all so busy asking me to lead . . ." Mare mumbles.

"We would've made a scene dancing together in that crowd."

Mare nods, eyes unfocused as he stares into the red of the stew until it bleeds into a sunset seen from the rooftop of a banquet hall in the old parts of Foundation. Mare wanted to learn, so he masqueraded as a student. Dream said Mare could teach him anything he needed, but as long as they were there, he may as well help out. Charismatic as he was, it was easy to land him a job as a teaching aid. Between the two of them, only Dream could ever have the patience to instruct. That was the first time Mare really understood Dream's effect on others, how it wasn't just Mare that so easily got swept up in the way he spoke.

"You had that entire city in love with you," Mare muses. "Logan was furious."

"It was supposed to be her city," Dream says. "Guess I stepped on her toes a little."

"Dreams are more romantic than logic," Mare whispers. "Only natural how they took to you."

"Mare."

He blinks, glancing behind him to see Dream holding his hand out.

"It's been ages. Surely you got one more dance in you?" His half smile makes Mare's chest ache, like Dream is already sure that Mare doesn't really want to. "If you can stand this face of mine for a few minutes."

Mare ignores his hand, crossing the few feet between them to glare at Dream, eye to eye. "There's *nothing* wrong with your face. Don't say that to me again."

Dream straightens up, eyes flashing bright as his lips curve into a real smile. "Shit, alright. Sorry."

"Push the coffee table aside or else there won't be enough room." Mare can feel his pulse thrumming in his neck as he makes the demand.

Dream looks like he's getting drunk off the sound of Mare's clipped voice. "Okay. Don't keep me waiting."

Mare crosses his arms. "Fine."

It's a blessing that Dream actually walks into the other room. Mare's breath shakes on its way out. Again, again with that look on his face. A velvet expression, like the only thing Dream has ever, could ever, will ever want is just to look at Nightmare.

Mare turns the burner down low before he goes to join Dream in the sitting room. The table has been pushed onto its end and rests against the wall, leaving them an open path. Dream has another cigarette in his mouth as he resets the needle to play the record from the beginning. One of the slower string pieces swells through the room.

"Might be a little rusty," Dream says, offering his hand again.

Mare approaches him on light steps, so painfully aware of how ready he is to split open. "You're stronger than you used to be."

Touching his fingers to Dream's immediately makes Mare wish he had his damn gloves on. Electricity and pure oxygen are soaking through his skin.

"That mean I can throw you?" Dream asks, his hand smoothing over Mare's hip, the cigarette still held between his knuckles.

"Fuck no," Mare breathes, his fingers curling over Dream's shoulder as his blood turns to sugar. "I don't know why you like swing dance so much."

"I don't, not really," Dream says, nudging Mare forward. "Just wanted an excuse to touch you like that."

"To throw me," Mare corrects, easing into a basic step.

"You gotta admit it'd look good," Dream says, guiding Mare forward.

They're moving at a quarter of the normal speed for a dance like this as they both remember how this goes.

"God, I forgot how stiff this is," Dream mutters.

"It's elegant," Mare chides.

"*You're* elegant," Dream scoffs. "This dance is stiff."

Slowly but surely, some of the dust loosens from their arms. Dream takes a drag in the lull between songs, refusing to let Mare's hand go. He sets the cigarette on the ashtray before the next song picks up, and Mare notices the space between their hips shaving away with every movement. At least now they have an excuse, even if Dream's hands are burning him up.

"Is this when I—?"

"Yes."

Mare braces as Dream spreads his hand over Mare's back to dip him, and maybe it's the song, maybe it's the heat, but the moment Mare leaves the weight of his body in Dream's hands, the shadow starts to overflow. It drips out of his head and onto the floor, rotting everything it touches.

"Oh, gods." Mare's voice rolls out of him as his vision swims. His eyes show him smoke filling the room as a fire builds beneath their feet.

"I got you," Dream says, coaxing Mare back up to face him. "It's alright."

Mare still feels like he's upside down, clinging to Dream as the world tips around him. Dream is the only thing that isn't spinning, or burning, or falling into ruin. He slides his hand up Mare's back, holding them chest to chest with a gaze as heavy as the entire sky crushing their house.

They're not dancing anymore, just standing in their sitting room as music plays and Nightmare's head cracks open.

"No, no, no," Mare's voice is a drunken whisper, and Dream catches it on his cheek, nuzzling his face to Mare's.

"It's okay, you're safe here." Dream abandons the semblance of a dancer's hold and hugs Mare against himself. "Look at me, look at me."

Mare doesn't want to become the man he is when he looks at Dream, but he can't say no either. Not when the house is on fire, not with Dream's concern filling his head with pollen. And of course, the second he meets that gentle gaze, he's already half lost. Panting, heart racing, legs going weak, Mare touches Dream's face again, one hand at a time. There's ash in his mouth as he stares in awe at his twin, made new.

"I can't believe it." Mare's hands are threatening to go numb. He must look wild, pushing harder into Dream's chest. "I never thought I'd get to see you look different."

Dream exhales, his gaze flicking up and down between Mare's eyes and his mouth. "You don't mind, do ya?"

Mare lurches forward as the ceiling begins to collapse, and Dream threads his fingers into Mare's grayed hair, catching him by the mouth. The sound of sparks and cracking wood begin to roar as Mare's hands clutch Dream's head, kissing him until it's all he can feel. He's so empty, but Dream is so full—full of life and hope and love and memories and forgiveness and patience. Mare tells himself he only needs a little, but his mouth wants more, wants it so bad that his teeth chatter and his jaw aches and he bites Dream's lip hard enough that they both taste blood.

"Fuck." Dream gives a breathy laugh and brings his finger to his lip.

Mare blinks out of the spell of his own pent up energy, the house no longer burning up and falling apart. Everything's back to normal, except for Dream, who really is bleeding. Mare sees the cut, and tries to pull away, but Dream is too quick. His arms clasp back around Mare's waist, hauling him up off the ground just to pin him against the wall with the weight of Dream's own body.

"Don't run away from me again," Dream growls at him, forehead pressed to Mare's.

"I'm sorry," Mare clings to his shoulders. "I'm sorry, I don't want to hurt you."

"I know." Dream lowers his voice. "But I don't give a shit, Mare. Fuck, I'll take another bullet if it keeps you outta trouble. Just don't leave."

The blood is threatening to spill across Dream's chin.

"How am I supposed to help you?" Mare's fingers tighten in the fabric of Dream's shirt. "All I want is to give you what you need, but if the only thing you ever ask for is *me*, I'll only ever hurt you."

"Then *listen* to me, you idiot," Dream snaps, and Mare freezes.

Fierce, in ways he never used to be.

"I don't need you to give me everything," Dream tells him. "But I do need us. Okay? I'll get the rest from other people. But I need this. I need you."

His hands are tight on Mare's hips, his breath hot, his own euphoria thick on his tongue, ready to spill just like the blood on his lip.

"Fuck, Mare, I need you so bad."

All he wants is to stop that drop of red from making a mess of Dream, but Nightmare crumbles on the taste of his brother's blood. As his tongue crests over Dream's bottom lip, iron and sap mixes in Mare's mouth, and the texture of Dream's sigh smooths out with anticipation, and Mare needs to drink it all—Dream's blood, his relief, his need, his spit and sweat and skin.

Another kiss is enough to set fire to the house again, but Mare hardly feels it when Dream picks him up off the ground. He's shivering through the heat as Dream carries him across the crumbling house. Only when Dream sits on the bed with Mare wrapped around him does Mare remember the second part of this equation.

"The scars . . ."

Dream starts unbuttoning Mare's shirt even as Mare leans away from him.

"You think I give a shit?" Dream yanks Mare's collar open to run his tongue over one of the seams.

Mare's mouth falls open as he tastes his own skin on his tongue. The new flesh pulls so slightly against the rot scars, and Mare barely hears himself moan over his own blood roaring in his ears. He's already hard, squeezing his thighs into Dream while the ceiling of their bedroom rains burning wood all around them.

Mare flinches as a cluster of sparks flies up toward his face, and Dream slides his hand up under Mare's shirt.

"It's alright, c'mere."

He burrows toward Dream's voice while Dream guides him toward the covers.

"What do you see, Night? Tell me."

Dream lays Mare down, holding the back of Mare's neck to direct their eyes to meet.

Mare finds himself again with Dream leaning over him.

"The house is burning down," he whispers.

Dream smiles. "Knew you liked this place. Open your mouth."

Mare's lips part as Dream cups his face.

"You remember how to do this?" Dream asks, only an inch away.

When he lays his hips down on top of Mare's, any annoyance Mare might have felt at being asked if he forgot how to *breathe* vanishes with a gasp. Mare's legs cinch against Dream's sides as it sinks in that they really are back together. This really is happening. He can see every one of the fifty years that separated them, but this is undoubtedly his twin. He's safe. Even if the house does burn down, even if every conceivable thing went as wrong as it possibly could, even if Mare fucks up so badly that nearly everyone else cuts him loose, Dream will still want him.

Dream wants him. He looks like he might cry, like he's just that happy to be close to Mare again. Dream's mouth is open, his hands gentle on Mare's face, his heart pounding at the ends of every one of his fingertips.

"It's really not fair that you got more handsome," Mare tells him in a whisper.

Dream laughs into a sigh, and Mare opens his mouth to fit against

Dream's. When their lips seal together, Mare has to temper his own desire just to keep himself steady while their bodies tune to each other. It takes several breaths for them to get it right, syncing their lungs together so that every exhale is the other's inhale. Mare can feel Dream's breath filling his entire body, from the ridges on his toes to the crown of his head. When he slides his fingers through Dream's hair, he feels it on his own scalp. When Dream moans so quietly into Mare's mouth, Mare echoes him automatically as his body bruises with *want*.

Winding his arms and legs around Dream, Mare stops fighting as euphoria pours into him. It's sweet and light and perfect, Dream's joy at getting to touch Nightmare.

It's Mare who shifts his head and Dream who takes a taste, and then they're not breathing, just kissing, and Mare doesn't give a damn what's happening anywhere but here.

Dream's hand snakes down over Mare's shirt toward his hip as the comfort brings their appetite back to the surface. With Dream's fingers slipping around his thigh, Mare breaks the kiss as his voice spills out of him. It's been so very long since he had this outside of a fantasy. Dream is pushing Mare's shirt off and kissing the seams of scar tissue while Mare watches the flames spread over their bed. It's licking up his arms, engulfing him in an awful heat that will surely boil his blood.

"Too hot, Dream, it hurts."

"I know, I know," Dream soothes while he unbuttons Mare's pants.

It's a relief to get the rest of his clothes off if only to cool him down a little. He's forgetting how to breathe again as his vision succumbs to a bright mess of burning orange, and he yelps when he feels Dreams hands smoothing up his leg, pulling it off the bed.

"I got you," Dream says, pressing his lips to Mare's ankle.

Dreams blows air against Mare's skin like he's breathing smoke from a cigarette again. His breath cuts through the heat of the fire and Mare's own panic, sending a rush of goosebumps sweeping over

Mare's body. It's just cool enough to fight the illusion of everything burning down. As Dream blows more air along the arch of Mare's foot, and the top of his shin, and over the scar of the spider's teeth marks in his calf, the flames around him begin to wane.

"We're gonna die in this house," Mare says.

"Not we're not."

"The town will turn on us."

"No they won't."

"The spiders are going to eat me." Mare's voice catches as he feels Dream's fingers drawing down his thigh.

"Not while I'm here," Dream says.

The fire is only embers by then, and Mare is left staring back at his twin, the scars Mare gave him, and the unbearable affection in his gaze.

"Dream, I'm sorry." Mare shuts his eyes against the sting of tears, pushing his hands over his face. "I'm so sorry. I hurt you. Oh god. I could've killed you."

"You almost did."

Dream's voice is in Mare's ear as his fingers glide over Mare's thigh and up the length of his slit.

"Is that what you want to hear?" Dream asks, and his hand has all the heat of the fire he just put out as he slides his fingers into Mare's body.

Mare's hips jump off the bed, so unused to this feeling, tighter than he remembered but that's what fifty years of solitude will do. Dream wets his fingers one at a time inside Mare just to smear the mess over Mare's cock.

"You want me to tell you how awful it was without you?"

Mare nods over and over as the heat he's been running from opens up underneath his skin. Dream pushes Mare onto his side so he can hold Mare against his chest, burying his face in gray hair while he coaxes Mare's body back to life.

"You left me." Dream's voice is choked, and it could be the pain of the words, or it could be his own need hot on Mare's back while he paints that slickness over Mare's skin. Mare reaches behind him for Dream's hip, digging his fingers into the fabric of his pants. It's been too long, he doesn't know how to do this anymore. He's choking on the sensation of skin that hasn't been touched in ages, handled so suddenly, and so roughly.

"You *shot* me."

There it is. Dream's fingers squeeze into Mare with an almost painful tightness, and Mare buckles against him, his voice twisting into a moan.

"Can't believe you fucking shot me."

Mare's vision skews as Dream works his hand faster over swollen skin, and the warmth melts through Mare's body, pooling in his cunt.

"You little monster." Dream breathes the words in Mare's ear and Mare hitches his leg up. It's all he can do not to fall apart.

Dream's anger is a sweet knife, and Mare writhes against it as he starts to come with nothing inside him, and it's wrong. He needs Dream there, he needs to keep the warmth inside or he'll burn every-thing again.

"*Dream, stop* . . ." Mare sounds just as hollow as he feels.

"Stop what?" Dream growls back at him. "Stop making you come? *No.*"

Mare grits his teeth as more and more heat spills out of him. It's not fair, it's not fair that this is what he needs, that he has to keep doing this to Dream over and over, but it makes his body sing when Dream refuses to give in to him. It's the sound of Dream punishing Mare the only way he knows how.

"I'm never gonna stop."

Mare's thighs are trembling, hands bracing against the bed. It wasn't just the spider that kept them apart. They hadn't been perfect for a long time before that. Years of tasting the alcohol in Dream's mouth as he tried to keep his mind under a veil, of stale routines and being afraid of telling the truth—it kept them untouched for more than just Mare's tenure as a prisoner of Innovation. It's been so long, Mare forgot just how good it could be.

"I don't care how terrible you are."

Dream is only merciless when it comes to Nightmare. He's seen it time and time again. All of Dream's loveliness turning razor sharp while he was defending Mare. It was always *for* Mare. Feeling it directed entirely at himself for once is electric. Another thing he could never have predicted in his years of dreaming alone.

"I'm not going anywhere."

Dream says it with a bite of acid that Mare has never heard. When Dream pulls his hand off of Mare to unzip his own pants, Mare holds his breath, eyes wide, heart ready to burst. Fear slices through him at the thought that Dream won't really want to, or that'll it be bad after all, or that Mare really won't be able to handle it, but he feels Dream's fingers and the head of his cock pressing against Mare's slit, and Mare automatically moves in concert to let him in. Mare has to know, no matter what.

Dream bites Mare's ear, snapping Mare's attention back to his mouth.

"I'm gonna love you until there's no more earth to hold us."

When Dream finally slides his cock into Mare's body, it's like he never left. Nightmare sings Dream's name with the unrestrained euphoria that only Dream can give him. He used to wonder what humans felt when they had sex, what thrills they could be chasing that make them act so uniquely strange, and how it inevitably couldn't compare to the sensation of Nightmare and Dream spilling the very core of their beings inside each other. It's not just the physical feeling either. Mare has no idea what a human feels when they orgasm, but he knows that when a human plants a seed, it's to grow another human that breathes their own thoughts and emotions.

When Dream fucks Nightmare, they bleed into each other until they can both feel everything they couldn't before. Mare can feel Dream's satisfaction at getting to do this again, and Dream can surely feel Mare's blistering relief at getting pinned down and smoothed over. He feels the pressure of his own body pulsing around Dream's cock, and around his own, like an unseen hand still wrapped around him. Dream must be getting the reverberation in his hips, and Mare pulls his own thigh up higher as he remembers that Dream will feel it in his own, the perfect aching fit of Dream thrusting into Mare's cunt. For a blissful moment, Mare can't tell the difference between their bodies at all, sensation swimming around his head and pouring over his skin twice over, and of course that's when Dream comes. Mare feels it in his blood and in every muscle, deep in his belly and through each of his fingers.

Dream clings to Mare's chest, breathing deep with his nose pressed to Mare's neck, and it takes a moment for their nerves to redistribute back into their own bodies, but Mare knows exactly which ones were taken from Dream—parts of his lungs, the backs of his knees, his earlobes, and navel, and the tips of his shoulder blades.

"Did you really not undress?" Mare asks with a metal button pressing into his backside.

"Are you really critiquing me? Fuck, it's been two minutes."

Mare laughs, winding his arms around Dream's. "Not self-conscious are we?"

"You still look like you could be a fucking student, you think I don't have the right?" Dream asks.

Mare smiles, sliding his fingers under the edge of Dream's shirt sleeve. "You've seen all of my rot scars. You can be self-conscious, but you don't have the right to hide."

Dream kisses Mare's shoulder. "Still hard . . ."

"Not an excuse, though I appreciate the honesty."

With a grumble, Dream pulls out of Mare and leans up to look him in the eye. "You better not get all pouty looking at my hip."

Mare lifts a heavy hand to touch Dream's face. "I won't."

Dream narrows his eyes as he starts to undo the buttons on his shirt. "Holding you to that."

"Try me, old man."

"We're twins, asshole."

Mare hasn't felt this full in decades.

"We'll have to be extra careful now," Mare says. "People will hate it twice as much if they see us touching in the wrong way with you looking like you could be my father."

"I swear to god."

Dream grabs Mare's jaw just to give him a rough kiss that Mare gladly opens his mouth for. It takes much too long with Dream attached to him by the lips, but Mare slowly wrestles Dream's shirt off of him until he can run his hands down Dream's chest. The hair is new, but Mare shivers at the feeling of it on his fingers. Dream pulls away to shove their clothes off the bed, and Mare smirks at him.

"I can't take your threats seriously when you punctuate them with a kiss."

Dream glares from his knees. "You want me to take my pants off or not?"

Mare pushes himself up to touch the webbing of scar tissue over Dream's hip, the texture of it more like poison ivy than skin. With his hands on Dream's waist, he kisses the old wound as Dream runs his fingers through Mare's hair.

"Don't worry, I got all my pouting done already," Mare tells him.

"Good."

Dream resumes undressing, and Mare sits up to wait for him, taking in all the new and different structures of muscle and lines in his skin. He's still a warmer shade than Mare, but that was true even before Mare was trapped underground for so long. Dream is the traveler, the one who *wants* enough to go and get things. Mare is his shadow, and that's where he loves to be.

Dream lays down beside Mare, one arm under his head, his left leg bent up, relaxing once again, and the picture is almost complete.

"I'll be right back," Mare says, sliding out of bed.

"What?" Dream reaches for him, but Mare slips out of his reach. "You get me naked and you leave me cold?"

Laughing, Mare pads down to the sitting room to get the book of matches off the table, as well as the ashtray, inspecting the abandoned cigarette to see if it's still good. Figuring Dream would prefer a new one, Mare grabs the half-empty pack as well, only to stop cold as he sees a familiar face staring at him through the window.

Val's mouth is agape, eyes open wide, but he quickly claps his hands over his face and yells at the window, "I'm sorry! We thought something was wrong! Bye!" before turning around and walking resolutely back toward the woods.

Mare barely has room left in him to be bewildered, so he just closes the blinds and goes back to bed.

"Did someone just yell outside?" Dream asks, brows furrowed as Nightmare climbs up to straddle Dream's stomach.

"Your boy just saw me naked," Mare says, setting the ashtray aside and pulling a cigarette out of the pack.

"What the fuck?" Dream takes the cigarette. "Val did?"

"He knows about us, right?" Mare asks, setting the pack down so he can get a match out.

"Yeah," Dream says. "They both do. Sorry."

Mare shakes his head. "It's easier that way, I just wish I could tell when Val was walking up to the house while the blinds are up."

Dream rests his hands on Mare's thighs with a smile, and Mare lights his cigarette. They both breathe in, they both taste the tobacco, and they both revel in the smoke. Mare slides back down to rest his face against Dream's chest with a sigh, and Dream fits his hands around Mare's waist. This time, when they are silent, the house does not interrupt.

"I spent a very long time thinking about how you'd eat me," Mare says quietly.

Dream cradles Mare against him, brushing Mare's hair away from his ear.

"I really didn't think I'd be able to leave that place," Mare tells him. "I thought I was ready. To live inside you. I thought about how lovely it'd feel to be swallowed by you."

Dream's heart beats steadily underneath Mare's cheek.

"And then I realized how selfish it would be to make you carry me like that," Mare says. "When I've hardly had the chance to carry you. And now you're all healed, so I can't even help with that."

Dream gives a smoky laugh. "Sorry, kiddo."

"Don't you dare." Mare closes his eyes. "I'm trying to be sincere."

"You're the one who put me in such a good mood," Dream says. "If you want to help, take a shift at the shop. Get to know Val and Hunter. Don't lock yourself away, okay? It's good to know other people."

Mare lifts his head up to look at Dream again. "Are you sure you won't get jealous?"

Dream takes a generous drag before he sets the cigarette aside. "I will. I can't help it with you. But I'll tell you next time. So you can tell me I'm being an asshole."

Mare starts to smile as Dream runs his fingers over Mare's face. "Is that it, then? We never change, we just . . . own up to the stasis?"

Dream smirks back at him. "We did change, Mare. We hardly look the same."

"That's not what I mean."

"You're such a pessimist."

He draws his thumb over Mare's mouth, smiling like he knows everything, and Mare wants to bask in the obnoxious warmth of it.

"C'mere," Dream says, tugging on Mare's chin. "Give me a kiss."

Mare is drawn right to him, hopelessly, helplessly. He crawls up closer to press his lips to Dream's, already anticipating the fall back into him. All it takes is Dream running his hands over Mare's body to forget, not just composure, but what it was ever used for in the first place.

If they only ever needed each other for a function of their beings, maybe this wouldn't take Mare apart so efficiently. But Dream touches Mare with the shamelessness of a teenager who only just realized that he could get away with this. No matter how many centuries pass, Dream still acts like he's lucky, looking at the oldest nightmare with all the wonder of a newlywed.

"I still—" Mare's tongue feels useless when it's not in Dream's mouth. "Will you . . ."

Dream slides his hands up the backs of Mare's thighs, squeezing Mare's ass with a smile, and it should be annoying, it should piss Mare off how crass he can be, but Mare's heart is pounding. It still bowls him over to feel Dream's attraction. That part isn't necessary, they don't need to *like* each other, not when they were built to love each other. Desire isn't required to make any of this work, and that's what does him in every time.

"What is it, beautiful?" Dream asks.

Mare *thunks* his forehead against Dream's with a sigh. "Have mercy and shut up."

"Make me." Dream says it with the shining confidence of a man who just knowingly ate poison and lived.

Mare kisses him again, already too warm as he shifts his knees further apart. Dream takes Mare's tongue while he slides his fingers over every part of Mare that was made for him. Drinking the moan right out of Mare's mouth, Dream circles Mare's cunt, smearing the beads of cum over his fingers.

"Got more for me?" Dream asks.

Mare's breath stalls in his chest. "Take everything."

The second time is always worse, better, numbingly beautiful. When Dreams fucks Mare because he *wants* to, not because he has to. When Mare feels like a reward, rather than a process. This must be the feeling that humans die chasing.

"Fuck, you're pretty." This new voice of Dream's riles Mare even more when he talks like this.

"Don't say that with your face between my legs." Mare's voice is the same, even when he's strangled by an impending orgasm.

"Why not? Everything about you's pretty."

Mare falls apart with Dream's tongue in his slit, Dream's hand on Mare's cock, Dream's words in Mare's mouth.

"Fuck, I missed you." Mare speaks into the covers, face pressed to their bed.

"Missed you too, Pumpkin."

Just as Mare can taste his own cum as Dream licks him, Dream must feel the ache in his own cunt as Mare tries to pull him deeper. Mare puts his hand around Dream's, weaving their fingers together over his own taut skin, working the heat out of them both.

Twined together, two flowers growing from the same vine.

Forever and ever and over again.

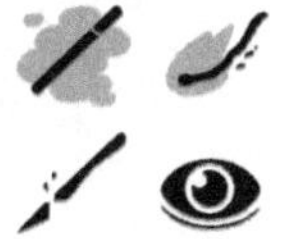

Characters

SPIDERS

Val – he/him

The Cardinal Major (Knives) – he/him

The North Sentinel (Arum) – she/her

The Queen (Raleigh) – any

HUMANS

Hunter – they/he

Lady Violet – they/them

HATCHLINGS

Moon – he/him

Matthew – he/him

The Doctor – they/them

Nora – she/they

PILLARS

Dream – he/him

Nightmare – he/him

Lux (Indulgence) – she/her

Rez (Restraint) – he/him

Etienne (Patience) – she/her

Liz (Impulse) – she/her

Sig (Foresight) – they/them

Vann (Vanity) – he/him

Austen (Austerity) – they/them

Ozzi (Curiosity) – he/him

Mis (Mischief) – he/him

Rae (Courage) – she/her

Hes (Hesitance) – she/her

Sully (Severity) – they/them

Gen (Generosity) – they/them

Logan (Logic) – she/her

Rom (Romance) – he/him

Acknowledgments

Thank you to everyone who has supported me through my patreon, my itchio, and my crowdfundr. And thank you to everyone who shares my works with others when you don't have to. This book would not exist without you.

There are too many people to thank. I'll do my best.

My first readers, including the handful of you who read the very first chapter before I had anything else written, and those of you I rambled over the phone to: Larry, KMO, V, Mal, Ambar, Asher, Zeda & Rinny.

And the people who found me after it was finished to grab me by the shoulders. You gave way more than I was ever expecting: Laurent, Frog, Nechama, Hydein & Danika.

Danika, you deserve your own page of thank yous. I love all your work—for this book and everything else.

And thank *you* for reading.

About the author

M. Loyd Gohty is a collector of tall tales. He attended the Northern University of Foundation with an interest in the way history shapes storytelling. After one too many classes missed from the private study rooms in the library, Loyd decided his time was better spent outside academia. Together with his twin, he traveled the country in search of fantastic tales from the mouths of the people who live here. This is his first published work.